Pegasus

With Warm regards

John Archer

John Archer

Note for Librarians: a cataloguing record for this book that includes Dewey Decimal Classification and US Library of Congress numbers is available from the Library and Archives of Canada. The complete cataloguing record can be obtained from their online database at:

www.collectionscanada.ca/amicus/index-e.html

ISBN 1-4120-3753-0

Printed in Victoria, BC, Canada

TRAFFORD

Offices in Canada, USA, Ireland, UK and Spain

This book was published *on-demand* in cooperation with Trafford Publishing. On-demand publishing is a unique process and service of making a book available for retail sale to the public taking advantage of on-demand manufacturing and Internet marketing. On-demand publishing includes promotions, retail sales, manufacturing, order fulfilment, accounting and collecting royalties on behalf of the author.

Book sales for North America and international:

Trafford Publishing, 6E–2333 Government St.,

Victoria, BC v8t 4p4 CANADA

phone 250 383 6864 (toll-free 1 888 232 4444)

fax 250 383 6804; email to orders@trafford.com

Book sales in Europe:

Trafford Publishing (UK) Ltd., Enterprise House, Wistaston Road Business Centre,

Wistaston Road, Crewe, Cheshire cw2 7rp UNITED KINGDOM

phone 01270 251 396 (local rate 0845 230 9601)

facsimile 01270 254 983; orders.uk@trafford.com

Order online at:

www.trafford.com/robots/04-1581.html

10 9 8 7 6 5 4 3 2

John Archer
Pegasus

Acknowledgments

This effort would not have reached fruition without the encouragement and support of several people. First, my thanks go to Dr. Tom Mann for his early reading, constructive criticism, and enthusiasm. I probably would not have gone forward with the project without his prompting. Also, to my editor, Lori Skinner, for her attention to detail and sense of humor during the editing process, I give my thanks. Thirdly, I thank Bryan Attaway for the cover art work.

Finally, and most importantly, I thank my wife Joan who followed me all over Europe for six years and most of the rest of the world for another twenty, where the ideas and characters for this book were born.

Prologue

Herr. Doctor Peter Weismann is the keynote speaker at the annual meeting of the New World Order in Munich, commonly referred to by world political extremist watchers as the neo-Nazi Hoot, but known by a growing number of political extremists and racists as the NWO. He had formed the NWO to collect and to integrate the myriad neo-Nazi splinter factions around the world into the most powerful international political organization in the world. His intent is to pick up where Hitler left off and to fulfill Hitler's dream of an Aryan world. The goal of the NWO is to support the suppression of all inferior races and the threat they represent to the progress and the well being of all Aryan people.

At precisely ten o'clock the morning of January 2, 1994, before a frenzied audience of over ten thousand neo-Nazis, he begins defining the New World Order platform according to the very same parameters set forth in the White Aryan Resistance Positions:

"My friends, our position on race is simple. The Aryan race must be protected at all costs and above everything else." Jumping to their feet, the audience screams their approval of his profound words of wisdom. He waits several minutes with his arms raised for them to calm so that he may continue his remarks. "Your extended family of racially conscious men and women must receive the same protection and priority as your own family. From time to time, we might disagree on given issues, but never on race. On issues of race we shall stand together." Once again the crowd erupts, cheering and applauding. He steps back from the podium and waits, arms folded across his chest, chin raised, allowing them to fully express themselves, while enjoying their praise. He steps back to the podium and resumes his address.

"Brothers and sisters, we also have a crucial responsibility for the environment. A polluted environment, one that is overpopulated by non-Aryans, is a direct threat to our very existence. It is our stance that any action that stems the tide of non-Aryan invaders is good. We must also be mindful of the effects of corporate greed on our fragile environment. Massive consumerism leads to overproduction and overproduction leads to waste. We must foster conservative lifestyles and resist the pontificating of the so-called Madison Avenue mentality. Their propaganda is designed to trick us into buying what we don't need. Conservation and common sense are the watchwords." The crowd begins another standing ovation, but this time he urges them, with his Hitler-like charisma, to allow him to continue, and they obediently quieted.

"Someone in the world is threatened with armed conflict everyday, but we Aryans must not support foreign military conflict for the benefit of global corporate greed. Aryan nations shall not war against non-Aryan nations except for food or for living space. We will learn to control our Aryan populations so as to live within our well-defined borders. You must understand that the primary need for conflict to Aryan nations arises from our need to protect the gene pool. Modern wars have been based primarily on trade disagreements, encouraged by capitalist overproduction and the seeking of new markets for products. None of these wars was for the benefit of Aryan people: millions of Aryans, both military and civilian, were killed in World Wars I and II. Some of the finest specimens of our race died in wars having nothing to do with the cultural and racial well being of Aryan people. We must never allow ourselves to be duped into armed conflict for the wrong reasons." More wild shouts and applause from the audience reverberate in the auditorium as testimony to his adeptness at propaganda.

"The NWO supports abortion and birth control for non-Aryans and encourages racially conscious Aryan women to produce Aryan children; however, we do not promote the forcing of Aryan women to have unwanted children. Non-Aryan races continue to breed with little control, while Aryans have voluntarily destroyed millions of healthy Aryan babies some of whom would have become doctors and engineers. Those who support the continuation of these circumstances will certainly, at some point in time, face Aryan justice." As expected, the shouts and cheers from the women in the crowd are heard well above the cheers of the men.

"Those who might one day hope to form a friendly relationship with NWO should be forewarned that we consider an ally as any group or individual who supports, or makes contributions toward, racial separatism. And they must also recognize that we consider an enemy as anyone who is opposed to us. You must remember, my friends, anyone who promotes or supports racial mixing contributes directly to our racial destruction. No matter what their motives, race, nationality, or religion, these people are the enemy. Never forget, my brothers and my sisters, that race is our only religion."

"NWO condemns priest craft and all other religions and will not allow religious theories and unproven myths to interfere with Aryan survival and advancement. We Aryans must deal with reality and the world in which we live, and shun those who attempt to control us with stories from the Middle East. Our religion is our form of government, an Aryan oligarchy based on genetic aristocracy.

"In regard to rights, my friends, the NWO does not support the myth that everyone has God given or natural rights; we choose to deal with evidence not faith. We support the right of natural aristocracy. The word rights has become one of the most misused words of our time and has been the cause of more bloodshed and sorrow than anything else to which I can point. In lieu of rights, we believe in privilege, that so long as a person is a dutiful citizen and follows orders he shall be privileged to enjoy certain benefits. But if that person acts not in accordance with the precepts of the New World Order, then his privileges may be taken away. There is very little that the strong cannot take from the weak; therefore, the Aryan people must always depend upon their intelligence and use their muscle to back it up. Strength doesn't lie in some abstract right." Electrically charged silence follows these words as the spellbound audience breathlessly awaits his next words.

"As Aryans we must be sensitive to the impact of political policies on economics, and when those policies threaten our way of life, we must be ready to radically change them. Because the so called Coca Cola society is a direct threat to the Aryan race and the stability of the world, we must see that economic determinism is placed second to racial determinism.

Many of you in the audience today are women, and for your benefit I want to make perfectly clear the NWO position on women. As Aryans, we recognize the basic difference between men and women, but beyond that we encourage women to involve themselves to the limits of their abilities to support the interests of the Aryan race." The women in the crowd become frenzied, their screams deafening. Nearly five minutes elapse before they are quiet enough for him to continue. Although he is concerned about loosing momentum, his concern is short-lived. They await his next words as if they alone sustain their very existence. "Qualified women are, and will continue to be, operating at all levels of the organization because you are considered equal partners. I urge you not to fall victim to the popular beliefs about women that are handed down by the Muslim, Judaism, and Judeo-Christian religions; their belief structures are clearly anti-Aryan. The Judaised concept of women is the most obscene of all. You must remember, my sisters that under the Aryan banner male and female are a team.

"Now, my friends, I want to make a statement about the NWO position on homosexuality. Everywhere I go, and I am certain that you all have had similar experiences; I hear comments that lead me to conclude that the outside world considers us a family of homosexuals. Whether this stems from the fact that some of Hitler's associates were homosexual, or from other drummed up assertions, is of no importance to us. The real question becomes does nature cull those she finds unfit for reproduction? Homosexuals must be encouraged to separate their lifestyles from the community at large, and we must refrain from teaching homosexuality as a positive lifestyle. The homosexual population is not a major threat to the Aryan people. It is the right-wing element of society that is obsessed with the subject and who devotes too much time and money on this segment of the general population. Homosexuals have existed for thousands of years; therefore, the best the Aryan heterosexual society can do is to limit their collective influence and keep the closet door shut."

"Finally, my comrades, I want to leave you with this advice: all racial activists should concentrate on freeing the Aryan world from non-white aliens and from racial suicide. We are currently in the midst of Necrophilia. European Aryans have problems unique to Europe, and North American Aryans have their own peculiar problems; both must address these problems in their own way. NWO does not recognize a border between Aryan nations. We are facing the ultimate challenge that will become irreversible at some point in time, and I salute all Aryans around the world." As he leaves the podium, the crowd goes out of control, wild, jumping up and down, waving their arms, screaming, chanting NWO, NWO, NWO.

He accepts a glass of water from an assistant backstage, drinks it, looks the assistant in the eye and says, "I find it more and more difficult every day to communicate with the common man, Dieter. Why must I resort to street babble to be understood by them?"

Chapter 1

July 1, 1994

Colonel Hampton H. Porter stepped from the bachelor officer's quarters in freshly pressed officer's greens. This would be, he thought, the last time he would wear the uniform in an official capacity. As "Hamp" walked the twenty meters to the waiting staff car, he noted the crisp South Carolina air and a sky void of clouds. "Yes, it is going to be a beautiful fall morning," he said to no one in particular. Under other circumstances Hamp would have looked forward to a new and challenging day full of excitement as he had done for the past twenty-six years of his Army career.

"Good morning, Colonel. I'm Staff Sergeant Sanders, your driver for the day. General Stone said I was to be at your disposal for as long you needed me. Where to, sir?"

Hamp returned Sergeant Sander's salute, and slid onto the back seat of the sedan, the customary position for a senior officer passenger in a chauffeured military vehicle.

"For a start, I'd like to see the old basic training area over near the water tower. If I remember correctly, that area is called Tank Hill."

Hamp expected the sergeant to say the Tank Hill area had been demolished. After all, Hamp's last associations with Ft. Jackson, and the infamous basic training encampment know as Tank Hill was many years ago when he was a frightened, new recruit.

"You bet it's still there, sir, and still extracting blood, sweat and tears from the slick heads. Sorry, sir. I meant to say recruits."

"We used to call them slick heads, too, Sergeant," Hamp said with a smile. "Some things in this man's Army never change."

Fighting a growing feeling of nostalgia and sadness, Hamp gazed out the window and tried to concentrate on a company of basic trainees out on their morning run. "God, they look young," thought Hamp. Could he have looked so young and trim when he was one of them so long, long ago? There were no women in his training company when he was a basic trainee at Jackson. Hopeful of fending off a growing mood of nostalgia, Hamp reminded himself that for a man of 48 years he was still trim, and was entirely capable of running the distance with those "Newbys." He took pride in being able to maintain physical fitness— in spite of the scar tissue accumulated over the years, and the stiff knees on cold mornings.

"Sir, Major Johnson over in Officer Out-Processing told me to remind you that the retirement parade will begin at 1500 hours this afternoon."

"Thanks, Sergeant. I would prefer to miss it, but even Colonels have to follow orders."

"Did you have breakfast, Colonel? I could drive you by the Officer's Club on the way over to Tank Hill."

"Yes, thank you. He walked over to the troop mess hall behind the BOQ and ate with the soldiers of the 1st Training Brigade."

The morning passed rapidly as Hamp visited old training sites. The rifle ranges, obstacle courses and all the other training areas were still as he remembered them. As a matter of fact, not much had changed. Many of the buildings constructed during the early 1940's were still standing and serving a useful purpose, greatly surpassing their supposed seven year life expectancy. Thousands of these same types of wooden structures with coal stoves and no air conditioning covered every military reservation in the United States during the early years of World War II. Many had endured. Hamp wondered if perhaps it was the several dozen coats of paint which held them together. Chuckling to himself, Hamp considered the great bargain the government had gotten in those old structures so opposite from the waste associated with today's military like the infamous hundred dollar toilet seats.

After lunch on the hand grenade range with a company of advanced infantry trainees, Hamp freshened up at the BOQ. Ten minutes later he and Sergeant Pike arrived at the parade field where a brigade of soldiers and the 17th Army Field Band stood at parade rest on the parade field. Most of the visitors seated on each side of the reviewing stand were families and friends of the retirees being honored. Hamp, with a noticeable tightness in the pit of his stomach, placed his gold braided service cap on his head and walked smartly toward the reviewing stand to assume his place of honor in front of the troop formation.

Hamp was intercepted and greeted by the post commanding general's aide de camp. "Good afternoon, Colonel Porter. General Stone is waiting for you up on the reviewing stand. You will be on his left, sir."

"Thank you, Lieutenant."

"Sir, General Stone said you and he were old friends."

"Yes. We served together several times over the years at Fort Hood, the Pentagon, and twice in Vietnam."

The aide led Hamp up the reviewing stand steps and to his assigned place next to General Stone.

"Hamp! How did your tour of Fort Jackson go? Did you recognize any of the old places of your younger years?" asked the general as he shook Hamp's hand.

"Except for the new troop billets, I found the post much as she was 26 years ago, sir. Thanks for the use of your sedan and driver," Hamp said, almost as an after thought.

"Fran would have thrashed me had I not arranged for your last day of active duty to be a little bit special."

"Tell her again for me how much I enjoyed dinner last night and how good it was to see her again," said Hamp.

"Hell, Hamp! This day is as sad for me as it must be for you. You and I have a history together. Frankly, your premature retirement grieves me. I was looking forward to pinning those brigadier general stars on your shoulders next year. You know you were a "shoe-in" for the promotion list coming out next month."

"Thanks for your confidence in me, General. Serving with you over the past few years will be one of my fondest career memories," said Hamp.

The sound of the bugler playing Adjutant's Call interrupted their conversation, and signaled the beginning of the parade, Hamp's last parade.

As the troops passed in review, and the Honor Guard marched by the reviewing stand carrying the Army and National Colors, Colonel Hampton H. Porter stood at attention with his friend and rendered the hand salute, Hamp's last salute. He hoped no one saw the tears brimming in his eyes. He was leaving the life he had known for so many years, and the certainty he had come to depend upon, but he now faced an uncertain future all alone. His precious wife of 15 years, with whom he had dreamed of living out his old age, had died two years ago from cancer. "She should be here," he thought to himself. He faced the future now much as that fearful new recruit had faced his new military life all those many years ago. He wondered if he would be as successful with this new life as he had been with the previous. Regardless of these uncertainties, he would retire to his old fishing spot in Florida.

July 2, 1994

Gwen Judith Williams was born and raised in the small, scenic community of Evergreen, Washington, where she married her high school sweetheart Greg Williams during their senior year in high school. She was the beautiful cheerleader and beauty queen and Greg the football idol of Evergreen High School. They each managed to receive a decent education at Washington State University, thanks to Greg's football scholarship and limited financial support from both their families. They also managed to have two children during their four-year stay at Washington State. However, the marriage had been difficult for Gwen. Greg remained the spoiled idol of the female gender. He spent most of his time off the football field drinking beer with his teammates and pursuing the many miniskirts that abounded on campus. Gwen spent all her time caring for two baby boys and trying to study. To make life even more difficult, they had their third child, a daughter shortly after graduation. Soon thereafter Greg chose to return to Evergreen to help his father farm, and Gwen, the dutiful wife, followed. However, after having received a bachelor's degree in journalism, Gwen reluctantly settled into the predictable life of raising three children in the small house given to them by Greg's father. She did manage to work part time with the local weekly newspaper to keep her skills in journalism honed. Gwen believed their life to be satisfactory by local standards, but something was missing, something she could not quite identify. She did know that she was not like the other wives and mothers in Evergreen who were content with their particular lot in life. She wanted more beyond her babies' cooing and kisses goodnight on the cheek. She wanted more than bread baked perfectly or a floor that shone. She wanted a career. She wanted to be a part of everything important going on around her.

However, something was about to happen to brighten her life, and she could hardly wait.

Gwen drove away from the ranch as though a dire emergency required her immediate attention. She was speeding to the airport to meet the shuttle flight from Seattle. It was due at noon. She hurried because she was meeting her dear, lifelong friend Hamp Porter. She smiled to herself at her excitement. Heaven knows there was no need to rush. Traffic was not a problem in Evergreen; only two traffic lights were present in the entire community, but she allowed fifteen extra minutes just in case. She did not want to be late because Hamp's visit was special; she had not seen him since his wife's funeral just over two years ago.

Gwen and Hamp grew up together in Evergreen and had been best friends since. Hamp's parents still lived in Evergreen, and Gwen saw them regularly. They were like a second family to her. That is how Gwen had learned that Hamp was having a difficult time adjusting to his wife's death and his retirement from the Army two months ago.

It seemed only natural for Gwen to share Hamp's emotional distress—even in absentia. After all, they had shared many emotions through the years. Each had always been there for the other. Gwen considered their relationship the epitome of true friendship. She didn't feel it fair to Hamp to burden him with her present problem; he had enough to worry about, and she wanted to offer him comfort and understanding. Her problems could wait—for now. She saw her responsibility as providing temporary relief from his pain. She would hide her own.

The Salt Lake City shuttle was on time. Gwen's excitement grew as she watched Hamp cross the tarmac on the way to the terminal. He looked tall, slim, and a little older than his 43 years, but he still walked with his usual hiker's gait and stride.

Hamp saw Gwen immediately upon entering the small terminal. He could not help but see her because she was jumping up and down and squealing like a star struck fan at a concert. Hamp swept her from the floor and swung her around in circles until they almost fell.

"Oh, Hamp! You great big handsome devil. Don't you ever stay away from me so long again," said Gwen with her usual exuberance.

"I cannot believe how wonderful you look, Gwen," Hamp said. "You're more beautiful than ever."

"You always were good for my ego," Gwen replied.

Their conversation from the terminal to Gwen's car covered everything from families to fantasies. Both talked as fast as possible and simultaneously, but that did not matter. Two old and dear friends were together again, and both needed the other as never before.

"Since when did you begin opening car doors for me, sir?"

"Since I decided that just maybe you will behave like a lady if I give you one more chance," Hamp laughed.

"Give me a break," Gwen said while sporting her best frown. They had, without effort, fallen back into a very familiar pattern of mutual and affectionate harassment. It made them both feel very much at home in that special way known only to very good friends.

They passed the entire afternoon and early evening together sitting at their favorite place. Overlook Point, about four miles north and overlooking Evergreen, had been the spot they had chosen for their more serious conversations since they were teenagers. Today it seemed even more special to them. Their conversation was easy, carefree, and was concerned with nothing of great significance except once when Hamp, at Gwen's insistence, related the details of his wife's illness and death. They talked for hours. Words were never difficult to find despite the years that had separated the two friends. Then as the sun approached the western horizon, and the clouds were splashed with red, and orange, they stopped talking. For nearly fifteen minutes they watched in silence. It was as if the red glow of sunset had silenced their talk, but not their thoughts. .

It was Hamp who broke the silence.

He took Gwen's hands in his and gazed intently into her beautiful brown eyes. He spoke slowly and tenderly. "Gwen, you know that I can sense when something is not right with you. You are hurting, my friend, and I want to know what or who is to blame."

His words released a flood of emotion of which even Gwen was not fully aware. She had been so busy being what she was supposed to be that she had pushed her own disappointments aside. Now they were released by her friend's gentle words. She began to cry uncontrollably. Her breath came in jerks. Rivulets of tears ran down her cheeks and caught the red glow of the setting sun.

"It's not fair, Hamp," she sobbed. You have your own problems. I want to help you, not burden you. "

"We will not leave here until I know," Hamp said sternly. "I mean it, Gwen. I'm your friend, too. Remember?"

As Hamp talked, Gwen regained some of her composure. She removed Hamp's handkerchief from his jacket pocket, and blew her nose. "Okay, Hamp. Oh, God! I do have to talk to someone."

"You and Greg still having problems," Hamp suggested.

"Yes, but that's nothing new. That's not really the problem. It's part of it, I suppose, but not the most important part." She really did not know where to start, but she did—at the beginning. She told Hamp all about her troubled marriage and her inability to find her niche in life. As she opened her heart to Hamp, the sky's red glow gave way to twilight, their signal to leave.

Gwen drove them home unhurriedly—the long way. Each was pensive and quiet. Gwen broke the silence. "I prepared your favorite dinner; the menu includes a medium-well steak smothered in mushrooms and wine sauce, corn on the cob, and lemon ice box pie. Going out is too much trouble. Besides, there is still not a decent restaurant in town."

"Gwen, you didn't say corn bread?"

"Don't push your luck, or the Burger King will be your host for the evening, Colonel," Gwen said as she shoved her right elbow into Hamp's rib cage.

"I wish I could say that I look forward to seeing Greg, but in all honesty I'm not looking forward to it. It's all that I can do to keep a civil tongue when I'm around him. I just can't tolerate the way he treats you, Gwen. Why do you continue to stay with him?"

"I refuse to talk about that any more," Gwen said sternly. "I want to enjoy what little time I have with you. I don't want to spend it pursuing pipe dreams, okay? Can't we put it to rest? Please?"

"All right, but don't be surprised if I punch him out if he starts mistreating you, and I'm certain he will."

Gwen turned sharply into the driveway of her little white bungalow. Greg's pick-up was in the driveway. He had probably been drinking for at least an hour, Hamp suspected.

As she opened the car door and swung her legs out to exit the car, Gwen reminded Hamp once more to behave himself. Greg greeted them at the door, his beer belly hung over his dirty jeans and strained his shirt buttons to the breaking point. He badly needed a shave. Greg escorted Hamp through the house to the back yard grill without saying a word. Hamp had been correct in his earlier assumption; Greg was well on his way to inebriation. The smell of alcohol surrounding him was overpowering.

The grilling and the eating went surprisingly well. With accustomed skill, Gwen managed to steer the conversation toward only safe topics, and Greg managed to behave almost decently until she began clearing the table of dishes.

"What's this I hear about your wanting Gwen to spend a month in Steinhatchee with you? I'm telling you right now, Colonel Hampton Porter, that it ain't going to happen. You got real nerve, boy," Greg slurred. You think I'm stupid?"

Hamp took a deep breath, counted to ten, and spoke slowly and softly. "Greg, first of all, she is not going to stay with me. It's as simple as this. Ben Fuller, a friend of mine in Steinhatchee has developed a trend-setting Victorian resort on the river down there, and is ready to launch a nation-wide marketing campaign to promote the resort. He needs someone with a journalism background to design and implement the campaign. I told him that I had a friend with the qualifications he desired and suggested that he talk with Gwen about the job. I took the liberty of setting up the meeting with Ben because Gwen told me the last time we saw each other that she wanted to use her college training just to see if she has any real talent in that arena. Ben wants Gwen to visit Steinhatchee and talk with him about it. If they agree on terms, the assignment would require Gwen's presence in Steinhatchee for about a month. She would stay in Sexton's Motel. The owners are my friends and will look after her. That's all there is to it, Greg. Don't make more of it than is there. As to whether or not I think you are stupid, I think you are acting stupidly. I am also sure that you are quite drunk."

"Well, all I can say is you and Gwen have been too close for too long, and I don't like it."

"Greg, you are just jealous," Gwen said in a wavering voice. You don't think I am capable of doing something special. Well, your contribution to the world was that you could play football well. Let me remind you that that was 30 pounds and many years ago. I have always put my life and dreams on hold because of you and the kids. Now the time has come for me to see what I am capable of doing. Her eyes were like burning embers. "I intend to go. Besides, your mother has agreed to keep the children here in our house. I am entitled to do something with my life other than keeping house, cooking, cleaning, washing your clothes, and putting up with your damned infidelity. I'm going and there is nothing you can do to stop me," Gwen shouted. Tears ran freely down her cheeks, her fists were clinched, but Gwen did not loose eye contact with Greg, nor did she show any timidity.

"Well, we'll see about that," Greg shouted, as he stormed from the room overturning his chair.

"I think I should leave, Gwen," said Hamp with a deep exhale of breath.

"I'll drive you." Gwen took the keys from the credenza next to the door, walked through the front door, and got into the car without saying another word. Hamp followed.

Gwen drove for a couple blocks in silence and then looked at Hamp. "I'm going, Hamp," said Gwen with great determination. Tell Mr. Fuller I'll fly to Gainesville Sunday and rent a car. He can expect me next Monday morning."

"But that is only three days from now," said Hamp, a little surprised.

Gwen looked straight ahead and said, "Not soon enough."

They arrived in front of Hamp's parent's home. Hamp got out of the car and leaned into the passenger window. "I'm sorry things are not better for you, Gwen."

"Things will be better soon one way or another. Don't forget your bag in the back seat. I'll pick you up thirty minutes before flight time in the morning. Good night and I'm sorry for Greg's behavior, Hamp."

"Don't be." He watched the tail lights of her car until they disappeared over the hill. He was ready for sleep, but doubted that it would come. Gwen hurt and he hurt with her. He had not realized that her marriage, and subsequent unhappiness, had deteriorated to shambles.

At seven thirty the next morning, Hamp peered through the living room window to see Gwen waiting in the car near the front door.

"'Morning," said Hamp cheerfully as he approached the car. "Are you okay?"

"Yes, thank you," Gwen responded with a half-smile. "Get any sleep last night?"

"My usual four hours, thank you," clipped Hamp with false sarcasm. "To the airport, madam, if you please."

They filled the fifteen minutes to the airport with light chitchat. Neither of them wanted to relive the events of last night. Gwen held Hamp's left hand tightly in her right hand as she drove.

"Will you be in Steinhatchee Monday, Hamp?"

"Yes, sure. As you know, I've been away from the place for over a year. I need to spend some time there getting the place back to some degree of normalcy. I also want to do some fishing and diving with my friend, Tom Adams. I'll be waiting with a smile. There is nothing for you to worry about. Sam and Winnie are expecting you at the motel, and Ben Fuller will be ready for you; I called him last night."

Hamp snatched his luggage from the back seat, kissed Gwen on the cheek, waved good bye, and walked directly to the connecting flight to Seattle. His next stop would be four hours later at Jacksonville International Airport in Florida. His good friend, Tom Adams, would be waiting for him at the airport. Steinhatchee was just a two and a half-hour drive from Jacksonville.

Chapter 2

January, 1995

Lieutenant Colonel Billy Joe Patterson, United States Army, from the sovereign State of Mississippi, settled into the back seat of his military sedan for the twenty minute ride from his quarters to the elevator level of the infamous Eagle's Nest. Billy Joe had been a very senior lieutenant colonel for the past five years, and had commanded the American Armed Forces Recreation Center at Berchtesgaden, Germany. Since there are only three US Forces recreation centers in Germany, his job was considered one of the most sought after assignments in Europe. He essentially waived any further career advancement in order to keep his job for as long as possible. Billy Joe, or B.J. as his friends referred to him, was a popular, flamboyant cavalry officer with good political connections which he used unashamedly to help land his present job.

Before World War II, all three American armed forces recreation centers in Germany were prime German ski resorts ranked among the best in Europe. At the conclusion of the war, Allied forces retained control of certain properties throughout Germany under special lease arrangements specified in the terms and conditions of the Allied occupation of post-war Germany. Most of the properties were army kaserns and Luftwaffe air bases. The kaserns were used as Allied troop bases, troop billets and family quarters. Three of the prime resort properties, Chiemsee, Garmisch/Partenkirchen, and

Berchtesgaden in southern Bavaria, were converted to recreational facilities for US Forces.

As B.J. pensively gazed at the surrounding mountains, he thought it remarkable that so much Alpine beauty could have part of its history entangled with the brief existence of Germany's Third Reich. He recalled that during the early days of Hitler's political career, Hitler's friend and mentor, Dietrich Eckart, introduced him to the Obersalzberg. Obersalzberg means "Upper Salt Mountain", which refers to salt residue left by the Ice Age at the 3,300-foot level of the Kehlstein and Hohen Goll Mountains. Several villages in the area, including Berchtesgaden, were old salt mining communities. Dietrich Eckart played a significant role in Hitler's early political thinking. He authored Deutschland Erwache (Germany Awaken), which inflamed Hitler's determination to become Germany's political savior, and held ideas similar to Hitler's regarding Germany's need for new politics. Eckart later helped Hitler form the National Socialist German Worker's Party (NSDAP), the party that eventually became the Nazi movement.

Eckart was also responsible for showing Hitler Haus Wachenfeld, a private Alpine dwelling on the Obersalzberg built by the Bavarian Director of Commerce in 1916. Hitler immediately fell in love with the house and always made a point of visually inspecting it during his many walks over the Obersaltzberg. He always stayed at Pension Moritz on the Obersaltzberg primarily because Haus Wachenfeld was less than a kilometer from the inn. In just a few short years, Haus Wachenfeld, Pension Moritz, and most of the unsuspecting residents of the Obersalzberg became victim to a remarkable transformation.

After his stay in jail in 1929, Hitler acquired Haus Wachenfeld and renamed it the

Berghof. Then, subsequent to his appointment as chancellor in 1933, Hitler moved to establish a secret, elaborate complex on the Salzberg from which he would rule the Third Reich, and, he thought, the world. Rudolf Hess, Hitler's party secretary, began the expansion, but it was Martin Bormann, Hess' replacement, who took over the expansion of the complex with a vengeance. If B.J.'s memory served him correctly, it was Bormann who brutally ousted farmers from their property in order to establish complete territorial integrity of the complex. Bormann was said to have fenced the entire compound. Then he constructed an inner fence to divide the area into the inner circle (Hoheitsgebiet, or sovereign territory) for the houses of Hitler's close associates, and the outer circle where employees and construction workers lived. Schutzstaffel, (SS) guards, were quartered in expensive stone barracks at the perimeter of the compound. Three hundred feet below the Berghof, accessible by elevator or stairs, Bormann constructed an extensive system of tunnels that interconnected other installations on the Obersalzberg. The system consisted of caverns and sub tunnels branching off both sides of a large main tunnel. The caverns were at the disposal of the Berghof inhabitants. Hitler had seventeen rooms, Hermann Goering, ten, and Martin Bormann, five. Even though the rooms were caverns in the side of a mountain, their furnishings were nothing if not plush. They included polished walls, inlaid floors, rugs, wainscoting, well-equipped offices, and safes built into solid rock. Ironically, Hitler did not own the property, but Martin Bormann held title to all of it.

Bormann even went so far as to dismantle the famous Pension Moritz and replaced it with a new hotel he named the Platterhoff. It was supposed to be an inn for all Germans who wished to spend a night close to the Fuhrer, but in actuality it was too expensive for the average German, and became quarters for Hitler's business guests and friends—just as Bormann had planned. The structure was elaborate. It consisted of a basement and two floors above ground built of marble and stone. The interior was comprised of a reception hall with paintings on the ceiling, a barber shop, a beauty parlor, a reading room, bowling alleys, a mirrored hall, a library, a beer room, a breakfast room, and 150 quest rooms. The furnishings were of the best available. This newly constructed transformation of the Obersalzberg quickly acquired the name of Hitler Territory.

This facility, since called the General Walker Hotel, or GW, was now B.J.'s domain and he lorded over it in the finest tradition of Conrad Hilton. Why shouldn't he? He lived like a king in a king's Alpine surroundings. He awoke every morning to the grandiosity of Alpine scenery, his wife was happy in these surroundings, and his staff was competent Germans who performed their jobs well and never caused problems. Most had been in the continuous employ of the center since the end of the war and the death of Hitler. B.J. and his wife were prominent members of the local social scene, and he had stature as a local businessman; the center meant 105 jobs and over five million US dollars a year to the community's economy. As an American soldier in a foreign land, he truly had the best of all worlds, and he knew it.

The center consisted of a well-stocked ski shop, two fine restaurants, a small Post Exchange store, and three well-appointed hotels, all of which were formerly part of the Hitler Territory. The buildings and grounds were immaculately maintained in the German tradition and according to local horticultural practices. The General Raymond D. Walker Hotel was the focal point and gemstone of the center with a commanding view of the town and the Obersalzburg. B.J. and his staff played host to more than 300 vacationing American soldiers and their families on any given day.

The time was 1940 hours and the snow-covered shops and homes of the community glowed with soft colors from stained glass windows and fireplaces. As his sedan negotiated the snow-packed streets, B.J.'s mind settled on the evening ahead. He was going to dine with Herr. Peter Weismann, the Bavarian Director of Museums, newly appointed by Herr. Heinz Teoffel, Germany's Minister of Interior Affairs. In three months, he would assume responsibility for and curatorship of the Eagle's Nest and all other pre-war Nazi Museum-quality structures and facilities throughout Bavaria including B.J.'s beloved recreation center. The Allied leases with the German government were about to expire and all three recreation centers would revert to German control. According to Herr. Weismann's telephone call two days earlier, they would discuss transitional topics after dinner. B.J. assumed Herr. Weismann wanted to discuss matters pertaining to the passing of the baton, so to speak. He also mentioned something about a chance to become better acquainted. Because Weismann had said that a few friends would also be present. B.J. thought it odd that his wife had not been included in the dinner invitation, but he assumed that the other guests must all be male. He was acquainted with Weismann, but knew very little about him. USAREUR (United States Army Europe) Headquarters in Heidelberg sent a brief biographical sketch on Weismann two days ago. The sketch included very little useful information, just the usual stuff on education, experience,

and family. It would be just enough to facilitate
dinner party small talk.

According to the sketch, Peter Weismann was
the son of a Jewish businessman, Franz Weismann.
He was born in Berlin where his mother was killed
in an Allied bombing raid shortly after his birth
in 1944. His father took him to Brazil after the
war and established an export business. He
attended Brighten Academy in England from age
twelve until his matriculation to the University
of Heidelberg in 1960. He graduated the
university with honors in 1964 and lived with an
aunt, Frau Ilea Weismann, while he pursued post-
graduate work in political science and history at
Humboldt University in Berlin. He worked in
various civil service posts in the Bavarian
government until 1994 when he was appointed
curator of the Eagle's Nest in Berchtesgaden and
other minor museums in Bavaria. In 1995 he took
a sabbatical from his governmental duties to
study somewhere in Turkey. The sketch also
mentioned Weismann's avid interest in the history
of World War II, and that he was considered an
expert on the Hitler era, especially the third
Reich, the Nazi Party and neo-Nazism.

"Oh, well. I'll play this evening by ear.
I've had practice doing that," said B.J. to no
one. B.J. mused that his role in Berchtesgaden
social circles had placed him in the company of
Herr. Weismann several times, but they had not
developed a friendship, nor had B.J. a reason or
desire to learn more about the man. He was a
nice looking, athletically built man who dressed
impeccably. Herr. Weismann was also a loner and
had the reputation of being an intellectual
eccentric with extreme political views. "Not my
cup of tea," thought B.J.

"Careful of this road, Pike; it's slick as
owl manure and narrow as a gnat's behind," said

B.J. to his driver in his characteristic Mississippi drawl.

The climb to the elevator level and parking area of the Eagle's Nest was five miles long and very steep. The road was one sharp curve after another with no guardrail. Several workers involved in the construction of the road were killed when trucks plunged over the side of the mountain.

There were no lights along the roadside, nor was there a moon this particular night. Total blackness surrounded them, and B.J. felt as if they were floating in space. The sedan lights on the road and the lights of the town below were their only points of orientation. A slight shiver ran across his shoulders and down his spine. As far as he was concerned, Alpine driving should be limited to daylight hours.

"I hope we don't meet another car," said Pike.

"If we do, stop and let it pass; don't jockey for position. Remember we are in the outside lane," cautioned B.J.

"How can I forget?" replied Pike in a shaky voice.

B.J. finally saw four quartz lamps on twenty-foot poles illuminating a parking area thirty yards ahead. The sedan lights illuminated a green, rectangular sign with the words "Eagle's Nest" printed in white. "We're here," said B.J. "Park next to that Mercedes."

"Sure looks different at night, sir. It's kind of spooky."

"Yeah, well, this whole damned evening is spooky if you ask me," drawled B.J. He thought to himself, "Why is this guy putting on a dinner party in the Eagle's Nest for heaven's sake? The place is just a tourist attraction; it isn't permanently staffed."

B.J. quickly walked the twenty-five yards from the sedan to the heavy bronze double doors guarding the entrance to the tunnel that led to the elevator anteroom. The first time he saw those doors, five years earlier, they appeared to be an entryway into the mountainside itself, like large bronze doors fastened to solid granite. In the poor light, he almost failed to see the man dressed in domestic servant's attire standing at the door.

"Welkohmen, Herr. Parker," said the man in formal German, as he opened the door for B.J.

"Danke," said B.J., a little surprise in his voice.

"Your driver may wait with me down here," said the man in perfect English. His remark sounded more like a polite order than a suggestion; B.J. could not help but be slightly taken aback by the man's temerity.

"This is really going to be an interesting evening after all," thought B.J.

B.J. remembered from earlier briefings that the tunnel was 170 meters long and wide enough for two cars to pass. The ceiling was high and supported an electric cable the full length of the tunnel from which a light fixture was suspended every ten feet. A special mortar mix protected the rock walls from humidity.

The tunnel led to another set of bronze doors that formed the entrance to a small anteroom of about a hundred square feet with ornately carved wooden benches along opposing walls. The floor was covered with heavy, gray slate. A very large set of brass elevator doors occupied most of the remaining wall. The doors were polished highly enough to serve as mirrors. B.J. pushed the single button on the left elevator door panel and the doors slid quietly open. "Not bad for fifty year-old doors," thought B.J. The interior walls of the elevator

were also made of highly polished brass. Crimson
wool carpet covered the floor. Crystal lamps
adorned three sides of the elevator and made the
polished brass walls appear even brighter. There
were cushioned seats, a telephone, and an
umbrella stand in the elevator. The doors closed
as quietly as they opened, and the elevator began
its ascent. The electric motor was so quiet and
the ride so smooth, that B.J. was barely aware of
any movement. Only the pressure change on his
ears assured him that the elevator was ascending.
He made the 200-foot ascent in about 20 seconds.
B.J.'s mind drifted to the history of the
infamous Eagle's Nest, the place to which he was
presently ascending for the third time in the
last five years.

He recalled that Martin Bormann ordered
work to begin on this mountain perch in 1935.
Although called a teahouse, it was to serve as a
very private conference center and place of
relaxation for Hitler. Work could only be done
during the months of May through October, before
the snow season. To reach the 5,500-foot peak of
the Kehlstein, the site Bormann selected for the
teahouse, a road five miles long had to be
constructed from the Berghof to the base of
Kehlstein. Long tunnels had to be blasted
through the mountain. Then, a long tunnel leading
to the site of the elevator, and a shaft for the
elevator, had to be blasted from the solid
mountain rock. Working conditions were horrible
and life was miserable for the workers. They
lived in barracks 18 men to a room, and were
allowed only a pillow, blankets, and a small
cupboard. Under Bormann's supervision, they
received extremely harsh treatment and many died.
Once completed, the tunnel, elevator, and
teahouse were protected by remotely controlled
poison gas. Bormann considered the tea house to
be a starting point for Hitler's and his escape

to South America, should the need arise. At a
cost of 30 million marks, the Eagle's Nest was
the most expensive teahouse ever built. Fritz
Todt, the project engineer, completed this
engineering marvel and construction in less than
two years. It literally perched on a mountain
crag 5,500 feet above Berchtesgaden. Even after
three visits to the Eagle's Nest, B.J. still
found it and the very idea of the place,
extremely fascinating and incredible. "There
certainly isn't anything like this in
Mississippi," mumbled B.J.

The elevator reached its only stopping
place twenty seconds later. The fifty-year old
machine had ascended nearly 200 feet through a
vertical tunnel cut from solid granite. The doors
slide quietly open again to reveal an image
easily remembered by B.J., and it was still
breathtaking. Before him was the huge, vaulted
tearoom, the largest room in the nest. Besides
the tea room, the nest contained a dining room,
study, kitchen, guard room, washrooms, rest
rooms, and a basement. Most of the rooms were
lined with stone, pine, or elm paneling. The
tearoom was lined with Untersberg and Cararic
marble. The huge fireplace was decorated with
bronze tiles. A collection of overstuffed leather
chairs and sofas served as two conversational
groups near the glass walls of the tearoom.
Wool area rugs of Turkish design and animal hide
rugs were carefully placed according to furniture
groupings. From the juncture of the support beams
at the center of the ceiling hung a massive
chandelier made from wrought iron which supported
sixty light fixtures. A long walnut dining table
inlaid with black ebony hunting scenes, and
twelve matching chairs occupied the space in
front of the fireplace. Hanging over the
fireplace, in lieu of the once present portrait
of Adolf Hitler, was a large oil painting of a

hunting scene. A roaring fire crackled and imposed dancing reflections on the glass wall panels. "This was definitely not how I remembered this place," said B.J. to himself.

Herr. Weismann immediately excused himself from the group of men standing around the fireplace and quickly walked toward B.J. with his right hand extended in greeting. "I'm so glad you could join us this evening, Colonel Patterson," said Weismann with a warm smile. "Come over here so that I might introduce you to my friends. And please allow me to offer you a drink. We are having wine."

Weismann took B.J. by the arm and led him to the group of men who were now observing him without any particular expression of interest. Weismann placed a glass of wine in B.J.'s hand and began the introductions. "Beginning on your left, Colonel Patterson, may I present Herr. Doktor Heinrich Dieppe, Herr. Erich Feltgeibell, Herr. Doktor Hans Reifenstahl, Mr. Zuni Anatole, and Mr. Tomas Popodopolus. Gentlemen, I present to you Lieutenant Colonel B.J. Patterson, commander of the US Forces Recreation Center Berchtesgaden. Well, Gentleman, I think that about does it. Shall we take our seats at the table for dinner?"

"I apologize for my tardiness, Herr. Weismann. The road was particularly slippery this evening, and my driver was a little apprehensive. I hope I have not delayed dinner."

"Certainly not. No apology is necessary. We were just discussing the business of Allied property leases that will expire soon. Please take the chair at the other end of the table, the place of honor," Weismann said as he gestured toward the chair. The other men began taking seats on either side of the table between B.J. and Weismann. "Perhaps you will be good enough to

share your thoughts with us on that subject,"
Weismann suggested.

Everyone appeared to be waiting for B.J.
to respond to Weismann's last request. As a heavy
oxtail soup was served, B.J. cleared his throat
and tried to appear as nonchalant as possible. He
thought, "I'm beginning to feel a bit outclassed,
but I'm not certain why."

"The expiration of the property leases was
not a surprise; the eventuality was anticipated
in the armistice agreement from the very
beginning," he said with a matter of fact tone.

"But do you see the transitional activities
associated with the expiration as problematical
for you or for us?" asked Weismann.

"I assume you mean the United States and
Germany, Herr. Weismann. In my opinion my
government will experience irritating, but
manageable, logistical problems in turning over
the kaserns and Luftwaffe bases. There could be
problems of a domestic nature in reassigning
troops to the United States and other foreign
bases, but I really do not expect problems of a
significant nature. I certainly do not expect
problems in turning over the facility here. As
for Germany, I expect your government might have
difficulty in deciding exactly what to do with
the facilities, but nothing serious. I should
imagine they already have a plan to deal with the
matter. Do you anticipate problems, Herr.
Weismann?"

"No, no, no. I expect no problems from the
German side. As you say, I, too, believe plans
have been drawn to make proper disposition of all
the properties. Of course, I am not privy to
these plans, Colonel Patterson —if they exist. I
am privy only to matters that might affect
properties located in Bavaria," responded
Weismann.

"Of course you know, Colonel Patterson, that Herr. Weismann has been appointed to the post of Director of Museums," said Herr. Feltgeibell, as though B.J. might not be aware of events going on in his own back yard.

"Yes, of course I am aware of that, Herr. Feltgeibell, and let me congratulate you once again on that honor, Herr. Weismann," replied B.J. smiling slightly.

"How kind. By the way, thank you for your kind note of acknowledgement, Colonel Patterson," said Weismann, with a slight bow of his head. "Now, let us dine, Gentleman; we have prepared for you a very good rouladen garnished with roasted almonds. Come. Eat."

It was obvious that Weismann wanted to change the subject, but B.J. couldn't figure out why, nor could he determine the reason for the presence of the other dinner guests. If Weismann wanted to discuss transitional matters in particular as they applied to the recreation center in Berchtesgaden, why would he have invited other guests who had no personal interest in the transition? Or did they have personal interests? "I suspect a hidden agenda here," mumbled B.J. to himself.

B.J. did expect further conversation on the subject of lease expirations. While waiting, he initiated dinner chitchat by asking, in turn, the occupation of each guest. He thought that might give him insight as to the reason for their presence. Remembering at least the last name of each guest, he began with Heinrich Dieppe.

Heinrich Dieppe was not a remarkable man. He was older, of average height and weight, slightly stooped, with graying brown hair. His clothing was typical of that expected of a university professor, and he wore small, wire-rimmed glasses.

"Doctor Dieppe, Herr. Weismann mentioned that you are a professor. What is your area of academic specialization and where do you teach, sir?"

"I teach the history of the Third Reich at Humboldt University, Colonel Patterson," he said without looking up from his dinner plate.

B.J. knew better than to ask what he did before and during World War II. "And how about you, Herr. Feltgeibell? What is your occupation, sir?"

Erich Feltgeibell was a man in his sixties, on the tall side, and bald. Although overweight, he had excellent posture and carried the weight well. His grooming and general appearance suggested that he took very good care of himself. His eyes commanded attention and respect.

"I am a business man, Colonel Patterson. I have an export business in Brazil. We export pumice found in South America to Europe, The United States, and Canada. Are you familiar with pumice, Colonel Patterson? It is the key ingredient in polishing compounds used in dental work and other polishing operations requiring precision," explained Feltgeibell.

"No, sir, I was not aware of the use of pumice. Thank you for enlightening me. Doctor Reifenstahl, may I ask you the same question, sir?"

Hans Reifenstahl was tall, thin, tanned, and had a very full head of blondish-gray hair. He was a handsome man of about sixty-five, and was dressed in well-tailored tropical linen.

"Yes, of course. I, too, am in the import/export business, in a way. I have a small company in the British Virgin Islands that deals in sailing vessels, Colonel Patterson. We broker boats for the many charter companies in the islands, and find buyers for them when the charter companies are ready to rotate their fleets."

"How did you come to meet Herr. Weismann?" asked B.J.

Weismann put his wineglass down with a noticeable firmness, cleared his throat, and said, "I will satisfy Colonel Patterson's curiosity, Hans. You see, Colonel Patterson, my father knew many people in the import/export business. They are a small fraternity in Germany; that was especially true just before and after the war. My father knew most of these men as competitors or occasional business partners. Many friendships formed among these men over the years. Some are still friends today, but most are now dead. Hans was my father's friend and now he is my friend --from father to son, as the saying goes. In fact, my friends here are on their way to Munich for an international import/export association conference and were kind enough to make a slight detour south to visit me in Berchtesgaden."

"Very interesting," said B.J. "Family friendships are apparently more common in Germany than in the United States. We have become too mobile to allow extended family friendships. You are lucky," smiled B.J. "Now it's your turn, Mr. Anatole. Am I pronouncing your name correctly? Please forgive me if I am not."

"Close enough, Colonel Patterson. As you might have guessed, I am Turkish. You Americans seem to have a difficult time with Turkish pronunciations," Anatole said in a very thick Turkish accent. "There is no need to ask your question of me, Colonel Patterson. I will tell you in advance that I, too, am an exporter. My office is in Istanbul, but I also have small offices in Ankara and Ismir. Are you surprised to hear that I am an exporter, Colonel Patterson?" With that explanation, Mr. Anatole rendered a loud belly laugh, and B.J. thought his belly ample enough to make the laugh much louder should the need arise. "I export carpets, Colonel Patterson, the kind of carpets that adorn the floor of this beautiful place."

"And that leaves me, Colonel Patterson." B.J. noticed that Mr. Popodopolus spoke English with an accent that was more near Eastern than European. "I travel a great deal throughout the Mediterranean and Asia Minor, Colonel Patterson. My interest is in flocatti wool. I buy the wool in Greece and Turkey, manufacture the famous flocatti rugs, and export them all over the world."

"Oh. Yes. My daughter is the owner of one of your rugs, Mr. Popodopolus. She will be impressed when I tell her of my meeting you," said B.J. humbly.

"Well, gentlemen, now that we are all acquainted, let us retire to the sitting area for a sip of brandy. Shall we?" Again, Weismann appeared to want the direction of conversation changed, thought B.J. "We have not yet gotten around to his agenda," thought B.J. to himself.

B.J. stood with his back to the fireplace, so he could see the lights of Berchtesgaden below. Two or three separate conversations were taking place as the men found seats in the grouping of furniture nearest the fire.

"I cannot help but notice, Herr Weismann that the Eagle's Nest has been completely furnished since I was here last. It was completely bare during my last visit." The conversations ended. All eyes were now on B.J.

"Yes. Yes, it has. I convinced the Bavarian Interior Minister to allow me to furnish the most famous, or infamous, buildings among the properties being returned to our control. The Eagle's Nest is sort of an experiment, if you will, before the minister agrees to explore the idea further. Since I am now curator and live in Berchtesgaden, it logically followed that the Eagle's Nest would be the first attempt. It will even enhance the value of the Nest as a tourist attraction, I believe. Do you agree, Colonel Patterson?" asked Weismann.

"These gentlemen and I donated the furnishings, Colonel Patterson," interrupted Mr. Popodopolus. "When Peter told us of his idea to refurbish these places, we thought it wonderful and decided to help in some small way. It is good for international politics, is it not, Colonel Patterson?" laughed Popodopolous.

"Yes. They were so generous and thoughtful, and I shall forever be in their debt," said Weismann.

"Remarkable," said B.J. "Gentlemen, I am impressed."

"I intend to move my personal quarters from the village to the Eagle's Nest once the transition with your people is complete, Colonel Patterson. I shall use the Commander in Chief's suite in the Platterhof Hotel for my office. What do you think?" asked Weismann.

"Great idea. The suite is very plush and would make a very comfortable business office," replied B.J. He noticed that Weismann did not use the American name for the hotel, The General Walker. Everyone nodded in agreement. Doctor Reifenstahl proposed a toast, as though a great victory had been realized, and everyone lifted their glasses. B.J. knew Weismann was about to change the subject again by the way he cleared his throat in preparation for speaking. He cleared his throat before speaking each time on a new subject, which was undoubtedly a habit.

"Tell me, Colonel Patterson, do you know if any physical changes will be made to the old storage tunnels under the Platterhoff and other

Berghof buildings before the transition of property is complete?"

"Bingo! The hidden agenda was about to be revealed," thought B.J. But what possible interest could he have in those tunnels? Weismann must have noticed the puzzled look on B.J.'s face.

"I'm sorry, Colonel Patterson. Allow me to be more specific. As all of us here know, the Allied forces, the Americans to be specific, were the first to reach Berchtesgaden during the last days of the war. They assumed, after a cursory examination, that the Nazis had removed anything of value from the tunnels and set off explosive charges that sealed the tunnel entrances except for four rooms. Do you know if there are plans to unseal the tunnels prior to your property transfer to me?" Weismann's tone and facial expression turned deadly serious as he asked his question. B.J. wondered if Weismann knew how obvious he was being. "He had said, 'Transfer the property to me,' " thought B.J.

"Well, no. To my knowledge there are no such plans," B.J. answered with a little surprise in his voice. "Quite frankly, Herr. Weismann, your question arouses my curiosity. What would be the point in opening the tunnel?" asked B.J.

"I apologize, Colonel Patterson. I had no intention of embarrassing you. The minister of interior wants to include the tunnels as added tourist attractions. As you can imagine, reopening the tunnels will be extremely expensive. It would be nice if you Americans would do that before leaving. Tell me, Colonel Patterson, just how much damage was caused to the tunnels by the explosives used to seal them?" asked Weismann.

Weismann's tone had grown suddenly cold. "You are beginning to piss me off," thought B.J. to himself, even if I am your guest.

"Herr. Weismann, I think you are asking me if we intend to clean up a mess we made earlier under very different circumstances. The answer is no, not anymore than we intend to rebuild every building that was destroyed during Allied bombing raids. And as for the amount of damage done to the tunnel, I have no idea, nor do I know of anyone else who might know." B.J. knew he had crossed the line and had demonstrated bad manners, but he could not help himself. The question was insulting to him and was an affront to the United States. The room was quiet. They all stared at B.J. expressionless. He knew the evening was over.

"The hour is late and the road down the mountain will have frozen solid," said B.J. "Thank you for your hospitality, Herr. Weismann. You may contact my office when you are ready to work out the specifics of our transition. Good evening, gentlemen." Not another word was said by anyone. B.J. collected his hat and coat and entered the elevator without looking back.

The electric motor faintly hummed, and the elevator began its descent. B.J. asked himself the same questions over and over:. "Why was Weismann so interested in the tunnel? Why were the other men, all export/import people, present? Was it coincidental to their visit to Weismann? And what were their interests in the transition? Who the hell were they?" The elevator stopped without a hint of a bump. When the doors opened, the man who had greeted him earlier was gone. When he exited the tunnel, B.J. saw exhaust vapor coming from the sedan and assumed Pike was in the sedan running the engine to keep warm.

"That's an excellent way to commit suicide, Pike," said B.J. as he entered the sedan.

"I had my window rolled down a couple inches, sir."

"I thought that fellow was going to take care of you. Have you been waiting in the sedan all evening?"

"Oh, no, sir. We ate bratwurst, cheese, and bread for awhile. Then he left."

"Chances are the road is frozen solid. Let's take it slow and easy going down," said B.J. as he closed his eyes and laid his head on the back of the seat. The questions kept coming: "Why the interest in the tunnel? Who are those men? What is their agenda and interest? Well, one thing is for certain, my transition with Weismann will be strained. Hell, I'm retiring in three months, so why the hell should I care?"

* * * * *

"Well, gentlemen, what did you think of our Colonel Patterson?" says Weismann as soon as the elevator doors closed.

"He is not as bright as I, for some reason, had thought he might be," said Dr. Dieppe.

"But I do not think he will present a problem," said Mr. Popodopolus. "How could he possibly be a problem?"

"Perhaps not a problem, my friend, but I failed to find out what I must know. Did the Americans leave anything in the tunnel when they sealed it, and how extensive was the damage to the tunnel? We still do not know the answer to those questions, gentlemen," said Weismann unhappily. "And do not underestimate Colonel Patterson's intelligence. I am told that he uses his Mississippi drawl to make everyone think he's just a good ol' boy, as the Americans say."

"The Americans will be in too big a hurry to complete the transfer of property to give a damn about the tunnel, Peter," said Zuni Anatole. "Why should they pay it any attention at all?"

"Do the rest of you think Zuni is correct in his assumption?" asked Weismann. Everyone nodded affirmatively. "Perhaps you are all correct. I just do not want any surprises. Our investment in Pegasus is too enormous for us to commit simple, stupid mistakes. We cannot afford clumsiness or sloppiness in our operation, gentlemen," said Weismann emphatically. "There can be no loose ends or unfinished business. Do we understand each other?" Again everyone nodded affirmatively. "If we are successful in our endeavor to trade nuclear warheads for heroin, we stand to earn enough money to finance the growth of the New World Order for at least the next five years."

"Now, let us get down to the business of Pegasus, shall we?" insisted Weismann. "Dieppe, you are the chief of staff for Pegasus, the floor is yours," said Weismann with authority. Weismann knew Dieppe was not exactly enamored with the name Pegasus because it came from Greek, not German, mythology, but Weismann liked it and Popodopolus loved it, so be it.

"The most significant problem we face, as I see it, is the fact that US Army Artillery Detachments have physical custody of the warheads at all the nuclear storage facilities in Europe and Turkey," said Dieppe pensively. "You each have the authority to do what you must to circumvent this problem. Please share with us how you are going to remove multiple warheads from those American facilities, gentlemen? Tomas, please begin," said Dieppe.

"Very well," said Popodopolus as he stood and began pacing in front of the fireplace. "I am most encouraged at the progress we have already made in Thessalonica. The disgruntled American soldier we found and cultivated has agreed to provide us with drawings of the warhead storage and assembly building on the US Army compound northeast of Thessalonica. My suggestion is that we tunnel under the compound to the storage and

assembly building. I know it will take much
longer that way; however, I believe there is no
other way to breech the compound security
measures. The Americans take nuclear security
very seriously, and they are meticulous in their
efforts to insure it. The buildings are enclosed
in double chain link fences, 14 feet high, 12
feet apart, with razor wire on top. There is a
guard tower at each corner of the compound, and
walking, armed patrols along the fences. Guard
dogs freely roam the inner fence line. The fences
are extremely well-lighted, and in case of a
power failure, there are emergency generators to
power the fence lights. There is a 44- man
reaction force to back up the normal guard
contingent. Guards have instructions to shoot
anyone inside the fences who are not properly
identified. We are ready to begin digging up to
the assembly room flooring at any time."

"I am concerned about the direct
involvement of an American serviceman, Tomas,"
said Feltgeibell. "Is that not risky? That means
he can identify at least one of your people. That
is very bad," says Feltgeibell, shaking his head
from side to side.

"Once we have the information we need,
Hans, the person liaising with the American will
meet with an unfortunate accident. Should the
American have a patriotic change of heart and
confess his transgression to the authorities,
there will be no one for him to point to as his
accomplice," says Popodopolus.

"Excellent," says Weismann.

"Mr. Anatole, please proceed," says Dieppe.

"Thank you, Heinrich. Gentlemen, I am
confident that the Turkish part of Pegasus is
ready to proceed. Colonel Sultoy, commander of
the Turkish security detachment in Boctoi, is
fully on board with us and has been invaluable in
helping with preparations. We will have the

advantage of the Turkish security forces being on
our side when the time comes. They have full
responsibility for perimeter security of the
American custody detachment compound. The nuclear
storage and assembly building in the compound is
in a natural tunnel at the base of a mountain.
Colonel Sultoy knows of a sub-tunnel that at one
time intersected the main tunnel near the storage
and assembly site. The Americans sealed the
juncture when they placed the storage and
assembly room in the tunnel. We have already
drilled our way through the old juncture at the
main tunnel using the many seasonal storms that
occur in that region to mask the noise. The work
will be far enough removed from the facility
entrance so as not to be heard. Working during
storms is just an added precaution we are taking.
When activity is planned inside the facility,
Colonel Sultoy's men will alert the tunnel crew.
That is an over-simplified explanation of what we
are doing, gentlemen. In the interest of time, I
omitted certain details." said Zuni Anatole.

"Who is this Colonel Sultoy? How do you
know he can be trusted? Did you cultivate him
personally, Zuni?" asked Reifenstahl. Dieppe and
Feltgeibell nodded their agreement with the
question.

"Colonel Sultoy is somewhat of a political
outsider," said Zuni Anatole. He hates the
present regime because of the treatment his
father received when they took over the
government. He retains his rank and position in
the Turkish army only because of his wife's
connections with the prevailing government. If
his feelings about the government are not
sufficient motivation to keep him quiet about his
involvement with me, I have promised him money
enough to leave Turkey for good. Should he elect
to stay in Turkey, I would expect that he might

have an accident—an accident permanently detrimental to his health."

"We will perhaps revisit your plans, Zuni," said Dieppe. "I am not comfortable with your reliance on thunderstorms. Yes. We will hear the others and then come back to you. Hans, please tell us of your preparations."

Hans Reifenstahl was standing near the windows. He turned slowly, removed the pipe from his mouth, blew a large smoke ring at the ceiling, and began speaking. "At least twice a week during the winter season, less often during the summer months, one of the boats we sell sets sail from Tortola heading for the Gulf coast of Florida. Almost always the crew is mine; however, a few buyers prefer to sail with their own crew. My office at Rodrigo de Freitas Lake in Brazil sells about two boats per month that sail for the Florida Keys or the Gulf coast. Eighty percent of the time the crews belong to me. The same can be said for boats going to France, Germany and Spain during the summer months. Transportation of our cargo from Brazil to the United States and Europe will not be a problem, gentlemen," said Hans with confidence.

"What about customs?" asked Zuni.

"US Customs inspections are cursory since my captains visit Key West, Miami, and Tampa ports so frequently. That will not be a problem. For deliveries in the Big Bend area of Florida, we will transfer cargo from the sailing vessels to sea anchors just off shore, thus avoiding customs. How and when the heroin will be retrieved is a problem for the buyers, Charo and Costellano, not for us."

"What about the US Coast Guard?" asked Dieppe. "Do they ever stop your boats for routine inspections?"

"Only once, one year ago, in Key West waters," replied Hans. "They are concerned only with safety. Their inspections never turn into a search of the boat unless they have a specific reason. Private sailing vessels like ours seldom arouse suspicion. I cannot, however, give you 100 percent assurance that they will not stop one or both boats."

"Thank you, Hans," said Dieppe. "Nothing is 100 percent certain. Continue, Erich," motioned Dieppe.

Erich Feltgeibell remained seated in an overstuffed chair near the fireplace. The Eagle's Nest grew colder as the evening became early morning. He drained his brandy snifter, placed it carefully on the table next to his chair, and rose. His hands were clasped behind his back as he began walking back and forth in front of the fireplace. His propensity for the dramatic was well known among the group. Finally he spoke. "Things in Brazil are not as politically stable as I would like them. It is true that the government in Brazil is presently more stable than in most South American governments, but there are problems. The country has more than twelve political parties, not counting those that periodically come and go. The export/import business enjoys favorable conditions some of the time and finds itself in the government's disfavor at other times. Right now conditions are good. In fact, some of the current government's problems appear to be in our favor. Brazil is having boundary disputes with Paraguay and Uruguay. Most of the border patrol forces have been moved to those areas to deal with the disputes, taking the pressure off the Colombian heroin traffic coming into Rio de Janeiro. Additionally, President Hernando Cardovan and the Congress are preoccupied with the left wing of the Catholic Church and labor unions allied to the leftist Worker's Party. They are playing havoc with the government's economic and social policies. Having said all that, I see no problem in getting the commodities to my warehouse on Vietra Way in Ipanema. The marina is only two blocks from the warehouse. The exchange of warheads for cocaine will be made in the warehouse. Are there any questions regarding my part in Pegasus, gentlemen?" asked Erich Feltgeibell.

"How large will the packages be, Erich?" asked Dieppe.

"I have arranged with our Colombian friends that packages be no more than ten kilos each. Packages any larger would be difficult to store in the boats. I plan to store the packages in the keel and flotation compartments of each boat for passage to the various destinations. The keel on these boats is not very wide; packages larger than ten kilos would not pack well."

"And how many kilos can you safely transport in each boat, Hans?" asked Dieppe.

"Not more than one thousand. I have to leave room in the keel for enough lead to keep the boat stable when it is under sail."

It was Dieppe's turn to stand and pace. While pouring himself another brandy, he turned to Zuni Anatole. "Now back to Colonel Sultoy, Zuni. Let's discuss him more."

"All right, Heinrich," nodded Zuni. "You do not think his animosity toward the government and the offers of money are sufficient to insure his loyalty?" asked Zuni.

"No. I do not. You have no assurance that he will not change his mind about his participation, nor do you have any assurance that he will not talk after the fact," said Dieppe.

"He will cooperate, Heinrich, because his wife will be held by my people until the warheads are safely in our hands. He loves his wife very much, Heinrich."

"You did not mention that part of your plan before, Zuni," said Dieppe.

"I did not feel it necessary," said Zuni, feeling a bit insulted.

"All right. But kill him when you have the warheads, and make it look like the theft was his doing. The matter is closed," said Dieppe. "Now I have a few concerns of my own that I would like to present for discussion, gentlemen."

"Go ahead, Heinrich," said Weismann.

"At our last meeting we only touched on the problem of getting the heroin from the boats to the buyers. You took that problem upon yourself, Peter," said Dieppe. "Have you formulated a solution to that little problem?"

"As a matter of fact I have," said Weismann rising from his chair. He stood before one of the giant windows overlooking the valley below and stared. "The warhead coming into Germany on Reifenstahl's boat will be integrated with museum shipments to Munich that I will have arranged in advance. I have already made arrangements with the Louvre in Paris to lend us an early Egyptian relic display. Museum items usually travel by train and rarely attract the attention of customs officials. I will simply move the warhead with museum shipments that I will arrange going from Bremen and Homburg to Munich. One of our museum trucks will make the final delivery from Munich to Berchtesgaden. The warhead will be inside an Egyptian sarcophagus that I will be moving from the Museum of Armaments in Munich to a public display I will arrange in the Platterhoff. Does this arrangement satisfy you, gentlemen?" asked Weismann. Everyone nodded their agreement except Dieppe.

"Shall I continue with the delivery problem, Peter?" asked Dieppe.

"Of course, please do."

"The Charo family in Miami has agreed to buy as much as we can deliver. We will deliver the heroin to their people in Key West, Tampa, and Steinhatchee. All three locations are making preparations. Only minor details of coordination remain unresolved, and I can handle those within the next six weeks." After Dieppe explained in great detail exactly how the delivery would be handled in Florida, Mr. Popodopolus raised his hand.

"How did you arrange to solicit the Charo family, Heinrich?" asked Popodopolus.

"Through our Columbian friends in Rio de Janeiro, Tomas," said Heinrich.

"That does seem strange," remarked Weismann.

"Not at all. The authorities in South America and the DEA in The United States are applying a great deal of pressure on the cocaine supply line running from Colombia to the Charo family in Florida. Charo is happy to establish a supply of heroin, and our Colombian friend is happy to retain a regular buyer. He is also ecstatic to acquire the nuclear warheads. No one gets hurt feelings except the DEA. Everyone wins," smiled Dieppe. "But, I can tell from the looks on your faces, gentlemen, that I should provide you with more background information. I will try to summarize circumstances in South America and Colombia in particular, that led me to certain decisions and conclusions," said Dieppe.

"There is a new order in narcotrafficking with far-reaching effects for the United States and for Colombia. We are taking advantage of this change. In 1980, the Colombian cartels had a virtual monopoly on cocaine trafficking to the United States. There were only two or three significant cartels in Colombia. They bought the raw materials from Peru and Bolivia, manufactured the cocaine in just a few large jungle factories, hired Mexican organizations to get it into the United States, and then ran their own distribution operations inside the US. The Cali and Medellin cartels alone are reported to have amassed fortunes in the $12 billion range. Just a year ago the composite Colombian narcotraffickers and their empire comprised one of the twelve biggest financial enterprises in the entire world with profits rivaling and even sometimes surpassing the largest corporations in the world." Dieppe paused for a moment as he stared intently at the leaping flames in the fireplace and then continued.

"The rapidly growing influence of Mexico in the drug world is bringing about the new order. Evidence of this can be found all along the Mexican border with the United States and in several large cities like Los Angeles, Houston and Dallas. Together, three of the Mexican cartels are shipping several hundred tons of cocaine into the United States every year and have established their own distribution system. The Colombian narcotraffickers have responded to the Mexican move into cocaine trafficking by trying to fulfill the growing US demand for heroin. Cocaine usage in the US is dropping, while heroin use has expanded from an estimated 500,000 users to more than 600,000 hardcore users. In short, gentlemen, heroin has replaced cocaine as Colombia's main drug export.

"In just a few short years the Colombians have gone from zero production of heroin to over six metric tons a year. Since they already have a distribution system in place, especially along the eastern seaboard, the transition from cocaine to heroin has been relatively easy and certainly smart. Their focus is now on establishing a reliable set of heroin buyers. Another coincidental benefit derived from the transition from cocaine to heroin is that heroin is easier to produce, and is worth much more money pound for pound. The street value of heroin is four to ten times that of cocaine, making it easier to transport dollar for dollar. The retail value of just one kilo of heroin is $100,000."

Waiting for his companions to digest this latest information, Dieppe poured himself another brandy and did not continue speaking until each man was staring at him, urging him to continue.

"There are other practical reasons for the transition. Newer manufacturing techniques allow heroin to be used in many different ways. It can be sniffed, smoked, taken by pill, or taken in combination with other drugs. Heroin no longer has to be injected, thereby reducing the users' chances of contracting the AIDS virus. The Colombian's coup de gras though during this transition period was to make heroin more enticing to the street user by cutting the street cost. Once their customers became hooked, they simply raised the prices again. Quite ingenious don't you think."

Dieppe continued. "Narcotraffickers have learned from the past mistakes of the old cartels. They live in modest houses and do not flaunt their fortunes. Instead of living lavishly, they invest their money in legitimate businesses and enterprises. Another advantage to their new enterprise is that heroin factories are small and scattered, unlike the former cocaine factories. Also, the poppy plants, which are grown on small plots high in the mountains of Tolima, Cauca, and Huila provinces, are more difficult to detect when mixed with other crops. The drug lords grow more than 5,500 acres of poppies that are harvested three times a year all the while not fearing police detection because they pay the Marxist Revolutionary Armed Forces of Colombia (FARC) to protect their poppy fields.

The FARC allows the growers to bring in seed and fertilizer, and they screen potential buyers and sometimes battle police who wander into the area. That, gentlemen," explained a rather confident Dieppe, "is why we are trading nuclear warheads for heroin rather than cocaine. Now, you asked me how I selected the Charo family."

"I selected Charo for the same reason I selected Estabo Sanchez as our heroin provider. Estabo, who as you know survived the recent ravages the cocaine drug lords have suffered, was smart enough to move into heroin. He also is one of the few survivors of the recent Mafia shake up, and is the man to be dealt with in the Southeastern United States. Charo has the cunning to succeed. Because of his business savvy, if you will, he has maneuvered until he now has the only connection to the man who controls the movement of all illegal drugs from Florida into the eastern seaboard of the United States, Joey Costellano. More importantly, he has the only organization capable of commanding enough cash to buy at our level," explained Dieppe. "Are there any questions, gentlemen?" he asked.

"A very good demonstration of your research thoroughness, my friend, but those circumstances could change unexpectedly," said Weismann. "We must begin to think about alternatives in the event something goes wrong with those arrangements. The hour is very late. Please put that on your agenda for our next meeting, Heinrich. Does anyone else have questions or comments regarding Heinrich's explanation?" asked Weismann.

"To whom will the warheads be sold, Peter?" asked Erich Feltgeibell.

"I really have not the slightest idea, Erich, nor do I care. The Colombians are giving us in exchange for warheads enough heroin to supply the southern United States and most of Europe with all their needs for a year," exclaimed Weismann. "After we sell the heroin, The New World Order will be wealthy beyond our dreams, gentlemen. The money will allow us to expand our organization ten-fold in just a few years. We will have cells in every city in the United States by the Year 2005. The sublimeness of the plan is that we will operate from a safe haven— Berchtesgaden, property belonging to the State of Bavaria in the Federal Republic of Germany," said Weismann, his face a picture of glowing pride. "I realize the hour is late, gentlemen, but I would like to ask a curiosity question of Heinrich. Where is Steinhatchee, and why did Charo choose it as a delivery point?"

"I can only guess that it is because of its remoteness and proximity to the state of Georgia and the major transportation arteries of the southeastern United States," replied Dieppe.

"Thank you, Heinrich. Let us stop for now and get some rest.

Chapter 3

Hamp stood on the deck of Hatchee Haven and watched the sun set over the Gulf of Mexico in brilliant splashes of red, silver and purple. Sunsets here were prettiest during the winter months, because the sun lowered itself precisely down the river to the gulf. He never tired of the sight and had included this vista in his late afternoon ritual since his retirement and move to Steinhatchee last July. Fifteen minutes prior to sunset every day, Hamp walked out onto the upper deck, opened a cold bottle of beer, took a seat in a lounge chair, and thought about his late wife. Judith named their retirement home Hatchee Haven, a local Indian name, but she never had the chance to live there. Her illness had made certain of that. Hamp almost decided to sell the house after her death, but couldn't bring himself to do it because she had loved it so much.

The house is everything they wanted in a retirement home. Perched high on 14-foot stilts, the house faces southwest and overlooks Dead Man's Bay where the Steinhatchee River empties into the Gulf of Mexico. From this point, he could observe boat traffic on the river and listen to activity in the bay on the marine radio. Hamp remembered how they had loved the community from their first visit ten years ago.

Tom Adams, a longtime friend of Hamp's, retired to the community in 1985 and established a charter boat service for offshore fishing and diving. He invited Hamp to Steinhatchee several times for fishing and diving, two of Hamp's favorite leisure activities. Judith joined Hamp on one of his trips to Steinhatchee three years ago and fell in love with the serenity, remoteness, and pristine beauty of the area. When the house became available, they immediately bought it.

Steinhatchee had been a Mecca for commercial and sports fishing people since the 1850's. Several seafood outlets, a half-dozen of fish camps, and numerous homes line the narrow highway that parallel the river to the sea. Three restaurants, a grocery store and market, a post office, a hardware store, a community center, four churches, an elementary school, two automobile repair shops, and three real estate offices support about 1,100 full-time and 700 part-time inhabitants. The nearest communities of any size are Perry, 34 miles to the north, and Cross City, 17 miles to the south. Traffic is not a problem in Steinhatchee, so there are no traffic lights, only stop signs where most residents only yield. Life there, though not totally unencumbered by adversity, seems to roll lazily with the ebb and flow of the tide. If some need arises and Steinhatchee businesses cannot fulfill it, folks can take a quick jaunt to the city. Gainesville and the University of Florida are 75 miles west, and Tallahassee and Florida State University are 90 miles to the northwest. Hamp found that life there among the beauty and southern hospitality was fairly idyllic.

Gwen had been in Steinhatchee for two weeks. Greg threatened to leave her and take the children if she made the trip, but she told him he should do what he felt he had to do. His name had not been mentioned since her arrival in Steinhatchee. Ben Fuller hired her on the spot, but for various reasons he postponed the marketing project kickoff until January. While waiting, Gwen rented an efficiency apartment at Sam and Winnie Pamona's Seawind Motel located on the bay just a block from Hamp's Hatchee Haven. Even though he had been sort of a catalyst to her moving to Steinhatchee, Hamp was uncomfortable with Gwen's presence in Steinhatchee, for reasons he could not explain. What he did know was that he was very pleased to be able to see her almost daily. He enjoyed being with her more than with anyone else and looked forward to their time together.

The ringing phone broke Hamp's pensive mood. "Hello," said Hamp lazily.

"Hey, are you awake?" It was the familiar voice of his friend, Tom Adams.

"Barely. Did you catch fish today, or did you send your party to the market for fish?" asked Hamp with a chuckle.

"As a matter of fact, I am about to place several beautiful filets of grouper on the grill as we speak, ol' buddy. Marian and I would like for you and Gwen to help us eat them. You two need a chaperon, don't you know? The lady is married," said Tom in his usual lighthearted manner.

"Sure. We would love it. I'll give her a call and let you know."

"No need, ol' buddy. Marian has already invited her. Pick her up on your way over. See ya." He hung up, precluding an expected retort from Hamp.

Gwen was standing on the motel dock talking to Winnie Pamona when Hamp drove up. Gwen waved good bye to Winnie as she hurried to the car. He thought that she looked very pretty in the little flowered sun dress and white flats—fresh and vibrant. Age had been her friend; she grew prettier with each passing year.

"You've smiled more since you've been down here than I can remember," Hamp said as she approached the car. "The sea air must agree with you. I have never seen you look more beautiful. You are simply radiant these days young lady."

"I have good reason for smiling. I'm happy where I am, I like what I'm doing, and I don't know where else I would receive compliments like that." Gwen replied, giggling.

"I can tell," Hamp said with a smile. "Tell me, how did your day go?"

"It was just great as usual, said Gwen. "Oh yes, I did hear some rather interesting trivia about Steinhatchee. You will not believe what I learned—or maybe you already know. Anyway, let's wait until we get to Marian and Tom's before I tell what I have discovered, "said Gwen with a certain amount of drama in her voice.

"Hold that thought. We're here," said Hamp, as he parked under the stilted house where Tom was busy at the large charcoal grill.

"Go on up, Gwen," said Tom as he motioned with a long pair of tongs. "Marian is in the kitchen preparing the salad, I think. Grab a glass and some George Dickel on the table over there, Hamp. There is some ice in the blue cooler under the table," Tom said. "These grouper will be ready in about two shakes of a blue fish's tail."

"You did good today, huh?" remarked Hamp, slapping Tom on the back.

"Yeah. We caught a little better than 150 pounds of grouper. Not a bad day, considering the fact that I had a lot of LOFT on the boat. My clients were happy campers and that's what is important."

"LOFT?" asks Hamp.

"Yeah, LOFT. That stands for lack of fishing talent," explained Tom with a grin.

"You fellows come on up. The potatoes are ready, and Gwen and I are starving," shouted Marian from the top of the stairs.

Happy small talk dominated the conversation at the dinner table between mouthfuls of the delicious grouper. Then Gwen remembered the information she had learned earlier in the day. "Oh! I'm almost forgetting to tell you guys what I learned today about our quiet Steinhatchee. How could I forget?" exclaimed Gwen.

"Let her rip, Gwen. We'll be all ears instead of all mouths for a change," laughed Tom.

"Well, I spent the entire morning interviewing Mrs. Hattie Collier for historical background information on Steinhatchee," began Gwen excitedly. "After an hour or so, she became rather relaxed with me and began speaking freely about various goings on around Steinhatchee. One thing she mentioned was that illegal drug trafficking was rampant on the river. She even told me that she had seen shrimp boats come into the river from Dead Man's Bay with decks piled high with bales of the stuff. Can you believe it?" asked Gwen with bewilderment in her voice.

The table grew suddenly quiet. Marian looked at Tom, and Tom looked down at his plate. Hamp gazed at Gwen over hands clasped under his chin and said nothing.

"Hamp, is what she said about the drug business really true?" pleaded Gwen looking first at Hamp and then to Tom and Marian.

"I'll defer to Tom for an answer to that, Gwen. He's been here longer than I and knows much more than I about what goes on around the river and bay."

"The short answer to your question, Gwen, is yes," stated Tom quietly. "Drug trafficking on the river used to be a major activity around here, and I place emphasis on the used to be. Besides knowing everything that goes on around here, sometimes Miss Hattie confuses times and dates. About ten years ago, huge quantities of marijuana and cocaine came into Steinhatchee from offshore. Colombian fishing vessels would transfer bales of marijuana to local fishing boats waiting at predetermined points about twelve miles offshore. Local boats moved the bales to remote transfer points along the river and on the coast, where they were transferred again to waiting trucks belonging to major drug traffickers. Some of the airplane traffic took place on the south end of Rocky Creek Road near Cow Creek. Some would say that a good chunk of the entire supply of marijuana for the southeastern United States was being funneled through Steinhatchee, a sad, but true fact of our history, Gwen. Is it going on now? I don't think so. Too many local people went to prison for doing it ten years ago."

"But why would local people become involved in something like that?" asked Gwen. "I don't understand," she said shaking her head.

"Money. You have to understand, Gwen, most people in this community, the people that have their roots here, are essentially poor. Their livelihood is directly related to the fishing industry in this area. When fishing is good, they make a living. When fishing is bad, they go hungry. The drug dealers came here and offered them more money for one night of transporting illegal drugs than they could earn fishing in a year. Many of them just could not refuse the big money and took their chances. It was not uncommon for a fisherman to make $5,000 or $6,000 in just one night."

"How long did it go on?" asked Gwen.

"Until the federal agents caught wind of it and built their case. A retiree that moved here from Georgia, a former lieutenant colonel in one of the armed services, blew the whistle. The feds planted an agent across the river; two months later they conducted a massive raid on the community and arrested 33 people. All served time. Most served from five to ten years; some are still in jail," explained Tom.

"These were basically good people, Gwen, who just could not deal with the temptation to have more money than they ever thought possible," explained Marian. "They didn't go into it with evil intent. They saw it as simply moving a commodity from one place to another."

"To my knowledge, the DEA was successful in closing down the Mafia's Steinhatchee connection," said Tom. "I have not heard even a rumor of drugs coming into the community via the river since the night of that infamous raid. I think I would know if something was going on."

"Did you know about this Hamp?" asked Gwen.

"Yes, I did, but it never occurred to me to tell you of it; that was over ten years ago."

"What happened to the man who blew the whistle?" asked Gwen.

"He received several anonymous threats to his life and property and eventually left Steinhatchee," said Tom. "This is a tight community, Gwen. There are three kinds of people here: those who were born here; those who live here, but were not born here, like Hamp and us; and those who own homes here, but only reside here part-time. The people who were born here are all related in one way or another. They protect each other from outsiders. If push came to shove, Marian and I would be considered outsiders, "explained Tom.

"I see," said Gwen thoughtfully. "But she also told me of Iggy's Restaurant, and that it was closed by federal agents just a year ago. She said it was later sold at auction when the owners were tried and found guilty of laundering drug money. Doesn't that mean drugs are back in Steinhatchee?" insisted Gwen.

"I don't think drugs are coming into Florida through Steinhatchee again, Gwen. Money laundering operations are not necessarily co-located with drug distribution points," explained Tom.

"It's fairly common for drug suppliers to geographically separate distribution and money laundering. They learned through experience that restricting their operations to one location made it much easier for the DEA to discover, to bust, and to prosecute an entire organization," said Hamp.

"Let's get this conversation back to happier things," said Marian as she got up and began clearing the table. "How is your project going, Gwen?" she asked.

"Oh! Great," said Gwen with a smile. "Southern Living magazine is coming down in two weeks to do a spread on the River's Edge, and Florida Living magazine will be here next week for a photo session. They plan to feature the River's Edge in their March issue. Ben appeared happy with the brochure layouts I've done, so I guess he's happy with my work so far. He wants me to move into the vacant town house at River's Edge; he thinks I should be on the premises to manage the project."

"What did you tell him?" asked Hamp blankly.

"Careful, girl" interrupted Marian. "Ben is a great guy and an asset to this community, but you are a married woman, and Ben is a very eligible bachelor," warned Marian.

"Thanks for sharing that with me, but I think he's right. I could be more effective if I were staying at River's Edge and had access to the corporate telephone, staff, and facilities," said Gwen. "Don't worry about me. I know how to handle myself."

"Terrific," said Marian. "How much longer do you think you will be in Steinhatchee?"

"I'm not sure," responded Gwen. "Ben keeps mentioning new ideas; one thing leads to two more—who knows?" remarked Gwen with a shrug of her shoulders. "I miss the children and want to see them badly. There are many things to think about in that arena; I guess I'll just have to play things one day at a time. Besides, he's paying me very well."

"That's the way to look at life," said Tom expansively, sensing Gwen's discomfort with the subject of home, and how long she might be away from her children. "One day at a time is the proper attitude for everyone. It has taken me a long, long time to convince my ol' buddy here of that. Right, Hamp?"

"Yes, smiled Hamp, but then you are a very convincing old salt."

"The boy has gone to hell, Gwen. He spends his days either fishing, diving, writing, or riding his motorcycle. I fear there is no hope for him; he's fallen into the famous Steinhatchee mode," exclaimed Tom.

"Steinhatchee mode?" questioned Gwen. "What, pray tell, is the Steinhatchee mode?"

"Utter and complete sorriness," replied Tom. "It's about two steps beyond laid back. Precisely, it means doing exactly what one wants to do when one wants to do it. Understand, now?"

"I cannot even fathom the idea," said Gwen shaking her head.

After more small talk and George Dickel, Gwen suggested that she and Hamp go home. She planned to meet with a group of advertisers in Tallahassee the next day and intended to get an early start. During the short return drive, neither spoke until Hamp pulled up in front of the motel.

"You know, Gwen, Marian was right about Ben. He probably will make a move on you, "cautioned Hamp.

"Like I said, Hamp, don't worry about me. I can take care of myself. If I have a problem,

I'll call for the cavalry to be led by you. Good enough?"

"Okay," said Hamp reluctantly. He did not want to spoil the enjoyment and satisfaction Gwen was deriving from her project with Ben Fuller. He was annoyed at himself though for feeling almost jealous of Ben; he did not have that right.

Gwen quickly kissed Hamp on the cheek and hurried to her apartment.

January 18, 1995

The weather was perfect for diving. The air temperature was 71 degrees, and the seas were glassy smooth. It wasn't necessary to go so far offshore to find clear water during the winter months. Moving through the 30-foot depths of Dead Man's Bay, Hamp could see rocks and grass on the bottom. The Cummins diesel engine in Tom's 30-foot boat throbbed quietly at 2,700 revolutions per minute. The water was a deep jade.

"I don't see a single cloud in the sky. What is the water temperature?" asked Hamp.

"It's going to be a little on the cool side. I hope you brought your long underwear," said Tom, jokingly.

"How cool, Tom?" insisted Hamp.

"It's 63 degrees at the three foot mark. That means it will be a tad colder at the depth we'll be diving."

"You guaranteed grouper today, Tom," reminded Hamp.

"You bet. Yesterday the bottom reader showed a lot of fish where we're going."

Twenty minutes later, Tom slowed the engine as the boat's Loran C navigation system signaled they were within a half mile of their destination. Hamp casually scanned the horizon with binoculars to see if other boats were in the area. Tom slowed the engine to an idle and went forward to man the bow anchor.

"Tom, look starboard," shouted Hamp. Tom turned and could barely see a large fishing trawler heading south at a very high rate of speed.

"What the heck is that, Tom?" asked Hamp. "I couldn't see that she's flying any colors."

"Looks like one of those South American trawlers that occasionally visit this end of the gulf, but I've never seen one so close to shore."

"She doesn't appear to have been fishing," said Hamp. "She's riding too high in the water and her nets are stored. Anyhow, she couldn't be moving that fast with a load of fish on board. Beats the hell out of me, Tom!", said Hamp.

They watched the boat out of sight then turned their attention back to the task at hand—spearing large grouper. Once the anchor was properly placed and secured, they labored into seven mill wet suits, strapped aluminum air tanks to their buoyancy compensators, buckled on weight belts, slipped into fins and masks, and made certain the A.B. Biller spear guns were uncocked. They checked each other's equipment to make sure everything was properly adjusted, then shuffled to the diving platform on the stern end of the boat. With each holding his mask in place with one hand, and his regulator with the other, they made a simultaneous split-legged entry. The initial shock of the cold water penetrating their wet suits caused them to breathe more deeply and rapidly than usual. From this moment on they would communicate with arm and hand signals developed over years of diving together. Tom took the lead; Hamp stayed behind and slightly above Tom so he could anticipate Tom's moves and shoot without fear of hitting him. At the 66-foot level they found bottom on the rocky edge of the freshwater spring they had targeted. They each equalized air pressure in their ears, adjusted their buoyancy, and remained in place while surveying the immediate area to find out what fish presently occupied the spring. A large school of amberjack swam ten feet above them. Hamp counted eleven good-sized grouper just inside the spring, and Tom pointed to a pair of very large barracuda approaching Hamp from his upper rear. Hamp remained very still so as not to excite the big predators. He knew from experience that if he remained calm the big silver fish, with long razor-sharp teeth, would give him a close once over and then go about their business. They did exactly that. The lead fish swam to within one foot of Hamp's face and momentarily peered into his mask. Having satisfied its curiosity, the fish swam away. His partner, having given Tom a similar inspection, swam away, too. Tom held up seven fingers to show his estimate of the barracuda's length. Hamp nodded and then pointed into the spring. Tom acknowledged Hamp's signal and began a descent into the spring. The twenty-foot wide spring shaft was vertical and bottomed out at 80 feet before becoming a nearly horizontal cave. Fish loved the spring during the winter months for the warmth the constantly 72-degree water coming from the cave afforded them. Hamp followed Tom to the bottom of the spring shaft. Immediately upon reaching the bottom, Tom shot a grouper large enough to break the retaining cord on the metal spear. The wounded fish headed for the cave, spear and all, with Tom in hot pursuit. Suddenly, Tom stopped pursuing the fish, went vertical, and began backing up in a sitting position. Hamp swam even with Tom and followed Tom's pointing finger with his eyes. The reason for Tom's sudden stop was evident. Lying in the entrance to the cave, no more than ten feet away, were two large tiger sharks. They were looking directly at them. Tom signaled a retreat, and both turned slowly and swam for the surface of the shaft. Once on the ledge of the vertical shaft, both men turned to make sure the sharks did not follow them. The grouper didn't like all the movement in the water and departed, so Hamp and Tom ascended to the 15-foot level where they stayed three minutes to decompress. Hamp frequently looked down to see if the sharks had changed their minds and followed. The stainless steel ladder on the teak diving platform was a welcomed sight.

"How long do you figure those tigers were?" asked Hamp as Tom helped him remove his buoyancy compensator and air tank.

"At least nine feet," replied Tom. "They must have had their fill of amberjack. That's why they didn't show any interest in us."

"Well, I'm glad for that, but they surely screwed up the spear fishing," fussed Hamp.

"I want to go back down in a few minutes," said Tom with a serious look on his face. "I saw something down there I've never seen there before."

"What did you see?" asked Hamp.

"A large, square chunk of concrete with a stainless steel hook-eye imbedded in it," said Tom rubbing his chin. "Funny thing about it is that it looked new. There were no signs of marine growth on it anywhere. Didn't you see it? It was just about ten yards south of the vertical tunnel."

"Nope. I must have been watching you too closely," replied Hamp.

"It's not part of a new reef," mused Tom. "The last addition to the manmade reefs in this part of the gulf went in the water last year at least twelve miles to the north of here."

"Well, let's take a look," said Hamp as he swung his buoyancy compensator and a fresh air tank on his back.

They descended again using the anchor line. Tom swam straight to the peculiar-looking concrete structure just a few yards away. Tom was correct. The structure appeared new. The square's sides were at least two-feet, and a shiny eye-ring protruded from the top side. They searched the ocean floor near the object carefully but noticed nothing unusual. There were no markings on the object except in one place near the bottom on one side. In handwritten letters Hamp saw the word PEGASUS. Seeing nothing else in the immediate area to offer an explanation for the object's presence, they made an ascent to the boat.

"Isn't Pegasus something or someone out of Greek mythology?" asked Tom.

"Yeah, it is," answered Hamp. "But what is that particular word doing on a concrete block on the bottom of the Gulf of Mexico?" asked Hamp.

"Beats me," Tom shrugged. "I can tell you, however, that it has nothing to do with fishing or those who fish these waters."

"That boat we noticed bothers me more than that concrete thing, Hamp. It's been a long time since a South American fishing vessel visited these waters," said Tom. "I think it's been about ten years."

"Do you think you could make a few discreet inquiries among your fishing buddies to see if they've seen other boats like it?" asked Hamp. "There could be a connection between the concrete block and that boat."

"Damn right I will," said Tom emphatically. "My curiosity is at a fever pitch."

The Steinhatchee Pool Hall was more of a bar than a pool hall, and many fishermen could be found there after six in the evening. It was the stopping off place on the way home for some of the working men, and some women. The juke box was playing a country tune about 200 decibels too loud when Tom walked in and saw four fishing guides that he knew well sitting at the corner table. They saw Tom, too.

"Come over here, Tom, and let me buy you a cold one," said Bob Pridgin as he motioned to Tom.

"Evenin'. You boys doin' all right?" asked Tom with a smile.

"Better than a starved fox in a new hen house," retorted Willie Smith.

Tom opened the beer the waitress brought to the table and listened to the chit chat for five minutes and decided the timing was right for his question. "Listen, fellows, I got a problem you boys might be able to help me with," said Tom with a serious look.

"Sure, Tom, be glad to," replied Bob Pridgin. "Lay it on us."

"Well, Hamp Porter and I went diving for grouper today out at the spring. About the time we got there a strange boat took off like a spooked mule. Funny thing about it was that it looked exactly like one of those South American fishing trawlers that used to occasionally show up in these waters. I'm just wondering if any of you guys have seen anything like that lately"

They all looked pensive for a moment then Willie Smith spoke. "Naw, I don't recall seein' any boat like that, Tom, but my cousin over at Keaton Beach said he seen one 'bout a week ago. It was headin' south fast. Said it looked like one of them South American boats, too."

The other fellows had no recollection of seeing a boat like the trawler, nor did they know of anyone else who had seen one. "If two were seen, then how many more went unseen?" thought Tom.

"Why you interested in South American boats, Tom?" asked Willie.

"I'm not really interested, just curious," replied Tom. "Thanks fellows. See you guys later." Tom left the pool hall and drove home. "Hamp would be interested to hear that at least one other South American boat had been spotted in these waters and just one week ago," thought Tom. "Or maybe it's the same boat," he said out loud to no one in particular.

January 21, 1995

I'm taking a chance trying to see the Coast Guard Station Commander without an appointment, thought Hamp as he negotiated the steps leading to station headquarters. Just maybe my rank, although I'm on the retired list, will help get me in the door.

He found the correct door leading to the commander's office without difficulty. In the outer-office Hamp was intercepted by Chief Petty Officer Byrd, who greeted Hamp with an uncertain smile, probably because he was in civilian attire.

"How may I help you, sir?" said Petty Officer Byrd as she rose from her chair.

"I would like to speak briefly with the commander," smiled Hamp.

"Oh. I'm afraid that is going to be difficult today, sir; Captain Miller has a full calendar and is running a little behind schedule. What is your name, sir, and the nature of your business?" she asked with a smile.

"Colonel Hampton Porter, US Army (Retired)," replied Hamp. "I just need a little information from Captain Miller—I will not require more than five minutes of his time. I will appreciate anything you can do."

"Please take a seat, Colonel Porter. I'll see what I can do." said Byrd as she walked toward Captain Miller's office. She walked out of Captain Miller's office in less than thirty seconds. She began talking as she took her seat behind her desk." Captain Miller will see you when he completes the meeting now in progress, Colonel Porter. "It shouldn't take long; they are almost finished."

"Thanks very much," said Hamp without rising.

Hamp thumbed through a US News & World Report magazine while he waited and had decided to read an article on how to invest money for the coming year when Petty Officer Byrd called his name. "Captain Miller will see you now, Colonel Porter," she announced as she opened the door to his office. Hamp walked quickly into the office and met Captain Miller who was walking toward him with his right arm outstretched and ready to shake hands.

"Captain Miller, I very much appreciate your taking time from your busy schedule to see me," said Hamp as he shook hands with the captain. "I promise not to waste a minute of it."

"No problem, Colonel Porter. I understand that you are a retired Army Colonel. What can I do for you? Please sit."

"I'll come straight to the point, sir" said Hamp as he took a chair across from Captain Miller. "Have your people sighted any South American fishing trawlers in gulf coast waters, especially around the Steinhatchee area and International Marker 18?"

"I don't recall reading anything like that in the daily patrol reports. It would have caught my attention because it's so rare to see them in gulf waters anymore," said Miller thoughtfully. "Why do you ask, Colonel Porter?"

"Deja Vu, I suppose. About ten years ago illegal drugs were delivered to that area by the ton in South American fishing trawlers.

Steinhatchee is my retirement home, and seeing one of those boats in my neck of the woods just two days ago concerned me enough to come here and make an inquiry of you personally. No one in Steinhatchee wants a repeat of the drug experience of ten years ago," said Hamp.

"I can certainly understand that. I do seem to remember something about the drug problem up there. Are you sure about the boat being South American?"

"If it were not, it was an identical copy. My diving partner saw it as well, and a fisherman from Steinhatchee said he saw one near Keaton Beach a week earlier," insisted Hamp. "They are both experienced seamen and are familiar with the appearance of all boats that fish the gulf."

"That's a very interesting story, Colonel Porter. I'll have my people review patrol reports for four weeks back. I would be interested in knowing if my people have spotted a similar vessel.

Tell you what, Colonel Porter, I'll give you a call if I turn up anything. In the mean time, if you hear of another sighting, please let me know personally." He gave Hamp a copy of his personal calling card. "And I think it might be best if we keep this between us until we know a little more. Don't you agree? Leave your phone number with Petty Officer Byrd, please."

"Good enough, Captain. Thanks again for seeing me."

All the way back to Steinhatchee, Hamp thought of his conversation with Captain Miller. Miller appeared interested and took Hamp's information seriously, but he had no way of knowing what he would do with it? Will he push it up the chain of command? There could be implications for the state department. "Maybe I'm just overacting," Hamp told himself. "The whole thing is probably just coincidence. But the fishing trawler is no coincidence, and there is not a local boat on the entire gulf coast that even resembles that trawler," mumbled Hamp aloud. By the time Hamp reached Steinhatchee, three hours later, he was thoroughly frustrated and still without answers.

Chapter 4

March 2, 1995

B.J. Patterson's morning had been less than pleasant. The daily meeting with his staff was longer than usual, and everyone seemed ill-tempered and short on patience, including B.J. Also, Herr. Weismann was being somewhat less than cooperative in matters regarding the transition of property. "Now he wants a tour of the tunnel complex under the General Walker Hotel," grumbled B.J. to himself.

Frau Gurter, B.J.'s secretary, knocked and entered B.J.'s office. "Herr. Weismann will meet you at the General Walker Hotel at two o'clock this afternoon, Colonel Patterson," she said in a tired voice.

"Thanks, Frau Gurter. Please alert my driver."

"Very well. And your wife called ten minutes ago to tell you that the movers arrived at nine o'clock this morning," she added. "Pike went home sick about an hour ago. Shall I find another driver for you?"

"No," replied B.J. "I'll drive myself. Nothing else is going my way today, so why should transportation go smoothly?" he said. He promised his wife he would help with the movers. "She would be real happy to learn that he was spending his afternoon with Herr. Weismann in lieu of the movers," he fussed to himself.

Herr. Weismann was waiting in front of the hotel entrance when B.J. pulled into the parking lot. "Look at the prick, standing there as if he were a Prussian emperor," mumbled B.J. under his breath. "All he needs is a damn monocle."

"Good afternoon, Colonel Patterson," said Weismann without extending his arm for a hand shake. "Shall we walk directly to the basement?"

"Yes. I have the keys we will need," said B.J.

They walked silently across the lobby, took the elevator to the basement level, and walked down the long main corridor to a large metal door at the end. Painted in six-inch red letters on the door in English and in German were the words Absolutely No Admittance Permitted. Two large brass padlocks secured the door— one at the top of the door and one at the bottom. The door also had been freshly painted so as not to distract from the hotel's decor. B.J. found the correct keys on his key chain, inserted them one at a time, and the locks clicked open.

"Who maintains custody of the keys to these locks?" asked Heismann.

"I do. They are kept in my office safe. There are no duplicates, and I am the only one who has the combination to the safe."

"Who were the last visitors here?" insisted Weismann.

B.J. quickly grew irritated at Weismann's game of twenty questions. "I believe the engineers who closed the tunnel shaft entrance were the last visitors; that would have been in early 1946. They were probably the ones to lock these doors, since they installed them. These particular locks, however, are not the original locks. As a matter of fact, I had the original locks replaced shortly after I assumed command of the recreation center. The old locks were made of iron and had turned to rust and had become an eyesore."

The heavy door swung open with a loud squeaking noise. Behind the door was nothing but total darkness and the smell of stale air and dust. "There is no electricity in the tunnel complex; it was turned off when the place was sealed. We will need these." B.J. produced two flashlights, turned his on, and gave the other to Weismann.

"Then we are the first in here since 1946?" asked Weismann.

"Yes. There has been no reason to open the complex. It probably isn't even safe in here as a result of the blasting that sealed the entrance." Their lights revealed about thirty feet of tunnel in front of them that ended in a pile of large rocks and dirt that reached to the tunnel ceiling. Two doors on either side of the tunnel led to empty rooms. The doors on the left had the name Rudolf Hess on them; the doors on the right had the name H. Goering. "This is like opening a damn time capsule," remarked B.J. as he flashed his light all around the tunnel.

"My God," exclaimed Weismann in an awe inspired voice. "One can only imagine the value of the art work and other treasures once stored in these four rooms and the fifteen rooms on the other side of the blockage. My research has revealed estimates of anywhere between thirty and fifty million 1945 US dollars. I suppose the rooms beyond the seal are empty?" questioned Weismann, as he looked into the four rooms off the hallway.

"I did not realize this is your first visit to the complex," said B.J. ignoring Weismann's question. "There is not much to see now, Herr. Weismann. "I really see no point in remaining down here any longer, do you agree?" B.J. was becoming impatient. He needed to be home with his wife helping with the movers.

"Very well. I suppose I have seen enough for now," said Weismann with resignation.

B.J. had difficulty closing the heavy door but finally succeeded, and then he snapped the big brass padlocks to the closed position. They walked back to the elevator without speaking. When standing outside the hotel entrance once again, Herr. Weismann informed B.J. that he would be out of the country for the next several days, thanked B.J. for the tour, and walked to his car.

It was almost dark when B.J. pulled into the driveway to his quarters. The moving crew appeared to be loading the last of the household packing crates onto the truck. He walked into a house empty of everything except government-issue furniture. All reminders that his family had lived were gone. His wife didn't answer his weak greeting. He suddenly felt very tired. "One thing is for sure. I'm going to make a note of Weismann's unusual interest in the tunnel complex in my final report to USAREUR Headquarters. I'll also mention his strange friends," said B.J.

March 30, 1995

The phone rang just as Hamp stepped from the shower. "Only Tom Adams would call me at 6:30 a.m.," thought Hamp. They had discussed going after grouper today. "Hello."

"Colonel Porter, this is Major Williamson in the Department of the Army Inspector General's Office. Please hold a moment for General Stone," the major said with authority.

Hamp was shocked enough that he let his towel fall to the floor. In about thirty seconds, a familiar voice said, "Hello, Hamp. Glad I caught you at home. I thought you might be fishing already," laughed the General. General Stone was promoted to Lieutenant General the month after Hamp's retirement and was presently Inspector General of the Army.

"I must say, General, you have surprised me," said Hamp.

"I wish this was a social call, Hamp, but it's not. I need your help. Could you possibly fly to Washington tomorrow for a most important meeting?" asked the general.

"Why sure, if you say so, sir," said Hamp, still a little surprised and puzzled. "What is the nature of the meeting, sir?"

"You'll have to wait until tomorrow for that answer, Hamp. Please try to be in my office no later than 1500 hours."

"Yes, sir," said Hamp as the General hung up.

Hamp walked around the room trying to decide if the conversation he just had had actually took place. "Maybe I'm not awake yet," thought Hamp. "Why would General Stone want me to attend a meeting in the Pentagon? Lieutenant General Stone is the Inspector General of the Army, now. Could I have information that might be of value to an IG investigation?" Hamp asked himself over and over again. He slipped into a pair of jeans, walked into the kitchen, poured himself a cup of fresh coffee, and paced on the upper deck of the house to help himself think. It was raining lightly, but he didn't feel it, or the hot coffee as it burned his lips. He had to figure this out. After pacing on the deck a half hour, Hamp decided to stop worrying about it and to get busy making flight reservations.

He was unable to book a flight out of Tallahassee or Gainesville that would put him into Washington in time for a three o'clock meeting. Hamp decided to play a long shot and called base operations at Moody Air Force Base in Valdosta, Georgia, just two hours away from Steinhatchee. They just might have something going that way, Hamp hoped.

"Flight Operations Desk, Sergeant Bill Robins speaking," says the voice.

"This is Colonel Hampton Porter, Sergeant Robins. Perhaps you can help me."

"I'll try, sir." said the sergeant.

"Good. The Inspector General of the Army just called me, and I have to make a meeting in the Pentagon at 1500 hours tomorrow. I live in Florida, and the local flights will not get me there in time for the meeting. Can you help?"

"The only thing we have on the books going that way right now, sir, is the weekly medical evacuation flight leaving here at 1300 hours going to Andrews Air Force Base. That flight makes three stops on the way and would not land at Andrews until 2030 hours, too late for your meting."

"Damn!" said Hamp. "Well, thanks anyway sergeant."

"Just a second, sir. The base commander's aide de camp penciled-in a flight plan for Andrews departing at 0700 in the morning. The fact that it is penciled-in means the flight plan is tentative. If you can wait a few minutes before you try something else, I'll try to reach the aide and check the status of his flight plan." Hamp gave the sergeant his phone number and began packing—just in case.

Fifteen minutes later the phone rang. "Colonel Porter, this is Sergeant Robins at Moody. I spoke with the aide and the flight is a go. There is just one problem, Colonel. The boss is flying a T-33, which is a two-seater. If you can do without luggage, he'll be happy to give you a lift."

"Fantastic!" said Hamp. "What time should I report to flight operations?"

"Be here ready to fly by 0630 hours, sir. You can borrow a flight suit here."

"I'll be there. Thanks a bunch, Sergeant. What do you drink?"

"Well, sir, I've been known to sip a little Wild Turkey on special occasions."

Hamp made a note about the Wild Turkey, then called Gwen and Tom Adams. He asked them both to say nothing of his destination or the purpose of his trip to Washington. "Hell, I don't even know why I'm going," Hamp had explained to Tom. He told them both he would return in a day or two, or as soon as he could get a flight back to Moody. Driving away, Hamp wished that he had told Marian to call Gwen.

*****

Brigadier General Elton Walker put the T-33 into a sharp left turn over Boling Air Force Base and lined the T-33 up with the Potomac River to make his approach to the Andrews Air Force Base landing pattern. It was 1045 hours. The flight had been late departing Moody, but otherwise uneventful. He and the general made small talk, but the general was busy on the radio most of the time checking into and out of various control points. There is not much to see from 30,000 feet at 500 miles per hour except just clouds. The general remarked that pilots, both military and commercial, detest the Washington area. Traffic and unusual landing patterns make the area one of the most dangerous places to fly in the country. He told Hamp that near misses among airplanes and near-river landings were not uncommon. Hamp wished the general had waited until they were safely on the ground to share that information with him. The T-33 kissed the runway perfectly—not the slightest jolt. Hamp had called General Stone's office from flight operations at Moody and informed his aide of his flight plans. The aide said he would have someone meet him at Andrews's flight operations.

"Thanks for the ride, General," said Hamp as they shook hands.

Hamp heard his name called as he entered the door to flight operations. The microphone voice called his name again, and Hamp noticed an Army staff sergeant holding a card pager above her head with his name on it.   He walked over to the sergeant and identified himself.

"I'm Staff Sergeant Nancy Johnson, General Stone's driver, Colonel Porter.   Welcome back to Washington, sir.   I have instructions to take you to the General's quarters at Fort Myer where you will be staying.   You will be having lunch with Mrs. Stone. After lunch, I'll drive you to the general's office, sir."

"Thank you, Sergeant," said Hamp politely. "Let me shed this flight suit, and I'll be right with you."   Hamp gave the flight coveralls to the operations sergeant and followed Nancy Johnson to the Army sedan in the VIP parking area.   He settled into the back seat for a nostalgic ride through the city.   Fort Myer and the Pentagon are on opposite sides of Washington from Andrews. The shortest route to Fort Myer was directly through the city.   The ride would take about half an hour.

"Did General Stone give you anything for me, Sergeant Johnson?" asked Hamp.   He had been optimistic that the general would pass him an information paper on the meeting, or even an agenda.

"No, he did not, sir."

Hamp tried to put the meeting and events of the past several days out of his mind.   He wanted the drive through Washington to Fort Meyer to be a reminder of happier days.   Judith had loved their tour of duty in the Pentagon.   She had enjoyed Washington thoroughly and had worked in the Museum of Natural History as a volunteer the last two years of their tour. They had bought a home near the Georgetown University campus.   She had liked the academic environment of that area and the quaint shops and townhouses that lined the streets.   It was also reasonably close to the Pentagon.   "Things have changed little," thought Hamp, as Sergeant Johnson negotiated the downtown traffic. "However," he continued musing, "as long as the seat of government remains on this unique piece of geography, Washington will continue to be a place of ambiguities and a place of national and international intrigue." Hamp remembered how many Pentagon people called it "the city of lies and deception."

It was precisely 11:30 when they pulled into the driveway of General Stone's quarters at Fort Meyer. The beautiful and spacious old two-story brick homes along General's Row seemed to have acquired even more character since his last visit to this street. The family dog, an old Labrador retriever named Goldie, greeted the sedan—probably expecting his master. Fran Stone walked onto the front porch ready to greet Hamp.

"You look as though you just posed for Vogue magazine, Fran," said Hamp with a smile.

"I see you have not lost your charm," she said as she hugged Hamp's neck. "No one has said that to me since you left Washington, Hamp," she said as she took his hand and led him up the steps to the front porch. Fran was the perfect Army wife. She was attractive, educated, intelligent, self-sufficient, and loved people. She had been a decided asset to General Stone's career, and he loved her very much. They lunched and then had a very good visit. Fran had been Judith's best friend, and being with her somehow made Judith seem close. Sergeant Johnson rang the front door bell. Hamp glanced at his watch, 1430 hours in the Pentagon; time for the meeting.

March 31, 1995

The Parthenon loomed awkwardly over the city of Athens as a constant reminder of another time. Herr Weismann never tired of the sight of it. It reminded him of an earlier time, a period in history that better suited him. He adamantly believed he had been born in the wrong century.

He fancied himself very much like General George Patton, Jr., in that regard, a man thrust into the world at the wrong time.

Weismann would call on his academic and professional friends at the Athens Museum on his way to the municipal dock and arrange to meet with them on the following day. His official purpose for visiting Athens would then be established; he was conducting business on behalf of the German Minister of the Interior, as far as anyone should know.

Weismann's taxi turned off the Apian Way and headed south toward the municipal docks. He would take the ferry to Mykonos where he would meet with his Pegasus partners who would be waiting for him. The ride would take about two hours, even though the ferry was a fast hydrofoil. He could have taken a plane to Mykonos, but he wanted the extra time to clear the cobwebs after his flight. The beauty of the Greek Isles with their white buildings surrounded by azure blue water calmed him.

It was almost time for phase one of Pegasus. He also needed the time to mentally review the operational plans again before his meeting with the group. If they were successful, history would record the first theft of nuclear warheads—warheads belonging to a superpower at that. He was counting on the cooperation of the President of the United States, due to the horrible embarrassment he would surely experience from such a thing happening to the United States of America especially on his watch. He had more confidence in the unwilling cooperation of the President than he did in his key Pegasus lieutenants. Heinrich Dieppe was of no concern. His loyalty and ability were beyond reproach. He would perform. Leadership and organization were his strengths, but the others were questionable. His Turkish and Greek associates were not Aryans,

so how dependable could they be? Their
motivation was greed, not the future well being
of the New World Order, he suspected. Motivation
stemming from greed does not breed the same kind
of dedication as does motivation resulting from a
belief in principles. For the Aryan,
preservation of the race was motivation enough
for one to sacrifice his or her life, if
necessary. Those motivated by greed were seldom
willing to sacrifice their own life for the
pursuit of money. Perhaps Dieppe could manage
their motivation; he would have to.

Tomas Popodopolus was hosting this meeting
because he lives in Greece; this was his
territory. He selected a remote hotel on the
northern side of Mykonos Island for their
meeting. The hotels of the Greek Isles are
accustomed to hosting groups of businessmen.
Greek businessmen prefer conducting serious
business away from stuffy offices and noisy
cities, so their group will not arouse suspicion
in a Mykonos hotel. Besides, his 300-pound body
required frequent sustenance, and the hotel
restaurant was excellent. He and Dieppe sipped
Ouzo, a popular and potent Greek liquor, on the
ocean-side patio while awaiting the arrival of
the others. The meeting was scheduled for 3:00
p.m. At 2:50 p.m., Erich Feltgeibell and Hans
Reifenstahl joined Tomas and Heinrich Dieppe on
the patio. Zuni Anatole arrived five minutes
later. All had rooms in the hotel. Weismann
arrived intentionally twenty minutes later.

"Good afternoon, gentlemen," said Weismann
as he took a chair at the table. "I apologize for
my lateness. I decided to take the ferry from
Athens," said Weismann with no further
explanation. "Shall we begin, Dieppe?" Dieppe
detested Weismann's propensity for aloofness in
the company of Anatole and Popodopolous. His
superior attitude made them uncomfortable.

Dieppe was going to have a difficult enough task keeping them loyal to the operation.

"Very well. Erich, Hans, Zuni, Tomas and I met all day yesterday and most of the evening. I believe everything is in order for us to proceed on schedule. Would you like a detailed status report from everyone?" asked Dieppe.

"No. That will not be necessary," began Weismann quietly. "I am familiar enough with each component of the overall plan. I shall leave the details to you, Heinrich. I would, however, like to hear of any concerns that any of you might have—no matter how inconsequential. All I have heard is that everything is just fine. I cannot believe that in an operation of this magnitude and complexity that everything can be just fine. We are about to attempt the theft of nuclear weapons from the number one super power of the world, and you say that all is well?" Weismann's voice was now an octave higher and several decibels louder. "It is time to lay all the cards on the table, gentlemen. There is too much at stake to hold back anything that has the potential of jeopardizing our efforts. For example, Zuni, at our last meeting most of us had some concern about Colonel Sultoy's reliability. Please tell us of the steps you have taken to assure his discrete participation and dependability."

Zuni appeared somewhat red-faced and a little nervous. Weismann clearly believed him to be the weak link in the operation. "Dieppe should have been more careful in his selection of the leader for the Turkish part of the operation," thought Weismann. Before speaking, Zuni finished a glass of Ouzo.

"I still have confidence that Colonel Sultoy can and will carry out his responsibilities for Pegasus," retorted Zuni rather loudly. "My threat to hold his wife hostage is the key, and it will work."

"Yes. You told us that before, Zuni, but how do we know he will not send her out of the country, or otherwise hide her?" demands Weismann, his patience growing thin. "The entire success of your part of the operation depends on that one circumstance, Zuni. If it goes wrong, everything will fall apart. Don't you understand that, Zuni?" said Weismann, with noticeable contempt in his voice. Zuni was now clearly shaken. His hands trembled and perspiration ran down his face in rivulets. The others became noticeably uncomfortable as well. Dieppe was about to intercede when Zuni answered. His face was beet red; his eyes were like burning coals; his hands gripped the chair arms, and his breathing was labored.

"I will take her into custody as soon as I return. Are you happy now?" says Zuni with suppressed rage in his voice. Weismann smiled and looked away, like a child having successfully played a joke on another child.

Dieppe felt it time to relieve the pressure. "Does anyone else have a concern?" he asked in a calming voice. "No. Good. Then can we agree, gentlemen, that the operation will be executed according to plan?" He knew Pegasus had to be a "go" or a "no go," at this very moment. Any further delay or questioning of decisions already made would serve no useful purpose and would only weaken everyone's confidence in the operation. He believed preparations were as sound and complete as he could make them. Any further questioning from Weismann would be detrimental to their interests. Everyone appeared to have sensed Dieppe's thinking. No further concern was forthcoming.

"Peter, do you have anything further?" asked Dieppe.

Weismann stared at Zuni for several seconds before answering. "No," he said curtly. "However, I do have a question. Have all tunnel diggings been completed?" he asked. All heads nodded in the affirmative.

"The tunnels have been completed for several days, Peter," says Dieppe. "Now, let us turn our attention to timing, gentlemen," said Dieppe. Dieppe had successfully diffused the situation. Everyone seemed noticeably more relaxed—even Weismann. "In my opinion we should move as quickly as possible," says Dieppe.

"I agree," said Feltgeibell. "The longer we wait, the better the chance for a leak in security."

"Yes. I agree also," said Popodopolus.

"Do you agree, Hans?" Dieppe asked Reifenstahl.

"Yes. We should move quickly," he said with a nod of his head.

"Then so be it," added Weismann. "Pegasus will begin at midnight on April 15."

"You wanted to discuss contingency plans during this meeting, Peter," reminded Dieppe.

"Oh. Yes. I have given the matter a great deal of thought, and I think we should let each component of the operation stand alone."

"What do you mean stand alone?" asked Dieppe, clearly surprised.

"For example, Heinrich, if the Thessalonica phase fails, it does not mean we have to call off the Boctoi part of the operation," says Weismann.

"I just wanted to make sure we all understand, Peter."

"Of course," replied Peter.

"Then we will proceed without contingency planning, but against my better judgment, Peter," says Dieppe firmly.

"So noted," replied Weismann.

March 25, 1995

Frau Gurter entered B.J.'s office without knocking and looked as though she had seen the ghost of Hitler—very uncharacteristic of her behavior. "Colonel Patterson, Lieutenant General Stone's Office is calling for you," she said breathlessly. Frau Gurter tended to be overly impressed by rank, thought B.J., but most Germans were.

B.J. picked up the phone wondering what could have gone wrong now. "This is Lieutenant Colonel Patterson speaking," he said in his official voice.

"Sir, this is Major Williamson in the Department of the Army Inspector General's Office. General Stone requires your presence for a meeting in his office at 1500 hours on 31 March."

"I assume the general knows I am in the midst of turning this facility over to the Germans," B.J. said, a little surprised.

"Yes, sir, he knows, but the meeting takes precedence over your other duties."

"May I ask the nature of the meeting?" questioned B.J.

"I am not at liberty to say, sir."

B.J. slowly placed the phone into its receiver and buzzed for Frau Gurter. She hurried into his office with pencil poised over a stenographer's pad as usual. "Frau Gurter, please book me on the Air Force Eagle Flight from Frankfort to Andrews Air Force Base on 30 March. Tell flight operations that my travel status is category one, and ask the personnel office to cut the travel orders today." Frau Gurter knew that category one was reserved only for top priority travelers. It would allow him to automatically bump anyone else for a seat on the flight, regardless of their rank. "How eventful can a fellow's retirement be?" B.J. asked himself as he scratched his head. "My wife will love this," he thought.

Chapter 5

March 31, 1995

Hamp was comfortably seated in General Stone's outer office along with Lieutenant Colonel B.J. Patterson, whom Hamp knew from an earlier assignment, and three gentlemen dressed in civilian attire like himself, whom Hamp did not know. The Aide de Camp, Major Williamson, opened the door to the General's conference room and asked everyone to enter. General Stone shook everyone's hand as they filed into the room and took seats around a conference table large enough to accommodate a dozen people comfortably. Hamp couldn't help but wonder what all of this was about, especially when General Stone asked him as he shook his hand to remain after the meeting. However, he did not have time to question him then because as everyone was seated, General Stone walked to the podium at the head of the table.

"Gentlemen, thank you for being prompt," said the General in a serious voice. "Hamp, I hope you and Colonel Patterson didn't have to break your necks to get here, but this is important. As soon as the Chief of Staff arrives, we will begin."

As General Stone talked, a full-length curtain that covered the wall behind the podium slid open to reveal a very large opaque screen. Hamp noticed that on the opposite wall of the room were two square openings; "Obviously they are for slide or movie projectors," Hamp thought to himself.

"While we are waiting, I'll make introductions," said the General: "Beginning on my left, Colonel (Retired) Hampton Porter, and

Lieutenant Colonel B.J. Patterson, Commander of the US Army Recreation Center in Berchtesgaden. To my right are Mr. Walter Gibbs, Deputy Director of the Central Intelligence Agency; Mr. James Gregory, Director of the Drug Enforcement Agency; and Mr. Wilbur Burns, Deputy Director of the Federal Bureau of Investigation." Everyone nodded and smiled as he was introduced, except Mr. Gregory. Hamp noted that they were all dressed exactly alike in dark blue suits, conservative ties, white shirts, and he guessed, black wing-tipped shoes.

"Gentlemen, the Chief of Staff," announced Major Williamson as General Gordon Beckman entered the room. Everyone stood as a courtesy.

"Sorry I'm a little late, gentlemen. Please go on General Stone," said the Chief as he took the seat at the end of the table opposite the podium.

"Thank you, sir," said General Stone. "Gentlemen, I want to keep this meeting as informal as possible. We have a lot of territory to cover, and there are a number of government agencies involved. I ask that questions be held until each briefer has completed his remarks."

"I agree," interrupted the Chief. "You can skip the introductions for my sake," he said. "I'll find out who everyone is as they brief," the Chief directed.

"Walt, please begin," said General Stone as he took a seat across from the Chief. As Walter Gibbs stood and moved to the podium, the room lights dimmed, a slide projector came to life, and an image of a man in military uniform appeared on the screen. Before speaking, Mr. Gibbs let the image of the man burn into everyone's mind. Hamp almost fell out of his chair from shock when he realized who the man on the screen was. He was Colonel Anton Sultoy of the Turkish Army. They had become friends when

Hamp was the USAREUR IG. Hamp had always loved Turkish history, and Sultoy was obliged to take him on many interesting side trips of historical interest while he was there.

"Gentlemen, meet Colonel Anton Sultoy. He is a Colonel of Artillery in the Turkish Army and commands the guard detachment for the American nuclear storage facility at Boctoi in eastern Turkey. For those not familiar with Boctoi, or our nuclear storage facility there, Boctoi is the eastern-most city in Turkey. It is where Turkey shares borders with Russia, Iran, and Syria near Mount Ararat. A Turkish artillery brigade in the area commanded by Colonel Sultoy provides perimeter security for the American nuclear storage facility," continued Gibbs. "My understanding is that this is standard procedure among NATO countries, General Beckman."

Hamp felt numb. "What had this covert meeting to do with Sultoy," he wondered.

Another slide appeared on the screen of an aerial view of the storage facility that houses the American custodial detachment, as well as the nuclear storage and assembly building. The third, fourth and fifth slides were various ground-level views of the compound perimeter, to include guard towers, fencing, and lighting. "As you can see, gentlemen, the compound is typical of more than eighty other storage facilities in Italy, Greece, Turkey, and Germany."

"I suppose you are going to eventually make a point with all this, Mr. Gibbs," said the Chief, as though his time was being wasted.

"Yes, I do have a point, General," replied Mr. Gibbs as Secretary of the Army Martin Griffin entered the room and took a seat next to B.J. Patterson.

"Sorry I'm late, gentlemen. Please go on Walter," he urged.

"Thank you, Mr. Secretary. As I was saying, General Beckman, all of this has been to point out Colonel Sultoy's proximity, access, and familiarity to the Boctoi storage facility. He has been in command of the Turkish troops there for over three years, and he is known and trusted by the Americans in the custodial detachment. Now, my specific point is that he entered the American consulate in Istanbul two days ago and insisted on speaking with the Counsel General. He persisted until Mr. Lake, the Counsel General, saw him."

"And?" urged General Beckman.

"He told Mr. Lake that someone was planning to steal nuclear warheads from the Boctoi facility," finished Gibbs with the proper amount of drama. General Stone then stood and walked very matter-of-factly to the podium. He, as well as General Beckman did not react with the same surprise as Hamp and B.J. who looked at each other in amazement.

"Gentlemen, I was the first on the Army Staff to learn of this incident when Mr. Gibbs called me late yesterday afternoon," said General Stone. "Obviously, I have been privy to everything these gentlemen will be telling you. I did not want to blow an unknown situation out of proportion, so I kept the matter quiet while I put this meeting together for today." General Stone paused for effect and then continued. "Before we rush into a discussion of this situation, I suggest that we hear all of the details so that the scope of this situation is very clear. Afterwards, we will discuss our plan of action, if that is acceptable to everyone."

The Secretary and the Chief nodded their approval. The Chief shifted in his chair and unbuttoned his blouse. Mr. Griffin stood, lit a cigar, removed his suit jacket, and sat down

again. Suddenly, the meeting had taken on an air
of gravity.

Mr. Gibbs continued his presentation. "Mr.
Lake called our station office in Istanbul
immediately after Colonel Sultoy walked into his
office. Within fifteen minutes of Mr. Lake's
call, Colonel Sultoy was in our Istanbul office
where our agents questioned him for over an hour
about the allegation he made to Mr. Lake. With
the exception of telling us he was certain of his
allegation, Sultoy refused to tell us more than
he had already revealed. He even refused to give
us any personal information—not even his address.
He showed our agents only his military
identification card. That was it. We had no
legal basis for holding a Turkish citizen who had
voluntarily approached us for the purpose of
providing information, so we released Colonel
Sultoy. Our Istanbul Field Office went to work
immediately with little more than a physical
description and the name of the Colonel. Through
highly placed contacts in the Turkish Army
Headquarters in Ismir, we did manage to learn the
following. Slide, please."

The screen filled with a page from Colonel
Sultoy's military personnel record jacket. The
usual personal data: name, address, date and
place of birth, education, family members,
military schools, promotions, awards and
decorations, and military assignments filled the
screen. Two more slides included notations in his
jacket concerning civilian work experience,
hobbies, and known associates. Gibbs commented
on significant aspects of Sultoy's records. "The
US Army would never get away with keeping that
kind of information on its personnel," thought
Hamp.

"Gentlemen, I draw your attention to this
notation made just six months ago," said Gibbs,
as his laser pointer highlighted a paragraph near

the bottom of the last page of the jacket.
"Colonel Sultoy was seen in the company of,
second projector please, this man on the campus
of the University in Istanbul. They met and
spent at least two hours together each day for
three consecutive days." The second projection
screen came alive with a picture of a rather
ordinary looking gentleman of about 65 or 66
years of age. Tall and slightly stooped, he
appeared fifteen pounds overweight, probably out
of physical condition, and wore rather heavy
looking glasses. "Through our contacts with the
Turkish authorities, we learned that his name is
Heinrich Dieppe. He is German born and holds a
German passport." A stunned B.J. immediately
recognized Dieppe and began to inventory all his
uneasy feelings he had had about the man. "Dieppe
resides in Berlin where he teaches history at
Humboldt University," continued Gibbs. "Our
office in Berlin confirmed with the university
that Dieppe is on a one year sabbatical."

"What is the connection between Dieppe and
Sultoy?" interrupted the Secretary.

"As you noted in Sultoy's military
personnel jacket, sir, Sultoy is an avid and
trained historian. He holds a doctorate degree
in ancient Turkish history from the University of
Istanbul and taught history at the same
university until entering military service.
Dieppe also holds a doctorate in history granted
by the University of Heidelberg in Germany. His
specialty is the history of the German Third
Reich and the Nazi movement. We have learned
that an international symposium on military
history was being held at the University of
Istanbul where the two were seen together."

"That proves nothing," remarked General
Beckman. "The two men have in common an interest
in history. So what?"

"A logical response, General," said Gibbs.
"My reaction was the same until I learned that
Dieppe has a propensity for being on the fringe
of neo-nazi movement activities in Germany and
has known connections to several active terrorist
groups in Europe and elsewhere. We confirmed
that information with our people in Germany
yesterday."

"How did you put the two men together?"
asked the Secretary.

"Our people in Istanbul had Dieppe under
surveillance hoping to get a lead on a particular
terrorist faction believed to be in Istanbul,"
replied Gibbs. "Learning of Dieppe's connection
to Sultoy was nothing more than a coincidence."

"Thank you Walter," said General Stone
rising from his chair. "Any more detail at this
point will only bog us down. Wilbur, your turn in
the barrel."

Wilbur Burns walked deliberately to the
podium. Burns was a tall, distinguished-looking,
thirty-one year veteran with the FBI and had a
reputation for being a hothead. Aside from that
fault, he was one of the best thinkers in the
bureau and had the ability to cut right to the
heart of an issue.

"Mr. Secretary, General Beckman, and
gentlemen, I am pleased to represent the Director
today. His wife's hospitalization and surgery
yesterday precludes his personal attention to
this matter. I can only hope my presence will
suffice," said Burns with just the slightest
touch of a sneer. "What an ass," thought Hamp.
"How does General Stone put up with these
pedantic megalomaniacs?"

"Gentlemen, the FBI is interested in this
incident because there is potential for
terroristic activity in this country, the
possible importation of illegal nuclear weapons
into this country, and the possible threat of

sabotage to federal government entities. I will
personally serve as the FBI representative should
a task force be formed subsequent to this
meeting. I will see that all the FBI resources
necessary are made available as needed." Burns
sat down. Hamp suspected that General Stone
invited the FBI to the meeting to cover the
Secretary of the Army's ass should something
really big develop from this incident. A glance
in General Stone's direction confirmed his
suspicion.

General Stone rose once again. "Mr.
Gregory, if you please," gestured the General.

"James Gregory would make a good dictionary
picture under the word Mafia," thought Hamp, as
Gregory took the podium. Gregory was about 45 or
50, short, stocky, and had prematurely white
hair. His cold, gray, penetrating eyes were
testimony to his fearing no man. Unlike many
Washington bureaucrats, he had the reputation of
being a straight shooter, a what-you-see-is-what-
you- get sort of man. "I would hate to meet him
in a dark alley at night," Patterson murmured to
Hamp.

"The DEA's interest in this is simple,
gentlemen. My agents have seen Dieppe on four
separate occasions with two of the biggest known
drug bosses in Florida," announced Burns.
"Slide, please," he called. "The man on the left
in this picture is Enrico Charo. He controls all
illegal drugs coming into the United States
through Florida. The man on the right you should
recognize as Heinrich Dieppe. The next slide
again shows two men. This time they are in West
Palm Beach. Dieppe is the man on the right. The
man to whom he is talking is Joey Costellano, a
mafia drug boss who we believe is presently
controlling most of the illegal drug traffic
moving from Florida to points along the eastern
United States. We have reason to believe that

Charo is Costellano's supplier. So far we have been unable to establish the link between Dieppe and these two prized citizens. We need to know the connection between Dieppe and these people. What is a history professor from Germany doing talking to known mobsters in the United States? Could Dieppe be their connection to European drugs? We have a man undercover with Charo's family, but he has not contacted us in over two weeks."

"When was Dieppe seen with Charo and Costellano?" asked the Secretary.

"Twice in November and on one occasion in December," replied Burns.

"Anything more, Wilbur?" asked General Stone.

"Yes, one more thing. The next slide shows Dieppe talking with a man on the patio of the Palm Beach Hilton Hotel. The picture was taken the day after we shot the picture of Dieppe talking with Costellano. We have been unable to identify him." The image appeared on the screen, and B.J. Patterson inhaled loudly enough for everyone in the room to hear.

"My God! That's Peter Weismann," exclaimed B.J. All eyes were on Colonel Patterson. He was pale as a ghost and visibly shaken.

"Who did you say that is?" asked Burns.

"Peter Weismann," repeated B.J. "He is the newly appointed Curator of Antiquities for the State of Bavaria. I'm in the process of transferring the US Army Recreation Center in Berchtesgaden to that man."

"Gentlemen, I think we need a short latrine break," interrupted Secretary Griffin as he stood. "Do you agree, Chief?"

"Yes. By all means," replied General Beckman. "It is now 1630 hours. We will reassemble here in twenty minutes, gentlemen. Not a word of this to anyone if you leave this

room.   Mr. Secretary, General Stone, will you
join me in my office for a moment, please?" asked
the Chief.

Gibbs and Burns went into a huddle in a
corner of the conference room.   Meanwhile, as
Hamp was trying to bring B.J. Patterson back to
earth, James Gregory walked over to B.J, grabbed
him by the arm, and looked directly into his
eyes.   "Are you certain that the man you saw in
the picture goes by the name of Peter Weismann?"
Gregory asked in a low unintentional growl.

"Yes. I am positive," replied B.J. pulling
his arm away from Gregory's grip.   "I've known
the man for three years. I would recognize him
anywhere," said B.J., miffed at Gregory's
manhandling him.

Gregory hurried over to a telephone near
the podium and placed a call.   "I can guess who
is on the receiving end of that call," said Hamp
to B.J.

"If that son of a buck grabs me again,
he'll be on my receiving end," replied B.J with
some of his Mississippi country boy attitude.

As the initial shock of recognizing
Weisman, B.J. appeared calmer and more relaxed.
B.J. explained his relationship with Weismann to
Hamp. "I'm beginning to put two and two
together," said B.J.   "I had concerns about
Weismann that I could not put my finger on," he
explained. "Now it's all beginning to make
sense."

Meanwhile, General Beckman, along with
Secretary of the Army Griffin, and General Stone
filed into his office. The Chief pushed a button
on his intercom and asked his executive officer
to come in.

"Ray, hold all calls and visitors. We will
require absolute privacy for the next few
minutes," directed the Chief.

"Yes, sir," replied the executive officer as he exited the office and closed the heavily padded door behind him.

"Gentlemen, we have the makings of one hell of a situation here," said the Secretary. General Stone, you seem to be ahead of the game at this point. How do you suggest we proceed? I think we need to alert the President."

"I would like to answer that question, sir," interrupted General Beckman. "Before we get down to decisions, we need to know more about what exactly is going on. I suggest we hear the rest of the story, assuming there is more and then meet again to discuss options and courses of actions," said the Chief.

"There is more to the story," added General Stone. "We have not heard from Patterson or Porter, yet," he continued. I had a reason for inviting them to the meeting. Their reason for being here will become clear, and with your permission, Mr. Secretary, I prefer you hear it from them rather than me." Stone was politic enough to defer to the Secretary's seniority in the group.

"Chief, do you agree?" the Secretary asked General Beckman.

"Yes. I do."

"Then let's get on with it, gentlemen," said Griffin. They departed the Chief's office and walked quickly back to General Stone's conference room. Everyone appeared present and ready to resume the meeting. As everyone took his seat, General Stone asked B.J. Patterson if he could now understand why he was invited to the meeting.

"Do you think you can add anything to this story, Colonel Patterson?" asked the General. B.J., now collected and poised, took the podium and began speaking confidently in his slow Mississippi drawl.

"Yes, sir, I certainly do have something to contribute," said B.J. "Just a few days ago, Herr. Weismann invited me to the Eagle's Nest for dinner. I thought it a little unusual that my wife had not been included in the invitation, but I assumed that it was because Weismann wanted to discuss the impending property transfer. When I arrived for dinner, I was surprised to see five other dinner guests. At first, I could not understand their purpose for being there. Three of the men said they were in the export/import business; one proclaimed to be a yacht broker in the British Virgin Islands; and the fifth man, Heinrich Dieppe, said he was a history professor at Humboldt University in Berlin. Herr. Feltgeibell reportedly ran his pumice export trade from Iponema, near Rio. Reifenstahl brokered yachts to and from the British Virgin Islands to the United States, France, Italy and Germany. Mr. Popodopolus was from Greece. He said he manufactures and exports Flaccoti rugs. Mr. Zuni Anatole is Turkish and explained that he exports fine Turkish wool rugs." B.J. paused for a moment to make sure everyone was following him. Gibbs, Gregory, and Burns were frantically taking notes. Mr. Griffin, the Chief, and General Stone looked spellbound. The silence persisted for several seconds and then Walter Gibbs spoke.

"Did Weismann give you any reason for the presence of these men at his dinner party?"

"Yes. But only after I asked one of the guests how he became acquainted with Weismann," replied B.J. "I distinctly remember Weismann's interruption to preemptively answer my question. Weismann explained that his father had been in the export business in Brazil after World War II and had formed friendships with these men over the years as business associates and occasional partners," replied B.J. "He further explained that all five men were attending a conference hosted by one of the trade associations in Munich and had made a detour to Berchtesgaden for the purpose of paying him a visit. Weismann said his father's friends had become his friends. And I believe Herr. Dieppe said that Weismann had studied under him in the graduate history program at Humboldt University in Berlin." B.J. paused again to allow everyone a moment to absorb this new information.

After a moment, Walter Gibbs spoke. "Well, so far, gentlemen, we have established some very interesting connections, but we still don't know what the connections mean."

"We know at least one of them: Dieppe is connected to Sultoy and the drug bosses in Florida," offered Burns.

"An interesting point, Wilbur, but it still proves nothing," challenged Gregory. "All we can say with certainty at this moment is that Dieppe and Sultoy have history in common."

"We have no choice, gentlemen, as representatives of our government, but to assume the worst," stated Secretary Griffin emphatically. "It is our decided responsibility and duty to assume that Colonel Sultoy has warned us of an impending disaster of unthinkable consequences. The burden of proof rests on our shoulders. It is up to us to discover Colonel Sultoy's motivation for telling his story in the first place; it's up to us to pursue these people's connections until we know what they mean and what the implications are. Chief, gentlemen, I'm going to talk with the President immediately and ask him to set up a joint task force to pursue this matter to its conclusion."

"Don't you think that might be a little premature, sir?" suggested Walter Gibbs. "We really have done very little homework on this thing." Gibbs paused for a moment. "I hate to say this, but we also have to consider the White

House staff's propensity for leaks and their utter disregard for secrecy. I say this in all due respect for you, Mr. Secretary. I do realize that you are the President's appointee," said Gibbs apologetically. "But I also realize the White House staff is a mess." Griffin's face flushed noticeably at Gibbs' remark. He stared at Gibbs acrimoniously. "I believe your boss is also a Presidential appointee, Mr. Gibbs," Griffin reminded him.

"Gentlemen!" said General Beckman in a firm voice. "This is getting us nowhere. A good argument can be made for each side of that issue, but let's be reasonable," he insisted. "We all work for the White House. The President is my Commander in Chief, too. I do agree, however, Mr. Secretary, that it is too early to bring the White House in on this. The laws of the country already provide us a mechanism for working together on joint operations; we don't need approval from the White House unless we intend to commit troops in a civilian or foreign environment, or unless sanctions are required by the CIA. Furthermore, Gentlemen, if nuclear storage facilities in the custody of the United States Army are threatened, it is clearly an Army matter. You have a piece of the action, Walter, because it is your responsibility to investigate threats to this country on foreign soil. And, Jim, the DEA certainly has vested interest should illegal drug trafficking be a part of this. Walter, you will have to become involved should any of these potential threats move on American soil." General Beckman stood and threw up his arms. "Hell, we all have a vital role and interest in this," he exclaimed. "Now, let's knock off the bull, gentlemen, and get down to work. General Stone, you are the Army's top investigator, and I trust your judgment. How do you see this thing going from here?"

"In my opinion, sir, we immediately do two things. First, we should refrain from alerting the White House until we know more. Secondly, we should form the task force this afternoon and determine its composition and leadership. I suggest that, since the perceived threat is aimed at the Army, my office head the task force. I further suggest that the civilians presently in this room serve as representatives of their respective agencies. With the exception of Colonel Porter and Lieutenant Colonel Patterson, I further suggest that no one else be brought into this investigation at this point."

Gibbs, Burns and Gregory nodded their approval of General Stone's proposal. The Secretary was still clearly perturbed; he just sat and stared at the wall. The Chief had not yet responded. All eyes were on him. Finally the Chief rose from his chair and paced in front of the conference table with his hands behind his back.

"General Stone is on the money. We will do exactly as he suggested, gentlemen," said Beckman with authority. Gibbs' eyes rolled back in his head. Gregory shook his head in disbelief. Burns showed no emotion whatsoever. "Does anyone have a problem with that?" he asked.

"Don't we civilians get a vote, General?" asked Gibbs.

"Not as long as it is an Army matter," replied Beckman. "But you will have a say every step of the way, and your input will be valued and respected. Fair enough?" asked Beckman.

"Does the same apply to Gregory and me?" asked Burns.

"Yes. Of course," replied Beckman.

"Burns, Gibbs, Gregory and I will meet here every day at 1600 hours to debrief, update and make necessary decisions," instructed General Stone. "Mr. Secretary, Chief, you know that you are welcome anytime you choose to come. One more thing before we call a halt to this meeting," said Stone. "Colonel Porter has not spoken, and no one has asked why he is here."

"I assumed you had good reason for his presence," replied Beckman.

"Colonel Porter and I have a history," began General Stone. "We served together several times over the years, and I have a great deal of confidence in him and I respect his abilities. Colonel Porter is now retired and lives in a small fishing village on the gulf coast. Before his retirement, Colonel Porter was the Inspector General of USAREUR and Seventh Army. He worked for me and for the Commander in Chief of USAREUR and Seventh Army. Inspecting all the nuclear storage sites in NATO at least annually was one of his primary responsibilities. He did that job well. I know of no one who has more knowledge of those storage sites than Colonel Porter. He also knows Colonel Sultoy very well. Hamp, would you care to comment on your knowledge of Colonel Sultoy?"

Hamp spoke from his chair. "Well, in a nutshell, sir, he is well educated, highly intelligent, articulate, and very well read. He is also a competent officer and a devoted husband and father. He is apolitical, but his wife comes from a family that is very active in politics. Her father in particular has frequently been the source of problems for their marriage. He wants Colonel Sultoy to adopt his politics and become active in local political activities; however, Colonel Sultoy has always resisted, and this does not sit well with his father-in-law. You already know of his training and interest in history. During my inspection trips to Boctoi, we would frequently visit historical military sites. I can very well remember on one occasion how excited he was to show me an actual ancient battlefield site of Attila the Hun. His genuine love for history and for his country made a significant impression upon me."

"Did he ever strike you as being the type of man who would just walk into the American Consulate and tell them someone was going to steal their nuclear weapons, and then clam up?" asked Walter Gibbs.

"Not at all," Hamp assures Gibbs. "He must have had very good justification for doing it. If I were you, gentlemen, I would pay attention to his allegation." Hamp had their full attention. Clearly Hamp knew what he was talking about, though what he had to say did not ease the tenseness of the situation.

With this said, General Stone turned to Mr. Griffin. "Mr. Secretary, may I have your permission to recall Colonel Porter to active duty in his retired rank?" asked General Stone. "To do so will require your personal approval and signature."

"You have my permission," said Griffin without looking at the General. Griffin showed no emotion, but was still obviously stinging from General Beckman's bite.

"Thank you," said the General. "Colonel Porter's help will be invaluable."

Reeling from surprise, Hamp thought, "I don't remember anyone asking me if I were willing to be recalled". Then he remembered that under the law the Secretary of the Army could recall him to active duty anytime, which suited the army's pleasure.

"Gentlemen, we have covered everything I had in mind for this meeting, and we have made the decisions necessary at this juncture," said General Stone.

"Sir, before we leave, I do have one more question to ask General Beckman," said Walter Gibbs. "General," he continued, "Will the storage sights be ordered to higher alert status?"

"No." Their usual alert status is high. There is no need to do anything more about security at the storage facilities," he responded.

"Now, if that is all, I suggest we adjourn until our first 1600 hour meeting tomorrow," said General Stone. Everyone nodded their agreement and left the conference room except Hamp and General Stone.

General Stone and Hamp were now alone. "I really don't agree with General Beckman's assessment of storage site security," said Hamp.

"Nor do I," replied General Stone. "You have to understand, Hamp, he's never been in the nuclear business."

"Don't you think the commanders of each detachment should at least be warned?" asked Hamp.

"Not just yet, but probably soon, depending on what our investigation turns up. I'm sorry as hell to drag you out of retirement, Hamp, but I think you can help us. You will not need to visit the Post Exchange at Fort Meyer tomorrow to buy uniforms; I want you in civilian clothes. I'll leave it to you to dream up any cover you need. You will have special travel orders and an Army American Express Card."

"I didn't know there is such a thing as an Army credit card," replied Hamp. "How long do you think you will require my services, sir?" asked Hamp. "I'll have to tell my friends in Steinhatchee something."

"You can tell them the truth -that you are helping me with an investigation. You will need to do some packing. You can tell them tomorrow in person," said General Stone. "Tonight you will be my house guest. Major Williamson is working on a flight home for you tomorrow as we speak."

"Where am I going, General?"

"To Turkey, first. I want you to make contact with Sultoy and find out what you can. Tell him you are vacationing in Europe and wanted to see him, or tell him the truth. I'll leave that decision to you. Perhaps he'll tell you what we need to know without your asking because you are his friend. Just play it by ear, but we have to know if he was telling the truth and soon."

"And after Turkey, sir?"

"Wherever you need to go, Hamp. You have complete freedom in this investigation. Just keep me informed on the secure phone. I'll give you the number."

Chapter 6

April 6, 1995

General Stone walked into his conference room with General Beckman at precisely 1600 hours. Everyone was seated around the conference table ready to begin. General Beckman glanced around the table nodding a curt, stone-faced greeting: "Mr. Gibbs, Mr. Gregory, Mr. Burns, gentlemen. I assume the Secretary will be here momentarily and we can begin," announced General Beckman. As though on cue, Secretary Griffin walked into the room and took a seat.

No one knew that the Chief and the Secretary had moments before met in the Secretary's office and had had harsh words. Griffin wanted to inform the President of what was going on and the Chief was adamant that he wait. The Chief was very much aware of how things were in the White House, and didn't trust anyone over there. The White House Chief of Staff had burned the Chief twice already by leaking highly classified defense information to the Chinese. He was not about to get burned again by that bunch of irresponsible, immature, drug snifters. Being civil to the Secretary of the Army as a Presidential appointee required every ounce of patience and fortitude at his command.

"Gentlemen, shall we begin?" said the Secretary, his face still flushed from his encounter with the Chief'.

General Stone took the podium. He had an idea of what had taken place between the Chief and the Secretary and hoped their differences would not spill over into their work here. "Gentlemen, before we begin the briefings, I want you to know that the information you will receive today represents five days of extremely intensive work on behalf of the CIA, the FBI, the DEA, my own staff, and countless staff members in those agencies. I want to thank each one of the agency representatives here today for their cooperative efforts. Mr. Secretary, you and General Beckman did not attend our last four daily meetings, so what you see and hear today will be entirely new to you both." General Stone knew what they were going to hear would capture their immediate attention. "Walter, will you begin, please?"

"Thank you, General Stone. Indeed we have been in a full court press for the past four and one-half days, but our efforts have paid off. Slide, please." As the room lights dimmed, the screen came to life with a full frontal photograph of Peter Weismann. "You saw pictures of this gentleman four or five days ago. Lieutenant Colonel Patterson gave us an impromptu rundown on his recent background and activities." B.J. began concentrating on what Gibbs was saying. He had always felt that something was not right about Weismann, but he didn't know what it was. "But what Lieutenant Colonel Patterson did not know was that his real name is Peter Franz Sturmer, III. He is gentile—not Jewish—and is the son of the late Colonel General Franz Sturmer of Hitler's Storm Abteilung, better known as the SS, and the former commandant of the Nazi extermination camp at Treblinka," said Gibbs with his usual drama. Gibbs knew this information would get everyone's attention and it did. The room became deathly silent.

He waited a few seconds for everyone to recover and then continued, "For those who don't remember the death camp at Treblinka, it ranked fourth among death camps behind Auschwitz, Buchenwald, and Dachau. Over 700,000 people were sent to Treblinka and only forty were known to have survived." B.J. could only shake his head in utter disgust and disbelief at such an atrocity. Gibbs continued, "Sturmer eluded capture by the Russians when the camp was liberated, and after the war, he made his way to Brazil with his one year old son, Peter Franz Sturmer, III. His wife had died earlier in a Berlin air raid. He then took the name Peter Weismann in Rio de Janeiro, started an export/import business, and lived the life of a Jewish businessman. Sturmer, Jr. did not send his son to public school in Brazil. Instead, he hired a private tutor for him, an ex-Nazi party member from Austria who had also escaped to Brazil after the war.

When little Peter turned twelve, his father sent him to a private boarding school in England where he remained until he was 16. However, the school became fed-up with Peter's political tirades and neo-Nazi speeches on the school commons and encouraged him to pursue his education elsewhere. He matriculated to the University of Heidelberg where he studied languages and political science for seven years. The university refused to grant Peter a doctor of letters degree, because they felt his political views too radical. He did not help his case when he rendered the Nazi salute while defending his doctoral thesis, which clearly pointed to the need for a rebirth of the Third Reich in Germany. Considering the heightened state of post-war sensitivity among Germans to Jews, Sturmer's attitude did not sit well with the faculty.

After leaving the university, he decided to remain in Germany and lived with an aunt in Freiberg. He apparently tired of Freiberg in 1967 and began hanging out with a neo-Nazi group in Berlin for about a year. In 1968, through old family connections, he landed a job as an assistant curator of antiquities in Bavaria. In 1982, he was promoted to senior assistant curator of antiquities and was transferred to Berchtesgaden to supervise the restoration of the Platterhof Hotel, Eagle's Nest, and other government-owned buildings of historical value in the region. He took a one-year sabbatical in 1989 to study Turkish antiquities at the Free University in Istanbul. There is no evidence of his ever having been married, but, so far as we can determine, he is not homosexual. He is an expert on the life of Hitler, the Nazi movement, and neo-Nazism since 1969. Athletics and frequent travel, especially to Turkey and Greece, occupy his leisure time. So far as we could determine, he has very few friends and is considered a loner." Gibbs was finished. A pregnant pause followed. Finally General Beckman stirred in his chair, cleared his throat, and spoke.

"What significance do you see in all this, Walter?"

"Not much, General, but when considered with the rest of the information I'm about to give you, I would say we have real cause for worry," replied Gibbs with genuine concern in his voice. "Are there questions before I continue, gentlemen?" Gibbs asked. "No. Then I will ask my specialist in right wing organizations to take the podium and continue the briefing. We had a lot of help and input on this from Wilbur Burns and his people. Dr. Martin," Gibbs nodded to his specialist.

Dr. Martin took the podium. He looked every bit the part of a scholar. He wore tweed, horn-rimmed glasses, and had bushy gray hair. His height was reduced by a noticeable stoop of his shoulders. He arranged his papers on the podium and looked directly at each person seated at the conference table as though he were taking the measure of his audience. He finally began speaking in a rather pleasant and strong baritone voice.

"Gentlemen, I am about to describe to you the most dangerous man I have ever had the duty to study. Franz Joseph Sturmer, III is Adolf Hitler reincarnated. His passion for the adult portion of his life has been devoted to assisting with the world-wide birth and development of neo-Nazism. His involvement in such movements in Europe, particularly in his homeland of Germany, has been profound. As near as can be determined, Sturmer has started more than eight hundred cells of what he calls the New World Order throughout Europe and the United States alone. These cells are made up of hardcore national socialists who hold all non-Aryan people, especially Jews, as the great destructive forces in the world today who are ruining Western civilization. Sturmer believes his New World Order will give back to the noble Aryan races their former consciousness of superiority by inculcating the principle that men are not equal. He preaches that the belief in human equality is nothing more than hypnotic dogma espoused by Judaism with the help of the Christian Churches. Whereas Hitler was nothing more than a street fight organizer, a master of mass meetings, and the leader of an almost non-existent political party, Sturmer is very different and has the intelligence to identify and learn from Hitler's mistakes. Sturmer believes that in political life there is no room for foreign policy. His party focus is on racial doctrine and the fight against pacifism and internationalism, and, like Hitler, Sturmer's answer to political roadblocks is bloodshed," continued Martin.

"Sturmer's leadership skills are clearly demonstrated in his ability to convince his followers that hysterical anti-German, thus anti-Aryan, outbursts have come from Zionist sources.

It is they, according to Sturmer, who have been responsible for world-wide German phobia when they should be more concerned about Japan phobia. He excuses contemporary examples of German atrocities by pointing to newspaper and journal pictures of President Lyndon Johnson posing as the host of the Ethiopian genocidal master, Haile Selassie. He points to allied atrocities committed by American, French and Russian forces like the Churchill-Lindemann program of saturation bombing of German civilians, the incendiary bombing of Hamburg, and the atom bombing of Hiroshima and Nagasaki. Sturmer also points to the fact that the Zionists' claim that over 25 million Jews died at Nazi hands would be quite impossible since there were no more than fifteen to eighteen million Jews in the world at that time. The massacre of Polish officers at the Katyn Forest by the Russians and the treatment of Japanese citizens living on the Pacific Coast of the United States are frequently among Sturmer's examples of allied atrocity." Martin paused for a sip of water, his audience entranced.

"In America, Sturmer has several things going for him and the New World Order. First, many Americans today have lost interest in the causes and results of World War II. Even more helpful to the NWO is the credibility gap generated by the Vietnam War. The working man's criticism of the government in general tends to support and give credence to radical movements such as the NWO. The rapid growth in such movements, to include fringe groups like the Ku Klux Klan, George Lincoln Rockwell's White Aryan Resistance (WAR) in the United States, and Haider's Freedom Party in Austria are evidence and testimony enough to explain how a man like Sturmer can exert such powerful leadership. A sociologist would tell us he fills a void left by the inadequacies of the present government. Secondly, since the death of Rockwell, Sturmer has obtained leadership of the WAR by default, and is in the process of transitioning its membership to the NWO. Based on what we have learned from undercover operatives, the transition is going smoothly. Much of the NWO literature our operatives are picking up now is simply recycled WAR documents with a new cover," explained Dr. Martin.

"Based on a joint analysis with Mr. Burns' people in the FBI research group in Quantico, we think what Sturmer needs most now, gentlemen, is money. With megabucks he can easily grow new cells across this nation and many others. It would appear that he has found a source for that money—the sale of nuclear warheads. I apologize for the shallowness of my presentation, Gentlemen; that is the best I could do in four and a half days. Are there any questions?" asked Dr. Martin.

"Thank you for an excellent, though alarming, presentation, Dr. Martin. Are we going to hear similar stories about the other five men Colonel Patterson told us about?" asked the Secretary.

"Yes, you are, Mr. Secretary," replied Gibbs as he replaced Dr. Martin at the podium.

"Go on, Walter," said the Secretary with a gesture of his hand.

Gibbs took a deep breath, sipped from a glass of water and called for the next slide. Hamp braced himself. He knew the news would not be good.

"This is Herr. Dr. Hans H. Reifenstahl. His parents were German citizens but lived in Argentina where Dr. Reifenstahl taught the locals how to raise cattle more productively. The Doctor was highly placed in Hitler's Third Reich, but like many Nazi party members, fled to South

America after Berlin fell in 1945. The Reifenstahls had money—old money that was made worthless by the war. When he fled to South America, he carried with him a fortune in diamonds, legal tender in any country. Young Hans was born in Argentina in 1946. As soon as he was old enough, his father sent him to a private gymnasium in Austria. Then, when the schools were reopened, he went to West Germany for his preparatory education. He graduated from the University of Heidelberg with a doctorate in animal husbandry. His specialty was beef cattle genetics. After graduation, he went back to work on his father's ranch in Argentina, but he was not happy. When his uncle died of a heart attack in 1975, Hans went to the British Virgin Islands to take over his uncle's yacht brokerage business. His uncle's business grew under Hans' leadership and is now one of the most successful yacht brokerage houses in the world. Even though he is of German parents, he gets along quite well with his British colleagues in the islands. His parents were killed by bandeleros in 1985 during difficult times in Argentina, and an automobile accident took his wife in 1991.

Now for the connection, gentlemen. Hans Reifenstahl and Peter Sturmer were classmates at the University of Heidelberg, where they developed a very close friendship." There were nods and head shaking in the audience.

"Next slide, please. "Colonel Patterson, you will recognize this man as Erich S. Feltgeibell, one of the men you dined with in the Eagle's Nest. Feltgeibell is his real name. He was born in Munich in 1924. His parents were members of the Nazi Party, and his father was one of the original Hitler Brown Shirts. As commander of the Munich battalion of brown shirts, he was present for the infamous Munich riot. He also fought in the Battle of

Stalingrad. Erich attended the University of Munich where he earned a degree in political science. He then did graduate work in macro economics at the University of Heidelberg. And whom did he meet there, gentlemen?" asked Gibbs. "You got it, Franz Peter Sturmer, III, aka Peter Weismann," said Gibbs, pronouncing Weismann's name slowly and deliberately. "His mother encouraged him to go to Brazil after graduation to work in her brother's well-established pumice export business. Feltgeibell took his mother's advice, joined the company, and ended up running it when his uncle took ill. You might have read about his uncle, gentlemen," said Gibbs. "Last year a military court absolved the former Nazi SS Captain of charges of cruelty and premeditation in the World War II massacre of 335 Italian civilians. In what was likely the last Nazi war crimes trial, the court found Priema guilty of taking part in the reprisal killings, which Priema admitted to, but cleared him of the more serious charges because he was only following orders. Priema, now 83, was hunted down in Argentina by Shimon Samuels, the European director of the Simon Wiesenthal Center." Gibbs took another sip of water and called for another slide. "This slide shows Erich Feltgeibell at a neo-Nazi meeting in Berlin two years ago. Next slide, please. This picture was taken at the same meeting—that's right, gentlemen, the man with Feltgeibell is Peter Weismann."

B.J. Patterson was feeling both anger and nausea. He really wanted to knock the hell out of someone—anyone. Hamp's mind began putting together an awfully dark picture. He had an overwhelming feeling in the pit of his stomach that Steinhatchee was about to be in the big time drug business again. . Hamp decided that General Stone must have concluded the same thing about Steinhatchee. "Why else would I be here?"

thought Hamp. He found himself wondering what Gwen would say if she knew all of this, not to mention Tom and Marian. Gibbs continued.

"Feltgeibell has become an influential businessman in Ipanema and enjoys the respect of his business associates and acquaintances. Are there any questions before I continue, gentlemen?" asked Gibbs.

"Yes," said Wilbur Burns. "I would like to know how you found out so much so soon, Walter. What did you do—stop everything and put all your field agents on this?" he asked with genuine amazement.

"Damned near all the field agents," said Gibbs. "Once we knew who Weismann really was, we pulled out all the stops. Our Berlin people had a very fat dossier on Sturmer, so we had a good starting point. Your people helped, too, providing us with the stateside file you were building on his neo-Nazi activities in the States. As the list of Weismann's, that is, Sturmer's connections with others who came from Nazi backgrounds grew, I became convinced that something big was going on," explained Gibbs.

"Please continue, Walter," urged the Chief demonstrating some impatience.

"Next slide, please," called Gibbs. "You have also seen this man before, and his name really is Heinrich Dieppe. Dr. Heinrich W. Dieppe was born in 1928 in Neustadt. He was too young to serve in the armed forces during World War II, but he was a member of the Young Pioneers, a Hitler youth organization. His parents were both members of the Nazi Party. After the war, Dieppe went to the University of Heidelberg where he earned a degree in history. His doctoral work was done at Humboldt University in Berlin where he earned a doctorate in history with a specialization in the National Socialist Party, or the Nazi movement, and the Third Reich.

Humboldt University hired Dieppe as an assistant professor, and he eventually worked his way up to the rank of full professor and chairmanship of the graduate department of history. He has frequently been seen at neo-Nazi rallies and meetings all over Germany, but he does not appear to be a key officer in any of the groups. He justifies his association with these groups on the basis of academic freedom. He once explained to his superiors that it was not possible to teach about new political movements unless one has experienced them," explained Gibbs.

"Dieppe gained some degree of notoriety in 1960-1970 with several professional papers he published supporting the thesis that the holocaust was a hoax perpetrated by Jews. His brushes with anti-Semitism have almost cost him his job. He has been frequently seen with Peter Sturmer, and Sturmer has been Dieppe's houseguest in Berlin on several occasions within the last year. Dieppe's former housekeeper was most cooperative with our agents. She was fired by Dieppe for no reason, according to her, and Dieppe still owes her two months wages and refuses to pay. Gentlemen, that concludes the European part of the briefing," said Gibbs. "General Stone, may I propose a short break before I go on with Greece and Turkey?"

"Yes, good idea. Let's take twenty minutes, gentlemen," said General Stone. General Stone motioned for Hamp to join him near the coffee urn. He was about to tell Hamp something when General Stone's aide ushered a civilian into the conference room. General Stone recognized him as Walter Gibbs's administrative assistant. The man looked very serious and headed straight for Gibbs and handed him a piece of paper, whispered something into his ear, and then left the room in a hurry. Gibbs read the note. Noticeably shaken by its contents, he started walking from the podium toward General Stone and Hamp.

"General Stone, you had better read this and tell me how you want to handle the announcement to the group," said Gibbs. General Stone read the note just loud enough for Hamp to hear. "To W. Gibbs from George Lake, American Consulate, Istanbul, Turkey. Eyes Only. Be advised that the wife of Colonel Sultoy was kidnapped from her home in Boctoi early this morning. Any details of the incident we are able to gather will be passed to you posthaste. The Turkish authorities are not aware of the kidnapping."

"My God," said General Stone as he looked at Gibbs. "Hamp, tell my aide to call the presidential flight detachment at Andrews and get you on a plane to Boctoi as soon as possible. Tell him to use Priority Red. Get in touch with of your friend Sultoy, and find out what in hell is going on. When you have done that, call me from our custodial detachment headquarters in Boctoi." Hamp left the room immediately and huddled with the aide. Priority Red meant the Jetstar's engines would be running by the time a sedan got him to Andrews Air Force Base. They would have to stop by General Stone's quarters on the way for him to throw some clothes in a B-4 bag. When everyone was seated again, except Hamp, General Stone took the podium.

"Gentlemen, Walter Gibbs would like to read you a message delivered to him just a few minutes ago." Gibbs took the podium and read the message. "Mr. Secretary, I think we have a new ball game," suggested General Stone without rising from his chair. "But I also think we should hear the briefers out. What they are going to say will be germane to any decisions we might subsequently make. Sir, I also took the liberty of dispatching Colonel Porter to Boctoi to see what he can learn."

"That's fine, General Stone, I agree on both counts.

"In view of what we have just heard, General Beckman, do you still insist that the President be left in the dark about this?" asked Secretary Griffin clearly perturbed.

"For the moment, yes, I do, Mr. Secretary. Can't we at least wait until the briefings are completed?" said the Chief.

"Let's go on with the briefings," said the Secretary.

Walter Gibbs took the podium once more. "Slide, please. This is Mr. Zuni Anatole, born in 1943 in Boctoi, Turkey. His parents were both killed during civil conflict in Turkey right after World War II. They were collaborators with the wrong faction, so the Turkish government shot them both as little Zuni watched. After the death of his parents, Zuni was pretty much on his own and became a survivor out of necessity. He lived because he became street smart. He was infamous for his ruthlessness and cunning personality. Somehow he managed to get through the university in Ankara where he was known for two things, a brilliant mind for business and a savage temper. Zuni went to Istanbul after graduating the university, and eventually established a thriving export/import business. He now owns at least thirty gold and leather shops in the Grand Bazaar, besides his interests in the exporting business. Among the business community in Istanbul, he is known as the hatchet man, based on his reputation for doing anything to anyone to achieve his business goals. His personal political philosophy is radical, but he supports incumbent politicians because it's good for business. While it has never been proven, he is believed to be a major arms dealer with an extensive client list in Africa and the Near East. We don't know how his connection to Peter Sturmer was established; however, we are working on it." Gibbs sipped from his water glass and continued.

"Next slide, please. Now you are looking at Mr. Tomas Popodopolus. He was born in 1944 on the island of Samothraki, just off the coast from Thessalonica. His parents are dead, and as far as we can determine, he has no living relatives. Tomas grew up on Samothaki and eventually went to Ankara to attend the university. He was expelled from the university during his second year for gambling, and subsequently got accepted by the university in Istanbul. However, he was thrown out of the university there for killing a fellow student in a fight. The death was ruled accidental, so Tomas served only one year in jail. After his stint in jail, he borrowed money from his grandfather to purchase a flacotti rug business. Under Tomas's leadership, the business quickly quadrupled in size, and he began exporting flaccoti rugs all over the world. Zuni built his own manufacturing plant to produce enough floccati rugs to meet world-wide export demands. He travels a good deal throughout Turkey, Greece, and the Greek Isles buying floccati skins to send to his factory. His net worth is thought to be in the neighborhood of seven or eight million dollars. As was the case with Anatole, we have not been able to establish his link to Peter Sturmer." Gibbs paused, closed his briefing book, and called for the room lights. "That concludes my part of the briefing, gentlemen," said Gibbs. "I'll take your questions now."

"Excellent briefing, Walter, but where does it leave us?" asked Secretary Griffin.

"I was about to ask the same thing," said the Chief. "This could mean nothing more than six men having in common a love for Hitler and the Third Reich. And the growth of the neo-Nazi movement is nothing really new—although shocking. Is there any evidence yet that any of these men are linked to Colonel Sultoy and his allegation?" asked the Chief.

"No, General, not yet," replied Gibbs regrettably. "Perhaps Colonel Porter will soon be able to shed some light on that subject for us, sir."

"By the way, Walter, I do hope your agents in Turkey will be instructed to cooperate with Colonel Porter," said General Stone.

"I'll personally see to it, General," said Gibbs.

General Stone nodded to Mr. Wilbur Burns, and he took the podium without comment. "Gentlemen, at this juncture this matter remains in the domain of the CIA and the Army. The FBI is not, however, sitting on its duff. We are redoubling our intelligence efforts in the anti-terrorism and extreme political faction arenas to identify any noticeable increase in activity that might signal something is afoot. Surveillance of Mafia activity in Florida has been going on around the clock for the last four days. Heinrich Dieppe was seen in Miami on 4 April talking with Enrico Charo and Joey Costellano. Gregory will brief you on Charo, since drugs are his domain, and I'll tell you of Costellano's activities. We know that immediately after the meeting with Charo and Dieppe, Joey called a meeting of all his lieutenants. They met in a little pizza joint on the outskirts of Valdosta, Georgia. They have used the pizza house as a meeting place before, but this time all Joey's people and three of Charo's lieutenants were present. We believe the meeting had to do with coordinating the movement of a large shipment of heroin coming into Florida. Our undercover man in Costellano's camp was not at the meeting, but he picked up enough information for us to reach that conclusion," explained Burns.

"Can your people tie this meeting or drug shipment to the reason for Dieppe's meeting with Charo?" asked General Stone.

"No. We were unable to bug the meeting, but we were able to video most of the meeting between Dieppe, Charo, and Costellano," said Burns, smiling. "Roll the film, please." The screen sprang to life with a color film of three men seated around a table on the oceanside patio bar of the Miami Hilton Hotel. Unfortunately, Dieppe was the only one facing the camera. "We had the best lip reader in the country flown in to look at the film. She had a difficult time reading Dieppe's lips because he speaks English with a German accent. She picked up enough of what he said for us to know they were discussing rendezvous points and some kind of cargo. She also picked up something about divers, but we don't know what kind of divers."

"Is that all she picked up?" asked Secretary Griffin. "Were any dates or times mentioned?"

"No, sir," replied Burns. "That is all she picked up, and no mention of time was made by Dieppe."

"Okay, Wilbur, thank you," said General Stone. "James, it's your turn."

"Thank you, sir. Gentlemen, my people, too have redoubled their intelligence efforts to find out anything that might give us a clue as to what is going on," explained Gregory. All we have so far came from one of our undercover agents last night. We believe a very large shipment of heroin is coming into Florida within the next two weeks. In lieu of the usual routing through the keys or Miami, our undercover man says that the shipment will be split, and that part of it will go ashore further up the gulf coast. Unfortunately, we don't know where on the west coast. My people also confirmed the meeting between Dieppe, Charo, and Costellano. We shot our video from a different angle and were able to pick up some of what Charo said. They talked about retrieving some kind of cargo from the bottom of the ocean using divers, but where—we just don't know. We are going to attempt to bring in our undercover man tonight. Perhaps we will get more from him if we are successful in bringing him in," said Gregory.

"Why would there be a problem in bringing him in?" asked the Secretary.

"He is in very deep cover, Mr. Secretary. One false move, and he is dead," replied Gregory.

.

"Gentlemen, I think what Colonel Porter might find out, or fail to find out, is the information we need to put this puzzle together," said the Chief. "General Stone, I think we need to send Colonel Patterson back to Berchtesgaden to keep an eye on things there should Sturmer be in the area. Find an excuse to take a closer look at the tunnels, Colonel Patterson. See if they have been tampered with since you inspected them with Sturmer. I'll make arrangements with the USAREUR CINC to delay the transfer of the recreation center for the time being."

"Yes, sir," said Patterson. Everyone else nodded their agreement.

"After we hear from Porter, we will discuss talking to the President, Mr. Secretary. Does that meet with your approval?" asked the Chief.

"Yes."

Chapter 7

April 7, 1995

The Jetstar touched down on the long runway at Boctoi without the slightest bump. The flight had been long, but comfortable. Hamp was the only passenger on the eight-seat jet besides the pilot, co-pilot, and steward. The C-140 Jetstar is an older military version of an executive jet. Its four engines make it safe, by military standards, for transoceanic flight of cabinet level government officials. After a first class meal of steak, baked potato, and stuffed mushrooms, Hamp slept until they landed in England to refuel. A new flight crew took over for the flight to Istanbul where they would refuel again before the last two-thousand mile leg to Boctoi.

As they took off for Turkey, Hamp's thoughts turned to his friend Sully, Colonel Sultoy's nickname that was usually reserved for use by his immediate family. He gave Hamp permission to use it the last time they were together over eight months ago. Thoughts of Sully's wife, Toffy, also played through his mind. Hamp knew from experience that Sully must be going crazy not knowing if his wife was alive or dead. "At least he has hope that she's alive," thought Hamp. "Who had kidnapped her? Why? Did this have something to do with Sully's visit to the American Consulate? Was Sully being blackmailed? What did they really know? The CIA, FBI, DEA, and the DAIG had collected but a few pieces of the puzzle. They knew that Peter Sturmer was an impostor. They knew that he and three of his friends had Nazi backgrounds, an interest in the Third Reich, and a neo-Nazi organization known as the New World Order. They also knew that Sully had warned them that someone was going to steal a nuclear weapon, and they knew that one of Sturmer's friends, Dieppe, had contacted a Colombian drug lord in Florida and a Mafia boss named Costellano." Hamp felt certain that Sully knew more than he had told them. He also believed that Sully's wife had been kidnapped to control Sully and to keep him quiet. "But who?" said Hamp aloud. Sully would have to talk to him. Hamp all of a sudden felt that he was under a great deal of pressure. He just realized that General Stone and everyone else on the task force were counting on him to find the missing piece to the puzzle. Hamp closed his eyes again and tried to sleep, hoping to ward off jet lag.

When the Jetstar landed in Boctoi four hours later, Hamp saw a US Army Colonel dressed in fatigues standing near the little terminal building. He appeared to be waiting for someone. "Me, more than likely," said Hamp to himself.

When Hamp got off the Jetstar, the Colonel walked over to him and introduced himself while shaking Hamp's hand. "I'm Ed Carter, the custodial detachment commander, Colonel Porter. General Stone's office called and instructed me to meet you. The General's aide said you would tell me of the nature of your visit."

"There is nothing to be alarmed about, Colonel Carter," said Hamp with a smile.

"Don't hand me that crap, Colonel," said Carter. "Army Colonels don't fly half way around the world solo in a jet from the presidential flight detachment at Andrews Air Force Base just for the fun of it. Those big blue letters spelling United States of America on that airplane mean it's reserved for people with power."

Hamp could see that Colonel Carter was more than a little upset by all of this, and rightly so. His little corner of the world was all of a sudden attracting the attention of top brass. "I'll tell you what I can when we reach your office. And please call me Hamp. I'm really not the enemy," said Hamp trying to calm Carter's fears.

"Fair enough, "said Carter. "You can call me Buzz; everybody else does." He had begun to relax a little.

The drive into and through Boctoi to the detachment headquarters took about forty-five minutes. Nothing had changed on the streets of Boctoi since his last visit, so far as Hamp could tell. It was all very familiar to him, the shops, the people, and the women with their veils. It seemed as though he were here just yesterday. They rode in silence for about five minutes, and then Carter spoke.

"I know you by reputation, Colonel Porter. You were the USAREUR Inspector General a year ago. I thought you retired after that job," said Carter.

"I did retire. I have been recalled to active duty for a special assignment. I'm going to tell you about it when we reach your office," replied Hamp. They talked about Boctoi and Turkish politics during the remainder of the ride. Hamp recognized the detachment compound immediately when they drove through the gate. It was about the size of a football field and contained twelve masonry buildings.

"I see you have spruced things up around here, Buzz. The compound looks great," said Hamp.

"We try, but money is tight. You know the story," reminded Carter.

They walked into the headquarters building, a small concrete block building with three rooms;

there was an office for the commander, an office for the sergeant major, and a reception room. They went directly to Carter's office. Carter gave instructions to the clerk that they were not to be disturbed. They took seats across from each other in leather easy chairs. Carter spoke first.

"Arriving in a presidential flight detachment aircraft was a mistake," said Carter. "If secrecy is important to why you are here, you've blown it. Word about the arrival of that airplane is probably going up the Turkish chain of command as we speak."

"Urgency takes precedence over secrecy, Buzz," Hamp said with solemnity. "The Turkish chain of command is someone else's worry, not ours."

"Does this have anything to do with Colonel Sultoy's absence for the past few days?" asked Carter.

"Yes. What I am about to tell you is for your ears only, Buzz; do you understand?" Hamp wanted Carter to understand the necessity for keeping information absolutely quiet for the moment.

"Certainly. Go ahead," urged Carter.

Hamp told Carter everything he knew about what was going on with Sultoy and the information that had been discovered about Weismann and his associates. When Hamp told Carter about Sultoy's allegation of nuclear weapons theft, Carter gripped the chair arms so hard his knuckles turned white. When Hamp finished, Carter stood and began pacing.

"Why in hell have we not been placed on red alert? Why in hell was I not informed of this before now?" Carter was understandably upset again. A threat had been made against the facility for which he was responsible, and he was the last to know. "For Christ sake, Hamp, will you please explain to me why I am the last to know about all this?" asked Carter.

"We couldn't tell you because we cannot trust the White House enough to tell them, Buzz. That's the long and the short of it," explained Hamp. "We have to be absolutely certain of what the threat really is and what the scope of the problem is before anyone outside the task force knows. You are the first outside that group to know, Buzz," explained Hamp.

"Who else is on the task force?" asked Buzz.

"Secretary Griffin, the Chief of Staff General Beckman, General Stone, the deputy directors of the CIA and the FBI, and the director of the DEA. There is one other minor player like me."

"What minor role am I supposed to play?" asked Buzz.

"First, you will need to provide me with a cover story. Maybe you could tell everyone that asks that I'm here on some sort of congressional investigation," Hamp suggested.

"There have been rumors that we might get new facilities here," said Buzz. "Suppose I say that you are here to do some budget leg-work for congress."

"Sounds good to me," said Hamp. "Now, I need to see Colonel Sultoy as soon as possible," said Hamp as he stood. "Can you get me a car and a driver?"

"No problem. I'll also let General Stone's office know that you are here," said Carter.

"He already knows, said Hamp. "The Jetstar crew radioed that message just before we landed."

Colonel Carter's driver asked Hamp his destination. "Do you know where Colonel Sultoy lives, Corporal?" asked Hamp.

"Yes, sir," replied the driver.

"That is your destination," said Hamp. Hamp did not call Sultoy to inform him of his presence in Boctoi, or that he was on his way to visit him because he was fairly certain Sultoy's phone would be bugged.

The drive took about twenty minutes. Sultoy lived on a hilltop across town overlooking the Turkish troop barracks. The driver stopped in front of the Sultoy residence—a modest, single story, stone structure in very good repair with plenty of flowers and shrubs. It was almost dark, and smells of evening meals cooking in the neighborhood filled Hamp's nose as he walked onto the Sultoy's porch. He knocked three times before the door finally opened. There were no lights on inside the house, and Hamp could not see who had opened the door. Then a familiar voice spoke.

"Hamp, I cannot believe it is you," said Sully in a hushed voice. "I did not ever expect to see you again." The two men embraced; Sully turned on a table lamp and gestured for Hamp to sit on the sofa. Sully looked horrible. His face was pale and drawn, and his shoulders were stooped. He looked fifteen years older than when Hamp had last seen him. His eyes showed no signs of life. This was not the man Hamp remembered.

"Sully, I know about Toffy," said Hamp with tenderness. "We need to talk, Sully. You have to tell me everything you know if you are to ever see Toffy again," pleaded Hamp.

Tears formed in the corners of Sully's eyes and he stared hard into the eyes of his friend. "I cannot tell you anything. I should not have visited Mr. Lake's office in Istanbul. Toffy would still be here if I had done as I was told," exclaimed Sully. "Don't you understand, Hamp? These people will kill her!" Sully pleaded.

"Sully, you must listen to me. Look, let's take a walk up the hill behind the house like we used to. It will make you feel better, and it will be safer. Your house might be bugged," said Hamp. Sully nodded in agreement and stood. They walked up the hill path for ten minutes in silence, and then Hamp told Sully about the task force that had been formed to deal with the threat. He also told him everything he knew about the people involved.

"Then they really are going to do it," said Sully as he stopped dead in his tracks and looked at Hamp.

"Do what, Sully?" pleaded Hamp.

"They are going to steal warheads from the Boctoi storage site. Sully made a conscious decision to tell Hamp everything. He realized it was Toffy's only chance for survival. "Look, Hamp, I got involved with a man named Zuni Anatole. I met him through a friend in Istanbul. I was attending a seminar on neo-Nazism at the university, and my friend, Peter Weismann, introduced me to Zuni at dinner one evening. We were all interested in neo-Nazism from a historical point of view, or so I thought. But I soon learned that their interest went far beyond history. You have to understand, Hamp, that at the time I was angry and confused. My father-in-law was doing everything in his power to entice me into his radical political arena. He began to persuade Toffy to his political thinking and encouraged her to pressure me to join his political party. He wanted to use me to plant subversive seeds among my soldiers. When Toffy threatened to leave me, I knew I had to do something. It was about then that Zuni Anatole offered me one million American dollars to help him steal three nuclear warheads. I thought that with that kind of money I could take my family away from Turkey forever, so I agreed to help him."

It was now totally dark, and Hamp could no longer see Sully's face. He didn't have to. Then Sully continued. "I gave Anatole a set of blueprints of the storage and assembly building, the combination to the security system on the entry door, and keys to the back-up padlocks. I also agreed to keep the guards distracted during their entry and visit at a prearranged time," explained Sully. "Can you believe that I did those terrible things, Hamp?"

"Yes, because I know how much you love Toffy, Sully. You love her like I loved my wife Judith. You never really get over that kind of love."

"When they took her yesterday, I knew what a terrible mistake I had made, but it was too late. I had no choice but to cooperate with them."

"Do your superiors know anything of this, Sully?"

"No. I've told only Mr. Lake. But I didn't give him the details that I just gave you."

"Are you on duty, Sully?"

"No. I called in sick yesterday evening. I am the senior officer in Boctoi, so I don't have to provide a detailed explanation of what I do."

"Sully, did they give you the date they intended to steal the warheads?"

"No, but . . ." Sully paused quite some time. Hamp could tell that he was turning his options about in his mind. Clearly, he was torn as to what he should do. He knew that the warheads could not end up in the wrong hands, but on the other hand, if he told, he could possibly be putting the nails in Toffy's coffin. Finally he said, "It will have to be before 15 April because they know the combination to the security system will be changed on that day. Forgive me, Toffy," said Sully looking even older now.

"Why have you not come forward with this information before, Sully?" asked Hamp.

"I don't know. I suppose it is because I know they will never let Toffy live. But I realize now that whether I talk or not, Toffy is dead. Exposing the plot is the only way I can extract some measure of revenge for Toffy's death. Can you understand that, my friend?"

"Yes. I can. But let's not assume the worst for Toffy just yet, my friend," said Hamp encouragingly.

They walked back down the hill in silence. Hamp's mind was racing. He had to get this information to General Stone.

Hamp returned to the compound. Colonel Carter was waiting for him in his office. A tray with sandwiches, hot coffee, and a bottle of scotch was on the coffee table in front of the couch. Colonel Carter sat in his chair with his boots propped on the desk. The smell of a Turkish cigar filled the room.

"Tell me what you found out, and then I'll give you the combination to that bottle of scotch," said Carter with a smile. Hamp skipped the sandwiches and poured two fingers of scotch in a coffee cup. He was suddenly very tired.

"You do know how to please, Buzz."

"Well, we do have one hell of a situation on our hands, if what my friend told me is correct," began Hamp.

"What are the chances of his being correct?" asked Carter.

"In my book, one hundred percent." replied Hamp. "I would stake my life on it."

Carter anticipated Hamp's thinking. "We have a secure line in the communications hut," said Carter. I'll show you the way." The operator in the communications hut put the call

through to the Pentagon Emergency Action Center.
Ten minutes later General Stone was on the line.
Hamp repeated the information Sully had given him
to General Stone.

"Okay. Good work, Hamp. That confirms our
thinking on this end. To bring you up to date on
today's activities, I'll give you the gist of
this afternoon's task force meeting. We now know
a huge delivery of heroin is coming into the
United States within the next few weeks, but we
don't know exactly when. We think Sturmer and
his cronies will steal several warheads from the
Boctoi and Thessalonica storage facilities. They
will then trade the warheads for heroin with
their Colombian contacts, and move the heroin to
Florida and Europe via sail boats from the
British Virgin Islands. It's our guess that
Sturmer will use the General Walker Hotel tunnel
complex or the Eagle's Nest to store most of the
heroin until they can market it. The remainder
of heroin will make entry into the States along
the gulf coast—probably around Cedar Key and
Steinhatchee."

"Excuse me for interrupting, sir, but did
you say Steinhatchee?" asked Hamp.

"Yes. Now listen closely, Hamp. We think
it best not to foil the theft of the warheads.
We want the drugs and the drug bosses. This will
give the DEA a chance to put Charo and Costellano
away for good, something they have been trying to
do for several years. If we bust their operation
on your end, DEA may never get another chance
like this to dry up a major supplier of heroin.
Are you listening, Hamp?" asked General Stone.

"Yes, sir, but I can visualize a thousand
things going wrong between here and the place the
warheads are to be eventually recovered—if they
are recovered," said Hamp. "What happens if they
are lost, misplaced, or somehow damaged along the
way?"

"That's a chance we are prepared to take,
Hamp. Secretary Griffin is on his way to the
White House to brief the President at this
moment. We need his approval of how we plan to
deal with this situation. I want you to check in
with me every day and to let Colonel Carter know
where you are. Find out all you can about the
details of the operation, Hamp, but do not do
anything to interfere with it. Do you understand
me, Hamp?"

"Affirmative, sir," replied Hamp.

"Colonel Carter, are you listening?" asked
the General.

"Yes, sir."

"I know how you must feel about our
allowing something to happen that you try to
prevent from happening everyday. Try not to feel
too badly." said the General.

"I'm afraid that will be difficult to do,
sir," replied Carter.

"Yes, I suppose so," said the General. The
line went dead. Colonel Carter was not pleased.

"How can they do this?" asked Carter over
and over as he shook his head.

"Look, Buzz, I think I know how you must
feel, but get over it. We have work to do. I
need to make contact with the CIA's man in the
area. Do you happen to know who he is?"

"I was going to tell you after you talked
with General Stone that he called while you were
with Sultoy. He will be here in half an hour,"
said Carter.

April 8, 1995

"I'm back," said B.J. as he walked into his
empty house. "My God! I must be loosing my
mind," said B.J. aloud. My wife has been staying
at the General Walker Hotel for four days. I've
come home to the wrong house," said B.J. to
himself. He couldn't believe his state of mind.

This whole thing about Peter Weismann, or rather Peter Sturmer, had really upset him and made him angry. Everything was on hold, now. His retirement and move back to the States would have to wait until this present crisis is over. Not only that, but his wife had no idea about any of this, nor was he allowed to tell her. All she knew was that B.J. had to go to an important meeting in Washington. She presumed the meeting had to do with the property transfer. Then B.J. saw the note on the counter top. "Dear B.J: We don't live here anymore. See you at the GW. Love, Your soon to be ex-wife." She knew him so well.

B.J. drove to the General Walker, parked, and went directly to the suite where they were staying until their flight home. B.J. knocked. "How long will you be here this time, B.J.?" Beverly asked as she opened the door.

"I have not the faintest idea," drawled B.J. with a shrug. "I need an anti-jet lag scotch. Do we have anything to drink around here, my darlin'?" B.J. took his wife into his arms and apologized, and she, of course, forgave him. She was a good Army wife, and all good Army wives were used to being left suddenly alone without an explanation.

The next morning B.J. walked into his office and told Frau Gurter to hold all calls and visitors except calls from General Stone or Herr. Weismann. B.J. needed time to think clearly. He intended to make it his business to bird dog the hell out of Weismann—using the old name was less confusing; he would make it his business to know his every move. "You shouldn't have screwed with me, Peter, you arrogant Nazi swastika," said B.J. to the window. B.J. was under orders from General Stone to observe Weismann and to learn anything he can about what Weismann might be planning, and that is exactly what he intended to do.

"Frau Gurter, would you get me Herr. Weismann's office on the phone, please?" said B.J. into the intercom.

"His office is usually not open until nine o'clock, Colonel Patterson. Do you still want me to try?"

"Yes, please. And keep trying until you get him," instructed B.J. "That is your top priority for the day, Frau Gurter." She obeyed with a confused look on her face. She had worked as the secretary to all the commanders of the recreation center since the end of the war, but she would never understand Americans.

B.J. planned his strategy: he would begin by inviting Herr. Weismann to tour the tunnel once again, since B.J. had hurried him before. He would also invite him to tour the abandoned salt mine tunnels under the location where the Berghof had stood. Weismann would go because he would either want to see what B.J. was up to, or because Weismann had something in one of the tunnels to hide. B.J. was going to enjoy this game.

Paperwork had piled up, and his staff needed to see him to discuss concerns and to get transfer problems resolved. B.J. occupied himself into the late afternoon meeting individually with key staff members. At four o'clock, he turned his attention to a stack of papers requiring his signature. At five after four, Frau Gurter buzzed the intercom and said that Herr. Weismann was calling.

"Hello, Herr. Weismann. I have been away for a few days and wanted to touch base with you."

"Thank you Colonel Patterson. I have been out of the country myself. In fact, I arrived in

Berchtesgaden just moments ago. How can I help
you?"

"You must be very tired, so I will not
detain you long. I intend to tour the General
Walker tunnel complex tomorrow and probably the
tunnel complex under the site of the old Berghof.
Since I rushed our last visit to the complex, I
thought perhaps you might want to join me," said
B.J. in his very best southern Mississippi drawl.
"I plan to begin about 0900 hours."

Weismann did not hesitate. "Yes, I would
like to go with you. Thank you for asking me."

"Shall we meet at the General Walker at
0800 hours for some breakfast before the tour?"
asked B.J.

"I look forward to it. Good by, Colonel
Patterson."

B.J. felt much better. Now he felt like he
was doing something besides sitting on his butt
listening to briefers. "Time to lock up and go
home, Frau Gurter," said B.J. as he passed her
desk on his way out of the office. He pretended
to be looking for his keys as Frau Gurter got
into her car and drove away. When she was out of
sight, B.J. hurried back into his office and
placed a phone call to Chief Warrant Officer Clay
Brinson of the US Army Criminal Investigation
Division in Munich. He had worked with Brinson
last year on a theft ring operation at the
recreation center where they had become good
friends.

"This is Lieutenant Colonel Patterson,
commander of the recreation center in
Berchtesgaden," said B.J. when the phone was
answered. "I would like to speak with Chief
Brinson, please." Brinson answered quickly.
After a moment of pleasantries, B.J. told Clay
the purpose of his call.

"Chief I need your help on a very urgent
matter. Do you suppose you could drive down here

this evening and talk to me? I'll buy dinner and drinks," offered B.J.

"If it's urgent, sir, I'll be there in two hours," replied Brinson.

"I'll meet you in the dinning room at the General Walker Hotel, "said B.J., and hung up the phone. It was a quarter of five. He called the hotel dinning room and reserved a table for seven o'clock. He then called Beverly and told her of dinner arrangements. B.J. was feeling better all the time.

Beverly and B.J. walked into the dining room precisely at seven o'clock and continued their conversation about their children. Ten minutes later, Brinson entered the dining room and joined them. All through dinner B.J. had difficulty following the conversation because his mind was on the reason he had called Brinson. Finally dinner was over. Being a good Army wife, Beverly realized that the dinner was merely a formality probably for her benefit, and that the real purpose of Brinson's visit would surface after her departure.

"I'll let you fellows get down to business." she said, rising from her chair. Clay, be sure to tell Nita I asked about her. Good night." B.J. waited until Beverly was out of the dinning room, and then he spoke.

"I'll come right to the point, Clay. Can you bug a residence for me?"

"Well, sure. My gear is in the trunk of my car. I'm assuming you have authorization and the rest of the obligatory paperwork," responded Clay. "I thought you might have something like that in mind when you called, so I brought along my gear bag."

"I don't have any paperwork, and no one knows about this but you and me, Clay. There is one more thing: You will have to break into the house of a German citizen to do the job." Clay

was speechless.   He could only stare at B.J. as
though he had lost his mind.   Finally, he
regained his composure.

"Nothing is that urgent, Colonel Patterson.
No way," said Clay with emphasis on the word
"no".   "Do you want us both to spend the rest of
our lives in Leavenworth?   With all due respect,
Colonel, you are nuts."

"Clay, I can understand your reaction, but
I can assure you that I am of sound mind—well,
almost anyway.   Clay, if I tell you that I will
get blanket clearance for you from the highest
Army authority, will you do it?   Will you trust
me to get it?"

"Well, yes.   With the clearance I'll do
it," said Clay hesitantly.

B.J. explained exactly what he wanted Clay
to do.   Clay would bug Weismann's apartment while
Weismann and he toured the tunnel complex
tomorrow morning.   The receiving device would be
placed in B.J.'s office.   They could do that
tonight.   B.J. wanted Clay to go back to Munich,
get personal items he would need for a two or
three day stay in Berchtesgaden, and return in
time tomorrow morning to get the bugs planted in
Weismann's apartment.   Should Weismann leave town
again soon, then he and Clay would bug the
Eagle's Nest.   B.J. also impressed upon Clay the
need for total secrecy.

"When am I supposed to sleep, Colonel?"

"When it's over. You really don't want to
know anymore, Clay. "

"You sure got that right, Colonel.   I
already know more than I want to know."

★★★★★

They set up the bug receiver in one of
B.J.'s desk drawers where Frau Gurter would not
likely see it.   Clay then left for Munich, and
B.J. placed a call on the secure line to the

Emergency Action Center in the Pentagon for General Stone. It was half an hour later when General Stone returned his call.

"What's up, Colonel Patterson?" asked the General.

B.J. explained his plan to bug Weismann's apartment. He also explained that he intended to bug the Eagle's Nest and Weismann's office, although Brinson was not aware of the office bug, yet. He told the General of his need for Brinson's services and clearance to use him.

"I'll have orders in Munich within two hours attaching Brinson to you for as long as you need him. Keep up the good work, Colonel Patterson. But please don't get caught. The last thing we need now is an international incident. I'll let Porter know what you are doing." The General told B.J. what Hamp had learned in Boctoi and about the task force's intention of allowing the theft of the warheads. General Stone terminated their conversation by urging caution once more and reminding B.J. to keep him informed via secure telephone.

Breakfast the next morning with Weismann went smoothly. B.J. and he discussed minor details of the property transition, and B.J. told Weismann that he and his wife would be staying in Berchtesgaden until the final property transfer took place. A slight look of surprise and concern flashed in Weismann's eyes at that news.

"Is the Army suggesting that the final transfer be delayed or postponed?" asked Weismann anxiously.

"No. I think you and I can proceed on schedule and pass the baton on 12 April. I'll just be hanging around a little longer than I had originally anticipated," explained B.J. Weismann said nothing, nor did his eyes tell B.J. anything more. They finished their breakfast, took the elevator downstairs, and walked the distance of the long corridor to the "off limits" sign at the far end. The door was easier to open this time, and they were inside in just a few seconds.

"I had the power turned on down here, Herr Weismann. We will not have to stumble around in the dark this time," explained B.J. as he flipped on the light switch just inside the door. This time Weismann took his time and thoroughly inspected every nook and cranny. He entered each of the four private storage rooms that had belonged to Hess and Goering, and he asked B.J. questions about ventilation, humidity control, and temperature in the complex. He even made notes as they spoke. Finally he asked B.J. when he might have the keys to the complex.

"I see no reason why I should not give you the keys now, Herr. Weismann," said B.J. magnanimously. "I certainly have no further use for them. You may have the blueprints as well. I'll have them sent over to your office this afternoon, if you like."

"I would very much appreciate it, Colonel Patterson. I thank you for making this little exception to the transfer protocol." According to the terms of the transfer protocol, all keys, papers, etc. were supposed to be transferred only on the appointed day and at the appointed time.

"I am happy to oblige, Herr. Weismann. But I do have a favor to ask of you in return, if you don't mind."

"Of course. What is it?"

"A friend of mine is visiting from the States. He has never seen the Eagle's Nest and would like to tour it before he leaves for Stuttgart tomorrow. I realize you are renovating it for your quarters, but do you think it would be too much of an inconvenience if I personally escorted him through the Nest tomorrow morning?" asked B.J. in his best drawl.

"Please, be my guest. It will not cause any inconvenience whatsoever," replied Weismann.

"In fact, I would be interested in your opinion of what I'm doing up there. I will let my housekeeper know that you will be visiting."

Clay Brinson had no difficulty entering Weismann's apartment. In less than ten minutes, he planted twelve thousand dollars worth of state-of-the-art miniature transmitters in four rooms and two telephones. Clay then exited the apartment through the rear door, removed the latex gloves, and climbed the fire escape ladder to the apartment building roof. His German workman's coveralls and hat made him an unobtrusive part of the morning activities in the neighborhood. There he fastened a small receiver/transmitter about the size and shape of an electric razor to the chimney. The device would pick up any signals from the miniature transmitters in Weismann's apartment and retransmit them to the receiver in Patterson's office. There the signals would be automatically recorded. Clay, clad in German workman coveralls, climbed down the ladder, mounted his plain black bicycle. As he pedaled away excitement surged up his spine. He didn't often get an opportunity to practice his clandestine skills.

B.J. and Weismann finished their visit to the tunnel complexes, and B.J. returned to his office to meet Clay Brinson. Clay was waiting for him when he got there to report his successful visit to Weismann's apartment.

"Want to have some more fun, Clay?" asked Patterson with a smile.

"Why not?" said Clay. "Just so long as I'm legally covered."

"We are going to bug the Eagle's Nest tomorrow morning," announced B.J. with a broad grin.   "I do hope you have enough equipment with you."

"I should have enough, unless it's a really big place," replied Clay.

Chapter 8

April 12, 1995

Weismann took a taxi from Ataturk Airport into Istanbul. This two-continent city was one of his favorites. He wondered what life had been like in this ancient, walled city when it was known as Constantinople. Weismann's countrymen looted an unimaginable plethora of art and antiquity treasures from Turkey during Hitler's Third Reich. Marble from archaeological treasure-troves like Ephesus were carted back to Germany to build the monuments of the Third Reich. The enormous sense of history Weismann experienced each time he visited this city invigorated him and set his imagination soaring.

On its way from the airport to his hotel, the taxi took him past the famous Topkapi Place, the imperial residence of the sultans, where some of the world's largest diamonds and emeralds are on public display with other Ottoman treasures. Then they passed St. Sophia, the beautiful museum that is home to magnificent mosaics and frescoes from Byzantine times. Finally, just a few blocks from the Kapali Karsi, or Grand Bazaar by its English name, they passed the famous Blue Mosque with its boasting blue tiles.

After dropping off his bag at the hotel, Weismann decided to walk the short distance to the Kapali Karsi to savor the culture of this remarkable, ancient city. Weismann too quickly found himself in front of the largest and probably the oldest covered market in the world. He found little wonder in the fact that people from all over the world come here to shop in the bazaar's 4,000 business establishments. He knew his way around the bazaar well enough to find the carpet store where Zuni Anatole made his

headquarters.   On his way to Zuni's store,
Weismann passed hundreds of women dressed in
traditional Purdah, with only their eyes visible
from behind their black yashmaks. Young Turkish
boys carried trays of tea in small glasses
through the heavy crush of people without
spilling a drop. A Gypsy beggar woman hustled a
group of European tourists. Life and business
there went on as it had for centuries. For
Weismann, fathoming that this place had its
beginning in 1432 was still difficult. Few
places in the world could boast of such a rich,
lengthy history.

Anatole's carpet shop was only one of 116
carpet shops in the bazaar. His office was
located in a small room in the back of his shop
and was furnished with a low, round, copper-
topped table surrounded by a half dozen thick
tapestry cushions on which he and his guests sat
to drink tea and to conduct business. Weismann
thought it one of the most private places in
Istanbul.

Weismann entered Anatole's shop and
proceeded directly to the back of the shop to
Anatole's back room sanctuary. There behind the
beaded curtain, he found everyone dutifully
present and seated around the table enjoying
three o'clock tea, as was the custom in Turkey.

"Heinrich, Erich, Hans, Zuni, Tomas," said
Weismann as he shook each man's hand. "I am glad
to see you all could be here. Well, shall we get
down to it?" said Weismann enthusiastically.
"Zuni, first I will tell you that Mrs. Sultoy is
resting comfortably at the General Walker Hotel
tunnel complex in a bounty room that belonged to
Rudolf Hess. Your messenger delivered her last
night on schedule."

"Yes," said Zuni. "He called just two hours
ago and informed me that it had gone well,"
replied Zuni, a little disappointed that Weismann

was unwilling to indulge the custom of afternoon tea. "We gave her a new psilocybin derivative so she was mobile enough to travel, but not aware enough to protest her abduction," explained Zuni. "I trust she will remain undetected in the tunnel complex?" asked Zuni.

"She is quite secure," Weismann assured him. "She could scream forever and not be heard down there, and I have the only keys to the complex," replied Weismann.

"I hope this trip will be worth the trouble, Peter," said Reifenstahl. "I need to be attending to business in Tortola. Pegasus is only a couple days away."

"I am more than curious myself, Peter," said Dieppe. "What is this meeting all about?" Zuni said nothing.

"I called this meeting for two reasons, gentlemen," said Peter. "First, I want to make certain that everything is still absolutely on schedule. Secondly, I am announcing a change in plans. We will steal a total of seven warheads, not six, one of which shall be kept in the tunnel complex for insurance," said Weismann slowly and deliberately, taking everyone by surprise.

"What kind of insurance? You made no mention of this before. I do not understand why you want to do this, Peter," said Dieppe with obvious concern and irritation.

"What the hell is this, Peter? Are you mad?" asked Zuni.

"Our plans are pretty much irrevocable, Peter. It's too late to make that kind of change now. We would have to hire more men for my part of the operation. No. No, Peter. It's just too late," insisted Tomas Popodopolus.

"Gentlemen, please do not argue with me over this decision. I have my reasons," insisted Peter.

"What reasons, Peter? They had better be good ones," said Erich Feltgeibell.

Dieppe glared at Weismann. Erich Feltgeibell got up from the table and began pacing and mumbling to himself.

"We have never discussed what might happen if we get caught, gentlemen. Have any of you thought of that? What if—just what if—someone gets away and talks, or has a last minute change of heart. What then, gentlemen? Do you not think it prudent to hold a trump card in the event something goes wrong with any part of the plan?" asked Weismann. "I ask you again— have any of you thought about it?" said Peter, an octave and ten decibels higher than before. No one spoke. Everyone just stared at him Weismann continued. "You should have thought of it, Dieppe. You are the chief operations officer for Pegasus. Why didn't you think of it? You asked me why I want to do this, gentlemen. I will tell you why. I am doing it because none of you had the sense to think of it—that's why," said Weismann emphatically. "We must have a hostage maker!" The room was quiet for a few moments, and then Dieppe spoke thoughtfully.

"All right. It does make sense, and perhaps I should have thought about it myself. It really never crossed my mind that we might fail. If we are going to do it, then I suggest we take it from the Thessalonica facility. Adding another warhead to the three we are going to take from the Boctoi site would be too complicated at this late hour. To do so would require equipment and men we do not have," said Dieppe.

"I think it's ridiculous, but, if you insist, I suppose I have no choice but to go along with your decision," said Hans Reifenstahl. Zuni Anatole, Tomas Popodopolus, and Erich Feltgeibell nodded their reluctant approval.

"Trust me, gentlemen. It is the intelligent thing to do," said Weismann. Anatole and Popodopolous were easy to convince, as he had anticipated, but he really had expected Dieppe and Feltgeibell to offer serious resistance to his proposal because their motivation was not one of greed but one of political passion.

"How do we get it to Berchtesgaden?" asked Dieppe.

"The boat taking the warheads from Thessalonica to Brazil will make a stop in Bremen to make hypothetical repairs. I will meet the boat after midnight. We will transfer the warhead to my government van, and I will simply drive it to the Eagle's Nest. When Colonel Patterson and I have completed the property transfer formalities, and I consider it safe, I will move it to the tunnel complex for safekeeping," explained Weismann.

"Why not leave it in the Eagle's Nest?" asked Dieppe.

"Because the Eagle's Nest will be opened to the public after renovations are completed next week," replied Weismann. "An American tourist accustomed to looking in every nook and cranny would be certain to stumble upon it."

"If we are finished with that subject, Peter, I have a question about another matter," said Erich Feltgeibell.

"Yes, Erich, what is it?" asked Peter.

"We have covered the details of everything concerning Pegasus except the disposition of the money. I am surprised that no one has shown concern about it," said Erich. Heinrich Dieppe stood to stretch his legs and gestured with the wave of an arm that he would address that topic.

"Of course the exchange of heroin and warheads will take place in the Ipanema warehouse. Once the exchange has been made, and Estabo's men have departed, the heroin packets will be stowed in the boats by the crews. The shipment will go to Florida on the same two boats that deliver the warheads to Ipanema. When Charo and Costellano receive the signal from the boat captains indicating that the heroin packets have been secured to the concrete pylons, their diver will go out to verify that the packets have been secured to the concrete pylons. The divers will inform Charo and Costellano that the heroin is secured, and Costellano and Charo will make payment to Dieppe. Any questions, gentlemen?" asked Erich.

"Yes. I have a question," said Zuni. "What is the weather forecast for the crossing of your boats, Erich?" asked Dieppe.

"This is the best possible time of year for crossing the Atlantic," replied Erich. "The winds are favorable and no major storm activity is expected. Anyway, the fifty-foot Beneteaus are very seaworthy boats. It would take a major storm system to cause me to worry about them."

"You see, gentlemen, I was correct in calling this meeting. Several of you had concerns after all," smiled Weismann. "All right, then. Pegasus will begin at one minute after midnight two days from now. The meeting is adjourned," announced Weismann with a nod of his head. "Zuni, may I have a word with you?" The other men began to leave, talking as they drifted out of Zuni's shop toward their separate destinations. Zuni and Weismann were alone.

"Will you kill the Sultoy woman, Peter?" asked Zuni.

"That is what I want to talk with you about, Zuni," said Weismann. "Is there any point in keeping her alive once the warheads have been taken?"

"I suggest that we do keep her alive until all transactions have been completed and Colonel Sultoy's suicide has been arranged. Sultoy will remain quiet as long as he thinks she is alive. You must allow her to call him so that he will be convinced that she is alive" said Zuni, not knowing that Colonel Sultoy had already divulged the Pegasus operation.

"Very well. I will allow her to live for a few days," replied Weismann.

"By the way, Peter, how do you intend to dispose of her remains?" asked Zuni. "I am just curious".

"She will be buried behind the rubble that blocks most of the tunnel," replied Weismann.

Weismann left Zuni's shop and began negotiating his way through the bazaar toward the entrance a quarter mile away. He did not see the CIA agent that followed him, nor did Weismann's cronies see the agents following them when they left the shop.

Agent Timothy Mulligan smiled as he listened to the tape of the conversation he had just recorded in Zuni Anatole's carpet shop. He planted the bug yesterday when he posed as a carpet buyer for a major carpet importer in the United States. Zuni Anatole and he discussed their business around the brass-top coffee table in Zuni's office where Mulligan planted the bug. The CIA now had the exact time of the operation, the operation code name, the exchange point for the warheads and money, the location of Toffy Sultoy, and all the details necessary to track the movement of the warheads, the heroin, and the money. Mulligan immediately relayed the information to his boss at Langley, Virginia. Walter Gibbs would be very pleased.

Chapter 9

April 13, 1995

Hamp, with the assistance of a sketch map drawn by Sully, estimated the location of the old tunnel running under the storage and assembly building in the Boctoi custodial compound. Colonel Carter and the detachment security officer accompanied Hamp to the storage and assembly building. Army regulations precluded anyone from entering the facility without the permission and presence of the security officer; therefore, they would have to be careful about what they said in his presence. Using Sully's map, they concluded that the old tunnel ran parallel to the assembly side of the building, and about six feet outside the building wall. This meant tunnelers would have to dig a connecting tunnel of six to eight feet in length to reach the sub-flooring inside the building. They wanted to make sure where the tunnelers would enter the building, not that it would make any difference since the thieves would be allowed to steal the warheads and make their escape. Hamp and Carter at least wanted to monitor each step of the operation, if possible, whether or not they were allowed to react to it.

"If I were they, I would try to enter the building here," said Hamp pointing to a spot three feet inside the wall. "It's in the middle of a fire lane, and I could be assured that nothing would be in my way when I punched through the sub-flooring."

"I agree," said Carter. "They have the same map we have, and that's the logical place to enter. They would not want to dig any more than necessary. From this position the thieves could just roll the canisters down the fire lane to the opening and drop them to someone waiting below."

"That is exactly how I would do it, Buzz," replied Hamp.

The security officer was standing to one side about ten feet away. He was straining to overhear their conversation, but, judging from the look on his face, he could not hear them well enough to understand what they were saying, and that was a good thing. The last thing Hamp wanted was to alarm the troops. They would go berserk if they even suspected they might experience a break-in. This had to be kept quiet.

"Any other ideas, Hamp?" asked Carter quietly.

"No. I would bet a month's retirement pay it will play just as we have surmised," replied Hamp.

"We've seen enough here. Let's see if we can find the old tunnel entrance," said Carter.

"Not a good idea, Buzz. They could be watching it or even working in it," said Hamp. "Let's wait until tomorrow night. We can find a good vantage point from midway down the hill where we can use night vision devices to observe them when they leave the tunnel. You do have starlight scopes don't you, Buzz?" asked Hamp.

"Sure. That will be no problem," replied Carter. "But we should get settled at our vantage point at least an hour after dark. We don't want to spook the swastikas when they arrive."

They left the storage and assembly building and headed for Carter's office. Hamp was expecting the CIA contact at four o'clock; it was now ten minutes before three. The agent was getting out of her car when they approached the headquarters building. A petite, slim, attractive woman of about thirty-five walked toward them. Her very red hair was short and curly. Her eyes were green and her attire was a dark business suit. That hair would stand out in a crowd of Turkish women, thought Hamp.

"Colonel Porter, Colonel Carter, I'm Special Agent Diane Wright from the CIA office in Istanbul. Glad I caught you two here," said Wright with a quick smile. They shook hands.

"Let's step inside to my office," said Carter. In Carter's office they took seats around the coffee table. Wright's mood quickly turned somber.

"I was told to speak with you, Colonel Porter," said Wright looking blankly at Carter.

"I understand, said Hamp. Carter can stay. He is fully aware of what is going on."

"Suits me," said Wright with another quick smile. "My partner in Istanbul had a major stroke of luck yesterday, gentlemen," she began. "He not only successfully bugged the carpet shop office of Zuni Anatole, but he managed to tape an entire meeting of Peter Sturmer, aka Weismann, and his associates: Misters Heinrich Dieppe, Erich Feltgeibell, Hans Reifenstahl, Zuni Anatole, and Tomas Popodopolus. How do you like them apples, boys?" said Wright flashing another quick smile. Hamp started to speak, but she held up a hand to indicate that she was not yet finished. "It was apparently a last minute coordination meeting. Here's what we learned. The name of their planned operation is Pegasus. It will kick off at one minute past midnight tomorrow night with the stealing of seven nuclear warheads, three from the Boctoi detachment and four from Thessalonica. We know the schedule and place of exchange of warheads for money. We know that one of the warheads will be held as a hostage-maker in Berchtesgaden. We also know that Toffy Sultoy is presently being held in the General Walker Hotel tunnel complex and will probably be killed a few days after the operation is complete. We know enough about the movement of the drugs, warheads, and money to track them every step of the way; and we know the Colombian connection is the Escovar and the Medellin Cartel. To top that off, we nabbed the goon that escorted Mrs. Sultoy to Germany." Wright paused for effect and to catch her breath.

"I have two questions, Miss Wright," said Hamp. "First, how did you know about Toffy Sultoy being taken to Germany? Second, how did you know who was taking her and how?" asked Hamp.

"Your buddy in Berchtesgaden, B. J. Patterson, bugged Weismann's apartment and the Eagle's Nest," replied Wright. "He listened to Weismann make all the arrangements."

"So that's how you knew about the meeting in the Grand Bazaar," said Hamp.

"Yeah. Just your basic spy stuff," replied Wright with another quick smile.

"And, of course, General Stone and the task force members are aware of all this," said Hamp.

"Of course," replied Wright.

"I assume I'll be getting this information again from General Stone tonight," said Hamp.

"Wrong," said Wright. Things are moving too fast to duplicate information flow," said Wright. "He wants you on your way to someplace called Steinhatchee ASAP. A Jetstar from Andrews Air Force Base awaits you at the Boctoi airport as we speak. I'll give you a lift. By the way, where the hell is Steinhatchee?" she asked.

Hamp didn't hear Wright's question because his mind had turned to Steinhatchee. He had been away for weeks. He found it difficult to imagine that life there was going on as usual, oblivious to the political squall brewing there. Tom was probably out on a fishing tour and Marian was probably cooking up something great for supper. Gwen was likely pouring herself into her new job with all of her energy. "I wonder how she likes her new job. I sure hope that Fuller guy doesn't try to romance her." Suddenly the aircraft jounced a bit from a little turbulence, rousing Hamp from his thoughts. "What did you say?" Hamp asked Wright.

"I was just wondering just where Steinhatchee is."

"Oh, what about this end of things?" asked Hamp.

"Colonel Carter is the man," replied Wright. "I've been instructed to cooperatively hold his hand—whatever that means."

"I can't just walk away from Sully and the situation with his wife," said Hamp.

"There are bigger fish to fry, Colonel Porter," said Wright. "Sorry. Oh! One thing more, Colonel Porter. General Stone wants you to call him for further instructions as soon as you are airborne."

"Guess I have no choice in the matter," mumbled Hamp. "Will you explain things to Sully for me, Buzz?" asked Hamp. "Better yet, why don't you bring him here for his protection?"

"You bet. Consider it done," said Carter.

Carter and Hamp said quick good byes, and Hamp was on his way to the airport. When the Jetstar reached altitude, Hamp called General Stone at the Emergency Action Center in the Pentagon. Their conversation was brief.

"Hamp, I want you to look over everyone's shoulder in Steinhatchee. You are the coordinator on the scene appointed by the task force. I realize that puts you in an awkward position being the junior man on the scene, but there are just too many agencies involved for me to feel comfortable. Besides, you know the area, and that will be important. Keep me informed, and, Hamp, get the swastikas. You know what's at stake—seven nuclear warheads."

"Will B.J. Patterson handle the Berchtesgaden end?" asked Hamp. "You know how concerned I am about Mrs. Sultoy, General," said Hamp.

"Yes to both questions. I'm counting on you, Hamp," said General Stone. "By the way, Gibbs, Burns, and Gregory's people are already setting up in your house," said General Stone. The conversation was over.

It suddenly occurred to Hamp that the Jetstar could not possibly get him to the United States in time, to say nothing of getting him to Steinhatchee. He walked to the flight deck to talk with the pilot. "What's the game plan, Flash Gordon," asked Hamp. "Are you two fellows going to get out and push this bird to Steinhatchee?"

"No, sir. Not exactly," replied the pilot. As soon as we land in Istanbul, you will climb into an F-16 and fly the second seat all the way to Gainesville, Florida. The plan calls for one F-16 to do the job by refueling in flight along the way. A Coast Guard chopper will be waiting for you in Gainesville. You will be in Steinhatchee for breakfast, Colonel. By the way, where is Steinhatchee?"

Hamp was thrilled about continuing the battle on his home turf, but felt badly about leaving Sully. He used the flight time to Istanbul to begin sorting out how he would put the interagency team together. Some people were going to be bent out of shape about his leadership role, especially the DEA people, but he was use to that. "Maybe I'm concerned about nothing," thought Hamp. There was too much at stake to allow childish turf battles, and Hamp was certain that Gibbs, Burns, and Gregory would pass the word to their people to cooperate. Hamp liked the idea of his house being used for their headquarters. It would be easy to secure and would accommodate the required communications gear.

The steward brought Hamp a tray adorned with Cornish game hen, wild rice, green beans, hot rolls, and a glass of chilled chardonnay. It was half past eight—dinner time. He was starved but too excited to have noticed. His call to B.J. would have to wait a minute. He had not eaten all day. Hamp finished the meal quickly and asked for the secure phone again.

"Colonel Patterson's Office," said Frau Gurter after two rings.

"Colonel Porter for Colonel Patterson, please," said Hamp.

"I heard about your bugging success. Good work, B.J."

"Thanks. Where are you?" asked B.J.

"I'm en route from Boctoi to Steinhatchee," replied Hamp. "I'm going to coordinate things on that end. B.J., I called because I need your help. I'm assuming you know that Toffy Sultoy is special to me and why. Please take every precaution to extricate her without harm. Will you do that for me?" asked Hamp.

"Look, Hamp, I understand exactly how you feel," replied B.J. "Don't worry; I'll make certain she survives Weismann. Like the good cavalryman that I am, I have a plan, Hampton. I also have some pretty good help. Mr. Gibbs has sent a covey of his boys from Munich, Berlin, and Frankfurt to watch me at work," drawled B.J.

"Thanks, B.J. Please call me when you have her."

Chapter 10

April 13, 1740 hours

The sleek, white Beneteau 50, dropped her foresail, turned into the wind, and then began dropping her mainsail. Her captain would anchor her for the night about two hundred meters from the shoreline. From his vantage point, the ruins of Ephesus were clearly visible about a kilometer beyond the shoreline. The boat's Loran C navigation system had allowed the captain to sail directly to the rendezvous point. Though they had arrived a day early, he and his crew of two needed the time to rest and to make minor repairs to the boat's rigging. Tomorrow morning, after the repairs were complete, he would sail out to sea and burn time so as not to attract too much attention. Once he had received the prearranged radio message, he would return to this same spot to receive his cargo from the rubber boats. With his cargo securely aboard, he would set sail for Ipanema, Brazil.

April 14, 1645 hours

The captain turned the bow of the fifty-foot Beneteau into the wind. The two deck hands quickly cranked in the foresail and lowered the mainsail. While one of the crewmen secured the mainsail, the other hurried to the bow to drop the anchor. They were right on schedule. They lost only a half-day of sailing time on the crossing from Tortola due to a torn mainsail; otherwise, their crossing of the Atlantic had been uneventful. The tide was at dead low, so the captain would wait until morning to enter the port at Thessalonica. He decided that they would wait out the night on the leeward side of Samothrake Island. Looking thoughtfully toward the sky, the captain hoped his cargo would arrive

on time. He did not want to spend more time than
necessary in port because the weather around the
Bosphorus Strait was looking unstable according
to the latest weather bulletin. He wanted to
have his boat well onto the Atlantic within
twenty-four hours. While in port, though, the
captain decided to make good use of his time by
taking on fresh water and food. The captain
looked once more at the bogus paperwork for
transferring the boat to a new owner. Although
cursory, he wanted the customs inspection to go
as smoothly and uneventful as the crossing.

April 14, 1700 hours

Weismann stepped from the elevator into the
main room of the Eagle's Nest. He quickly poured
himself a drink and walked onto the deck to watch
the sun drop behind the mountains. Sunsets were
different in the mountains. The colors are
brilliant and unfiltered by clouds and ground
surface pollution. He thought how nothing in his
peaceful surroundings hinted at the intricate
maneuvers that he had set into motion. Most
certainly nothing in his manner bespoke of his
malicious intentions; however, he did feel
nervous. This was the eve of Pegasus, and he was
alone in the Eagle's Nest. At the moment, he
felt very much out of touch with what was about
to happen in Turkey and Greece, and powerless to
do anything about it. He could only trust that
each man was doing what he should be doing, and
that no glitches had occurred. He hated feeling
powerless, and being at The Eagle's Nest did not
help his mood. Being perched high in the sky in
the midst of the vast surroundings intensified
Weismann's feeling of loneliness and seemed to
amplify his feeling of fallibility.

The endless planning was finally over, the
pieces of the operation were all in place, and
the go signal was about to be transmitted. The

heroin was on a highway in Northeastern Brazil on its way to Ipanema. Reifenstahl's boats were anchored off their rendezvous points; Anatole and Popodopolus were readying their tunnel crews; and Mrs. Sultoy was insuring the cooperation of the security detachment guard force in Boctoi. Everything was ready. All he had to do was pick up the telephone and call Heinrich Dieppe who was waiting in Erich Feltgeibell's office. A chill ran across his shoulders. It was still cool at this altitude at this time of day—or was it fear that he was feeling? His mind began wandering aimlessly; he could not focus his thoughts. He drained his glass of the remaining schnapps and went inside to the fireplace.

His housekeeper had prepared a light dinner for him before leaving. He could feel the warmth of the fireplace on the right side of his face. His thoughts again ran rampant. What had he forgotten? Who will make the first mistake? Had they gone this far without detection? What if someone has talked and the authorities are watching them? Weismann felt uneasy with his feelings of doubt. He would certainly feel better after he had the warhead in his possession; he would no longer have to be concerned with who knew what. Until then he reserved the right to worry. Weismann picked up the telephone and placed the call to Brazil.

"I expected your call sooner, Peter," said Dieppe.

"Is everything ready, Heinrich?" asked Peter.

"Yes."

"Then let us begin. Keep me informed." He placed the phone back in its cradle and poured himself another shot of schnapps.

April 15, 1830 hours

Dieppe placed the telephone in its receiver and turned to face Hans Reifenstahl. "It's a go," said Dieppe. "I'll call Zuni and Tomas." In less than five minutes Dieppe had talked to both men and had given them the go ahead for Pegasus. "Shall we get some dinner, Hans?" asked Dieppe.

* * * * *

B.J. turned off the recorder and closed the desk drawer. Weismann's conversation with Dieppe had come in loud and clear. He turned to Clay Brinson and to Gary Turner, one of the CIA agents from Munich; even though there was a plan in place to stop Weismann and his cohorts from completing their mission, the thought of allowing them to steal the warheads and the thought of what could happen if they were not stopped before their mission's completion weighed heavily on B.J. and his companions' minds. Detecting Turner and Brinson's mood, B.J. said, "It's really going to happen. There's no turning back now."

"It's time to move, gents," said Turner snapping out of his disbelief. "I'll give the word to my men to be ready in five minutes. We need to get Mrs. Sultoy out of the tunnel complex while Weismann is in the Eagle's Nest." Turner then turned and quickly left the office to begin his part of the counter attack.

"We'll meet you in the lobby of the GW in fifteen minutes," called B.J. to Turner as he left the room.

B.J. placed a secure phone call to the Pentagon Emergency Action Center for General Stone. In less than a minute the General answered. "It's a go, sir. We are going in for Mrs. Sultoy while Weismann is in the Eagle's

Nest. Do you want us to pick up Weismann next?" asked B.J.

"No. Leave him alone for the time being. Let's allow Pegasus to unfold; he will be of more use to us where he is for now. He's not likely to go anywhere until Pegasus is well under way. By then, the German officials will be involved and will deal with Weismann."

"Okay, sir, we will just keep an eye on him." The General hung up the phone.

B.J. and Clay Brinson then left the office and headed to the GW Hotel lobby. Upon their arrival they discovered that the three CIA agents were already waiting for them. .

"I still think you should leave this to us, Colonel Patterson," said Turner.

"This is still Army business, my friend," reminded B.J. "I appreciate your position on the issue of jurisdiction, but I will appreciate more your willing assistance and acceptance of my leadership."

"Okay," said Turner reluctantly. "Let's do it. How do you want to proceed?"

"We will browse the shops in the corridor downstairs until we can determine if Weismann has anyone watching the tunnel complex entrance. The hotel has very few guests because of the transfer about to take place, so there should be very few people around. If no one is watching, we will go in expecting one or more of Weismann's people to be inside. I'll go in first to be followed by you and your men. I want Clay to close the door after us and stand watch outside the door in the corridor. If there are hotel guests around, I don't want to draw any attention to us or our activities if at all possible. I really don't think Weismann will have anyone here, either inside the complex or in the corridor. He thinks he has the only keys to the door and knows that I don't have any reason to visit the complex again," explained B.J.

"You left out the part about what we do if he does have someone watching the entrance," said Turner, unsure of the plan.

"Two of your men and Brinson will handle it," clipped B.J. "Now, let's go."

The men walked leisurely down the steps to the corridor and strolled along the shops on either side of the corridor as though they were guests. They even paused momentarily to watch a basketball game on the lounge television. Five minutes later they reached the last shop on the corridor about fifteen meters from the tunnel complex entrance.

"I don't think anyone that we've seen down here is the least bit interested in the complex door," said Turner.

"Okay. Then lets go on in," replied B.J. as he removed two large keys from his pocket. B.J. opened the door very slowly; when he had it opened about half way, he unholstered the 9-milimeter Smith & Wesson pistol and completely opened the door. He paused for a moment to listen for movement. The lights were off. Only a small sliver of light from the main corridor illuminated the tunnel corridor. There was no sign of anyone, so B.J. flipped on the lights. After the last agent was inside, B.J. told him to close the door. Still suspicious that someone might be in the room with Mrs. Sultoy, B.J. motioned for each agent to take a position near one of the storage room doors. He stood next to the remaining door. With sidearms at the ready, the agents awaited B.J.'s signal to enter the rooms. B.J. nodded to the agents, quickly opened his door, and entered the room with his pistol drawn. His room was empty.

"This door is locked," said one of the agents.

Apparently the other doors were open and the rooms were empty. All agents, and B.J., converged on the locked door. B.J. placed himself in the lead position in front of the door.

"Mrs. Sultoy, my name is Lieutenant Colonel Billy Joe Patterson. I am the commander of the recreation center where you are being held by Herr. Peter Weismann. I am here to get you out and take you to your husband and family. Can you hear me, Mrs. Sultoy?"

"How do I know you are who you say you are," replied a frightened woman's voice from behind the door.

"We have a mutual friend, Mrs. Sultoy. His name is Hamp Porter. I also know that your nick name is Toffy," said B.J.

"Thank God. Oh, please get me out of this place," she pleaded.

"Please stand back from the door, Mrs. Sultoy. Place your back to the wall next to the corridor. We will have to shoot this lock off," explained B.J. With that statement, the agents began moving for cover. B.J. stood to one side, placed his left arm across his face, and took aim at the lock with his right hand. His first shot did nothing but ricochet around the corridor causing the agents to stoop a little lower. The second shot did the trick. B.J. opened the door and saw Toffy Sultoy still standing next to the wall with her eyes tightly closed and her fists and teeth clinched.

"It's over, Mrs. Sultoy. You can relax" said B.J. Slowly Mrs. Sultoy opened her eyes, and as she realized that the ordeal was over, she rushed to B.J. He said, "No one can hurt you, now." Mrs. Sultoy tried to respond, but she couldn't; she could only bury her face in B.J.'s shoulder and sob.

April 15, 2345 hours

Emal Topaki finished briefing his three-man tunnel crew and asked them if they had any questions. They shook their heads indicating no questions. They walked to the old tunnel entrance two hundred meters away and removed the brush and old planking they had been using to cover the entrance. The tunnel once had been part of a very old mineshaft that had long since been closed and forgotten by the locals. While the three assistants made their way into the tunnel with miner's lamps on their hats, Emal began preparing the army mule just inside the tunnel entrance. Having made sure everything was in working order, Emal cranked the mule and drove slowly to the intersection where his assistants would be installing explosive charges.

Meanwhile, Colonel Buzz Carter and Special Agent Diane Wright placed the starlight scopes down and conversed quietly. From their observation point fifty meters above the tunnel entrance, they observed the four men arriving and entering the tunnel. They also heard the faint, muffled sound of an engine starting.

"It's going down," whispered Wright.

"Yeah, and right on schedule," whispered Carter.

"I'm going to let my partner know." Wright took a small hand held radio from her pocket and called for Sponge Two, obviously her partner's radio call sign. She listened for a minute using a miniature ear phone in her right ear.

"He's in position in a clump of trees by the road. He can observe the truck clearly. It's about twenty meters off the road in the tree line," she reported.

"As soon as the goons leave the tunnel, we'll follow on foot," replied Carter. "I hope you're in good physical condition, Agent Wright," said Carter.

"Five miles every day," replied Wright.

It was now five minutes before midnight. Emal observed as his three assistants carefully placed detonating cord in a circle three feet in diameter on the sub-flooring of the storage and assembly building. The detonating cord would drop a perfect three-foot circle of flooring from the floor. About eighty percent of the noise would be confined to the tunnel side of the explosion. One would have to be inside the storage and assembly building to hear it. Since the guards would be nowhere around, no one would hear it.

"We are ready," said one of the assistants. Emal nodded, the assistant pulled the firing cord on the fuse, and the four men took cover behind the mule about fifteen meters away. Five seconds later Emal heard a dull thudding sound and felt pressure in his ears and on his body. An acrid odor and thick dust hung in the air making it difficult to breathe for a few minutes. Emal then turned his flashlight on the roof of the tunnel at the blast site and saw an almost perfect three-foot hole in the building floor. The four men quickly moved the rubble aside and positioned the mule directly under the hole. Two of the assistants climbed into the hole and disappeared into the darkness. Emal could hear something rolling on the floor above. In a few seconds the first warhead container was being lowered to him through the hole. Emal and the other assistant strained to load the 90 kilogram container on the mule. Another container waited for them on the edge of the hole followed by another. Within fifteen minutes after punching through the floor, all four warhead containers were on the mule. They left the tunnel and began the downhill journey to the main road. The mule was operating at maximum capacity. Emal could not help wondering if the brakes would hold the load down the steep incline.

Wright and Carter watched them depart the tunnel with one man driving and the other three walking beside the mule. Carter's heart leaped into his throat at the sight of the four warheads. He was supposed to be guarding those containers with his life and the lives of his soldiers. As the warheads moved down the mountain, Carter and Wright followed at a safe distance seeking cover in the trees. The road was little more than a one-lane dirt path, and was just wide enough to allow the mule passage without hitting trees along the way. Carter and Wright had no difficulty keeping pace with the mule. Niki was being overly cautious with his nuclear cargo, apparently afraid to bump or jar it. Obviously, Colonel Sultoy kept the guards occupied as planned. Everything went as planned without arousing any suspicion: the security reaction force's pursuit was yet undetected and the alarm within the compound had not been sounded.

The mule stopped at the edge of the clearing near the main road. Carter and Wright watched the men load the four containers onto the truck and secure the rear canvas flaps. Within two minutes, the truck and men were on their way to Ephesus. Carter and Wright returned to the compound where they reported the night's activities to the Pentagon EAC. With their portion of the counter attack completed, Carter poured Wright and himself a large scotch as he waited for General Stone to answer.

April 16, 0016 hours

Niki Stafros helped his crew load the third and last warhead into the truck, secured the rear cargo flaps of the truck, and climbed onto the passenger side of the front seat. He told the

driver to go and then settled into the seat to
catch his breath. The operation had gone
flawlessly. He should be happy, but sweat ran
from every pore of his body. His hands shook and
his ears rang until he thought they would burst.
He was shocked that his excitement had reached
such a state. Never had he felt such fear at
being discovered. Stafros was very thankful that
Tomas was not present just then to see him this
way. He was also thankful that he had the forty-
five minute ride to the municipal dock in
Thessalonica to recover. "I must pull myself
together," thought Niki. "Tomas will be at the
dock."

Tomas Popodopolus stepped onto the dock
from his boat when Niki's truck pulled up next to
the boat ramp. Two men from the boat immediately
joined Niki's two cousins, and they began the
process of moving the three containers from the
truck to the boat. The transfer was complete
within five minutes and the truck, with Niki's
cousins, departed. Niki stayed behind.

"Any problems, Niki?" asked Tomas.

"None," replied Niki. "Everything went
exactly as planned. We were not detected." Niki
had calmed down, but was still shaking a bit.

"Good work, Niki. I knew I could depend on
you," said Tomas. "Captain, are you ready to set
sail?" asked Tomas.

"Yes, sir. I'll run out under diesel power
until I'm clear of the harbor markers. It is low
tide, now."

Tomas and Niki watched as the crew cast off
lines and pushed clear of the dock. The quiet
rumble of the boat's diesel engine was the only
sound on the dock. A derelict lying against a
lamp post a few meters away apparently in a
drunken sleep was the only person Niki saw.
Tomas felt good. So far, things had gone well.
He would go to his office and call Weismann.

"Niki, check on that drunk over there and make sure he is indeed just a drunk," said Tomas. Niki walked over to the man, pushed him over with his foot, bent down, and smelled the man's breath. He reeked to the heavens of alcohol.

"This man will be drunk for a month, judging from the way he smells," said Niki.

"Okay. Niki, let's go to my office. You would like a little ouzo, would you not?" asked Tomas.

Ten minutes later when the boat had cleared the harbor, and Tomas and Niki were gone; the drunk got to his feet, pulled a cell phone from his pocket, and dialed a number. "This is Agent Briggs, sir. The boat just cleared the harbor with the cargo on board."

April 16, 0110 hours GMT

Dieppe put the telephone into its cradle. He turned to Hans Feltgeibell and smiled. "We are precisely on schedule, Hans. That was Tomas. His end of Pegasus is complete. No problems encountered," says Dieppe. "I'll call Weismann, and then we can call it a day. It's hard for me to imagine that it's one o'clock in the morning in Turkey," yawned Dieppe.

Chapter 11

April 16, 1995

Hamp's house was bedlam personified. The great room was filled with sophisticated communications gear and takeout food cartons—some two days old. Six DEA agents and two FBI agents had been calling Hamp's home their office for the past couple of days. Sam and Winnie Pamona had been good enough to dedicate their six motel rooms to Hamp's friends for an entire week. To explain their presence in Steinhatchee, Hamp told everyone who asked that he had agreed to allow the Defense Department to use his home for the conduct of tests on new communications gear. He told them they wanted to conduct the tests from homes and buildings over salt water. Hamp explained that he was doing it for an old military buddy. By the time anyone figured out what was going on, it would all be over.

Hamp felt like he had a solid game plan. Their secure communications link to the Pentagon EAC, along with fully integrated satellite communications with the rest of the world, put information from a variety of sources at their fingertips. Through the secure radio/telephone links, Hamp, or any and all of the team members, could talk simultaneously or independently to any agency no matter how far away. Immediate access to intelligence satellites allowed them to track any boat, no matter how large or small, to within ten feet at any distance. They could also monitor any type of audio or video transmission from the same boat. To cap it all off, a US Air Force Blackbird SR-70 had been dedicated to their exclusive use.

At least a dozen antennas protruded from Hamp's deck and roof top making his home look something like a futuristic space station. Never had he witnessed a better example of teamwork and technology. He was impressed by how smoothly everything was going: There had not been even one turf battle. All agencies were cooperating in good spirit. Hamp had catered to Gregory and the DEA boys simply because this part of Pegasus, the drug intercepts, were legitimately in their sphere of responsibility. Gregory had taken the initiative in planning without being an ass. The arrangement pleased Hamp because the DEA fellows were good at this. It was their bread and butter. They had been hacking away at the Charo and Costellano operation for over two years. Now they had a chance to put them away forever, and at least slow the flow of heroin into the United States for a while.

Hamp received the call about Toffy Sultoy from B.J. Patterson yesterday, and Carter had reported an hour ago that Sully and Toffy Sultoy had been reunited in Boctoi. Perhaps the whole Boctoi part of Pegasus could be kept quiet, and Sully would not have to face a Turkish Army court-martial. Hamp looked at the six clocks on the mantle that represented six different time zones: Brazil, British Virgin Islands, Germany, Greece, Turkey and the United States. It was still yesterday in Turkey. B. J. also reported that Weismann was still in the Eagle's Nest. It was Saturday in Germany, so Weismann would not be expected in his office.

"The latest satellite fixes on the Beneteaus are coming in," said one of the FBI agents.

"Where are they?" asked Hamp as he walked over to the global plotting map someone had tacked to his wall.

"The Turk is at latitude 72 degrees north, 102 degrees east; the Greek is at 56 degrees north, 89 degrees east," replied the agent.

Referring to the boats as Greek and Turk helped them to keep up with which boat was which.

"They're making good time," Hamp remarked.

"Yeah, but take a look at this," said the agent monitoring the weather satellite. The Turk is sailing right into one hell of a storm line, and the line is too long for her to sail around." Hamp and several of the agents gathered around the monitor. An ugly blob of yellow and red appeared about an inch from the boat on the screen.

"When will they hit it?" someone asked.

"In about two hours," said the agent monitoring the screen. "They are on a collision course with the storm. I'll switch satellites and get a reading on the surface conditions at the storm's center."

"I thought this wasn't storm season in the Atlantic," said Hamp.

"A storm like this one can pop up at any time," said the agent. "But it is unusually large for a spring storm. Wait a minute. I have the other satellite. Damn! This baby is kicking up eight to ten foot waves at its center and is packing winds up to 65 miles per hour." They were about to be in danger of loosing the warheads. Hamp called his buddy, Tom Adams.

"Tom, got a question for you. How much of a problem can ten foot waves and 65 mile per hour winds cause a fifty-foot Beneteau with a moderate to heavy load?" asked Hamp.

"Ouch! Tough one, Hamp," replied Tom. "It depends on several factors like wave interval, the experience of the captain and crew, and the handling characteristics of the boat. Right off the top of my head I would say a boat sailing under those circumstances would be in deep trouble. Why do you ask?"

"Just curious, Tom. I'm having a nautical discussion with a weekend sailor at my house and needed an expert opinion. Naturally, I thought of you first."

"I'm glad you recognize and acknowledge my superior seamanship, Hamp. It's about time," laughed Tom. "By the way, Tanker Bartlett saw a South American trawler near the spring yesterday heading south. I thought you would be interested."

"Really," said Hamp.

"He sure did. Marian and Gwen's imaginations have been working overtime since I told them. Anyway, ol' buddy, how long are you going to put up with that crap in your house? Gwen said something about not having seen you since you returned from your trip. You do know that she left for home this morning, don't you?" asked Tom. Hamp didn't respond for a few seconds then spoke.

"No. I didn't know," said Hamp. "Why?"

"I don't know. She asked Marian to drive her to the airport in Gainesville this morning," "Give her time to get home, Hamp, and then call her."

"Yeah, I'll do that," said Hamp, a little irritated at Gwen for leaving without saying good bye.

* * * * *

Gwen could feel her heart pounding in her chest as she drove through the familiar streets of Evergreen. Although she had missed her children terribly, she surely did not feel like going another round with Greg. "Maybe he will be at work or gone fishing," said Gwen to herself. Gwen had almost not come home to visit, but when her children had called her and had begged her to come home, she had no other alternative but to return for a quick visit. They would not be home from school yet. Gwen was glad because she needed a few moments to gather her thoughts. She had had so much on her mind lately.

More and more she had felt herself getting closer to Hamp. Their friendship had started down a different path that she was not all too certain she could travel. She was a mother and a wife even if her husband didn't act like a husband. Gwen had never been unfaithful to Greg even though no one would ever blame her if she had. Greg had had so many affairs over the years and had not really put too much effort into concealing them. "About the only thing he never did was sleep with someone else in my own house," Gwen mumbled sarcastically to herself.

As she pulled into the driveway of her home, Gwen noticed that Greg's truck was parked in the back yard. "What's he doing home so early from work?" questioned Gwen aloud. "I didn't want to see him yet." As she trudged up the steps and onto the front porch, Gwen thought that she heard voices, but she knew that the kids were not home yet and that her mother-in-law was not home either because she had gone to get the kids from school. Quietly, Gwen slipped into the house and followed the sound of the voices, now laughing. As she passed by her bedroom door, Gwen found the source of the voices: There was her husband and some peroxide blonde she didn't know lying entangled in her bed. Although most wives' response would be to yell at the infidels, Gwen simply stood there in shock. She wasn't shocked to see her husband having yet another affair. She was amazed that she really didn't care. Actually she felt glad. Gwen knocked on the opened door. As the two looked to see who had discovered them, Gwen walked over to the woman who was scrambling to conceal herself and said, "Thank you. You have just done me a great big favor. He's all yours." With that Gwen spun around, walked out of the house, and drove to meet her mother-in-law and children before they returned home.

Gwen discovered her mother-in-law's car parked in front of the ice cream parlor. Taking a look in the rear view mirror to make sure her face did not hint at what she had just witnessed, Gwen exited the car and went to see her babies.

"Mama," they all yelled in unison as they rushed to hug her.

"Whoa, don't knock me down. There are plenty of kisses for everyone. Look at you. You have each grown six inches. Mom, what are you feeding them?"

"Gwen, we're so glad to see you. These kids have missed you terribly"

"Well, I've missed them, too, and you," said Gwen. "Heh kids, go place your ice cream orders and get me a hot fudge sundae." When the children left the table, Gwen turned to her mother-in-law and said, "Mom, I wanted to have a moment alone with you to tell you something. I just left the house. I got home early only to find Greg there with some woman in our bedroom. Mom, I love you so much, but I just can't take his infidelity anymore. Why couldn't he be more like you?"

"Gwen, I'm so sorry. I don't know what is wrong with Greg. I don't think he has ever grown up. You have put up with so much from him over the years. I know that. Even if Greg is my son, he is terribly wrong. What are you going to do?"

"Mom, I'm not exactly sure, but I know that I can never go back to my old life. I have discovered so much about myself, and most of it has been great. I love feeling like I matter. To be honest, Mom, I really don't feel anger toward Greg. I used all of that up a long time ago. I mostly feel thankful, thankful that he resolved the debate going on inside my head as to whether or not I should give up my new career and return home or whether I should continue with my new life. I am going to stay in Steinhatchee. My boss Ben Fuller has offered me a full-time position with his company. I just decided that I am going to take him up on his offer. Would you mind staying with the kids a few more weeks until school gets out for the summer?"

"You know I would do anything for you and the kids, Gwen. Are you sure this is what you want to do?" she asked.

"Yes, Mom, I am sure" Gwen said.

Driving into Steinhatchee from the airport, Gwen felt nervous. She realized that she was not merely returning to her job, but that her life had taken a completely different path and that her future now had so many possibilities, one of which was, of course, Hamp. She had so much to tell him.

*****

James Gregory came rushing through the front door of Hamp's house with a very tired-looking, youngish man in tow. Gregory had left the house two hours ago to pick up his undercover agent in Gainesville who had been under deep cover with Charo's mob in the Miami area for over nine months. "This debriefing should prove interesting," thought Hamp.

"Gather around, men," barked Gregory. "This is Agent Lewis Ramerez, our undercover man with the Charo mob. I just brought him in this morning. Listen closely to what he has to say." Lewis took a deep drink from the soda someone put in his hand, and then began speaking.

"You already know that the heroin is coming in to Florida near Key West, Cedar Key and Steinhatchee. I picked up the exact Loran C numbers of the rendezvous points last night. I was assigned to drive Mr. Charo. He held a coordination meeting with one of his lieutenants

in his car while driving around Miami. I
overheard Charo read the coordinates for the
lieutenant to write them down. I memorized them—
at least I think I memorized them. They are
14487 and 48941," Ramerez recited as Gregory
plotted the numbers on the wall map.

"They look reasonable," said Gregory.
"Take a look, Colonel Porter."

The Key West numbers were at the western
bay limits near marker number six, about 500
meters out of the shipping lane, and away from
the port entrance. The location didn't mean much
to Hamp, but they would mean something to Captain
Miller. The Cedar Key numbers pointed to a spot
immediately west of a little island eight hundred
meters off the Cedar Key pier. Hamp could
visualize the spot and the surroundings. But the
Steinhatchee numbers really got Hamp's attention—
they pointed to a spot directly over the fresh
water spring where he and Tom had seen the
concrete pylon on the ocean bottom.

"Are you familiar with that spot, Colonel
Porter?" asked Gregory.

"Yes, sir. Tom Adams and I dive that area
regularly. That's where we spotted the concrete
pylon with the word Pegasus imprinted on each
side," replied Hamp.

"There's more," said Ramerez. "Charo and
his lieutenant also discussed the landing points
for the recovery boats. The Steinhatchee landing
point is going to be at the bridge at a place
called Cow Creek. The Cedar Key landing point
will be on the western side of the little island
just off the Cedar Key Public Dock," explained
Ramerez.

"That's where drugs were transferred to
light aircraft ten years ago during the massive
influx of drugs into the country through
Florida," said Hamp as he moved to the map of the
local area on the wall. "This is called Rocky

Creek Road," Hamp pointed on the map with a pencil. "It runs from the community of Jena, across the river, past the Rocky Creek community here, on to the Gulf of Mexico where it abruptly ends. Just before the road reaches the gulf, it crosses Cow Creek, right here, a small rivulet that empties tidal water from the surrounding marsh land into the gulf. A small boat could easily navigate the two hundred meters from the gulf to the bridge without difficulty. The bridge is no more than six feet above the creek, making it easy to off load cargo from a boat to someone on the bridge," explained Hamp. "That is exactly what they did ten years ago. The aircraft used the road as a runway, because it is straight and has clear shoulders—there's nothing but saw grass on either side of the road for two or three miles."

"I find it hard to believe that they would use the same entry point again," remarked Gregory with doubt in his voice. "Charo is no dummy."

"Or he might be just smart enough to repeat history," said Hamp pensively. "He would assume anyone would take for granted that history would not be repeated. He's counting on it," said Hamp.

"I believe in the possibility enough to cover that base," said Gregory. "Hamp, I want you to take me on a tour of this road to nowhere."

Gregory huddled with Ramerez and several of his agents to work out the details of dealing with the new contingency identified by Ramerez.

"I want to make a quick phone call, Mr. Gregory, if you will excuse me," said Hamp.

Gregory nodded, and Hamp placed a call to Captain Miller at the Tampa Coast Guard Station. They spoke briefly, and then Hamp returned to the wall map and motioned for Mr. Gregory to join him.

"Captain Miller, commander of the regional coast guard station in Tampa, said his people sighted another South American fishing trawler north of Tampa sailing due north day before yesterday. The cutter shadowed the trawler to Steinhatchee, where it made a brief stop and put two divers overboard for about twenty minutes, then headed south making similar stops at Cedar Key and Key West. Divers were put overboard at each location. After the Tampa Bay stop, the trawler headed for South America. The Key West station picked up the trawler in their waters and shadowed her due south to Cuban waters. They assumed she sailed on to South America. She was not flying national colors. No attempt was made to board her as per instructions from the Pentagon EAC," explained Hamp. "Mr. Gregory, I think it's time for Tom Adams and me to dive the spring again. I'm going to recommend that General Stone ask the Coast Guard or Navy to dive the Cedar Key and Key West dump sites," said Hamp.

"Okay, but remember that Tom Adams is not in on any of this. How will you keep him in the dark?" asked Gregory.

"I'll find a way."

Hamp called General Stone and asked him to arrange the Key West and Cedar Key dives, and to approve Tom's participation in the Steinhatchee dive. He then called Tom, but Marian said he was at the marina preparing his boat for a fishing trip. Hamp decided to walk to the marina since it was only three blocks from his house and he needed a break from the noise and confusion in his living room. For now, everyone was huddled around the computer monitor that was tracking the weather satellite. The fate of the boat that was about to do battle with the storm was out of his hands. He was content to let others worry about it.

Strolling along the water toward the marina, Hamp could feel the ocean breeze lightly brushing his skin. He stopped for a moment to let it embrace him as the late afternoon sun washed over him. He took in a deep cleansing breath of the salt air and exhaled slowly. These past few days had certainly been hectic. "I thought I had left that kind of busy life behind me when I retired," he muttered to himself. Just then the aroma of cooking seafood caught Hamp's attention as he walked past Roy's, one of the local seafood restaurants, which reminded him of how hungry he was. He had barely eaten in over two days, and there was no telling how much longer he might have to wait for that luxury. While standing there watching the sun slip closer to the horizon, Hamp glimpsed the neon marina marquee blink on spelling Ideal Fish Camp in blue cursive letters. Out of the corner of his eye, he spotted Jeff Tuckman, the owner of the marina, and Tom loading a large cooler onto the Caroline II, Tom's offshore boat. Eight heavy duty Penn rod and reel rigs leaned against the stern waiting to be placed in rod racks on the boat. It was a familiar scene to Hamp. He had helped Tom with this pre-fishing ritual dozens of times. From the looks of the equipment, Tom was going grouper fishing. He was going to be unhappy about being asked to cancel a fishing party. Tom ran an exceptionally ethical guide service and believed in giving his clients the best of his talent and equipment. Hamp hoped the party was not a favorite client of Tom's.

"You're too late to be of any help, Hamp," said Tom without looking up from his work. "Besides, Jeff is better help than you."

"I hope you pay Jeff better than you pay me," teased Hamp. "Have you got a minute to talk, Tom?" asked Hamp.

"Well, since you aren't smiling, Ol' Buddy, I guess you mean talk as in serious business. Come aboard."

Hamp stepped over the gunnels and followed Tom into the cabin. Tom took two bottles of beer from a small cooler in the cabin, opened them, and gave one to Hamp. Tom took a long drink from his bottle, made himself comfortable on the captain's chair, and waited for Hamp to speak.

"Tom, it's time for us to go diving again—at the spring," said Hamp quietly as he looked out the front wind screen. "Before you ask me why, there's something you should know. May I have your word that you will tell absolutely no one of what I am about to tell you, not even Marian?" asked Hamp with solemnity.

"You have my word," replied Tom, equally solemn. He sensed Hamp was deadly serious about whatever it was he was about to tell him.

Hamp patiently told Tom the whole story of Pegasus, and described to him the task force's plans to deal with the situation. Tom listened attentively without asking questions. When Hamp finished speaking, Tom called to Jeff who was near the stern completing the refueling of Caroline II. Jeff entered the cabin.

"Jeff, do you think you could get another guide to take my party in the morning? Something has come up that Hamp and I need to attend to. Maybe Bill Musgrove could take them. Give him a call and tell him I would consider it a personal favor. Thanks, Jeff."

"No problem. I'll call Bill now. He left here just before you arrived heading for West Wind Marina," replied Jeff. "If he can't do it, I'll find someone."

Jeff could be trusted not to ask questions, or to offer unsolicited comments about Tom's business. They had been friends for a long time, and Tom had helped Jeff get his start with the marina. He would assume Tom had good reason to ask someone else to take his party tomorrow. Jeff left the boat and headed for the marina office.

"Let's get the gear," said Tom as he stood and walked through the cabin door and down on deck. "We might as well take advantage of the weather and do it now. It has been a while since our last night dive."

Tom kept their diving gear in a shed on the marina premises. He used the shed for storing fishing gear, boat supplies, and other paraphernalia. While the men were readying the diving gear, Tom said, "Hamp, while we've got a few minutes, there is something I think you might want to know."

"What's that?" he asked.

"Gwen came back home late last night. She called Marian and me about 11:30 last night," he said.

"That sure was a short trip home."

"That's not what I wanted to tell you. She caught Greg with another woman."

"That jerk," said Hamp. "Someone ought to teach him a lesson or two."

"Well, Gwen's not as upset as you might think. Actually, I think she is relieved. She is planning on moving her kids down here right after school lets out."

"Oh really," said Hamp. This last piece of information pleased him more than he had expected.

"Well, that ought to about do it. Are you ready to go yet?" said Tom as he completed loading and inspecting the gear.

"Yep, let's go," Hamp replied.

Only fifteen minutes had passed by the time they had loaded the diving gear and entered the river for the one mile run to marker number one in the gulf. From marker number one they would follow a heading of 172 degrees for 26 miles, or until the Loran C told them to stop. While Tom kept the Caroline II on course, Hamp assembled and checked their diving gear. They brought along only two eighty cubic foot tanks. That would allow them about 35 minutes of bottom time, enough time to see what they needed to see.

Hamp had no idea of what to expect, nor did he have reason to expect to see anything new or different than before, but his gut told him to investigate. If everything was the same as they had found it the last time they dove the spring, why had the South American trawler been in the area again? They would find the answer to that question in about an hour. The sea was relatively calm and water clarity was better than usual, and the cloudless sky meant some ambient light on the bottom. The conditions were perfect for a good dive.

The Loran C beeped a warning that their destination was one half mile away. Tom slowed the Caroline II to ten knots and turned on the bottom reader. Five minutes later, the Loran C beeped another warning indicating the programmed destination had been reached. Tom began circling the area slowly while watching the bottom reader. During the second circling maneuver, the entrance to the spring appeared as an abrupt depression of the ocean bottom. Tom closed the throttle and shifted the transmission into reverse gear to stop the Caroline II and yelled for Hamp to drop the anchor.

"We're right on the money," Tom called out as he shut down the engine.

"Then let's dress out and swim down," replied Hamp.

They squirmed into their wet suits, hefted air tanks onto their backs, buckled on weight belts, slipped into fins, and adjusted their face masks. They shuffled the few feet to the diving platform on the stern and made simultaneous split-legged entries into the water. The 64 degree water was cold enough to cause a slight shock, but after two or three minutes the wet suits absorbed water and began acting as an insulator by trapping body heat. They descended using the anchor line as a guide. Hamp had difficulty clearing pressure in his left ear at twenty feet—probably a clogged sinus cavity. After two more tries his ear cleared and he continued the descent toward Tom who was waiting for him on the bottom. They immediately swam the twenty meters toward where they had last seen the concrete pylon. They were not disappointed—the concrete pylon was exactly where it had been before. Nothing had changed. Then Hamp saw something else.

A silver colored box a cubic foot in size with a globe-like glass fixture on its top had been fastened to the top of the block. Hamp thought, "That's what the trawler had been doing in the area again. But why hadn't the men on the trawler affixed the box to the pylon when they had put it there in first place?" He and Tom both examined the box closely but to no avail. Neither diver had any idea what the device might be. One thing was for sure— they needed to know its purpose, so Hamp decided they should remove it and take it to the experts. Hamp used hand signals to indicate to Tom his intention to remove the device and to take it up. Tom shook his head in the affirmative, but suggested he be the one to disconnect it from the block; however, before doing anything, both men looked carefully for a booby trap wire though luckily they did not find one. Tom recognized the fastener that secured the device and began unfastening it as Hamp watched. Upon completion, Tom grasped the device with both hands, and the men began their ascent. Of course they could have tied a lift balloon to the device and floated it to the surface, but they didn't want to take any chances that might damage the device. After a three minute decompression wait at the fifteen foot level, they surfaced and climbed aboard Caroline II.

Hamp radioed Ideal Fish Camp where Jeff answered the call. Hamp asked Jeff to telephone Mr. Gregory at Hamp's house and to ask him to meet them at the fish camp dock in an hour and a half.

As Caroline II made her way back to the marina, Hamp examined the device closely. The box weighed approximately thirty pounds and was made of stainless steel. There were no buttons, leavers, or switches on the box. A metal appendage about the size and length of a paper straw protruded from one side of the device. The glass globe on the box top was about the size and shape of a water glass and appeared to contain some kind of light—perhaps a strobe light. One side of the box appeared to be detachable and was held in place by 20 small stainless steel screws and surrounded by a gasket, which apparently made it waterproof. Hamp decided not to tamper with the box. That would be better left to the experts. Making an educated guess, Hamp decided that the device was intended to be a guide of some kind for divers making a night dive. "That's it," said Hamp to himself. "They are going to put the heroin packages overboard and anchor them to the concrete pylons. Since the containers will have to be airtight, they will tend to float or move about under water. The pylons will be used as anchors to hold them in place until divers recover them later. A boat with a lift of some kind will have to be used to recover the packages—probably a fishing boat of the netting variety." Hamp concluded that the devices must have been added to the concrete blocks as an afterthought. "Sloppy work for an operation of this magnitude," thought Hamp.

Gregory was standing on the dock waiting for them when Caroline II made her way to the dock. As Tom secured the dock lines to Caroline II, Hamp explained to Gregory what had taken place. Gregory handed the device to one of his agents and told him to fly it to Gainesville.

"Your speculation as to the use of this device seems reasonable, Hamp. The DEA has contacts in the science community at the University of Florida. They can sort out the particulars of the device," remarked Gregory. "We had better get that thing back to where it belongs as soon as possible. We don't want to screw up their operation."

"I agree," said Hamp. "By the way, what is the status of that boat in the Atlantic?" asked Hamp.

"The captain must be one hell of a sailor. The boat is hanging in there. The storm is expected to dissipate in another hour or so," answered Gregory. "It looks like they might make it."

"Let's go to Roy's, Mr. Gregory," said Hamp. "I'll buy you and Tom the best grouper dinner on the gulf coast."

"Why not?" said Gregory.

Chapter 12

April 17

Weismann stepped from the elevator and entered the great room of the Eagle's Nest. He walked immediately to the bar, poured himself a drink, and hurried to the deck. "Perhaps the cool air and the whiskey will calm me down and clear my thinking," he said aloud. He paced, ignoring the breathtaking effects of the setting sun surrounding him. Waves of apprehension and anger alternately shook his body. He did not expect to find an empty room when he had slipped unnoticed into the tunnel complex an hour ago to check on Mrs. Sultoy's condition. It had to be Patterson. No one else would have keys to the complex. How did they get on to him? How much do they know about Pegasus. From whom had the leak come? Who is "they"? He was a man accustomed to having the answers. Not knowing was more than he could bear. Could they stop Pegasus? Yes. Would they stop Pegasus? He was not sure.

Weismann went inside and dialed the number for Heinrich Dieppe's hotel in Miami. Heinrich would monitor the Charo side of Pegasus from there and collect the money from Charo when the heroin had been delivered to the sea anchors at Tampa, Cedar Key, and Steinhatchee.

Twelve hours had passed since Heinrich had called. As Weismann waited for the call to go through, the idea suddenly occurred to him that his office and the Eagle's Nest were probably bugged. "Where else could Colonel Patterson have gotten information about Mrs. Sultoy's whereabouts? It had to be Patterson. His delay in leaving for the United States, and the delay in transferring property were nothing more than ploys to buy him time to spy on me," he mused. The hotel operator answered.

"Would you connect me to Dr. Heinrich Dieppe's room, please?" asked Weismann.

"One moment, please," replied the operator. "I'm sorry, sir, but Dr. Dieppe's room does not answer. Would you like to leave a message?"

"No. Thank you. I'll try again later."

Weismann was getting jittery. He began mumbling to himself. The abduction of Mrs. Sultoy had shaken him badly, and he briefly considered calling off Pegasus: however, after re-thinking the ramifications of doing such a thing, he changed his mind. "What good would it do to call off Pegasus?" he asked himself aloud. "The warheads had been stolen and are on the way to Brazil. The Americans dare not turn him in to the German authorities for fear of loosing the warheads, and for fear of creating a public panic," he said in a high-pitched voice. "As far as he was concerned, the loss of Mrs. Sultoy changed nothing," he told himself. "After all, there is no reason to be upset." However, he was certain that he would feel much better about things if only he could talk to Heinrich.

Weismann, however, did not have time to obsess over what had happened to Mrs. Sultoy. Other matters needed his attention. He walked over to the television and tuned it to the evening news channel in Munich where the national news and weather already had been on for ten minutes. Settling into one of the overstuffed leather chairs near the fireplace, Weismann listened intently. He had heard on the noon news that an unusual storm had popped up in the Atlantic near the Mediterranean. He wanted desperately to know if the boats were in danger from the storm. The commentator made no mention of an incident involving nuclear weapons or American Armed Forces. Also, the weather report, though it reported the storm, did not mention the loss of any vessels. "That was good," said Weismann aloud, "although they could have gone down without anyone knowing it." He felt the tension mounting. He needed to talk to Dieppe. As if reading his mind, the phone on the side table next to his chair rang, startling him.

"Hello, Weismann here," he answered.

"Peter, this is Heinrich. The desk clerk informed me of an overseas caller earlier," said Dieppe.

Weismann turned on the stereo player and turned up the volume as Dieppe spoke.

"Someone may be listening, Heinrich, so we must be careful," said Weismann. "I have been concerned. It has been fourteen hours since you called. Is everything on schedule? Are there any problems of which you are aware?" asked Weismann.

"No. None," replied Dieppe. "Why do you ask? You sound upset, Peter."

"Our guest here has left us without a word," said Weismann. "I went by to visit her today, and she had gone without leaving a message or a forwarding address."

"Perhaps our American friend picked her up for a drive," replied Dieppe, trying to sound nonchalant. "Will this change your plans, Peter?"

"I think not, unless you can think of a reason to change them, Heinrich."

"Let me think about it for awhile. I'll call you back within two hours, if I think of a reason to change anything," suggested Dieppe.

"Very well, Heinrich. By the way, has there been a report from our sailor friends?"

"No. I am afraid not, Peter, but I would not be concerned yet," replied Dieppe.

"Call me if there is anything we need to talk about, Heinrich." Weismann hung up the

phone.   He felt much better having talked with
Dieppe. "Now, to find Colonel Patterson's little
bugs," said Weismann aloud as he unscrewed the
cover of the telephone mouthpiece.

*****

Frau Gurter was gone for the day, so B.J.
had the office to himself.   He picked up the
telephone receiver and dialed Weismann's number
at the Eagle's Nest.   After the third ring,
Weismann answered.

"Herr. Weismann, I thought you would be
interested to know that Mrs. Sultoy's flight will
be landing in Izmir in about half an hour.   I
drove her to the airport in Munich myself.   She
said to tell you thanks for your hospitality
during her stay in the Hess Room. I want to tell
you something, too, Herr. Peter Sturmer.   You
screwed with the wrong Mississippi boy in the
wrong army, you Nazi son of a bitch. Your days
are numbered, Adolf," drawled B.J., with all the
contempt he could muster.

"I refuse to listen to such imbecilic
trash, especially when it comes from an American
red neck," replied Weismann with ample sarcasm.
"I believe redneck is the correct terminology, is
it not, Colonel Patterson?" asked Weismann as he
slammed down the phone.

"At least he knows my feelings," said B.J.
aloud to the empty room.

B.J. knew it would be impossible for him to
keep tabs on Weismann, now. It was time for the
CIA boys to do their thing. He checked in with
the Pentagon EAC and left a message for General
Stone outlining most of his conversation with
Weismann, and suggesting that he had lost his
usefulness as far as Weismann was concerned. At
least he could hang around until time to nail
Weismann. He wanted to be in on that before he
retired. "What a way to retire!" said B.J. aloud

with a chuckle. B.J. dialed Clay Brinson's room in the G.W. Hotel.

"This is Warrant Officer Brinson speaking," answered Clay.

"Clay, Colonel Patterson here. You've lost your gadgets. Weismann is on to us. You might as well pack it in and go home."

."I figured that would happen when we nabbed Mrs. Sultoy. You sure there's nothing else I can do?"

"No. It's a CIA show, now. Thanks for your help, Clay. You did a great job. You'll be able to read about your role in this mess someday. In the mean time, say nothing about this to anyone. If your boss hassles you about your activities down here, give me a call. Bye for now."

B.J. felt better than he had in years. He left the office and decided to take his wife to one of the local gasthauses for dinner.

* * * * *

According to the cockpit clock, it was six o'clock in the morning, but there was no sign of the sun. The captain struggled to keep the Beneteau headed into the wind. The waves were high enough to capsize her if she was allowed to slide sideways. The hull and cargo might be able to survive should she capsize, but the rigging and mast would be stripped from the decks. The storm was taking its toll on the seamen: Both crewmen had been seasick for the past 24 hours and were in their bunks below, and the captain was exhausted. He had been fighting the tumult for the last eighteen hours without rest, but like a woman scorned, the sea kept attacking the Gatsby passionately and indiscriminately, tossing them about upon her whims. Several hours ago, he had lashed his safety harness to the cockpit for fear of being washed overboard. The mainsail

hoisting sheet snapped two hours ago, and he had
to roll in a third of the foresail to keep it
from ripping loose, but he could not afford to
roll in more; he had to keep the Gatsby under
sail in order to keep her into the wind. He had
even started the engine five hours ago to make up
for the lack of sail. Doing so had helped to
keep her into the wind, but could not do the job
alone. All he could do now is hope for the storm
to pass quickly. Having pushed himself beyond
his physical limitations, the captain soon was
unable to fight off the acute fatigue which
racked his body and drifted off to sleep.

The captain awoke with a start. Someone
was shaking him by the shoulders. It was one of
the crewmen. Something was blinding him—if only
his head would clear.

"We made it, captain!" shouted the crewman
repeatedly.

His senses slowly returned. He felt the
sun on his face. The Beneteau was still, and the
wind had vanished.

"How long have I been out?" asked the
captain shaking his head, still trying to clear
his thoughts.

"I don't know, captain. I came up on deck
just a moment ago and found you asleep at the
wheel," replied the crewman. "Are you all right,
captain? We made it! We made it!"

"Help me out of this harness. We must
assess the damage and begin repairs. Where is
Bartoli?"

"He is below cleaning up the mess."

The captain slowly looked around surveying
the damage. The mainsail lift sheet was
shredded; the port spar on the mast had snapped
at the capstan; and the mainsail was split from
top to bottom. The UHF and Loran C antennas were
missing, and the mast light was gone. The stern
bilge pump was not working, and there was ankle-

deep water below. Aside from that, the boat was in surprisingly good shape. A closer inspection, however, might reveal other problems. There was a backup GPS on board, so navigation would not be a problem. They could get by with the single side band radio. He flipped the engine's ignition switch to the off position to conserve fuel. They had been extremely lucky; damage could have been much worse. It was eleven o'clock in the morning, and the repairs would take the rest of the day. They should be under way by evening.

The captain put the crewmen to work and went below to fetch the hand held GPS. He wanted to know how far off course they were as a result of the storm. He returned to the cockpit, turned on the GPS and waited for it to receive at least three satellite readings, four would be better. The fourth satellite appeared on the tiny screen after a few more minutes. He pressed the location button and the Beneteau's longitude and latitude, to an accuracy of ten feet, appeared on the screen after three seconds. "A marvelous little device, this GPS," said the captain aloud. He hurried below to plot the coordinates on a chart. The coordinates were not on the chart he had been using before the storm had hit them, so he decided to check the charts immediately ahead and behind the last chart used for plotting. The coordinates did not appear on the chart behind. The chart ahead rendered better results. The Gatsby had actually made headway during the storm—about fifty kilometers, as near as he could tell. A shot with the sextant would verify the GPS readings. The captain had many years experience navigating with the sextant; the GPS was new, and he did not trust it completely. He moved to the bow and took a shot on the sun. When he plotted his sextant reading on the chart below, it matched the GPS coordinates exactly. "This boat has a patron saint," exclaimed the captain with a laugh. Now he would try to make a satellite phone call to Herr. Dieppe. He would surely be worried about them. Dieppe would have been watching the weather in the Atlantic. They had a pre-arranged code for such an occasion. If the boat was on schedule and without problems, the captain would ask to speak with Mr. Smith. If problems were encountered, but were under control, the captain would ask to speak with Marie. Problems of a severe nature would be reported in the clear. He dialed the number and waited. After a minute, the hotel desk answered. He asked to be connected to Herr. Dieppe's room. The phone rang. Dieppe answered.

"Hello. May I please speak with Marie?" asked the captain.

"I am sorry, but she is not here at the moment," replied Dieppe.

His message delivered, the captain turned his attention toward his vessel and his men. His first priority while the crewmen were working on the repairs was to go below to prepare his crew a meal. They had gone without food for almost two days.

* * * * *

The second Beneteau was making eight knots under full sail. The weather was perfect, and the wind was being very cooperative. They had missed the storm, but had experienced heavy seas for a day. The captain noted in the logbook that the boat was in perfect condition and was a half day ahead of schedule. They had been very fortunate. However, they were uncertain of their sister ship's condition. All the crew aboard the second Beneteau had heard the news of the storm on the weather broadcast and knew that the ship was somewhere in the storm's general vicinity. Abiding by some code of honor among thieves, they

were concerned and decided to risk a call to
ascertain the Gatsby's situation.

Chapter 13

April 19

Heinrich Dieppe walked from the hotel lobby to the hotel parking garage below, located his rental car, drove onto Biscayne Bay Boulevard, and headed south. He followed the signs to US Highway One and turned south again. It was ten o'clock in the morning, and he was meeting Enrico Charo for lunch at a place in Key Largo. Charo called the meeting. Dieppe thought he was probably nervous about something and wanted to play questions and answers.

Dieppe felt nervous himself. Despite all of his self assurances, he couldn't seem to shake an uneasy feeling that all was not well. He had hoped to gather himself during the long drive through the swamplands to the Keys, but he was not having much success. "It's taking too much time," he said aloud. "There's too much room for error." Because of this same time factor, Dieppe had objected to Weismann's insistence on using boats to move the warheads across the Atlantic in the first place. Then, after ignoring his instincts and agreeing with Weismann, the unexpected storm had struck. "That damn storm almost ruined everything," he complained out loud. The storm was not the only problem: There was the business with Mrs. Sultoy and Weismann's office being bugged. The latter disturbed him more than anything else. He wondered how much the Americans knew about Pegasus, and if they had informed the German authorities. Weismann had been so sure that no one would ever dream of their plans or intentions. He had assumed that he was the only person in the world to have superior intelligence since Adolf Hitler. "What an assuming fool," he said.

Dieppe believed that Weismann was an intelligent man, but he lacked street sense and had difficulty thinking and speaking like a common person. He thought of Weismann sitting in the Eagle's Nest like Adolf Hitler and thinking the world will readily embrace neo-Nazism. He said. "Well, it will take more than money to make him another Fuhrer." Dieppe considered that that was probably why Peter had wanted to retain a warhead—to force those who opposed him to become part of the rebirth of the Third Reich. "You are mad, Peter, and I am just as mad for being involved," Dieppe concluded.

The swamplands suddenly ended, and Dieppe found himself on the causeway leading to the Keys. He had no idea why Charo wanted to meet this far away from Miami but assumed he would find out soon enough. Key Largo was only eleven miles away.

Dieppe drove into Key Largo and continued following US Highway One. He drove for about a mile before he saw the restaurant marquee. Upon arrival at the restaurant, he immediately noticed two large, black Cadillacs parked conspicuously in front of the restaurant. Dieppe couldn't help but wonder why gangsters felt compelled to own large black cars. They weren't exactly inconspicuous. Maybe that was the point—to let people know who was present. While Dieppe parked in a space next to one of the Cadillac's, he noticed that there were no other cars in the parking lot. "I guess the big cars scared everyone away," he said to himself. Charo's gangster lifestyle was alien to Dieppe as were his habits. However, Dieppe concluded that most of the Nazis he had known were just as much an anathema.

Dieppe entered the restaurant and found it completely empty except for Charo, several bodyguards, and a waiter who looked harried and very nervous. Charo smiled and waved Dieppe over to his table. He was dressed in his usual white suit and dark shirt. One of the bodyguards pulled a chair away from the table for Dieppe, as though Dieppe might choose the wrong place to sit. Dieppe sat down, shook hands with Charo, and made a remark about Charo having the restaurant to himself.

"I often come here for business meetings. The proprietor is indebted to me and is happy to see that I have complete privacy," explained Charo proudly. "Our lunch will be here shortly, Herr. Dieppe; in the meantime, let us talk about our business venture."

"Do you have a concern about our business arrangements, Enrico?"

"Frankly, I do, my friend," smiled Charo. "I learned about a woman named Toffy Sultoy yesterday. I am told that she was being held in Germany for insurance purposes. You want to enlighten me, Herr. Dieppe?"

Dieppe was dumbfounded that Charo could have found out about Sultoy. How could he possibly have access to information about Pegasus to that degree of detail? Dieppe tried to hide his shock and to compose himself before answering. Charo was obviously enjoying himself, as if this were a game and he was winning.

"How did you get your information?" asked Dieppe calmly.

"I am disappointed, Herr. Dieppe. You underestimate me. Do you really think me fool enough not to have my own intelligence network? How do you think I stay alive?" asked Charo, raising his voice as his fist came down hard on the table top. He was obviously insulted.

"Forgive me, Mr. Charo. I did not ask the question to insult you; I asked the question because I am concerned that we might have a leak in our organization," insisted Dieppe calmly. If we have a leak, I must know about it. Surely you can appreciate my position, Mr. Charo."

Charo cleared his throat and put his perpetual smile back on his face. "Yes, I can appreciate your position and concern—as one businessman to another. But you have nothing to worry about, Dieppe, my information did not come from a leak in your organization. I own people in the DEA, Herr. Dieppe—that is how I know. I have several DEA agents on my payroll. You are an intelligent man, Herr. Dieppe. You should not be surprised."

"No, I suppose not. What else do you know, Enrico?"

"I know enough to tell you that we, both you and I, are being watched twenty-four hours a day. I know that your associate, Mr. Peter Weismann fell victim to American bugs. I also know that the name of your operation is Pegasus, and that your organization is transporting nuclear cargo across the Atlantic as we speak," said Charo, intensifying his smile.

"While I find all that interesting, Enrico, I fail to see how your newly found knowledge changes our business arrangements."

"Basically it makes no difference, except that the lack of discipline in your organization concerns me, Herr. Dieppe. How do I know that someone in your organization will not mention my name? Will I soon hear that the DEA has monitored some or all of our recent conversations, Herr. Dieppe? Unless you can assure me that you will immediately tighten your organizational security, I will terminate our association here and now. Do you clearly understand what I am saying, Herr. Dieppe?"

"Quite clearly. I can give you that assurance right now," says Dieppe.

"Good. I am pleased, because if I get any further indication that information is being leaked, you will be history, Herr. Dieppe, if you get my meaning," said Charo, slowly and deliberately. "Now, eat your lobster," said Charo with a broader than usual smile.

Charo joked and talked during their meal as though nothing of an unpleasant nature had passed between them. He spoke of his love for Latin music and women, the stupidity of the United States government, and his fear that controlled drugs might be legalized in America. No further mention was made of Pegasus. Dieppe said nothing. He ate, trying to enjoy the lobster in spite of a tense stomach. One of the bodyguards walked up to the table and whispered something into Charo's ear. Charo listened intently, rose from the table, said goodbye, and departed quickly without an explanation.

The lobster on Dieppe's plate remained half eaten. He did not feel well. The meeting made him very uneasy and left him with feelings of despair, and preeminent danger. He truly had underestimated Charo's intelligence, or he had overestimated his own. He felt as empty as the restaurant.

The drive back to Miami seemed endless. Dieppe had to contact Weismann immediately and emphasize the need for security. He had believed all along that the two of them should be directing this operation from a single location, not with Weismann in one place and him in another. How would they communicate now? He made a decision that would solve that problem. As soon as he reached the hotel, he would send a telegram to Weismann. It will read: "Urgent that you meet me at our friend's house in Brazil as soon as possible. Heinrich." Peter would have no alternative. He could not take the chance of turning his back on something that might be critical to the success of Pegasus. "Yes, he will be there," said Dieppe aloud.

When he finished packing, Dieppe called the airport and reserved a seat on the first available flight to Rio. He then went to the main lobby in the hotel and sent telegrams to Weismann and Feltgeibell. The telegraph to Feltgeibell informed him that he and Weismann would be arriving in Brazil within the next twelve hours. He drove to the airport, turned in the rental car, and proceeded to the American Airline counter to pick up his ticket. Dieppe found a seat in a remote part of the waiting lounge, and made himself comfortable for the two hour wait until flight time. He decided to use the time to sort out the mess Pegasus was becoming. Although Dieppe had no idea of what might be transpiring in Brazil, the benefit of having Weismann, Feltgeibell, and himself together at one location to have secure communication once again far outweighed the chance that all was not well. He needed not to worry about communicating with Anatole and Popodopolous because they were essentially finished with their involvement in Pegasus, and Reifenstahl would be fine by himself; his job was little more than providing transportation. "A short nap might be beneficial," he said to himself, and quickly fell asleep.

Chapter 14

April 21

Weismann's flight from Frankfurt International Airport to Rio had been dreadful. Thunder and lightning storms followed them across the Atlantic. He hoped the storms had not reached the surface and endangered the boats carrying their volatile cargo. It concerned him enough to have one of the flight attendants ask the captain if he thought the storms were reaching the ocean surface. The captain thought not.

Dieppe's frantic call for a meeting, especially in Brazil, annoyed Weismann to no end. "I think more clearly in the Eagle's Nest," he mused. He found the ghost of Hitler there inspirational. Sometimes he even thought Hitler spoke to him from the grave. "If only you were alive today," said Weismann sighing. His thoughts were interrupted by an announcement.

"Please fasten your seat belts and return your seats to the upright position, ladies and gentlemen," said the voice of a flight attendant. "Please notice that the captain has activated the no smoking sign. We will be landing in Rio in approximately fifteen minutes. The local time in Rio is 2200 hours, and the ground temperature is thirty-two degrees centigrade. There is light rain in the area."

When Weismann entered the arrival terminal, he saw Erich Feltgeibell and Dieppe, who had arrived two hours earlier, waiting for him. Dieppe looked very tired. Feltgeibell appeared as calm and as unperturbed as ever. Sometimes Weismann thought Feltgeibell's propensity for unflappable calm was really a cover for inferior intelligence. He truly missed not having an intellectual equal among his associates.

"I'm glad you decided to come, Peter," said Dieppe nervously. "We really need to talk."

"Yes, obviously. You look quite troubled, Heinrich."

"My car is waiting, Peter. We will go to my office and have a late dinner. I have arranged to have dinner catered. We will talk there," responded Erich.

The car ride was unexpectedly quiet on the way to Erich's office. Weismann did not trust the driver, so he sidestepped any attempt at conversation about Pegasus. Dieppe soon got the message and withdrew into his thoughts. All the while, Erich chatted about the weather, politics, and the status of the export business. They soon reached Erich's office in Ipanema.

Erich led them upstairs over his office where he had his quarters, a rather tastefully furnished apartment with large, open rooms. The dining area was open to the street and presented a pleasant view of the ocean. Food was being placed on the table as they took their seats. When the last glass of wine had been poured, Erich dismissed the caterer and invited his associates to eat. Erich and Dieppe patiently waited for Weismann to begin the conversation. Both men had learned to handle Weismann's moods like this by deferring conversation to him. Weismann finally spoke.

"What is the latest on the boats, Heinrich?" asked Weismann quietly.

"They are both a full day ahead of schedule, and report no problems. They were both fortunate to have survived the storm," replied Dieppe.

"Good. And when are you going to tell me why we are having this meeting?" asked Weismann calmly.

"I suppose as soon as we finish our dinner, Peter, if that is satisfactory to you," replied Dieppe.

"Very well," said Weismann.

In a few minutes Erich finished his dinner, pushed his chair back and carefully lit a large cigar. Dieppe took Erich's cue and pushed his chair back from the table, and declined Erich's offer of a cigar. Finally, Weismann meticulously arranged his plate, wine glass, and napkin and pushed his chair back from the table as well. He accepted a cigar from Erich and allowed Erich to light it.

"So, Heinrich, why are we here?" asked Weismann.

"We are here, Peter, because too much has transpired to allow us to continue Pegasus with you in the Eagle's Nest and me four thousand miles away. Things are happening too fast, and secure communication between us over distance is no longer possible. We have to assume the Americans know everything about Pegasus, Peter. I no longer want the sole responsibility of making decisions not knowing how you will react to my judgment. We have to be co-located, Peter," said Dieppe with calm deliberation.

Weismann said nothing. He stared at Dieppe without expression, as though his mind were a thousand miles away. Erich stared at Weismann with growing concern for what might happen next. He fully expected Weismann to explode into a fit of rage, but he did not. Dieppe remained relatively calm to his own surprise.

"Of what are you afraid, Heinrich? Are you afraid that the Americans know enough to interrupt Pegasus and arrest all of us? Are you afraid that the Brazilian authorities will wait in ambush at the docks to seize the boats and the warheads? You said you assumed they know everything. I am telling you, Heinrich, that they know nothing beyond the fact that the warheads were stolen and are on the high seas on the way to somewhere. Are they tracking the boats? Certainly. Will they stop and board the boats at some point? Of course not. They would not take the chance; they would assume the captains have orders to scuttle the boats if anyone attempts to stop and board them, and they would be correct in their assumption, would they not?

That is correct, is it not, Heinrich?" repeated Weismann.

"Yes. Yes, of course the captains have orders to scuttle the boats if someone attempts to board them, Peter. But that is not the issue. At some point, Peter, the authorities will intercede. American, Brazilian, German—who knows? They will not simply stand aside and allow us to complete Pegasus," countered Heinrich. Now they were getting to the real issues that concerned Heinrich.

"Heinrich, my friend, we will complete Pegasus—just as we planned. I agree with you to some extent. I know that they are tracking the boats and monitoring any electronic emissions from the boats with satellites. They also probably have at least one submarine following the boats, but they do not know the details of the rest of the operation. They do not know of our association with the cartel in Colombia, nor what we intend to do with the warheads."

"Then why did they let us steal them, Peter?" asked Heinrich. "Why did they not stop our people inside the storage and assembly buildings? I'll tell you why, Peter. They didn't stop us because they know precisely what we intend to do with the warheads. They want us, Charo, the warheads and the heroin," said Heinrich in a firm and slightly agitated voice.

"You forget, Heinrich that we have a warhead in reserve to deal with the unexpected." replied Weismann.

"No. I have not forgotten, but I think you are placing too much value on the hostage effect of that warhead. Besides they will certainly look first around Berchtesgaden for that warhead," replied Heinrich with growing irritation.

"My friends!" exclaimed Erich as he stood. "What are you doing? You sound like two school boys having a debate. It does not matter what they know or do not know. We still have the upper hand so long as we have possession of at least one warhead that can be well hidden," said Erich. "Peter, we must preempt their advantage by letting them know we have a warhead in reserve that can be easily employed to destroy any city we choose, at any moment we choose. Why are the two of you making things more difficult than necessary?"

All three men were silent for a moment. Weismann and Dieppe were looking at Erich with intense interest. Weismann decided he might have been wrong about Erich Feltgeibell's intelligence. Dieppe was appreciative of the fact that Erich had broken the confrontation with a suggestion that made sense.

"You are correct, Erich," said Dieppe. "Preempt their advantage. It makes sense. What do you think, Peter?" asked Dieppe. Weismann paused before he spoke.

"I agree. That is exactly what we shall do," said Weismann.

"Then we should send the message to the Americans via your point of contact, Peter. Lieutenant Colonel Billy Joe Patterson of Mississippi," said Heinrich imitating Patterson's drawl.

"Excellent idea, Heinrich. I'll prepare a place for him on the other side of the rubble in the GW tunnel complex. It will not occur to them to look there for Colonel Patterson or the warhead," said Weismann.

"What about Geiger counters? Could not a Geiger counter be used to detect the warhead?" asked Erich.

"Not through twenty feet of rubble," replied Weismann.

"What is in the tunnel on the other side of the rubble?" asked Erich.

"More storage rooms. The rooms that belonged to the Fuhrer and Eva Braun," replied Weismann.

"I recommend you use some of our friends in the Munich group of The New World Order to handle the kidnapping of Colonel Patterson and for doing the tunnel work," said Dieppe.

"Yes. I had already thought of that, Heinrich," replied Weismann. "They can be trusted and will not ask too many questions. It will please them to become more actively involved in NWO activities."

"So you will kidnap Patterson?" asked Erich.

"Yes, why not? He can keep the warhead company and increase the hostage value of the warhead," said Weismann with a smile. "I shall enjoy making that uncouth imbecile squirm. Heinrich, I am pleased that you insisted on this meeting; however, I will be unable to stay with you. I must attend to matters in Berchtesgaden immediately, and I would like you back in Miami, Heinrich. That mobster Charo is not to be trusted."

"Very well, Peter," said Dieppe. "That means we will be forced to communicate in the clear unless you wish to use pay telephones." Weismann ignored Dieppe's remark.

"I am very tired. Would you be so kind as to show me to my room, Erich," asked Weismann. "Heinrich, please book me on the next flight to Frankfurt A.M. Good night."

At ten o'clock the next morning Weismann departed Rio for Frankfurt A.M. and Dieppe's flight to Miami departed an hour later. Dieppe had not accomplished all that he had hoped for during their meeting, but he now felt better about their insurance arrangements. He was still very uncomfortable about how much Charo might know, but was glad that he had not broached this subject with Weismann. That would have just added fuel to the Weismann fire and clouded the primary issue at hand. Dieppe was satisfied that the meeting had accomplished more than he had expected. He would let well enough alone.

Upon arrival in Miami, Dieppe took public transportation from the airport to Coral Gables, just north of Miami. He checked into a modest motel and sent for the remainder of his things from the Miami hotel. He called Charo from a nearby pay phone to let him know of his new location.

Chapter 15

April 23

Watching sailboats on satellite monitors, combined with the constant noise level of the agents that filled his crowded living room, was getting to Hamp, so he was pleased when General Stone called and said that he was flying in with one of the President's personal advisors for a first hand situational briefing. It was ten o'clock in the morning when Hamp got to the little grassy air strip outside Steinhatchee, and ten forty-five when the helicopter sat down at the Gainesville airport to meet General Stone's flight. He was flying commercially to avoid the publicity of an air force plane landing at the municipal airport. An occasional plainly marked DEA helicopter landing at the airport did not arouse suspicion. The flight was right on schedule. Hamp met the General and the President's man Miles Honeycutt in the baggage claim area of the small terminal. From there, Hamp escorted the two gentlemen to the waiting DEA helicopter. Since the pilot was a DEA agent, they could talk freely using the helicopter's intercom system.

"What's new on your end of things, sir?" inquired Hamp.

"Actually I just wanted to get the hell out of Dodge for awhile, Hamp. However, I do want a detailed run down on your end of things, and the President wants us to give Honeycutt a detailed operational briefing. I also thought it might be a good idea to update the entire group on the Washington perspective. Is Gregory crowding you too much, Hamp?"

"Not at all, sir. In fact he has bent over backwards to be cooperative," replied Hamp with genuine sincerity. "The same goes for the FBI boys—no problems at all."

"Glad to hear that. If you don't mind, Hamp, I would prefer to wait until I can brief everyone to say much more about this operation. I'm too tired to repeat myself for two hours."

"Suits me, sir. "Just one question of a personal nature and I'll let you catch a catnap, sir. What is Colonel Sultoy's situation? Do the Turkish authorities know anything about what's going on?"

"As far as we are able to surmise, they don't know anything. They believe Colonel Sultoy to be on legitimate sick leave. Also, Mrs. Sultoy is at home once again. There is no reason to expect any further action against either one of them from Weismann or the Turkish authorities at this time," replied the General. "But down the road could be another story when the Turks find out about the theft of the warheads. They will not be happy campers. Colonel Sultoy did decide of his own free will to participate in the theft, even though the circumstances were extremely mitigating."

General Stone closed his eyes as he spoke, then laid his head back and drifted off to sleep, something he had not been able to do in two days. Hamp was relieved that Sully would not fall under immediate Turkish disciplinary action. The Turks have a reputation for being harsh on those who violate military regulations. They would really throw the book at him for assisting with the theft of nuclear weapons. Hamp could not even imagine what they would do to him. He would have to think of something to make Sully a hero rather than the villain. He also wanted to ask the General about Patterson's status, but it would have to wait. Hamp radioed in their expected arrival time and closed his eyes for a catnap,

too.   He had barely closed his eyes when
Honeycutt shook him by the arm.

"Who is Sultoy?   How is the Turkish
government involved in this?   Does the State
Department know what's going on?" demanded
Honeycutt in rapid fire mode.

"A Colonel in the Turkish Army.   They are
not involved.   Yes, State knows what's going on,"
said Hamp without looking at Honeycutt.   "Now if
you will excuse me, I would like to get some
sleep."   Hamp noted a slight smile on General
Stone's face.

Gregory was waiting for them at the
airstrip when they landed.   He shook the
General's hand first, then Honeycutt's, and, for
the sake of protocol, Hamp opened the car door
for all three.

General Stone and .Gregory chatted about
Washington politics during the drive back to
Steinhatchee while Honeycutt kept looking out of
the window as though he were in a different
country.   His facial expression looked as though
he had detected a bad odor.

"A bit of culture shock, Honeycutt?" asked
Hamp with a smile.

"Now   I   understand   the   expression
boondocks," replied Honeycutt.   "This place is
something out of a Deep South novel."

"First time out of the city?" suggested
Hamp with an even bigger smile.   "Some of us call
this place civilization." Honeycutt looked at
Hamp with distinct displeasure but said nothing.
Hamp decided he was going to enjoy disliking this
man.

When their contingent arrived at Hamp's
home, now referred to as Pentagon South by the
agents working there, Hamp called everyone
together.   He wanted to give General Stone an
opportunity to make remarks to the assemblage so
General Stone could get some rest.

"It's my pleasure to be here gentlemen. I just want to make a few remarks, and then you can go about your business. You can brief Mr. Honeycutt and me in the morning. The President wants Mr. Honeycutt to get the full dog and pony show; you will need a little time to prepare," said the General. "Now allow me to bring you all up to speed on where we are in Washington."

The General stood in front of the fireplace, and the ten or so agents gathered around in a semicircle in front of him. He was in civilian clothes, and Hamp noticed how tired and old he suddenly looked.

"Gentlemen, I came here directly from the White House. The Chief of Staff and I briefed the President, in detail, on what was going on with Pegasus. Frankly the President is less than pleased that we allowed seven nuclear warheads to be taken from the custody of US Armed Forces."

"The President is pissed," interrupted Honeycutt. "He thinks you all are fumbling idiots to have allowed this abomination and fears for the safety of the world," yelled Honeycutt waving his arms as he spoke. "I can assure you that heads will roll in the Pentagon hallways if something happens to those warheads, people—and the FBI and DEA as well! You have all handled this situation badly. Hell, according to White House legal counsel, your agencies have acted illegally by forming a task force without the President's knowledge or approval. You and your bosses could all go to jail for that alone."

General Stone stared at Honeycutt without a trace of emotion. Gregory was red-faced and chewed on his cigar butt furiously. The senior FBI agent was visibly gritting his teeth. Hamp couldn't believe this jerk's behavior. The rest of the agents wore looks of disbelief. Finally, General Stone spoke again, this time ignoring Honeycutt.

"Jim, will two of your men escort Mr. Honeycutt to the airstrip, please? Have them take him to Gainesville and see that he makes his way onto the next flight north." said General Stone. Jim Gregory smiled as he nodded acknowledgement.

"That will be my distinct pleasure, General," replied Gregory. Gregory motioned to two of his men who each took one of Honeycutt's arms and escorted the wide-eyed, dumbfounded man from the room.

"You will hear from this. It will be the mistake of your career, General," yelled Honeycutt in a squeaky voice as he was hurried through the door. "You are all going to be sorry."

"Now where was I, gentlemen, before that foul-mouthed pipsqueak interrupted me?" asked the General calmly.

"You and the Chief briefed the President this morning, sir," replied Hamp as he smiled.

"Oh, yes. Thank you. I must reluctantly agree with Mr. Honeycutt that the President was indeed upset with us, but that's nothing new. The Pentagon stays in a running gun battle with the White House that is kept quiet by both sides. The President wants the public to think he supports the military establishment, and the military establishment wants the public to think they support the President as Commander in Chief. I doubt seriously that he would allow a White House leak on this issue. He's afraid the Pentagon will say they had Presidential approval—and we did initially, until his staff caused him to get a bad case of cold feet. But that has little to do with Pegasus; I have digressed too far."

"You all know that Colonel Patterson's electronic surveillance of Herr. Weismann is over, but at least it accomplished something.

Mrs. Sultoy was reunited with her husband, and we gleaned a good deal of information from Weismann's telephone conversations with his associates. That, too, is now over. Walter Gibbs' people learned that two local men were found murdered near Boctoi, and that three bodies had washed onto the rocks near Ephesus. Apparently, Weismann and his associates are eliminating witnesses by killing their workers as they go. Two days ago Weismann flew to Rio, was met by Dieppe and Feltgeibell, and was taken to Feltgeibell's home. We do not know the purpose of his trip to Brazil. We can only conclude that he had Pegasus business with Dieppe and Feltgeibell. The question we have now, gentlemen, which has top intelligence priority, is will they change their plans now that they know we are on to them? We must have an answer to that question and soon—the boats will make port somewhere, if not Brazil, in a few more days. To make matters worse, another villain has raised his head. Walter Gibbs has learned the Brazilian government is planning a massive campaign against the drug traffic lanes that run through their country from Colombia. The cartel's shipment will be somewhere between the jungles in western Brazil and the plains along the Amazon basin during the raids. Should the shipment be intercepted by the Brazilians, there is no telling what Weismann might decide to do with the warheads. The last thing we need is for the warheads to go on the market for sale to the highest bidder, but we fear that is exactly what would happen," explained the General.

"So how do we ensure the safety of the shipment?" asked Hamp.

"We tip the cartel off," interrupted Gregory.

"The Chief, Wilbur Burns, and the President agree with you, Jim," replied the General. "We want your input as to how to accomplish the tip-off."

Gregory walked to one of the big windows overlooking the gulf and stared silently at the sea for a moment. The hotline from the EAC in the Pentagon interrupted the silence with its peculiar ring. One of the agents answered and talked briefly with someone on the other end. He watched General Stone as he listened to the voice from the EAC.

"General Stone, Lieutenant Colonel B.J. Patterson has disappeared from his quarters at the General Walker Hotel in Berchtesgaden," announced the agent gravely.

General Stone let out a deep breath and rubbed his forehead with both hands. "The plot thickens, gentlemen. Okay, let's handle these situations one at a time. Jim, have you thought of a way to get to the cartel?"

"Yes, General, I have. I'll meet with their man personally," replied Gregory.

"I can't believe that you, the Director of the DEA, are suggesting a one on one meeting with your number one adversary," said the senior FBI agent.

"Is that the smart thing to do, Jim?" interjected the General.

"Yes. It is the smart thing to do," Hamp heard himself say. "How could he refuse to meet with Mr. Gregory—his nemesis—his archenemy? It's perfect!" blurted Hamp. "But there is a damned good chance you wouldn't come back, sir," said Hamp as an afterthought.

"Jim, that's too big of a chance to take," said the General.

"I'm willing to take it. Unless you and the Chief have very strong objections, General, I'll call the President now and get his clearance," responded Gregory. He waited for the General's response. He of course didn't need the

General or the Chief's approval; he was simply being courteous.

"I think I can speak for the Chief. Do it," said the General. "Gentlemen, that about concludes what information I had to share with you. Please do what you can to brain storm the intelligence gap I told you about. I would like to leave here tomorrow with a solution. Let me hear what you think of the Patterson disappearance, too."

The General took Hamp by the arm and walked out onto the deck. He breathed in deeply savoring the salt air and cool breeze. Hamp waited patiently for him to speak.

"I have one of my inexplicably bad feelings, Hamp. You remember an occasion or two when I've had them, don't you?"

"Yes, sir, I certainly do remember. You had one of those feelings just before the North Vietnamese Army attacked down the Street Without Joy," replied Hamp with a smile.

"Well this one is of the same nature. Hamp, I think Weismann is holding at least one warhead, maybe more, as a hostage-maker. I think that's why he doesn't care that we are tracking his boats. I didn't want to say anything about it during my remarks a moment ago. Gregory would think me insane."

"Do you think B.J. Patterson's disappearance has anything to do with it?" asked Hamp.

"Probably so. Aside from Patterson's value as a hostage, I'm not at all clear as to Weismann's reason for kidnapping him."

"You do think Weismann kidnapped B.J.?" asked Hamp.

"Without a doubt. I'm hoping that Walter Gibbs and his people in Germany will have some additional insight. I'll call Walter when we go back inside. By the way, Walter's researchers at

Langley have been burning the midnight oil on Weismann's background and on his ties with many of the neo-Nazi organizations in Europe and the United States. Their efforts might produce a link to his present behavior we have so far overlooked."

"You want me back in Germany, sir?" asked Hamp.

"No. At least not yet. We'll cut Clay Brinson and the CID in on Patterson's probable kidnapping. For the time being, I want you here. If I'm correct in my assumptions, Weismann and Charo will stick to their plan and bring the heroin in by way of the gulf. When are you expecting the boats to reach Brazil?"

"They are about eight hundred miles from Brazil now, and expected weather conditions over the next week between their present location and Brazil favor sailing. I would say they could dock in four or five days," replied Hamp. Gregory came out on the deck and joined them. He apologized for breaking in on their conversation.

"The President will not allow me to go to Brazil, General. I suggest we send Hamp. He can take a chopper to Gainesville in about ten minutes and catch the last shuttle flight to Miami. That will get him there in time to catch the American Airlines redeye flight from Miami to Rio. He'll be there by eight o'clock in the morning."

"I'm very uncomfortable with your plan, Jim, but I believe you are correct. Hamp, how do you feel about going?"

"I have no problem with it, sir."

"I'll contact my man in Rio, Hamp. He'll meet you at the airport in Rio," said Gregory. "On another subject, General, what is your best guess on Patterson's disappearance?" asked Gregory.

"Hamp and I were just discussing that. I'm fairly certain Weismann kidnapped him. For the time being, we'll let CID handle it with help from Walter Gibbs and his people. If Gibbs thinks it necessary, we will ask the German authorities to help as well. In fact, I need to call Walter now. If you will excuse me, gentlemen," said the General as he walked back into the house.

"Hamp, may I drive you to the airstrip?" asked Gregory.

"Yes, I'd like that, Jim. I'll throw a few things in a bag and meet you downstairs in five minutes." That was the very first time Gregory had called Hamp by his first name. Hamp was impressed and a little honored. Gregory was a tough cookie and devoted little time to friends and social frills.

On their way to the airstrip, they talked about the DEA's role in the anticipated interception of Weismann's drug shipment to Charo and company, and Gregory told Hamp something of his agent in Rio that would meet him at the airport.

"Our street sources of information have completely dried up, Hamp. We are getting absolutely nothing. The snitches are running scared. My undercover man, Lewis Ramerez, said even Charo's men are not talking to each other," bemoaned Gregory.

"Charo has really put a lid on his organization, huh?" replied Hamp. "Do you think he has learned Weismann was being electronically monitored?"

"A good probability. Their intelligence system can be better than ours at times. It's not unusual for snitches to get lockjaw just prior to a big drug transaction, but not this tight," explained Gregory. "There is something going on that I can't quite put my finger on."

Hamp pulled up to the Huey and stopped. The blade was turning at idle; the crew was ready to fly. Quickly the two gentlemen said their goodbyes, and Hamp boarded the aircraft. As soon as he was secured aboard, the Huey lifted into the night sky and faded away, its lights becoming indistinguishable from the stars.

Chapter 16

April 24

B.J. tried to focus his eyes, but could make out only a blurred light immediately in front of him. His head was exploding, he was nauseous, and his mouth tasted like a bivouac site of the Russian Army. His thoughts were muddled. Had he been in an accident? Slowly, what had happened to him began to come back. He recited the details as they came to him. "He pulled into the GW parking area in the rear of the hotel about nine-thirty last night, got out of the sedan, then someone—or something—hit him from behind on the back of his neck. Someone—yeah, there were two of them—held him on the ground and put a cloth over his mouth and nose."

He remembered a very strong odor, then nothing, just blackness. "Where the hell am I?" he shouted at the light, and then lost consciousness again. The darkness felt warm and protective.

When B.J. regained consciousness he was painfully aware that his hands and feet were tied to the chair in which he was sitting. His head was still in a state of volcanic eruption, but his vision had cleared. He was in a room with concrete walls and floor, no windows, a single metal door, and one exposed light bulb that hung glaringly from the low ceiling. There were no furnishings in the room, just the chair in which he sat. He was thirsty enough to empty the Rhine and Danube rivers. More than anything else, he was angry. He was lucid enough to believe that Weismann had kidnapped him, but for what reason he was not sure. B.J. sat in the cool, damp room for what seemed like hours thinking about his predicament and thanking the Lord that he had sent his wife on to the States to look for a house. The silence in the room was suddenly replaced by the sound of a key turning in the latch of the door. The door opened and Weismann entered the room with an exaggerated smirk on his face.

"You have rejoined the living I see, Colonel Patterson. I am truly sorry about the bump on your head and the aftereffects of the chloroform, but I assumed that you would of course resist my associates. Do you recognize the room, Colonel Patterson? You are in one of the Hess rooms."

"You assumed correctly, you son of a bitch," said B.J. through clinched teeth. "Untie me and I'll show you how much I would have resisted."

"Ah. Such a passionate man. You know, Colonel Patterson, the intelligent man learns how to control his temper," said Weismann mockingly, obviously enjoying himself. "But not everyone is intelligent. Tell me, Colonel Patterson, are there intelligent people in Mississippi?"

"Cut the crap, Weismann. Why am I here and what do you want?" demanded B.J.

"You are here, Colonel Patterson, because you are going to deliver a message to your superiors. While I consider you a most unpleasant and marginally functional person, I do realize that you will lend credibility and authenticity to my message," explained Weismann.

"And what message might that be, you pedantic ass?"

"My, my. Don't you know, Colonel Patterson, that profanity is considered a cover up for one's inability to express oneself adequately?" sneered Weismann, enjoying his temporary advantage over B.J. Then Weismann suddenly turned deadly serious. Leaning down and moving his face to within inches of B.J.'s face he stared intently into B.J.'s eyes, and then he spoke very slowly and deliberately in a whisper.

"You will make a phone call to the superior of your choice. I do not care whom. You will tell this person that Peter Weismann has in his possession a twenty megaton nuclear warhead. You will tell this person that if any action is taken to interfere with the impending business transaction between Mr. Charo, Mr. Estabo, and me, that I will use the warhead to destroy a major city, the name of which will not be divulged. You will tell this person that the warhead is already located in the city that I have chosen," explained Weismann. He continued to stare into B.J.'s eyes for several seconds.

"How am I supposed to authenticate your possession of the weapon? Are you going to show it to me?" asked B.J.

"Yes. I am going to show it to you, Colonel Patterson. All we have to do is walk a few steps across the hall," replied Weismann.

Weismann untied B.J.'s feet and helped him stand. It took a moment for him to gain control of his balance and feet. Weismann made certain that the bindings on his arms and wrists were secure, and then led B.J. by the arm out the door, across the hall to another room just like the one in which he was being held captive. The vintage sign on the door read simply "HITLER".

"As you may have surmised, Colonel Patterson, we are in the section of tunnel that has been closed off since 1945. We dug through the rubble and built a temporary mini-tunnel to allow us access to this end of the tunnel. Should anyone attempt to enter the tunnel complex through the familiar doorway, an electrical switch will trigger a device that will quickly close the mini-tunnel to this side. No one would ever suspect the rubble had been disturbed. My associates from Munich engineered that little

mechanism. Its quite brilliant, I think,"
bragged Weismann. "By the way, your gift of the
blueprints was most helpful, Colonel Patterson."

Weismann opened the door and pushed B.J.
into the room. A single light bulb hung from the
ceiling just like the one in the other room.
B.J. remembered from the tunnel complex
blueprints that for all practical purposes all
the storage rooms were identical. A youthful
looking man dressed in work pants and a pullover
sweater was sitting on a folding chair behind a
small table. He was tall, blonde, blue-eyed, and
powerfully built. No doubt he was one of
Weismann's Aryan specimens. The young man stood
at attention when Weismann entered the room.

"This is Dieter, Colonel Patterson; he will
be your companion for a short while. He is also
here to guard this," said Weismann as he pointed
to an object on the floor behind the little desk.
"Yes, Colonel Patterson, it is a nuclear
warhead," said Weismann as he nodded to Dieter.
The young man, with great difficulty, stood the
heavy container up on end and carefully slid the
protective cylinder from the container revealing
what B.J. instantly recognized as a high yield
nuclear warhead fitted for use on a U.S. Army
Pershing Missile. He stared in disbelief. The
warhead appeared to be in the fifteen to twenty-
five megaton range. B.J. suddenly felt sick, and
his head began to pound again. "You crazy
swastika you're not bluffing," blurted B.J.

The young man put the protective sleeve
back on the warhead and carefully laid it back
down on the floor.

"Now you will make the telephone call, and
I warn you, Colonel Patterson, if you make a
mistake, your wife will be the one to pay for it.
We have many associates in the United States,
Colonel Patterson. Her demise can be instantly
arranged by one simple phone call."

The young man held the telephone receiver to B.J.'s head, and asked what number to dial. B.J. gave him the number of the USAREUR Headquarters Emergency Action Center. The EAC operator answered on the first ring.

"Please identify yourself," demanded the voice from the EAC.

"This is Lieutenant Colonel Billy Joe Patterson from the Armed Forces Recreation Center in Berchtesgaden. My social security number is 111-78-0098," replied B.J.

"One moment, please," replied the operator. Then the voice said, "How can I help you, sir?"

"Please put me through to the Pentagon EAC. This is an emergency call."

There is a brief pause of about ten seconds as the autovon switching mechanism connected the two EAC facilities utilizing a defense department satellite. The Pentagon EAC answered instantly.

"This is Lieutenant Colonel Billy Joe Patterson. I have a priority one message for Lieutenant General Stone, the Department of the Army Inspector General," said B.J. He knew the priority one message status would trigger two things. First, it would start an immediate hunt for General Stone. Second, it would mean convincing the EAC duty officer of his identity. He was prepared to do that. The duty officer came on the line.

"This is Major Stockwell, sir, the EAC duty officer. You are not on the ready access roster. I need proof of your identity in order to process your request."

"My name should appear on your situational report board as missing from duty, Major Stockwell," replied B.J. There was a short pause.

"That is correct. Your request will be processed. Please stand by." Thirty seconds passed.

"Colonel Patterson, this is General Stone. Where are you? What is your situation?"

"I'm in the custody of Herr. Weismann, General. I can only read to you from a piece of paper Herr. Weismann just handed me. Please listen closely, sir; he's sitting on a high yield Pershing Missile warhead. I've seen it. Message follows: 'Should any action be undertaken to thwart the business dealings of Enrico Charo, Pablo Sanchez Estabo, and me, the nuclear device in my possession will be detonated in a major city on the European continent." B.J. paused. "I believe the crazy swastika means it, General."

"Hang tight, Colonel Patterson. I wish I could say everything was going to be all right," said the General. "Tell Weismann we believe him."

Weismann took the receiver from B.J. and returned it to its cradle. Dieter guided B.J. back to the other room and secured his legs and feet to the chair again with heavy tape, and then left the room as Weismann entered with a Walther PPK in his right hand. "I understand that you Mississippi rednecks like to go hunting. I also hear that sometimes you hunt with dogs—something about the excitement of hearing the dogs run your prey through the woods.—very sporting of you. I, too, love to hunt; however, I find the "thrill of the chase" is quite overrated. I prefer the "thrill of the kill", Weismann drawled, mimicking B.J.

Realizing that he was about to become Wesimann's prey, B.J. said, "Go ahead and kill me you Nazi swastika, but I promise you, that you will get what's coming to you."

"I'll be anticipating the feeble act of retribution, Colonel. Patterson," replied Weismann. "Meanwhile, I'll have to rely on the pleasure of killing you as entertainment." Weismann raised the Walther, placed the muzzle just behind B.J.'s left ear, and pulled the trigger—the same technique employed thousands of times by Nazi SS guards and officers in a dozen concentration camps in Germany and Poland. Having done so, Weismann took a handkerchief from his jacket pocket and wiped droplets of blood from his right hand, jacket sleeve, and the pistol. He then walked to the other room.

"Dieter, dispose of the body in the rubble pile, and then continue your work with the warhead. Will you and the others have any difficulty in preparing the warhead for movement by tomorrow night?"

"No, Herr. Doktor. The Egyptian sarcophagus is complete except for applying the gold trim. The paint should be dry in two or three hours. All we have to do tonight is move the warhead to the museum work shed in Munich and place it in the sarcophagus. We plan to do that about three in the morning when no one is moving around. Tomorrow afternoon it will be on display in the Munich museum with the Egyptian collection," Dieter proudly explained.

"Very good. Professor Albrecht will join you tomorrow morning to install the timer and detonating device. Call me at my office when everything is complete."

Professor Albrecht was a retired teacher of physics who had supported the birth and growth of the neo-Nazi movement in West Germany from the very beginning. He led the German research and development of the jet aircraft and V-1 rocket near the end of the war. He had happily agreed to assemble the warhead arming device for Weismann.

Weismann departed the GW tunnel complex through the back door to the electrical equipment room and drove to the Eagle's Nest. He poured himself a drink and contemplated the blood stains on his jacket sleeve. "What a shame. This was a new jacket," said Weismann aloud. He removed the jacket and threw it into the fireplace.

It would be about 0700 hours in Coral Gables— a good time to catch Dieppe in his room. He dialed the number Dieppe had given him. The phone rang three times before Dieppe answered.

"Dieppe here."

"Heinrich, the insurance policy has been delivered. Have you anything to report?"

"No. Everything is as it should be," replied Dieppe, and hung up

Weismann stared into the flames in the fireplace. The brandy warmed him and allowed him to relax enough to concentrate on the success of Pegasus thus far. He thought through the risk of what he had just done and recited his thoughts aloud. "What could they do now? Would they start an international man hunt? Hardly. Not a nation in the world would run the risk of the consequences. After all, I could have more than one nuclear warhead in reserve. How would they know? They might be able to monitor the whereabouts and electronic emissions of the boats, but they have no way of knowing how many warheads are on board. Undoubtedly the Americans will alert the German authorities, now that a threat has been made against a European city. Will they arrest me? Not as long as the hostage-maker remains undiscovered. They cannot risk it."

Weismann then considered all who were part of this magnificent scheme. "What if someone involved decided to become disloyal." He wondered if there was a possibility of Dieter or the others talking. "No. They are proud Aryan supremacists who are loyal to me ,and to the New World Order until death."

The logs shifted in the fireplace causing the flames to leap higher and then to burn steadily again. Unmoved, Weismann continued his musings. "Will Charo or Costellano do anything

stupid? No. They need the heroin to fulfill
major purchase contracts. To renege on purchase
orders worth more than a billion dollars would
put him out of business and in a grave. Estabo
certainly won't back out because he is anxious to
establish himself in the heroin trade."

Weismann's thoughts, unimpeded by the
brandy and the fire's warmth clipped along full
speed. He considered obstacles closer to home:
"What about my five lieutenants' defecting? No.
Dieppe, Feltgeibell, and Reifenstahl all have
strong backgrounds of Nazi heritage. Their
fathers played significant roles in the SS and in
the Third Reich. They were Hitler loyalists
until the end. Anatole and Popodopolous were a
different story, however, and will have to
receive special treatment at the proper time. If
there is a weak link, it will be one or both of
them. Their stake in Pegasus is greed. Their
profession of belief in the New World Order is
nothing more than a convenience for helping them
achieve their financial goals. Why should they
share in the riches of the New World Order?
Dieppe will give them special attention at the
appropriate time. For the time being, they will
conform and remain loyal in anticipation of
becoming wealthy.

"I wonder, though, if they sincerely
believe that I have the warhead." Weismann
questioned. Remembering Patterson's call to
General Stone shortly before his untimely death,
Weismann said, "Of course they believe me.
Patterson saw to that." Finally, with all points
of consideration covered, Weismann succumbed to
the warmth of the crackling fire before him and
the sweet brandy now flowing through his veins
and drifted off to sleep in his belief that all
was well.

Chapter 17

April 25

Hamp's flight to Rio had been uneventful, but the humidity of South America, combined with his fatigue, were sapping his energy and clouding his ability to think clearly. Gregory's key man in Brazil, Bill Sanderson, picked him up at the airport and took him to a moderately priced, indistinguishable hotel on Rio's west side. The room would be used for nothing more than a place to leave his meager traveling things and perhaps a place to grab a little sleep later.

He took a cold shower as the agent stood in the bathroom doorway and briefed him on arrangements. Sanderson had not been given much time, a mere seven hours, to set up a meeting with Estabo. The meeting would take place in a small village five hundred kilometers west of Rio called Mia Minas. Hamp was to arrive only in the company of Sanderson, and was to use local bus service for transportation. The transportation arrangements were demeaning and indicative of Estabo's disdain for the DEA, but Hamp thought it a minor irritation considering the stakes involved.

"When do we have to be in Mia Minas?" asked Hamp.

"We have to leave in about two hours. It's a seven hour drive. The road conditions are good, but we will be pushed to make it on time," replied Sanderson. "We'll travel in my land rover until we are several kilometers from our meeting place, and then we'll park and take a local bus into Mia Minas."

"What else do I need to know?"

"You need to know you are taking one hell of a risk meeting with Estabo alone on his terms. He might very well kill us both."

"Maybe, but I doubt it, Bill. I think the subject of the meeting will make him grateful enough to spare out lives. Besides, if he kills me he knows someone else will take my place."

"What is the subject of the meeting, sir?" I had a tough time getting Estabo to buy off on the meeting without knowing the reason," explained Sanderson. "He agreed to the meeting only because I told him you were Gregory's personal representative."

"I'm going to warn him of a massive Brazilian Army raid on the drug route he uses through Brazil," answered Hamp.

Sanderson was dumbfounded. His mouth fell open, and he stared at Hamp in disbelief. Hamp broke into a smile. He then explained enough to Sanderson about what was going on to relieve his shock. Hamp slipped into khaki trousers, a loosely fitting short-sleeved khaki shirt, and a comfortable pair of walking shoes as they talked. Hamp placed his wallet in a trouser hip pocket and dropped his military identification in a shirt pocket.

"Lets grab a bite to eat somewhere on the way," said Hamp as they left the room.

They lunched at a corner cafe not far from the hotel and were on the Trans-Amazon Highway one-half hour later. In spite of the nature of Hamp's mission today, he found himself enjoying the ride through new surroundings. It was good to be away from the minute to minute demands made on his time and authority. He let his thoughts drift to Brazil, the country in which he suddenly found himself. His college training had included a great deal of study about the South American countries. His memories of Brazil began to slowly drift into his consciousness.

The northern part of the country where they were stretches from the headwaters of the Paraguay to the mountains of Minas Gerais and is a part of the central plateau. It's a peneplain, an ancient land surface that was eroded down to sea level and then thrust upward. Much of it is flat in spite of the fact that it reaches up to 4,000 feet above sea level. Further along to the northwest, near the border with Venezuela and Colombia, is another uplifted peneplain similar to the central plateau. The two peneplains were once a single surface but became separated when a block of the earth's crust slipped downward to form a trench called a graben. The gap created by this action is where the Amazon River now flows to the Atlantic Ocean. Just to the south of the highway they were traveling, about halfway between Brasilia and the coast, the landscape changes to low rugged mountain ranges. On the western side of one of the ranges, the Serra do Espinhaco, is Brazil's extremely productive mining region. The area produces iron, manganese, lead, zinc, and aluminum ores, as well as quartz crystal, mica, diamonds, 90 percent of the world's semiprecious stones, and gold. As he recalled, Morro Velho gold mine boasts a 9,000 foot shaft, one of the deepest mine shafts in the world.

After Brasilia's inauguration in 1960, the nation focused its attention on the critical lack of surface transportation. The government began a crash program to build new roads and to improve those already in existence. The military government made roads its top priority when it came to power in 1964, and by 1970 the number of miles of paved road had doubled, and new roads were being extended to the most distant parts of the country. The most ambitious road building project was the Trans-Amazon Highway, completed in 1975. Railroads, already in existence at that time, were not suitable for meeting the country's surface transport needs. They were privately owned, constructed of different gauge track, and were designed to move agricultural and mining products to the seaports, not to link different parts of the country.

The constant hum of the land rover's engine and the consistent whine of the tires on the highway finally lulled Hamp to sleep. He awoke when Sanderson stopped the land rover at a gas station. Nature was calling, too. While Sanderson saw to the fueling of the land rover, Hamp found the rest room. He then walked back and forth near their vehicle to stretch his legs; however, he soon decided the heat and humidity were too much for any form of exercise and got back into the land rover. As soon as Sanderson visited the rest room, they were again on their way.

"How far have we come?" asked Hamp.

"About half way. You had a pretty good three hour sleep," replied Sanderson.

"Three hours? I don't even remember going to sleep," remarked Hamp.

"How are you going to approach Estabo?" asked Sanderson.

"Head on," he said. "One can't dance with a man like Estabo. He lives at a primal level we don't understand, Bill. His world is black and white; all decisions are absolute; life is lived from minute to minute; and his world is devoid of trust. He believes only in what he can see, or in what he can personally control. Power rules in his world—ruthless power."

"But what's going to keep him from killing you? I don't think his gratitude will be reason enough to restrain him."

"If it isn't, then his respect for me as a man brave enough to face him will have to be enough to restrain him. He might hate me, but he has a great deal of pride. That pride dictates that he show me the same respect he would want shown to him under the same circumstances," explained Hamp.

"You're the boss," said Sanderson.

"I notice that you don't wear a wedding band. Have you ever been married, Bill?" asked Hamp to change the subject and to fill the time.

"I never have had time for a serious relationship although I am seeing a young lady in Rio.'

"How is it that you ended up in this line of work," asked Hamp.

"As you might have guessed, I was born in Brazil. My father was a mining engineer with one of the diamond companies. My mother was Brazilian and taught languages at the university in Belem. I attended high school in Belem, and then went to the University of Florida where I majored in criminal justice. After three years on the Florida Highway Patrol, I joined the DEA. They sent me back to Brazil after two years as a field agent in the Miami office, and here I am."

Hamp took over from Sanderson at their next fuel stop and drove until they reached the village just east of Mia Minas. He roused Sanderson, and they decided to park the land rover at the village police station. They used their badges and Sanderson's language ability to make the arrangements to leave it there until their business in Mia Minas was completed. From the police station they walked a hundred meters to the bus stop and took seats on a dilapidated wooden bench on the side of the street. For the first time that day, his nerves were beginning to question his intelligence. When Sanderson offered Hamp a cigarette, he obligingly accepted it, his first cigarette since he gave them up twelve years ago. He had forgotten how good they tasted.

The bus arrived twenty-five minutes later. It was not quite like the colorful, dilapidated, stereotypical buses often seen in the movies, but it certainly resembled one of them. The passengers also seemed to walk straight from a movie screen. Two such passengers, neither having teeth, got off the bus carrying white chickens in homemade straw baskets.

Hamp and Sanderson boarded and found seats near the back of the bus. Judging from the substance on the seat cushion, the previous occupants had been the two men with the chickens. Fortunately the ride to Mia Minas would be short, and the serious nature of their impending meeting with Estabo pushed aside any further thoughts of travel conditions. In about thirty minutes Hamp noticed a small sign on the side of the road that read Mia Minas. The village appeared to be typical of the smaller villages found along the highways in this part of Brazil. All the buildings were single-story masonry structures with tin roofs, and the sidewalks were dirt.

The bus stopped in front of a cafe with tables and chairs in an open courtyard. Hamp and Sanderson were the only passengers to get off the bus. The bus departed as soon as they cleared the door leaving them in a cloud of yellow dust and black diesel smoke. As soon as the dust and smoke began to clear, they saw four men approaching them from across the street. A pair of men each took Hamp and Sanderson by the arms and lead them down a narrow dirt street to an alley behind the cafe. A late model Jeep Cherokee awaited them. They said nothing until they reached the vehicle.

"Are you armed?" asked one of the men in accented English.

"No," replied Hamp.

They decided to search them anyhow. They made them lean against the car and spread their legs. Two of the men made a police-type search of their persons. Satisfied that Sanderson and Hamp were unarmed, they pushed them into the car. Hamp was placed in the front seat between two of the men and Sanderson in the back seat between the other two men. Hamp noticed that all four men were armed. Two were wearing shoulder holsters, and two were wearing belt holsters. They appeared to be professionals. They worked quickly and their movements were well coordinated, indicating that they were well trained and that they worked together as a team. They spoke only when necessary.

"I presume you are taking us to see Mr. Estabo." said Hamp.

No one answered. The man on the passenger side next to Hamp placed a blindfold over Hamp's eyes and tied it tightly behind his head, while one of the men in back did the same to Sanderson. They began their journey over what felt and sounded like a dirt road. Many turns and about thirty minutes later, the car came to an abrupt stop. They could hear several men talking nearby. Estabo's people appeared to be excited over their visit. The blindfolds were removed, and they get out of the car. They were in what appeared to be an abandoned camp of some kind, deep into the boondocks. Two small tin buildings and several tin sheds formed a circle in the midst of a thick, triple-canopied forest.

Two more Jeep Cherokees were parked next to the one in which they had arrived. Hamp counted eight men standing around the area, all heavily armed. Estabo sat under one of the sheds in a folding chair. Two more chairs were placed in front of him. Two of the men nudged Hamp and Sanderson to the vacant chairs in front of Estabo and motioned for them to sit. The talking they heard when they arrived had subsided. All eyes and ears were on the three men seated in front of each other.

Estabo was dressed in a gray, silk, short-sleeved shirt with an open collar, white slacks, and black and white wing-tipped shoes. A very heavy gold necklace hung about his neck, and a large gold ring with a four or five karat diamond adorned the ring finger of his left hand. His clothing did not show a single trace of perspiration. His head was full of black hair that surrounded a handsome face of about thirty-five years of age. His body was that of an athlete. "He looks younger than his pictures," thought Hamp. Estabo spoke first.

"This is your meeting, Mr. Porter. Please state your business. I am a busy man and I've come a long way to meet with you," said Estabo in heavily accented English. He snapped his fingers and one of his men appeared from behind them carrying a tray with three glasses. "Have some refreshment, Mr. Porter. I can see that you are not accustomed to the climate here." Ignoring Sanderson, he took a glass from the tray and waited for Hamp to state his business. Hamp took a glass, sipped from it, and then began his explanation for being there.

"For a reason very important to many people, I am interested in your impending business transaction with Herr. Weismann, Mr. Estabo," said Hamp. He noticed a distinct twitch in Estabo's right cheek at this news, but Estabo said nothing. "What I am about to say is as difficult for me to say as it will be for you to believe, Mr. Estabo, but I ask that you hear me out. I am privy to the fact that the Brazilian government intends to launch a massive raid on your traditional transportation routes through Brazil beginning tomorrow. My government wants your merchandise to be delivered to Weismann unharmed," explained Hamp. Hamp waited to get a reaction from Estabo, but there was absolutely no indication of an emotion of any kind. "This guy is as cold as an Eskimo's fanny," thought Hamp to himself. Estabo's eyes were impenetrable, and Hamp was getting no feedback from him at all.

"I don't know if you are playing me for a fool or if your government is just stupid," said Estabo without emotion. "We will find out."

Estabo snapped his fingers again and held the palm of his right hand out. The man standing immediately behind him stepped to his side and placed a semi-automatic pistol in his outstretched hand. Without a pause or a change in expression, Estabo aimed the weapon and shot Sanderson precisely between the eyes. The impact of the bullet knocked Sanderson and the chair over backward. Hamp felt the warmth of Sanderson's blood on the left side of his face and upper arm. For a moment, the shock of the moment paralyzed him: He stopped breathing and felt light-headed. He saw Estabo staring at him to read his reaction. After a few seconds though it seemed much longer, Hamp regained control of himself and returned Estabo's stare. His shock slowly turned to anger. "Control yourself, Hamp. Control yourself," he repeated.

"Now, what is your real business? If you lie to me, Mr. Porter, I will shoot you just like I did your friend," said Estabo as he aimed the pistol at Hamp's head.

"Weismann is holding my government hostage with a nuclear device. Unless your merchandise is delivered as scheduled, Weismann has threatened to detonate the weapon in a large European city. By warning you of the Brazilian Army's impending raid on your delivery routes, we hope to ensure the safety of your merchandise. If you deliver your merchandise as scheduled, you will in return receive your merchandise from Weismann. Weismann is insuring your business transaction with the threat of using the nuclear device. It's as simple as that, Mr. Estabo. No hidden agendas or ulterior motives."

"How do I know that your government will not be lying in wait for me once I take possession of my merchandise in Brazil?"

"Our government cannot operate in a foreign country without an invitation, Mr. Estabo."

"They have done it before many times," said Estabo angrily. "What about the rescue of hostages in Iran? Was President Carter invited to send in military troops? You insult my intelligence, Mr. Porter." One of Estabo's men moved to his side and placed a hand on his pistol. Hamp wondered how many men had died by pushing Estabo this far.

"It is not my intent to insult your intelligence. Based on what I have read about the size and equipment of your security forces, Mr. Estabo, you are quite capable of defending your merchandise from anything less than a US Marine Landing Force," countered Hamp. "I would expect nothing less from a man of your intelligence and experience."

"You are a smart man yourself, Mr. Porter. What have I to loose by believing your story?" He tossed the pistol to one of the men standing nearby. "You are lucky that I am a trusting soul," said Estabo with a broad smile, his first display of emotion. "Pablo, take him back to Mia Minas."

Two men escorted Hamp back to the Cherokee, tied the blindfold in place, and helped him onto the backseat. Half an hour later the Cherokee stopped, his blindfold was removed, and he was told to get out of the car. They didn't have to tell him twice.

Hamp walked the short distance to the police station. The land rover was parked where Sanderson and he had left it. Fortunately, the ignition key was also where it was left—in the ash tray. He drove east on the Trans-Amazon Highway. As Hamp looked into the rearview mirror before passing a truck, he suddenly realized why two old women had stared at him near the police station. Sanderson's dried blood covered the left side of his face and left upper arm and shirt sleeve. He would have to do something about that when he stopped for gas later.

Hamp drove for miles numb and oblivious to meaningful thought, then the tragedy of what had taken place an hour earlier fell on him like a ton of bricks. The senseless murder of Sanderson was testimony to the kind of people with whom they were dealing. At least Sanderson didn't have a wife and children. Hamp could not help but think of little, calm Steinhatchee at a time like this. There life seemed so innocent and meaningful. Hamp passed the time during the long drive back imagining Tom and Marian sitting in their back yard during the evening, laughing over a couple of drinks. He also imagined Gwen pouring over the minute details of her latest resort public relations campaign while she was chewing on her pencil. "What a beautiful mouth she has," thought Hamp.   .

Hamp's escape from the realities he was facing was all too brief. He looked toward the afternoon sky. It was late. The sun was sinking rapidly behind the jungle canopy, and it was a long way to Rio. He stopped for gas and cleaned the blood from his skin and shirt as best he could in the rest room. He bought coffee and crackers, and then continued the journey. His thoughts turned once again to Sanderson's murder. Even though Hamp had cleaned the blood from his face, he could still feel its warmth on his skin. He wondered why Estabo had let him live. He decided that Estabos motivation had been merely so Hamp could tell his superiors that the message of warning had been delivered.

The lights of Rio appeared as Hamp rounded a curve coming out of the foothills of the Serra do Espinhaco. It was three o'clock in the morning. He entered the suburbs of western Rio, but had difficulty recognizing anything in the darkness. Soon he realized that he was lost. Finally, after nearly ten minutes, Hamp found an open business establishment. He parked in front of what appeared to be an all night bar and grill and went inside. After several tries, he finally found someone who spoke English. The young woman knew of Hamp's hotel and gave him directions. He bought the woman a drink, thanked her and began the search for the hotel while the directions were fresh in his tired memory. Twenty-five minutes later he pulled into the hotel parking lot. There was no desk clerk in sight so Hamp took the key to his room from the cubby hole behind the desk, climbed the stairs to the second floor and walked slowly to his room. Once inside, he dialed the hotel switchboard. A sleepy sounding man answered the phone on the eleventh ring. Hamp gave the man the number of the Pentagon EAC and asked him to place the call. The clerk told him that the call would take a few minutes to place, and that he would ring Hamp's room when the call went through. The clerk's English was as poor as Hamp's Portuguese, but they finally managed to make each other understand.

Hamp was half way through a cold shower when the phone rang. He wrapped a towel around himself and grabbed the phone. The clerk told him to hold on.

"Pentagon EAC," answered the voice on the other end.

"This is Colonel Hamp Porter speaking. Please put me through to General Stone."

"One moment, sir. He is here in the EAC," replied the operator.

"Hamp what's going on?" asked the General. "The President and the Joint Chiefs are having fits. Weismann sent a message by B.J. Patterson that he would detonate a Pershing warhead in Europe if we interfered with Pegasus. He is holding B.J. prisoner somewhere. The President had no choice but to bring the Germans in on Pegasus based on Weismann's threat. They want to find and arrest Weismann. I don't know how long we will be able to hold them off.

"I'm afraid the news is not good from this end either, General. I spoke with the main man over here and gave him the message, but I lost my assistant in the process," said Hamp gravely.

"I'm sorry to hear that, Hamp. I will of course pass that on to Gregory."

"I'll catch the first flight out tomorrow morning, General. There are no flights at this late hour."

"No. Stay where you are, Hamp. Another one of Gregory's men will contact you soon. I want you around to monitor the exchange of merchandise in Iponema. We need to know when the boats sail from there on their way to Florida. Go to the consulate in Rio tomorrow morning and call me here at the EAC. To be perfectly honest, things are about to reach a crisis point around here, and I am not certain where I will need you tomorrow," said the General.

Hamp got back in the shower and let the cold water run on the left side of his face and left upper arm for a long time. He could not forget the image of Estabo's stone-like face void of emotion as he murdered Bill Sanderson.

Chapter 18

April 26

The knock on his hotel room door awakened Hamp with a start. He had been sleeping the sleep of the dead, and for a moment or two he was disoriented and unsure of his whereabouts. "Did someone knock on my door, or did I dream it?" Hamp thought to himself. He forced himself out of bed and moved toward the door. He heard the knock again. "I guess I'm not dreaming," he said aloud. "Who is it?" said Hamp in a loud voice as he reached for the door knob.

"Gary White. CIA. Walter Gibbs sent me over to see you, Colonel Porter," replied the voice on the other side of the door.

"Slide your credentials under the door," said Hamp. An unfolded set of CIA credentials appeared under the door face side up. Hamp picked them up and managed to focus his eyes well enough to read them. "They look genuine, but so does zirconia. Stand back from the door," said Hamp as he opened the door about an inch to get a look at the man. The face matched the picture on the credentials, so he pushed the door the rest of the way open and invited Gary White into his room.

"I apologize for the caution, Mr. White, but I had a rough day in Mia Minas yesterday." said Hamp. "Give me a second to get my clothes on." He remembered that all he had was the suit he wore on the airplane the day before yesterday or whatever day it was when he arrived in Brazil.

"I heard about Sanderson. Too bad," said White. "Estabo would have made a good SS officer in the Third Reich."

"What time is it? Did you come here to hold my hand, Mr. White? General Stone said one of the

DEA boys would come by to see me," said Hamp ignoring White's comment about Sanderson.

"It's nine-thirty a.m. No. I didn't come to hold your hand. I came by to give you a lift to the consulate and to see if I could be of other assistance to you," said White, a little stung by Hamp's hand holding remark.

"Sorry about that crack," Hamp said. "I am appreciative of your gesture, and I do need to get a call in to the Pentagon EAC."

"No harm done. They have a secure line at the consulate so your call will be no problem. The consulate general is expecting you," replied White.

"Any chance of getting something to eat on the way? I haven't eaten in a while," said Hamp.

"No problem. The consulate has a small, but good, dining room. I'm sure the cook will be able to make you something," replied White.

"Then let's be on our way," said Hamp as he slipped on his suit jacket.

After a quick visit to the consulate kitchen for eggs, toast and juice, Hamp paid a brief courtesy call on the consulate general, and then headed for the message center to call General Stone on the secure telephone. Since it was mid-morning in Washington, General Stone answered in a matter of seconds.

"Sorry to hear about your experience in Mia Minas, Hamp, but I am happy that you survived the ordeal. How did Estabo receive the warning?" asked the General.

"He bought it, sir, so far as I could tell, but how much does one trust a narcotrafficker?" asked Hamp.

"He will act on the information, Hamp. He has too much to loose not to do so. Hamp, I regret jerking you around like this, but I want you back in Washington today. Walter Gibbs and Gregory can handle things down there. I'll have someone meet you at Washington National Airport. Your CIA contact down there can notify the EAC of your flight arrangements. See you later today, Hamp," said the General.

"When can I get a flight out of here to Washington?" asked Hamp of Agent White. White looked at his watch pensively, and then picked up a telephone and dialed a number. He talked to someone for a few minutes, then hung up.

"A flight to Miami leaves in an hour and a half. You should be able to make a connection to Washington from there," said White. "By the time we get to the airport and check you in, it will be time to lift off. You ready to go?" asked White.

"You have no idea how ready I am," said Hamp.

*****

When Hamp entered General Stone's office, the Aide de Camp ushered him directly to the EAC in the basement of the Pentagon. The Aide briefed Hamp on the way down that a meeting had been called for 2100 hours for the Pegasus task force group, and the President, the Secretary of Defense, and the Chairman of the Joint Chiefs of Staff would be present. That's all the Aide knew, and Hamp could not even guess what had prompted such a meeting unless something had gone badly wrong.

Hamp found the EAC office impressive. Although the room is not huge, nor is it elaborate, the knowledge of what decisions had been made and would be made there was awe inspiring. The room's furnishings were simple: a very large oval conference table surrounded by at least twenty overstuffed, high-backed chairs, which occupies the center of the sunken room. An opaque screen about fifteen feet wide and eight feet tall occupies the upper center part of the room. The opposite - wall hides projection equipment as evidenced by four square cubby holes at the top of the wall. Communications gear with world-wide capability and seating for aides and assistants line the two remaining walls. There is no podium; however, Hamp noticed small pencil-like instruments lying at each place at the table that appear to be some type of laser pointing devices. A small reading light, note pad, name plate, and pencil have also been placed on the table at each seat.

Those already present for the meeting would make an impressive guest list. Standing in a circular group near the platform and screen are the Chief of Staff of the Army, the Chairman of the Joint Chiefs of Staff, General Stone, Mr. Burns, Mr. Gibbs and Mr. Gregory. General Stone saw Hamp come in and motioned for him to join the group. Hamp was suddenly very nervous.

"Welcome back, Colonel Porter," said General Beckman. "General Stone tells us that you had a bad time of it in Brazil day before yesterday." Hamp shook the Chief's hand and just smiled.

"Glad you're back, Hamp," said General Stone as he shook Hamp's hand warmly.

The others shook Hamp's hand and mumbled obligatory congratulatory remarks except for James Gregory. He held on to Hamp's hand and said "I was worried about you, Hamp. I know how badly you must feel about loosing your companion, but don't blame yourself. Just feel fortunate that you survived the incident." Hamp appreciated Gregory's gesture.

"We are waiting for the President and Secretary Defense to arrive," said General Stone. "I assume that Secretary Griffin will be with them." Hamp knew better than to ask the subject of this meeting. Another two minutes passed, and then the door to the EAC was thrust open and the guard at the door announced "Gentlemen, the Commander in Chief." The President walked in with a smile on his face, followed by the Secretary of Defense, Griffin, and Miles Honeycutt. Hamp noticed that Honeycutt was full of himself. He strutted into the room like a preening peacock. "It might not go well for General Stone," thought Hamp.

The President shook hands with everyone in the room saying to each person "Glad to see you." As task force commander and meeting host, General Stone allowed the President time to finish his greeting ritual, and then asked everyone to take his seat. When everyone was seated, General Stone exercised his host's prerogative of speaking first.

"Mr. President, gentlemen, thank you for being here." The General paused for a moment to allow everyone to settle down and focus on matters at hand. "The purpose of this briefing is to bring the President, Secretary of Defense, and members of the task force up to date on developments regarding Pegasus. There have been significant incidents over the past forty-eight hours, and, in my opinion, we are approaching the critical stage in expected events. First slide, please." A picture of the Atlantic Ocean and the surrounding continents appear on the big screen. With his laser pointer, the General highlighted two small dots of light north of the chain of islands northeast of the South American continent.

"As you can see gentlemen, the boats carrying Sturmer's bounty are rapidly approaching their destination—Ipanema, Brazil. Winds favoring the sailing objectives of the boats, and highly skilled crews have enabled them to reduce their anticipated sailing time by two days. They should reach Ipanema within forty-five to fifty hours.

Around the clock satellite surveillance of the boats indicate they have not made contact with another vessel; therefore, we assume the warheads are still on board and the boats still intend to make port in Ipanema," explained the General.

"We learned two days ago that the same boats we see on the screen made port in Bremen, Germany, for two hours before resuming their course. We suspected that at least one of the boats transferred at least one warhead to Sturmer during the stopover. An authenticated telephone call from, Lieutenant Colonel B.J. Patterson verified our suspicion. Sturmer apparently has one warhead in custody. Within hours of Colonel Patterson's phone call, we received a report that Patterson is missing and that his whereabouts is unknown. Our belief is that Sturmer kidnapped Patterson for the purpose of verifying to us the fact that Sturmer possesses the warhead. Sturmer will obviously use the warhead as a hostage maker should the need arise. The President immediately advised the German Prime Minister of these events. The German government has reluctantly agreed to withhold action against Sturmer until our task force has had the opportunity to react to the situation. Whether or not we will be able to restrain any action on their part long enough for Pegasus to run its course is highly questionable and a matter for concern," explained the General, pausing for a sip of water before continuing.

"Three days ago we learned of a massive military raid on known narcotrafficking routes through Brazil by the Brazilian Army. The raids were planned in response to American pressure on the Brazilian government to cut the supply routes used by the cartels in their country. Realizing the danger the raids would pose to Sturmer's business arrangement with Estabo, I sent Colonel Porter to Brazil to warn Estabo of the impending government raids. We lost one of Mr. Gregory's agents during the meeting but Colonel Porter managed to accomplish his purpose. In our opinion . . ."

"You screwed up, General," interrupted Honeycutt. "It's a damned good thing the President didn't allow Mr. Gregory to go to Brazil or he would have been killed instead of some lowly field agent." Honeycutt was seizing the opportunity to repay General Stone for having him removed from Steinhatchee and dispatched back to Washington. The President allowed Honeycutt's outburst without saying a word or showing any sign of emotion. All the while Honeycutt was oblivious to the dagger-like stares of Gregory, the Chief of Staff and the Joint Chiefs Chair piercing his back. The General continued.

"As I was saying, gentlemen, there is every reason to expect the remainder of Pegasus to be executed according to Sturmer's plan. In our opinion, Sturmer feels secure from harms way now that he has a warhead with which to hold the world hostage. We now know each step of the plan, and we know when and where the steps will be taken. Wilbur Burns is fully prepared to deal with events once they reach Florida waters."

"You know, General Stone, I find it highly out of the ordinary—and an affront to the President—that you have placed yourself in charge of this mess. Gregory, Gibbs, and Burns should be speaking for themselves. But that's not the worst of it. You have allowed—no, you have encouraged—the theft of seven nuclear weapons that could, and maybe will, be used to create havoc and destruction in Europe and who knows where. You are just lucky, you idiot, the President has not already stripped you of your rank and commission and jailed you, but that can still happen," ranted Honeycutt now clearly out of control. Even the President looked uncomfortable. Honeycutt had gone too far. Hamp found himself gripping the arms of his chair to keep from leaping over the table to throttle Honeycutt. Gregory's eyes espoused pure hatred. The rest of the group stared, not at Honeycutt, but at the President for allowing this outburst.

"General Stone, may I suggest a short break to allow us to refill our coffee cups and digest what you have told us," said the Secretary of Defense. General Stone nodded his agreement, and the group broke into smaller groups of two and three speaking in hushed voices.

Hamp moved quickly to Honeycutt's side, grabbed him firmly by the arm, and escorted him from the President's side through the EAC entrance to the hallway outside. Hamp's grip on Honeycutt's arm was so vice-like that Honeycutt was afraid to protest... The security guard looked at the two men and was about to say something when Hamp told him to get lost. Sensing what the situation was, the guard complied. With the Security guard at a safe distance, Hamp grabbed Honeycutt by the jacket lapels and pinned him to the wall, moving one hand to Honeycutt's throat and tightening his grip. Hamp's facial expression and physical actions struck terror in Honeycutt. His eyes widened and he stopped breathing.

"I'm going to tell you something you little mouse, and you had better listen carefully because I'll not repeat myself," Hamp hissed. "Are you listening, punk?" asked Hamp as he tightened his grip on Honeycutt's throat. Honeycutt made a gurgling sound, which Hamp took for a "yes". "I'm not a presidential appointee, nor am I an active duty officer any longer. I'm just a plain John Doe, so you can't threaten me like you just did General Stone, you little slime ball. Here's the way it's going to go. We are going back inside, and if you in any way show disrespect to General Stone, or to anyone else, I'm coming after your ass across that table and you'll wish you had never been born." Hamp tightened his grip on Honeycutt's throat still more. "And by the way, that's not a threat; it's a promise." Honeycutt's face was turning purple and he was near unconsciousness. The security guard, who had been standing at a respectful distance away, felt compelled to intervene.

"Allow me to straighten this gentleman's clothes before you two go back inside, sir," said the guard to Hamp as he separated the two men. Honeycutt slid to the floor gasping for air. The guard picked him up and began straightening his clothing. Hamp stepped back, regained his composure, and then walked back into the EAC.

"You saw what just happened," blurted Honeycutt to the guard in a raspy voice. "You are going into the EAC with me and you're going to tell the President of the United States that Colonel Porter just tried to kill me," commanded Honeycutt.

"I have no idea what you are talking about, sir. All I saw was a man who passed out in the hallway. I don't know about anyone else being out here," protested the guard.

"I'll have your job for this," threatened Honeycutt.

"I doubt that, sir. I'm retiring next week," replied the guard with a smile.

Inside the EAC everyone was talking in groups of two or three. The President, Secretary of Defense and Griffin were huddled in a corner. Gregory, Burns and Gibbs stood together near the entrance, while the Army contingent formed the remaining conversational group. Hamp joined the Army contingent.

"I told you before, Mr. President, that this thing was out of control. Now we are looking nuclear disaster in the eye," said Griffin.

"I find that interesting, Martin, since you are the Secretary of the Army and the Chief and Stone work for you," said the President with irritation. "Obviously you are incapable of controlling either of them. You should have told me about this mess sooner, Martin. Maybe something could have been done about it. Now I'm faced with world embarrassment and possible blame for a nuclear disaster."

"Your personal advisor's propensity for showing his ass didn't help us any either," remarked the Secretary Defense to the President. "The Chairman of the Joint Chiefs and the Chief of Staff of the Army are good soldiers, Mr. President, but if you push them too far they will resign and go public in a heartbeat."

"I don't give a damn how good they are, or what they might do, I should have been brought in on this Pegasus mess sooner," exclaimed the President.

The Army group was a little more relaxed. "I understand why you waited to bring the White House in on this, Chief, but it surely put me in an uncomfortable situation with the President," said the Joint Chiefs Chairman.

"I'm sorry about that, sir, but you are as familiar with White House leaks as I. Someone like Honeycutt would have gone public and we would have had a real crisis on our hands. The public would have panicked," retorted the Chief apologetically.

"Perhaps it's time to tell the President and the others about the warheads," suggested General Stone. "Maybe that would defuse the situation somewhat. There is no telling what the President will do now or the fools around him."

"Sir, what about the warheads?" Hamp heard himself ask without thought. He was embarrassed at having questioned the Army top brass.

"Later, Hamp," remarked General Stone as he gave Hamp an oblique glance.

"Well, let's get the show back on the road, shall we gentlemen?" asked General Stone.

"Wait a minute. Are you going to tell them about the warheads?" asked the Chief.

"Unless either of you can give me adequate reason not to," replied General Stone.

"But a leak at this stage of the game could prove disastrous," protested the Joint Chiefs Chair.

"Not if we get the President's attention on the level where he lives," said General Stone without an explanation. Without a pause General Stone called the meeting back to order and asked everyone to take their seats once again. Hamp had no idea what General Stone was going to tell them about the warheads, but he assumed it would be earthshaking. The President glanced around the room obviously looking for Honeycutt, but quickly turned his attention to General Stone. For the first time, Hamp noticed a look of concern on the President's face and the faces of the Secretary of Defense and Griffin.

"Now, gentlemen, I am about to tell you of something that will require absolute confidentiality. If what I am about to tell you leaves this room, there is an excellent chance that Pegasus will be successful, and the world will end up as Sturmer's hostage." General Stone spoke with an unmistakable firmness and resolve. He paused a few seconds for everyone to consider his remarks. "When the task force made their decision to allow the theft of nuclear warheads to facilitate the capture, and or destruction, of the largest heroin transaction and narcotrafficker round-up in history, the Chief and I alone made another decision. We kept that decision to ourselves for the purpose of preventing even the remotest possibility of a leak. Only one other person knew of the decision because his participation and cooperation were necessary. To make a complicated story short, gentlemen, the warheads presently enroute to Brazil, and the warhead being held by Sturmer in Germany, are not live warheads. They are training devices used by the custodial detachments for practice in assembly and disassembly of the weapons." General Stone again paused. The President's head dropped forward and all could hear the audible sigh of relief coming from him. Groans of joy, curses of exclamation, and expressions of relief could be heard all around the table.

The President began to speak, and everyone grew quiet. "Are you saying that you allowed me, the President of the United States, and the Prime Minister of Germany to labor under such a horrible deception on purpose?" asked the President in angry disbelief. "Why on earth would you do such a thing?"

General Stone took a deep breath in preparation to answer the President's question, but the Chief interrupted. "Mr. President, as Chief of Staff of the Army, I will answer that question. The White House was not informed because we could not take a chance on a security leak." Hamp admired the Chief for having the courage to step up to bat to tell the President the unpleasant truth. General Stone deserved not to be the one to tell him. The room was quiet enough to hear the proverbial pin drop.

"Is that feeling unanimous among everyone here? Do you all feel that I, or my staff, cannot be trusted with the secrets of this nation?" asked the President obviously shaken and angry. Again, there is total silence in the room. The presidential appointees cast their eyes downward. The military contingent and Mr. Gregory stared hard at the President in confirmation and condemnation. The comprehension of these men's lack of faith in him washed over the President in one debilitating wave. Hamp saw this man's transformation from a confident leader to a broken man and a fallen President happen right before his eyes. Hamp would respect the office of Commander in Chief, but the constitution of the United States of America did not require him to respect the man currently holding the job. Hamp had the distinct feeling that others in the room felt the same as he.

The President stood and stared a moment at the faces around the table. "Very well, gentlemen. Please keep me informed on the remainder of Pegasus. I will inform the German Prime Minister and beg his forbearance and confidentiality." The President left the EAC followed by the Secretary of Defense, Griffin, and Wilbur Burns.

Those left in the room stood captivated for a moment, and then the Chief spoke. "I want to say to each of you how proud and fortunate I am to have served with you. No matter what the future consequences of any actions we might have taken together in our efforts to silence a lunatic of international gravity may be, you did your duty. You are honorable men. Mr. Gregory and Mr. Gibbs, my remarks apply to you as well. General Stone, are we finished here for today?"

"Yes, sir, I believe that we are. However, I do have further work for Colonel Porter," smiled the General. "Let's go to my house and see if we can talk Fran into making a late dinner for us, Hamp." After a few cordial words among those remaining, the EAC emptied. On the way out, Hamp noticed that Honeycutt was no longer in the hallway.

"What happened to the gentleman I talked to out here?" Hamp asked the guard.

"He took sick and said he was going home," replied the guard with a smile.

When they were in the General's sedan and on the way to Fort Myer, Hamp remarked to the General that he had never experienced a meeting so highly charged with emotion and intensity. "That meeting is one I'll not likely forget anytime soon," said Hamp.

"Nor will I," replied the General. "I'll more than likely be asked to retire, but not before we wrap up Pegasus."

"General Beckman, too?" asked Hamp.

"Yes, I think so," responded the General. "But don't feel badly for us. Sometimes, defending what one believes in is more important than one's career. Anyway, we've both had good career experiences and we're both ready to retire and to turn the Army over to younger fellows like you. I always wanted to go out fighting," smiled the General. "I'm ready for a drink. How about you, Hamp?"

Fran had anticipated the lateness of their meeting and had dinner ready when they walked into the house. The General's aide told her that Hamp was in town, so she was not at all upset with them and appeared very happy to see Hamp. The General put a tumbler half filled with scotch into Hamp's hand, poured one of equal proportions for himself, and kissed Fran on the check.

"You fellows hurry with those drinks. I don't want Hamp to accuse me of serving cold food," said Fran happily. "Go on and sit down at the dinning table. I'll be along in a minute."

"You are one lucky man, General," remarked Hamp.

"That is both an understatement and a mystery," said the General.

Fran served a delicious meal of prime rib, baked potatoes, spinach salad, and hot yeast rolls. Hamp and the General eat voraciously and with little talk. The emotional stress of the meeting had given them both a surprisingly good appetite. Fran enjoyed watching them consume the dinner with so much satisfaction, and made small talk that did not require their participation. After dinner she kissed them both on the cheek and excused herself to attend to things in the kitchen. Fran genuinely enjoyed doing things for those she loved. It was this quality that had first attracted Judith to her. They had been very much alike.

The men retired to the General's study, poured themselves a snifter of brandy, and relaxed in the big overstuffed leather chairs next to the fireplace. "You know, Hamp, it's the fight for what is right that I'll miss most about the Army," said the General pensively. "Soldier's rights, moral integrity, and an ingrained sense of duty and responsibility are qualities that have to be fought for in today's environment, because the general public cares less and less about those qualities and there is always a politician around the corner who will take advantage of their absence. I have made fighting for these qualities my job as the Inspector General of the Army. That's why I like my job, Hamp, and I have enjoyed it more than any other job I've ever had. I worry that whoever follows me in the job might be one who is more concerned with the politics of Washington than with the quality of life of the American fighting man," said the General as he stared into the empty fireplace. Hamp did not comment. He knew the General was thinking aloud.

"Sir, what job do you have for me?" asked Hamp quietly.

"Oh! Yes. Your job," said the General as he roused himself from deep thought. "B.J. Patterson is still unaccounted for, and two critical transactions must take place, Hamp; those are my concerns at this juncture. I'm not sure what we can do about Patterson at the moment, but we need to ensure the transfer of the warheads and heroin between Estabo and Sturmer's people in Ipanema, and the transfer of heroin for money among Sturmer, Charo, and Costellano in Florida. If we can manage the completion of those three tasks, we are home free," explained the General.

"I agree, sir, but how do you want me involved?" asked Hamp.

"I want you at Steinhatchee for the transfer there. When that transfer has taken place, and Costellano is in the custody of the DEA, I want you to go to Germany and see what you can do about Patterson. Gibbs's people have been working on it, but they don't have a real feel for the circumstances involved there, Hamp. I think you will be an asset for them. Will you go?" asked the General.

"Of course I'll go, sir. May I ask a sort of related question, sir?" asked Hamp. The General nodded his permission. "Was Colonel Carter the other party privy to the warhead scam?"

"Sure. Who else could have made the swap between the trainers and the real warheads?" asked the General smiling.

"Just one more question," said Hamp. "I know from experience how realistic the trainers are. For all practical purposes, they are the genuine article with the exception of the uranium bullet and the uranium target rings. I am assuming Carter, or someone else, put enough radioactive material in the trainers to make a Geiger counter sound off should someone decide to check the weapons for authenticity?"

"Right again, Hamp. Hollow lead dummies filled with depleted uranium training bags were substituted for the actual uranium bullets. As you know, they emit enough radiation for a Geiger counter to register a believable reading without placing anyone in harms way. The uranium rings were also removed and replaced with training rings. Only an expert who is trained in American nuclear devices would ever be able to tell the difference, and they would require specialized equipment to detect the difference."

"I thought so. There could not have been another answer," replied Hamp, his curiosity now satisfied. "I'll leave for Steinhatchee in the morning, sir. That will give me a few days to prepare for the arrival of Sturmer's boats. By the way, sir, is Sturmer still in Berchtesgaden?"

"As of 1700 hours local time today, yes," replied the General. "Are you ready for some rest?" asked the General.

"You bet."

Chapter 19

April 27

The shuttle flight from Athens to Thessalonica had been bumpy and turbulent all the way. Dieppe could not sleep, read, or write. All he could do was think about his purpose for visiting Tomas, and how many hours he had spent in an airplane during the last three or four months. The twenty- passenger, twin-engine airplane behaved like a bucking bronco. Dieppe had never been air sick, but he was getting close. He needed to use the rest room, but did not think the turbulence would allow him to walk to the rear of the plane. Finally, at 1538 hours the little plane landed at Thessalonica thirty-two minutes late. His legs were so shaky Dieppe could barely walk down the ramp to the tarmac. Tomas Popodopolous waved to him from behind the chain link fence that separated the taxiway from the terminal building. Dieppe did not have to

wait for luggage to be unloaded, because he had
none on this trip for his stay would be very
brief.

The two men shook hands. I am pleased and
impressed that you took the trouble to travel
from Brazil to bring me up to date, Heinrich,"
said Tomas.

"The pleasure is mine, Tomas. You did your
job well, and you are still a part of Pegasus.
Weismann wanted me to tell you personally how
much he appreciates you and what you have
contributed to the NWO movement," said Dieppe.
"I am very hungry, Tomas. Do you think we could
take the ferry over to Samothraki Island and have
dinner in that little restaurant you introduced
me to on my last visit?" asked Dieppe.

"Yes. Of course. That will be my
pleasure. My car is over there; let us be on our
way. We can just make the next ferry." They
hurried to Tomas's car and drove to the municipal
dock, arriving just in time to get on the ferry.
The air was cool and was made cooler by a light
drizzle beginning to fall. Dieppe shivered and
moved his shoulders up and down in an effort to
shake off the chill. Tomas babbled on and on
about how devoted he was to the NWO and how much
he wanted to help the organization grow in
Greece. His incessant jabber was too much for
Dieppe. Heinrich knew that Tomas was in NWO for
the money he thought he was about to make and for
no other reason.

The ferry sounded its horn to announce its
arrival at the Samothraki dock. They drove off
the ferry and turned onto the main north-south
road bisecting the island. The drive across the
island took about half an hour. They took their
time because the last rays of the setting sun
playing on the hillsides were quite beautiful.
No conversation was necessary. Dieppe sincerely

felt a kinship to Tomas. He became more and more depressed over what he was about to do.

The little restaurant was perched on a cliff of rocks overlooking the sea. Most of the dining tables were on a large deck overhanging the cliff, which is where Dieppe and Tomas chose to dine. The two men enjoyed a delicious meal of fresh clams and squid, Tomas' favorite, and then made small talk about the NWO and how the organization could be made to grow in Greece under Tomas's leadership. After they finished their meal, Dieppe suggested that they walk down the winding stairway to the sea below and view the last rays of the sun as it sank behind the ocean horizon. They made their way down the long, steep stairway to the beach below. To their right a group of large rocks blocked the view of anyone on the beach, the stairway, or the restaurant above. Dieppe walked leisurely to the ocean-side of the rocks with Tomas at his side. In one swift coordinated movement, Dieppe turned and plunged a five inch stiletto blade in Tomas's upper stomach and twisted it upward into his heart. Tomas's eyes widened in disbelief and then became fixed as his life quickly flowed from his body. "I am truly sorry, Tomas," said Dieppe to the dying man as he allowed him to collapse on the sand.

Dieppe quickly wiped his fingerprints from the knife and threw it into the sea. He then dragged Tomas' body well behind the large rocks on the ocean side making sure to remember to retrieve the car keys from Tomas' jacket pocket. Dieppe found moving Tomas' three hundred pound body very difficult and time consuming because he could only manage moving the body a few inches at a time. By now the sun had set, and darkness had covered the beach. Dieppe was alone on the beach, so there was no need for him to worry about being seen. Standing still a moment to catch his breath, Dieppe then climbed the stairs and walked from the stair landing near the dining deck to the car without drawing attention to himself. Satisfied that he had time to get back to the ferry dock, make the crossing back to Thessalonica, and take the last shuttle flight to Athens before the body was discovered, Dieppe drove slowly into the night. The body would not likely be found until tomorrow at the earliest.

April 28

Dieppe's flight landed at Helenicon Airport at precisely 0930 hours. He was right on time. Zuni Anatole told Dieppe that he would not be able to meet him at the airport due to a pressing business engagement, but would meet him at his office in the Grand Bazaar no later than 1030 hours. After processing through customs, Dieppe quickly walked the four hundred meters to the front of the airport and hailed a taxi. The ride to the bazaar would take from thirty to forty minutes depending on traffic, so Dieppe used the time to think about matters in Florida, specifically the transfer of merchandise and money. He did not expect trouble from Charo. He had too much to loose to double cross them. However, Costellano was a continual thorn in Dieppe's side. The man could not be trusted, but when would he make his move against them, and how would he do it? These were questions to which Dieppe had found no answers. Would Costellano attempt to kill him at pay-off time after Costellano had the heroin in his possession? Why not? What or who was to keep him from doing just that? What could Dieppe do about it? "All questions and no answers," said Dieppe aloud. "Perhaps Peter expects Costellano to kill me. Peter knows the man hates anyone or anything associated with Nazism. Maybe Peter has arranged for my death. My God, Heinrich, wake up!"

mumbled Dieppe to himself. "If I cannot trust Peter, who can I trust?" He knew Peter needed him because Peter had no business sense at all, and had to have someone around he could trust to run the finances of the organization, especially at a time when the organization would be growing so rapidly. After all, the mechanics and details of Pegasus had been his brainchild. He had been the one to make Pegasus work in spite of Peter at times." The taxi came to an abrupt stop in front of the south entrance to the bazaar. Taking the south entrance would mean a longer walk to Anatole's shop, but he had no choice now. He had been daydreaming when he should have been paying attention to where the driver was going.

Since it was mid-morning and a work day, the bazaar was full of shoppers and tourists. It took Dieppe almost twenty minutes to reach Anatole's shop. The door was unlocked so he assumed Zuni was present. Dieppe walked through the shop to the back room where he found Zuni talking on the telephone. Zuni motioned for him to sit, and poured him a cup of tea while talking on the phone. The conversation ended, and Zuni hung up. "I apologize for not being able to meet you at the airport, Heinrich. My meeting was with a buyer from Germany who is one of my best customers. I usually do a quarter million marks worth of business with him every year," said Zuni. "Please allow me to make a note to myself and I will be right with you, Heinrich." Zuni turned his attention to a small stand-up desk on the back wall of the room. He did not see Dieppe empty the contents of the cyanide capsule into his tea cup. "There, my business is taken care of. Thank you so much for your visit, Heinrich. I have been very anxious to learn of our progress with Pegasus. Are things going well?" asked Zuni excitedly.

"Yes. I am pleased with our progress. The boats should make port at Ipanema tomorrow evening. By the way, Zuni, I took the liberty of pouring you a cup of tea while you were writing yourself a note. You know I don't like to drink alone," said Dieppe with a smile.

"Thank you, my friend. I need a cup of tea after that extended telephone conversation a moment ago," said Zuni as he drank the entire contents of the small cup. "Now, tell me Heinrich, do you expect any trouble from these mafia fellows we are dealing with?" asked Zuni as he belched and rubbed his stomach as though he was in discomfort.

"No. Charo has too much to loose to botch the plan at this point. Costellano is another story. I really do not trust him, but there is nothing I can do about it now," said Heinrich as a look of distress came over Zuni's face. "Zuni, are you all right? You do not look good at all."

"I don't know. I've got this pain in my stomach. I cannot breathe. Help me Heinrich," said Zuni between spasms of abdominal pain. He struggled to his feet holding his large abdomen with both hands. His eyes rolled up into his head, and he fell heavily across the table smashing it. Zuni's eyes stared blankly at Dieppe. He was dead. Dieppe carefully wiped his fingerprints from his tea cup and from the tea pot handle. He left the shop quickly before someone came in to browse and saw him. Dieppe thought that he should be able to get out of the bazaar before Zuni's body was discovered. Even if he didn't, the bazaar was so crowded that it made no difference.

Dieppe made his way to the west entrance of the bazaar and hailed a taxi. He arrived at the airport in time to relax a few minutes before boarding the twelve noon flight to Rio. The cumulative effects of fatigue were beginning to take a toll on Dieppe, but he decided that he could sleep on the long flight to Rio. He would need all his strength and mental stamina for the next several days, and then the worst of Pegasus would be over.

Heinrich regretted the necessity of killing Anatole and Popodopolous. He especially detested having to do the deed himself; however, they had become a liability to both Pegasus and the NWO. Hiring the task done would have only meant an added security risk. Thankfully, Feltgeibell and Reifenstahl are loyal to the Nazi movement and believed in the New World Order. Furthermore, they have no compunction about relegating their own interests to the interests of the movement, and they will continue making significant contributions to the movement in many ways. Heinrich had a personal reason to be happy that Reifenstahl would be spared. They shared similar backgrounds and had over the years become close friends. In fact, Hans was Dieppe's only friend.

"Peter Sturmer, on the other hand, is another story," thought Dieppe. Heinrich admired Peter's intelligence, his unrestrained willingness to pursue a dream, and his vision for a new world order, but his admiration ended there. On a personal level, Peter was a cold-blooded loner who tolerated people only when they could serve his purposes. Dieppe's relationship with him was probably as close to having a friendship as Peter was capable of having. Presently, Peter's relationship with and acceptance of Dieppe was based on need. Dieppe had the organizational and managerial skills that Peter lacked. In essence, Dieppe was filling an ability deficit in Peter's makeup.

Dieppe wondered what difference all this made. He was an old man and only hoped to live long enough to see the NWO firmly established among Aryan people. He laid his head back on the

chair, closed his eyes, and waited for his flight
to be called.

Chapter 20

Hamp had grown accustomed to living in the midst of pandemonium. The number of government agents working in his home had not increased, but they had settled in for the long haul by making his home theirs. He got occasional respites when Marian and Tom invited him and Gwen to dinner, but these visits failed to relax him. They really seemed to frustrate him more because he wanted to be with his friends and Gwen more than he could at the moment. He wanted to be with Gwen especially now because she was forging a new life for herself, and he wanted to be there for her. Hamp had to push them from his thoughts so he could focus on the task at hand: reading agency reports, tracking Reifenstahl's boats, or attending strategy sessions with Jim Gregory and the FBI representative. Gregory came back to Steinhatchee the day after Hamp had returned. Despite the tense moments at the last EAC meeting, neither had discussed the fallout from that last meeting. Neither of them felt it necessary.

Reifenstaahl's boats were presently splitting the distance between Cuba and the Bahama Islands, and would probably make Key West by late afternoon or early evening tomorrow. Gregory's people were set up and ready in Key West, Cedar Key and Steinhatchee. Captain Miller and his Coast Guard contingent had been included in the operation and would play an active role in the seizure of the heroin, money, boats and narcotraffickers. Hamp and Gregory had analyzed their preparations a hundred times, playing the role of devil's advocate. Gregory was now in charge of the operation because his agency had most of the action and responsibility. Hamp fully expected to go to Germany just as soon as things were wrapped up in Steinhatchee.

It was now 1600 hours, time for the afternoon briefing. This would be the final briefing of DEA team leaders before the arrival of the boats. Gregory had essentially divided the operational area into four sectors: Key West, Miami, Cedar Key, and Steinhatchee. Each team leader was responsible for a sector, and the four teams would operate as a whole. Captain Miller's role in the operation would be briefed at this meeting. The addition of the team leaders and Captain Miller's team to the normal contingent of agents had packed Hamp's house to full capacity. Miller stood in front of the fireplace, which had become the podium.

"Gentlemen, may I have your attention, please," said Gregory in a firm voice.

Everyone stopped what they were doing and gathered around Gregory. "So far, all we have briefed has been the land part of this operation. Incidentally, I have decided to name this operation "Gotcha", just to prove the DEA has a sense of humor. This afternoon Captain Miller, Coast Guard Region VII Commander, will brief you on his plans. Be assured they are my plans as well. If you have a problem, or see a glitch with anything he has to say, take it up with me after the briefing, but before he departs the area. Captain Miller."

"Thank you, Mr. Gregory. Gentlemen, allow me to begin by saying that the Coast Guard is pleased to be a part of this operation. Like all of you here, the Coast Guard has been battling narcotrafficking in American waters for a long time and it has been a loosing battle. We are proud of our past history with DEA. I truly believe that Gotcha has a chance to deal a severe blow to heroin traffic in this country. Now, at 1500 hours tomorrow afternoon, two of my Island-

Class patrol boats, the Cuttyhunk and the Key Largo at Key West, and two Point-Class patrol boats, the Hobart at Cedar Key and the Wells at Steinhatchee, will each pick a two-man DEA coordination team who will patrol with us. The Cedar Key and Steinhatchee teams will be picked up at our Tampa station at 1000 hours in the morning for the longer runs north. We will be using the Point-Class boats up north because their shallower drafts will be better suited for those waters; otherwise, my boats will be following normal patrol times and procedures so as not to arouse suspicion in anyone Charo might have been watching us. In addition to our usual ship to shore radio routine, we will be monitoring your operational FM frequency, Mr. Gregory. My people will be exchanging frequencies and call signs with you while we are here this afternoon. Our mission, gentlemen, is simple. We will stop, board, and take into custody the boats and the crews, but only after we are certain they have secured the heroin to the sea anchors. My people will leave with you this afternoon, Colonel Porter, an underwater signaling device and will instruct you on its use. Once the ship's crew has secured the last bag of heroin to the sea anchor, and the boats make way, all you will have to do is to activate the signaling device. That signal will be the cue for my boats to move in and begin boarding tactics. We will allow the bad guys ten minutes or so of undisturbed sailing time, so that they will think their work was not observed. I do not want the bad guys to be prepared for a boarding engagement and increase the odds of someone's being killed unnecessarily. That is why I prefer the use of the underwater signaling device. As soon as the boarding party engagements have been completed, Mr. Gregory, your liaison people will notify your land-based teams via the FM radio command frequency. At that

time, you may safely send out your dive teams to
secure the heroin packages. I will place on
standby a squadron on HH-60 Jayhawks and HH-65A
Dolphins, half on the ground in Key West and half
on the ground in Tampa, to fly support missions
as required. I think that about covers it,
gentlemen. Are there any questions?" There was a
question from Colonel Porter.

"Captain Miller, for the sake of us
landlubbers who are not as informed about our
Coast Guard as we should be, would you please
describe more thoroughly the major
characteristics of the boats you will be using?"
asked Hamp. There were several affirmative nods
in the group.

"Yes, of course. Thanks for reminding me of
that oversight. The Island-Class boat, known as a
WPB, is a 110-foot boat with a 21-foot beam, and
displacement of 185 tons. She has a range of 1800
miles and a maximum sustained speed of 26 knots.
Her armament consists of a 20 mm cannon and two
M-60 machine guns. She carries a crew of 16. They
are primarily used for law enforcement operations
like this one, and illegal alien interdiction
duties. The Point-Class boat is smaller at 82
feet. Her beam is 17 feet, and she displaces just
over 67 tons. She is powered by two diesel
engines that will push her to a top sustained
speed of 22 knots. She carries a crew of 10 to 18
and her range is 490 miles. Like the Island-Class
boat, the Point-Class boat is used primarily for
law enforcement and search and rescue
operations."

"Thank you, Captain Miller. The DEA is
happy to have you working with us again. Colonel
Porter, will you brief your role, please?"

Hamp stepped to the fireplace. "When the
DEA liaison team on the Steinhatchee patrol boat
signals clearance, Mr. Adams and I will go out to
the drop site in his boat. Everyone around here

is familiar with his boat and it will not likely arouse anyone's interest or suspicion. Night diving is becoming more popular in these waters, and Mr. Adams does a fair amount of it. We will anchor over the pylon site, and I will dive to verify the presence and quantity of the heroin. After making a count of the packets, I will surface with a small sample from a packet and perform a field test to verify that the packets do in fact contain heroin. Mr. Adams will radio the test results to Mr. Gregory in code. If the test is positive, Mr. Adams will call for Carolyn II on the marine radio. If the test result is negative, Mr. Adams will call for Slim Jim on the marine radio. Should the radio fail for some reason, flares will be used to signal the results. Red will indicate something is askew, and green will indicate a positive result. We will head back to the dock immediately upon signal completion. Any questions?"

"Yes, I have a question," said Captain Miller. "Mr. Gregory, I understand that you

have to verify the drop, but why is Colonel Porter performing the dive - with a civilian at that -rather than DEA people?"

"Colonel Porter has been assigned to me for the operation by the task force commander. He and Mr. Adams are familiar with the sea anchor and surrounding dive site, and people around here are used to seeing Mr. Adam's boat going and coming," explained Gregory with a little irritation in his voice. "Does anyone else have a problem with this? No? Good. Now for the benefit of those who have not been privy to the detailed planning of the operation, I'll summarize the ground side of the overall plan

"The entire DEA organization in Florida and most of Georgia has been drafted for this task force. A couple of the new faces you've seen around here this afternoon belong to my regional commanders," continued Gregory. The mobile command group will consist of Captain Miller, the Senior FBI agent, two of my operations officers and me. The command group will initially be located aboard the patrol boat Hobart. When necessary, the command group will transfer to a Jayhawk and move to Cedar Key or Steinhatchee, depending on the situation. We will rely on satellite tracking until the bad guy boat or boats drop anchor. The patrol boats will remain out of sight near Key West, in port if necessary, until I give Captain Miller the go ahead."

Gregory paused for questions. Getting none, he continued. "The Miami ground team will be led by the Miami DEA Station Commander. His team will monitor Charo and his people, and, we assume, Dieppe. When the heroin drop is made at the sea anchor, we expect one boat to continue on to Cedar Key and Steinhatchee, and the other boat to return to Tortola. If our assumption is correct, then one of the patrol boats will stalk the northbound boat and the second patrol boat will pursue the southbound boat. The southbound boat will be followed until out of radio range of its sister boat, and any of Charo's people on the ground in Key West, before closing in and initiating boarding procedures. Should both boats proceed north to Cedar Key and Steinhatchee, then both patrol boats will follow at a distance until the bad guys are passed off to the patrol boats waiting in the waters near Tampa. Not until the final drop is made in Steinhatchee will the patrol boats take action against the bad guys. Are you clear on that Captain Miller?" said Gregory looking directly at Miller.

"Yes. I understand perfectly, Mr. Gregory," replied Miller.

Gregory continued. "The ground teams in Cedar Key and Steinhatchee will, with any luck, be in close proximity to Costellano's people. I know it will not be easy. Cedar Key is a small island community on which to play cops and robbers. Steinhatchee is even smaller, but there are more places in which the bad guys can hide."

"We expect Dieppe or his designated representative to drive to Cedar Key, and then to Steinhatchee to collect payment from Costellano. When Dieppe meets with Charo and Costellano's people in Key West and Cedar Key, we will wait until Dieppe has left before our people close in and take the bad guys. Only in Steinhatchee will Dieppe be arrested along with the rest of the trash. That, gentlemen, is the short version. Oh! I almost forgot. Teams equipped with the FM secure radios need to pick up punch card codes from the operations officer before leaving. Anyone requiring the long version of what I have said may meet with my operations officer after this meeting. Any guest ions?" asked Gregory. He recognized the raised hand of Bill Mowry, the Miami Regional Commander. "Yes, Bill, you have a question?"

"Under this scenario, Dieppe is really going to be pushed to drive to Cedar Key and arrive before the boats. Are we chasing the wrong assumption here? Why would he not wait for payment in Steinhatchee? Why two payoffs?"

"In all honesty, Bill, my hunch is that Dieppe will fly to Tampa and rent a car for the rest of his collection route. I'm assuming he will demand payoffs from the Cedar Key and Steinhatchee drops in case something happens and the Steinhatchee drop goes sour," replied Gregory. "Keep in mind that a sailboat will require a good deal of time under very good sailing conditions to go from Key West to Cedar Key and then to Steinhatchee, especially when at least a two hour stop in Cedar Key is required for a drop."

Bill Mowry shook his head still questioning the assumed travel plans of Dieppe. Gregory continued.

"Bill it really doesn't matter who shows up for the payoff. No matter if it's Dieppe, or three different people, we will take whoever shows up," replied Gregory. "Any more questions, gentlemen?" Gregory looked around the room to make certain everyone was clear about the details of the operation. He knew this was no time for crossed signals or misunderstandings. "No more questions? Okay, then thank you."

*****

Gregory and the mobile command group had been aboard the patrol boat Kay Largo for about an hour when the skipper handed Captain Miller a written message. Miller read the message and handed it to Gregory saying, "Both boats have dropped anchor about a mile west of the Dry Tortugas."

"How far is that from our present location?" asked Gregory.

"About thirty miles," replied Miller. "But we don't need to move yet. Remember our speed advantage. It will take them at least an hour to drop and secure the heroin, even though they are more than likely using both crews to do the job. The water depth is only about twenty feet where they are," said Miller while looking at a nautical chart. "The bottom is very irregular and there are numerous holes in which to hide things." A call on the FM secure radio from Bill Mowry interrupted their conversation, "Gotcha One, this is Gotcha Two. We're on the west end of the key across from the Green Dolphin Motel. Charo and six of his goons just got into two cars and headed in the direction of South Point Marina. We're going to tag along in a minute or two. Over."

"Gotcha Two, this is Gotcha One. Any chance they might be going somewhere else. Over?"

"Gotcha One, this is Gotcha Two. There's nothing else down that way except several private homes. Over.

"Gotcha Two, this is Gotcha One. Keep us informed. Out."

"Charo is behaving predictably so far. He owns the Green Dolphin Motel and South Point Marina," said Gregory to Miller. "Both are among his legitimate business holdings," explained Gregory."

"Gotcha One, this is Gotcha Two," said Mowry again. "Someone else just came out of the motel alone, entered a car, and is headed in the same direction as Charo. I couldn't tell who it might, have been. Over."

"Gotcha Two, this is Gotcha One. That was probably Dieppe. Out."

"Dieppe is driving his own vehicle so he can head for the airport in Miami after he collects from Charo. They think big daddy Weismann is holding the ultimate trump card," said Gregory to Miller.

"Shall I send a status report to the EAC in the Pentagon?" asked Miller.

"Yeah, thanks; do that."

* * * * *

Reifenstahl was tied off side by side, port to starboard. Three crewmen and both captains worked feverishly to bundle the heroin packages in small cargo nets. A fourth crewman donned diving gear and entered the water with a line in one hand. Since the heroin was literally vacuum-packed, the netted bundles would sink quickly. Each bundle was threaded to the line the diver had secured to the sea anchor. The diver remained on the bottom with the sea anchor to make certain the bundles did not become entangled on the way down. When all the heroin had been placed securely on the line, a crewman secured a heavy lead weight to the free end of the line and dropped it overboard. The diver waiting on the bottom with a halogen lamp pointed toward the surface waited for the weighted end of the line to hit bottom, and then he secured the line to the sea anchor. The heroin bundles were now snugly arranged around the sea anchor.

The two boats separated, hoisted mainsails, rolled out foresails, and made way in opposite directions. The boat that had just emptied her cargo set course for Tortola. The remaining boat set her course for Cedar Key. As per instructions from Reifenstahl, the senior captain called for Uncle Mike on the single-sideband radio. This radio had a much greater range than the standard marine radio. Reifenstahl had them installed on both boats precisely for this occasion. The call to Uncle Mike was monitored by one of the men standing next to Charo on shore.

"So far so good," said Charo to Dieppe. Charo then said something in Spanish and two of the men standing nearby hurried to the marina dock. Moments later, a 25-foot Maco outboard sped away from the dock heading in the direction of the sea anchor.

"My men will dive on the sea anchor to verify the presence and authenticity of the heroin," explained Charo."

"I would expect nothing less," replied Dieppe.

"We might as well return to the hotel and relax with a glass of wine. The verification process will take a little time," said Charo. Two of his men remained at the marina to monitor activities of the verification process. The rest accompanied Charo back to the motel. An hour and a half later in the motel dinning room, Dieppe and Charo sat at a table with a bottle of wine.

Dieppe, however, had only coffee, not wanting to impair his ability to stay awake and drive.

"I still have a very long night ahead of me," he thought to himself. He noticed the ever present contingent of bodyguards hovering in the background, saying nothing, but watching everything. The lights in the room were out so as not to draw attention to their presence. The only light in the room came from the neon marquis in front of the motel, which cast shadows across part of the room.

"You amaze me Dieppe," said Charo, breaking the silence. "You are always the business man, never smiling, to the point without mincing words, and focused only on matters at hand. I could see a man like you in my organization." Dieppe did not reply.

"Tell me, Dieppe, how someone of your intelligence got involved in this Nazi crap?" asked Charo.

Dieppe said nothing for a moment. He actually wanted to give Charo an honest answer, but decided it would be futile. "The same way you got involved with the Cosa Nostra, I suppose," replied Dieppe with a hint of a smile on his face.

"But I chase money, and you chase a political pipedream," retorted Charo.

"Do you call the value of 2,000 kilos of heroin a pipedream, Mr. Charo?" asked Dieppe.

"No, but what you will do with the money is a pipedream."

"We shall see. Time will prove one of us wrong," replied Dieppe. Charo had leaned forward in his chair to pursue the argument when one of his men entered the room, hurried to their table, and whispered into Charo's ear.

"My divers have completed their work. The heroin is present and authentic," announced Charo with a smile.

"When will you collect it, Mr. Charo?" asked Dieppe.

"When I think it is safe to do so." He snapped his fingers and one of the bodyguards produced a large satchel and placed it on the floor next to Charo. "There is enough money in this bag to start a Fourth Reich, Dr. Dieppe. Please start it somewhere else." He got up from the table and left the room with his bodyguards without another word. Seconds later, Dieppe heard them drive away.

Dieppe quickly rose from the table, picked up the heavy bag, and walked quickly to his rental car. He was running a little behind schedule. Reifenstahl's boat would be well on its way to Cedar Key, and he had a two hour drive to the Miami airport. Dieppe didn't bother to count the money…there was no need. Had there been a shortage, Dieppe would not have signaled the captain on his cellular phone, and the captain would have departed with the heroin. "Dealing with Costellano might not be as easy," he thought aloud.

Mowry and his men packed up the starlight scopes. From vantage points on the dock and the roof of the residence across the street from the motel, they had monitored the movement of Charo and Dieppe. Mowry radioed the mobile team that he was on his way to pick up surveillance of Charo's car. It was time to make a report to Gregory.

Dieppe made it to the airport in Miami in time to get a bite to eat before his flight to Tampa.

The flight to Tampa was uneventful. He picked up a rental car and headed north on US Highway 19 to Cedar Key. It was ten minutes past midnight and traffic was light on the four-lane road. The trip would take about two and a half hours, but there was no rush. The boat would not arrive at its destination near Cedar Key until late afternoon.

Costellano and his people were set up in a rental house on the northwest side of the key overlooking the Gulf of Mexico. Dieppe had no trouble locating the house with the directions Costellano provided. One of Costellano's men met Dieppe as soon as he pulled into the driveway of the rental house. He informed Dieppe that Mr. Costellano had made a reservation for him in a condominium near the dock in downtown Cedar Key. He gave Dieppe a key and directions. He also told him that he would be contacted at the condominium when the boat arrived. Costellano's rudeness came as a welcome relief to Dieppe. He had not relished the thought of spending more time in the vulgar man's presence. Dieppe would go to the condo, call Weismann, and then get some rest. For all he knew, the German authorities might have stormed the Eagle's Nest and placed Peter under arrest.

It was two in the afternoon when Dieppe awoke. "I must have been more fatigued than I thought," he mused. Dieppe regained his bearings and began to think out loud. "Had the boat already reached its destination? No. Surely Costellano's people would have contacted him if it had." He stepped out of his underclothes, got into the shower and turned the cold water on full force. The sudden shock of the cold water jolted him from his lethargy. Back among the living, he completed his shower, dressed and decided to get something to eat while he waited. He retrieved the money satchel from the closet and took it with him downstairs. His better judgment told him to put the bag in the trunk of his car so as not to draw attention to himself. Dieppe drove back and forth along the street where all the restaurants were located until he saw one that looked acceptable. He was nervous about leaving

the car unattended, considering the contents of
the trunk, but his hunger took priority.

The waiter seated Dieppe among several
tables of young couples. They reminded Dieppe of
another pleasure of life that had passed him by.

His lunch of grilled grouper and heart of
palm salad was delicious. He was about to enjoy
his second helping of grouper when he noticed two
of Costellano's men enter the restaurant. They
took a table next to his. They were dressed like
tourists, but their appearance still drew looks
from the guests around them.

"Has the boat arrived?" asked Dieppe when
they were seated.

"No, but it close enough to have contacted
us by marine radio," said the spokesman of the
pair. "Mr. Costellano wants you to come to the
house at five o'clock. The verification divers
will go out after dark."

"I will be there promptly at five," said
Dieppe. "Is there anything else, gentlemen?

There was no further conversation. The two
men left without another word. Dieppe finished
his dinner, and then he strolled on the dock
watching fishermen returning to dock.

At precisely five o'clock, Dieppe parked in
front of the rental house and walked to the
screen porch where Costellano and four of his men
were playing cards. One of the men vacated his
chair and motioned for Dieppe to sit. Costellano
did not acknowledge his presence. Dieppe took the
seat opposite Costellano. The card game continued
for several minutes. Finally, Costellano laid his
cards on the table and stared at Dieppe for
several seconds without expression. The other men
left the porch and walked toward the beach.

"I am concerned that things are going too
smoothly. My men have not seen even one DEA agent
on the entire key and we have been here since
last evening," said Costellano, concern showing

on his face. "The DEA usually tails me wherever I go, but for two days now I have seen not one agent," said Costellano, his voice filled with irritation.

"Perhaps it is because they know we hold a very powerful trump card," suggested Dieppe.

"What trump card?" asked Costellano, with a puzzled look on his face. "What are you talking about?" It was obvious to Dieppe that Charo had not shared certain information with Costellano. "How interesting," thought Dieppe. "He obviously did not trust Costellano, but of course he didn't trust anyone," mumbled Dieppe to himself.

"I am truly sorry, Mr. Costellano. I thought you knew. We retained a nuclear warhead in Germany and have threatened to use it on a major European city should anyone interfere with our transaction," explained Dieppe calmly.

Costellano said nothing, but his eyes revealed total surprise and skepticism. His mouth moved, but words were not forthcoming.

"Did Charo know?" he managed to ask.

"Why, yes, he did," replied Dieppe.

Costellano's look of surprise turned to anger—his face flushed. Without saying another word he stormed from the porch into the house. Dieppe saw a cooler near the table. He opened it and retrieved a cold bottle of beer and walked on the sand near the water. He took a long drink from the bottle. "Perhaps one day I'll learn to like American beer…just perhaps," he said just loud enough for Costellano's goons to hear.

Suddenly Dieppe heard the sound of a voice obviously coming from a radio inside the house. In a moment, one of Costellano's men came to the porch door and informed them that the boat had arrived and was presently dropping anchor off Cedar Key. It was almost dark. "Soon the boat crew would be undertaking the arduous task of bundling, sinking and securing the heroin," thought Dieppe out loud. "That means that at 2000 hours, Costellano will send out a dive team to check out the heroin," he murmured to himself. But would Costellano turn over the money. Dieppe did not trust him; however, there was nothing he could do but wait.

Dieppe noticed three of the men speeding away in one of the cars, presumably to make preparations for conducting the heroin check. He decided to sit in a nearby lawn chair and wait until someone required his presence. The warm May sea breeze felt good.

* * * * *

Two of Mowry's men sat anchored in a rented fishing boat just offshore of Costellano's rented house. Inside the small cabin, one of the agents refocused the powerful spotting scope aimed at a man who had just taken a seat in a lawn chair on the front lawn of the house they had under surveillance. "Hey, Tommy, I think this guy is Dieppe. At least he sure looks like Dieppe's picture."

"Well, he's supposed to be there, or somewhere nearby," said the other agent.

"Give the boss a call and tell him three of Costellano's men have left the house and appeared to be going in the direction of the dock. And tell him Dieppe is here, too."

Gregory and the mobile command team had set up shop in a condominium rented by the DEA for that purpose. The condo faced the ocean from where the community pier and docks could be seen to the south. They needed the place to get out of sight, and had to have a base of operations from which to communicate. The call came from the boat surveillance team shortly after they had monitored the sailboat's call to Castellano.

"Well, Captain Miller, I do believe this is going to go as smoothly as the Key West part of this thing," said Gregory. Agent Johnson has men at the docks, near Costellano's house, and on your patrol boat offshore. The backup team will be joining us in about five minutes, and your helicopters are standing by on the backside of the key. Can you think of anything we've missed?"

"Have Costellano and Dieppe been positively identified on site?" asked Miller.

"Yeah. We photographed Costellano coming in last night and Dieppe as he entered his condo early this morning and when he left this afternoon headed for Costellano's house."

"Then it's just another waiting game until the transaction goes down," said Miller.

"Yeah. From this point on, I believe Charo and Costellano will operate independently of one another. Besides, once Dieppe gets the money, he couldn't care less when the bad guys pick up their dope from the bottom of the ocean."

"I don't know about that," interrupted an agent who was talking to someone on the phone. "That tropical depression behind Cuba we've been watching is now a full-blown hurricane according to the weather boys in Miami. If it remains on its present course and maintains its present speed, it could be knocking on the door between here and Steinhatchee within the next twenty-four hours."

"That could be good or bad. It is good if it pushes Charo and Costellano to pick up their heroin before the storm hits, but bad if they wait the storm out," suggested Gregory. "We need to go ahead with the conclusion of this operation as quickly as possible. The longer we are forced to wait, the better the chance of something bad happening," continued Gregory.

"I'm just afraid the damned sailboat will sink before it makes it to Steinhatchee," said Miller with concern in his voice. "The captain

has been on that boat and under a lot of pressure
for a long time. Too bad he's not on our side."

"Why? Do we have sailboats in the Coast
Guard or Nary," asked Gregory in jest, trying to
break the tension everyone was feeling.

"No. But we still need good ship's
captains," replied Miller.

An hour passed while the mobile command
team made small talk and drank bad coffee.
Gregory broke the silence addressing Miller with
a serious look on his face.

"I re-think the grand finale of this
operation over and over again. Success depends
entirely on the right people being in the right
places at the right times doing the right things.
Too many variables exist to suit me. I can't
count the times one little mistake, or just one
unplanned incident has completely blown an
operation like this one. And allowing Chavez to
walk away last night was a hard thing for my
people to allow." Gregory began to pace back and
forth as he thought out loud. "Now, tonight we're
going to do it again. Costellano and Dieppe will
be allowed to walk away. If something goes wrong
tomorrow night in Steinhatchee, there will not be
another chance. This storm that's blowing our way
could automatically ground the helicopters. Hell,
anything could go wrong," he proclaimed, his
voice full of agitation. This operation has the
potential of spanning two counties and a lot of
water; the helicopters are a must."

"If the storm continues to threaten this
area, Costellano might go ahead and make a move
on the sea anchor fearing the hurricane might
cause damage or even destruction to the heroin
bundles," said Miller.

"Yeah. Well, we'll just have to wait and
see," replied Gregory. He closed his eyes. He was
dog tired and was snoring within seconds. Miller
wished he could do the same thing, but the stress

and tension produced in him by the circumstances had his adrenaline flowing.

Miller tapped Gregory on the shoulder. "It's 2100 hours," he said. The heroin bundles have all been secured to the sea anchor, and Costellano's divers have completed their verification routine. Dieppe is probably being paid off about now," said Miller.

*****

Dieppe was still in the lawn chair when the two men who made the verification inspection returned. Costellano came out onto the porch to meet them. Dieppe walked to the porch and stood out of the way, listening intently. The verification was positive. The heroin was in place and of a very high quality.

"Come with me Dr. Dieppe," quipped Costellano. They went into the kitchen and Costellano took a blue nylon satchel from the refrigerator. He tossed it to Dieppe saying nothing and walked from the room. Dieppe took the bag to his car and placed it in the trunk with the other satchel. One of the men stood beside Dieppe until the satchel was secured in the trunk..

"Mr. Costellano wants you to meet him at the end of Rocky Creek Road in Dixie County tomorrow evening at exactly eight o'clock. Here are the directions," said the man as he handed Dieppe a piece of folded paper. "Don't be late."

Dieppe drove away quickly, glad to be rid of Costellano and his people. "As far as I am concerned, the man is about one step above an animal," thought Dieppe aloud.

Dieppe drove carefully through the congested island traffic. "The last thing I need is to be stopped by a law enforcement officer and have the car trunk searched," said Dieppe to himself as he made his way to the small town of

Fanning Springs. Costellano had made a reservation for him at the town's only motel. That would put him about thirty-five miles from Jena where he would locate Rocky Creek Road. Costellano obviously wanted to keep an eye on him until their business was completed.

*****

The next morning Hamp found Pentagon South strangely quiet. There were no planning sessions, liaison meetings, or briefings to attend. As he looked around the place, Hamp realized the show was almost over. Only periodic incoming reports from the field teams and outgoing reports to the Pentagon EAC briefly broke squelch on the radios. One agent was monitoring the satellite positioning system to track the boat's progress as it neared Dead Man's Bay and Steinhatchee. Gregory was making phone calls to take care of other DEA business. Meanwhile, Hamp decided to take a break and visit with Tom Adams. He called Tom's number and Marian informed him that Tom was working on the big boat at the marina. He decided to stop by Roy's Restaurant on the way to grab a bite to eat.

"Hey, Hamp," said Tricia as he walked through the front door. "What can I get you this morning?"

"Pancakes without butter would be fine," replied Hamp as he took a seat. He picked up a copy of the Gainesville Sun someone had left behind and turned to the sports section to see how the Braves were doing. "It's strange how one can suddenly relax when so much is at stake," thought Hamp to himself. He was deeply involved in one of the most important events of his life, yet he suddenly found himself with nothing to do but wait. He read the sports page until the pancakes arrived.

"There are some really weird dudes in the other dinning room, Hamp," said Tricia as she placed Hamp's food on the table. "They came in about and hour ago, four of 'em, and they've been in there since just talkin' in low voices like they got a secret," she continued. "Kind of spooky, if you ask me."

"What do they look like?" asked Hamp.

"Like very tough customers from the city. They sure ain't from 'round here," she continued. "And I saw somethin' that looked like a gun butt under one of 'ums arm when he got up to go to the rest room. You think I ought to call the sheriff, Hamp?

"No. No sense in provoking trouble so long as they aren't bothering you or the customers."

Hamp knew exactly who they were and why they were in Steinhatchee. Hamp finished his coffee, paid his bill, and left the restaurant. On his way out he got a good look at the group; they were definitely of the mob. As Hamp mounted his motorcycle, he noticed two of Gregory's men in a car across the street. They were there to keep tabs on Costellano's people he surmised. Hamp cranked his bike and headed for Ideal Fish Camp to see Tom. He found him in the engine compartment of his boat changing an air filter on the big Cummins diesel engine.

"You all set for tonight, Tom?

"You bet. Just as soon as I get this air filter on and change the fuel filter, the Carolyn II will be ready to go. I've already taken care of the dive gear, and I put two extra air tanks in the tank rack."

"Good man," replied Hamp as he sat down near Tom. "You know, Tom, you don't have to do this. Gregory has trained divers and so does the Coast Guard. If something were to go wrong out there, you could be killed. These people play hard ball, Tom."

"Yeah, I know they do, but this is my town, and I don't want those swastikas bringing drugs in here again like they did ten years ago. I'm going. Don't give me an argument, Hamp."

Hamp knew he was serious and he knew when to back off.

"What time do you think we should head out?" asked Tom.

"The Coast Guard will give Pentagon South a call when the boat reaches the spring. That will be our signal to get ready to move in. How close will we need to be for you to identify the sailboat on your radar?"

"As far away as 2,000 yards, or as close as you want me to get."

"I think we should stand off at least 500 yards. We'll be able to see them depart on the radar," said Hamp.

"Sounds reasonable to me. I'll be ready to go about dark," said Tom.

"By the way, Tom, does Marian know about this?"

"No and I want to keep it that way. I mean it, Hamp," said Tom adamantly.

"If that's the way you want it," replied Hamp. "If anything happens to you on this operation, I would never forgive myself, nor could I ever look Marian in the eye again. That reminds me—I think I'll go call Gwen before we head out. I haven't spoken to her in awhile."

"Don't waste your quarter. She's not home. Marian said she drove back to Evergreen yesterday."

"What. Why?" asked Hamp, trying to ignore the feeling of panic this news gave him.

"I don't know. I didn't talk to her."

"Okay, well, I'll see you around five-thirty or so," said Hamp as he climbed over the stern platform and onto the dock.

As soon as Hamp got home he went to his bedroom to call Gwen. No matter her reason for going back to Evergreen, he wanted to talk to her just in case something happened to him tonight. .

It would be noon in Evergreen.. The phone rang four times before someone answered. The voice belonged to Greg.

"Hello," said Hamp in a voice a little grumpier than intended. "Greg, this is Hamp. I'm calling to see how you all are doing," lied Hamp.

"Bull, Hampton H. Porter, I know who you want to talk to, but she doesn't live here anymore thanks to you - you asshole," said the drunken voice on the other end of the phone.

Hamp hung up the phone without responding to Greg's insult and called Gwen's mother.

"Hey, good looking, it's your favorite boy friend," said Hamp playfully.

"Why Hamp. How good to hear your voice."

"Good to hear your voice, too, mom. I tried to call Gwen a moment ago, but her drunken husband told me Gwen wasn't there. I thought she had gone home for a visit. Where is she?"

"She and the children are visiting a friend in Oregon, Hamp - her old college roommate, Mary Ellen Hightower."

"How long will she be out there?" asked Hamp, disappointed.

"I'm not sure. She didn't know how long she would be away when she left, Hamp. Do you know that she left Greg, and that she has filed for divorce?"

"Yes, she mentioned that that was what she planned to do, but I thought maybe she had changed her mind since she went back for a visit," said Hamp.

"No, no. She is standing firm in that decision, and I can't blame her one bit. She came back just to pick up the kids for a weekend visit. Shall I tell her you called when I hear from her?"

"Yes, thanks. Good to talk to you, mom. Goodbye."

The news of the real reason for Gwen's visit home left Hamp with an odd feeling. On the one hand, he was happy Gwen was out of that mess; on the other hand, it frightened him for some unknown reason. Hamp left the bedroom and decided he needed to clear his head for the long night ahead. He needed to be totally focused. Things could get dicey before all was said and done.

*****

The captain of the Gatsby heard the beep of the Loran C announcing that the boat was a half mile from their destination. He turned off the navigation lights and ordered the foresail rolled in and the mainsail lowered a quarter. The winds had been favorable at fifteen to twenty knots, but the seas were running three to four feet, a little rough for what they were about to do. But there was no choice. He watched the Loran closely, steering as precisely as possible. It was time to turn on the bottom reader so he could see the sea anchor when the boat passed over it. Trying to pinpoint something as small as the sea anchor on the bottom of the ocean in sixty feet of water from a sailboat would be an extremely difficult task. He would be forced to use the diesel engine in order to maneuver the boat precisely. The Loran alarm beeped five times announcing their destination. He ordered the mainsail lowered, turned on the diesel engine, and watched the bottom reader carefully. He saw nothing but flat, sandy bottom.

"Coming about to port," he announced in a loud voice.

He would reverse his course and make a pass over the programmed coordinates and hope to pick up the sea anchor on the bottom reader. The boat moved along at two knots. The bottom reader showed nothing. The captain reversed course once more. He saw nothing but sand. Then, suddenly, the bottom reader revealed a deep hole, then a sharp hump on the ocean floor.

"I have it," shouted the captain to his crew as he reversed the engine to stop the boat's forward movement.

"Drop anchor!"

When the boat's forward motion stopped, the captain shifted the engine into neutral and shut it down. The anchor and chain did the rest. They were directly over the sea anchor.

A crewman began putting on diving gear, to include double air tanks, while the other two crewmen began breaking out the netting. The captain secured a small anchor line to a stern cleat, attached a five-pound weight to the line, and threw it overboard. The line would be used by the diver to make his way to the bottom, and then it would be used to guide the heroin packages to the bottom. Finally, the line should be used to secure the heroin packages to the sea anchor. By the time the captain had the line rigged and in the water, the diver was ready.

The diver entered the water off the stern platform, swam to the line and began following it down. The diver's light could be seen clearly from the boat. On the bottom, the diver used his light to make a methodical search, hoping to see either the sea anchor or the shaft of the fresh-water spring. He made three passes before seeing the sea anchor. Visibility with the light was only ten feet. He unfastened the five-pound weight from the small anchor line, secured the line to the steel eye imbedded in the top of the sea anchor, and blinked his light three times in the direction of the water's surface. The captain saw the signal and ordered the remaining crewmen to begin lowering the packages. One by one, the ten-kilo packages were fashioned into bundles and wrapped in the nets.

Exactly one hour and five minutes later the last bundle was lowered and the diver surfaced. While the diver was climbing aboard, the captain ordered the anchor and mainsail raised. It was time to make a swift departure from the area. They were still a long way from the British Virgin Islands and a storm was blowing between them and their destination. Once underway, the captain gave the helm to a crewman and went below to radio his report to Mr. Costellano.

"They're leaving," said Tom Adams, as he watched his radar screen.

"Good. Let's give them twenty minutes to get underway before we move in," replied Hamp.

"What if bad guys come out to check the stash? What do we do then?" asked Tom.

"Pray," replied Hamp.

"I'm serious, man," retorted Tom.

"So am I. In addition to praying, we will just have to be quick about our task."

"I still don't understand why we're going to plant a sound beacon on the sea anchor," said Tom.

"So the Coast Guard will be able to find it quickly," explained Hamp. "The patrol boat and the helicopters will be able to zero in on it when the bad guys come out to play. Now remember, Tom, if the bad guys come out while I'm down, you immediately leave the area and stand off to the southwest. I'm diving with two tanks and you're going to lower another one to me, so I'll be able to stay down almost two and a half hours," Hamp said.

"Where are you going to hide when the bad guys dive to check out the booty?" asked Tom.

"In the spring, unless you have a better idea," replied Hamp. "Remember, Tom, do not wait for me if the bad guys come out earlier than expected. Read my lips. Do not stay! It could screw up the entire operation."

"Yeah, yeah, okay. I'll stand off about 500 yards to the southwest. Can we go now?"

Tom began moving the Carolyn II very slowly toward the sea anchor, staring alternately at the bottom reader and the Loran. Tom used the time to put on his diving gear.

"Bingo," said Tom, as he reversed the engine and hurried forward to drop the anchor.

With Tom watching, Hamp entered the water from the diving platform on the stern and swam around to the front of the boat so he could follow the anchor line down.

While Hamp was making his descent, Tom prepared the extra air tank for lowering by attaching a large snap link to the Velcro strap on the tank. He lay on his stomach on the bow with the tank next to him, snapped the link onto the anchor line, and released the tank allowing it to follow the anchor line to the bottom where Hamp would be waiting.

Tom tried to stand on the cabin roof to scan the horizon in all directions, but the sea had become too choppy. He worried about being able to get Hamp out of the water if the wind velocity continued to increase. He called Gregory and reported their status via a prearranged code.

On the bottom, Hamp used his halogen lamp to look for the sea anchor where he saw it almost immediately about fifteen feet away. He turned back to the anchor line, retrieved the extra air tank, and moved it to the edge of the spring shaft on the opposite side of the sea anchor. Having secured the tank to a rock with parachute cord, Hamp swam back to the sea anchor to plant the sound beacon.

As the remaining rays of daylight were fading, Gregory's voice came over the radio.

"Carolyn II, this is Gotcha One, over."

"This is Carolyn II, over."

"This is Gotcha One; put your eyes on the channel. Out."

That meant the bad guys were on their way out to the sea anchor.

"Shit. I don't want to go, but I have to," said Tom as he began retrieving the anchor.

Hamp heard the engine come to life directly over him. He placed the beam from his halogen lamp on the spot where the anchor was and saw it being pulled upward.

"Tom is leaving and Costellano's people are on their way here," thought Tom to himself.

A cold, hard knot formed in the pit of Hamp's stomach. "Being alone on the ocean floor at night was bad enough…now this," mused Hamp. He quickly completed the planting of the beacon and swam to the edge of the spring where the spare tank was secured. He turned off his lamp, secured his regulator to a snap link on his gear, and took the regulator from the spare tank into his mouth and cleared it by exhaling hard. He had no idea just how black darkness could be, nor did he know he could feel so alone. At least he thought he was alone. Chances were good that two or more sharks were enjoying the warmth of the spring just twenty feet below him. The noise of his breathing through the regulator sounded extremely loud in the total blackness. There was nothing to do now but wait. He tried, with little success, to occupy his mind by checking his gear. He especially wanted to make certain his signal flares were still attached to his weight belt. Having checked all his gear, Hamp fine-tuned his buoyancy so that he could hover indefinitely at his present position. His slow, rhythmic breathing moved his body gently up and down.

*****

The crew launched the cigarette boat from the public boat ramp in Jena, just across the river from Steinhatchee carrying a driver, a diver and a third man. The twin water jet engine pushed the boat through the river channel very slowly until the boat cleared marker number twenty-six, and then she quickly planed at sixty miles per hour. A bright halogen bow light illuminated the way. At marker one, the driver punched in a set of LORAN coordinates and set course for the sea anchor. The diver was ready by the time the boat reached its destination. The search for the anchor took about fifteen minutes. Once it was discovered, the crew lowered the anchor. The diver rolled off the starboard side of the boat, back first, into the water, found the anchor line and began his descent.

Below, Hamp clearly heard the anchor hit the water and then the whirring sound as the anchor chain plunged through the water. The anchor must have taken hold between Hamp and the sea anchor as near as Hamp could tell without turning on his lamp. Suddenly Hamp could see a light above; it was a diver making his descent. Hamp exhaled slowly and made his breathing shallower to lower his profile a foot or so into the spring shaft. He didn't want the diver's lamp to pick him up if the diver decided to look around the area before going to work.

The diver found the sea anchor without difficulty and cut one of the nets enough to free a package of heroin. He put the package in a dive net attached to his weight belt, and in the process, dropped his lamp. Hamp thought he saw the diver poke at something as he retrieved his lamp. "Did he see the sound beacon antenna sticking out of the sand?" thought Hamp. The diver's lamp must have fallen right on top of it. A chill ran down Hamp's spine. He realized the man was rigging a booby trap device in case someone tried to tamper with the heroin before they could retrieve it. "That probably means the other two sites were booby trapped as well," thought Hamp. Somehow he had to get word to Gregory, and he had to eliminate this diver before he armed the booby trap. Without thinking further, Hamp pulled his dive knife from its sheath on his right calf, replaced the spare tank regulator with his primary regulator, and swam rapidly for the diver, hoping to achieve the element of surprise. Since the diver's back was facing Hamp, he was able to reach the diver undetected. He reached around the diver with his free hand and yanked the diver's regulator from his mouth. Before the diver could react, Hamp stripped his facemask from his head and pulled the diver's octopus out far enough to cut it through with his knife. The diver no longer had access to air and would be forced to surface. Not waiting to see who or what had done this to him, the diver swam frantically for the surface. Hamp quickly sheathed his knife, turned on his lamp, found the signal beacon, and turned it on. Now the Coast Guard would be on their way, and Gregory would be moving in on Costellano and his friends.

Hamp turned his attention to the booby trap. He found it secured to the side of a net. It was a simple device; a pound of plastic explosive with a wire trigger attached to the sea anchor. Should anyone attempt to lift the bundles, the wire trigger would be pulled loose thereby igniting the blasting cap imbedded in the plastic explosive. Hamp carefully removed the trigger wire from the device then sat down to see what would happen next. He had burned up nearly a thousand pounds of his air during his tussle with the diver. He would have to conserve air as much as possible. The spare tank he had been breathing from was about empty. He slowed down his breathing and concentrated on maintaining a shallow breathing pattern.

*****

The Coast Guard Patrol Boat Wells picked up the signal beacon's squeal immediately and began a full-throttle run for the sea anchor, which would take about ten minutes. The DEA liaison team on board signaled Gregory via a prearranged radio message. The crew automatically went to battle stations without being told. The WPB Wells was ready for anything.

Within three minutes of receiving the signal, two HH-60 Jayhawks were airborne and on their way to the sea anchor site.

Meanwhile, Costellano's diver broke the surface about fifty yards from the cigarette boat yelling to his companions that he had been attacked by someone. The boat didn't wait to pick up the diver; it took off at full throttle in the general direction of the coast. Chances were that the cigarette would outrun the WPB Wells. It would be up to the Jayhawks to intercept the boat. The Wells was now close enough to track the cigarette boat's course on radar. It would be a simple matter for the Wells to relay position information to the Jayhawks; they would use the information to vector in on the cigarette boat.

Within minutes the Jayhawk's spotlights illuminated the cigarette boat which immediately opened fire on the Jayhawks with automatic weapons. The Jayhawks returned fire with M-60 machine guns, and the cigarette boat stopped dead in the water, smoke billowing from the engine compartment. The Jayhawks' spotlights revealed two men standing in the cockpit of the boat with their hands raised in the air. The Jayhawks remained at a hover over the boat to light the area while the Wells pulled along side. The boarding team made short order of cuffing and transferring the bad guys to their patrol boat.

Hamp heard the cigarette boat leave, then another boat arrive several minutes later. When he looked up, he could see a light blinking overhead. Hamp decided to take the risk of surfacing in hopes that Tom was the one waiting for him up there. He turned his lamp toward his dive computer on his wrist and inflated his buoyancy compensator slightly to begin his ascent. Keeping his light on the computer to monitor his rate of ascent, he rose slowly to 15 feet then waited for a three-minute decompression stop. When he finally surfaced, the beam of his light revealed the stern of the Carolyn II. She had never looked better to Hamp.

*****

Costellano and Dieppe stood silently next to Dieppe's rental car at the end of Rocky Creek Road. There was nothing at the road's end but the Gulf of Mexico. On both sides of the narrow paved road were large expanses of saw grass and tide water. A half mile up the road was a bridge that crossed Cow Creek, a small tributary that empties into the gulf. Two car loads of Costellano's soldiers stood within twenty-five feet of Costellano and Dieppe...eight men in all. One held a portable military-type FM radio that had been monitoring the cigarette boat. The rest of Costellano's men were armed with automatic weapons. They formed a protective barrier around Costellano and Dieppe. At the Cow Creek Bridge was another group of Costellano soldiers armed with automatic weapons. Parked on the road between the bridge and Dieppe's car was a civilian version of the Bell OH-58 helicopter. Costellano had arrived by helicopter and undoubtedly intended to leave the same way. There were no dwellings or any signs of human life for several miles. The south end of Rocky Creek Road was now Fort Costellano. Dieppe leaned patiently against the car. One of Costellano's men could be heard talking excitedly to the crew of the cigarette boat.

"Boss, the dive team has been ambushed," yelled the radio operator.

Next, several things began happening simultaneously. As the radio operator spoke to Costellano, gunfire erupted in the vicinity of the bridge. Dieppe saw dozens of muzzle flashes coming from both sides of the road. Then, coming from the ocean, right down the road at an altitude of about twenty-five feet, flew four HH-65A Dolphins with search lights blazing on the men and vehicles on the road. One of the helicopters hovered directly overhead, and the voice over its loudspeaker demanded that everyone drop their weapons and raise their hands.

Costellano's men opened fire on the helicopters causing them to pull out of range of the automatic weapons. The firefight by the bridge grew more intense. Neither Costellano nor Dieppe had moved a muscle.

Suddenly, without any warning, Costellano turned slowly toward Dieppe, pointed a semi-automatic at him, and shot him between the eyes.

"You tried to double-cross me, you Nazi swastika," screamed Costellano, as he shot Dieppe again twice.

Meanwhile, Jayhawks followed the Dolphins in and landed two DEA assault teams at the end of the road. The teams slowly worked their way up both sides of the road as the M-60 machine guns of the Dolphins poured fire down on the uncovered mobsters. A sniper in one of the assault teams saw who he thought was Costellano in his infrared telescopic sight and witnessed the shooting of a man looking like Dieppe. The sniper placed the crosshair of his telescopic sight on the center

of Costellano's chest and squeezed the trigger of
his Mouser rifle. He saw Costellano's knees
buckle and then   Costellano fall to the
ground.

The M-60 machine guns were taking a heavy
toll. Five of the eight men who were guarding
Costellano lay dead, or severely wounded. The
remaining three, having seen Costellano go down,
dropped their weapons and raised their hands in
surrender. Assault team members quickly cuffed
them.

The four gunmen at the bridge did not fair
as well; all were killed by the DEA ambush team.
Unfortunately, so was one of the DEA agents

One of the Jayhawks landed and Gregory and
Captain Miller dismounted and assembled the team
leaders.

"Did we have any casualties?" asked Gregory
quickly.

"One man dead and two wounded," responded
the Alpha assault team leader.

"Two men wounded, one seriously," reported
the Bravo team leader.

"No casualties," said the Charlie team
leader.

"One wounded," reported the Coast Guard air
team leader.

"Get the wounded and dead on the Jayhawks
and get them out of here," ordered Captain
Miller.

"Scotty, bring the support vehicles in and
get our boys and the prisoners out," ordered
Gregory. "And don't forget Dieppe's car. Let's go
to Steinhatchee and find out what happened in
Cedar Key and Miami," suggested Miller to
Gregory.

They flew directly to the parking lot next
to Roy's Restaurant. It not longer mattered that
they were being observed by local citizens. This

part of the operation was over. Gregory would report to General Stone after he checked on Hamp.

Chapter 21

Hamp was once again the only passenger on the C-141 Jetstar. The sun was sinking behind the horizon as the Jetstar lifted off the Andrews Air Force Base runway following a flight plan to Munich, Germany. It had been a long day after a very long night, and Hamp was exhausted. He would use the flight time to get some badly needed rest. For the moment, his thoughts drifted back to the events of the past twenty-four hours.

Charo escaped Gregory's net in Miami, but seven of his men were now in custody and the heroin had been recovered. Charo would for the time being remain a thorn in Gregory's side—if the mafia allowed him to live after his failure of last night. The Coast Guard intercepted the Gadfly and took the crew into custody without incident. Interpol had arranged Reifenstahl's arrest in Tortola. Within two hours of his arrest, he committed suicide by swallowing a cyanide capsule. Feltgeibell was missing. Either he fled the country, or Estabo abducted him because he discovered the warheads were useless. It was Hamp's guess that his body would turn up within a few days somewhere in Brazil. So far, the good guys were ahead; they had two thousand pounds of heroin, a dozen or so major narcotraffickers, and almost a billion dollars of the mafia's money. The money and the heroin were on board this aircraft to give his negotiation position credibility. Sturmer would almost certainly want a look at the bartering goods.

General Stone talked to Sturmer in the Eagle's Nest last night. When Dieppe failed to report in, Sturmer called the EAC to demand an account of Dieppe's well-being and whereabouts. In an attempt to buy time, General Stone told

Sturmer that Dieppe had been taken into custody by the DEA to protect his life, because Costellano thought Dieppe had double crossed him. Sturmer had no choice but to believe the General and gave him forty-eight hours to deliver Dieppe and the heroin, or he vowed to detonate the warhead. Hamp was going to the Eagle's Nest as the task force negotiator. Theoretically, he was to deliver Dieppe and the heroin to Sturmer in exchange for Patterson. He and Sturmer were to mutually agree to the precise details of the exchange process during a meeting between just the two of them in the Eagle's Nest. The German authorities were panic stricken, and had a bad case of Nazi phobia, but they were reluctantly cooperating with the task force. Since they were not entirely convinced the warhead had been rendered harmless, General Stone did not expect their patience to last much longer. Hamp's attempt to negotiate the release of Patterson was a one shot only deal.

Hamp's plan was simple. He would confront Sturmer in the Eagle's Nest and listen to his demands. Regardless of the nature of Sturmer's demands, Hamp would demand the release of Patterson in exchange for money and the heroin. He would allow Sturmer, or his representative, to inspect the heroin and money on board the Jetstar, but would insist that Patterson be set free before any further exchanges could take place. Once he knew Patterson was free, he would simply tell Sturmer the truth. If Sturmer chose to shoot him, he hoped the armored vest he would be wearing would keep him alive.

"Are you ready for some dinner, sir?" asked the steward. "I can offer you a filet mignon with baked potato and a salad."

"That would be great. Would you happen to have a little scotch in the galley, sergeant?" asked Hamp hopefully.

"I might be able to locate some, if you will agree to forget about it, sir," said the steward with a smile.

Hamp finished the scotch in two swallows and promptly fell asleep. The steward didn't have the heart to wake him when his dinner was ready.

*****

Sturmer paced back and forth on the deck of the Eagle's Nest ranting and raving at the audacity of the Americans thinking they could challenge the New World Order without fear of retaliation. Dieter Obermyer, Sturmer's trusted operations officer, stood stoically next to the railing gazing out on the valley below and ignoring his beloved mentor's questions because he knew that Sturmer did not want or expect him to answer. Nearby, Sturmer's lieutenants were at their posts awaiting instructions from their master.

"How are the men taking the news of this debacle, Dieter?" asked Sturmer still pacing and not looking at Dieter.

"Sir, the men do not know of these events. The government is keeping the whole thing very quiet, I imagine, so as not to cause panic among the people," replied Dieter. "They are completely unaware that anything has happened to threaten our plans." Sturmer ignored Dieter's response. He could not have cared less what the men thought about anything.

"Not only did the Americans interfere when I warned them not to, they took Dieppe into custody. I am certain the DEA has tortured him to get information about us," yelled Sturmer throwing his arms about like a madman. "And they are stupid enough to think that the Mississippi Neanderthal, Patterson, is still alive. People always underestimate me, Dieter, did you know that? The professors at the University of Heidelberg accused me of being a political radical. One even went so far as to compare me with the American racist George Lincoln Rockwell, when it was I who filled the leadership void in America left by Rockwell's premature death, and showed his ignorant, misguided followers the way to true Nazism. It was I who gave the fledgling neo-Nazi movement in Europe true political meaning and direction. It was I who gave them the vision and wisdom to look toward and work for a new-world order." Sturmer paused, spittle dripping from his chin. His face grew grim. He walked slowly up to Dieter and put his face in Dieter's nose, the way a football coach would show his displeasure to one of his players who had committed a gross mistake. His breathing was labored and his fists were clinched. His eyes were like burning coals. Dieter braced himself expecting the worst. "And they call me radical, Jew basher, racist, hate monger, and a madman," he hissed. "They should thank God that I am here to save the Aryans from the barbarous nature of all the impurities of humankind, but, instead, I am labeled an iconoclastic lunatic." Sturmer was trembling. Spittle showered Dieter. Dieter had never seen him this much out of control, and it frightened him. Then, as though someone had pushed a button, Sturmer began to relax. He flexed his hands, let his shoulders drop, and exhaled slowly and deeply. He stepped away from Dieter a little, smiled, and nodded his head as though to say, "All is well. I'll be all right." He resumed pacing.

"And now, Dieter, I am expected to meet with this emissary of the American government to negotiate," he whispered. "Negotiate, Dieter! I have in my possession an atomic weapon and they want me to negotiate." Sturmer laughed an artificial, hollow laugh. Dieter was chilled as he saw for the very first time a chink in his master's armor. It just might be possible that he truly was mad. Against his better judgment, Dieter spoke.

"But, sir, we need Dieppe. Is he not worth the effort of negotiation?" asked Dieter. "You still hold the warhead. The outcome of any negotiations, no matter how humiliating for you, will have to be resolved in your favor," urged Dieter. Sturmer, unaccustomed to a response from his trusted comrade, turned abruptly and faced Dieter. His eyes flashed and his mouth dropped slightly open. Dieter prepared for the worst, but a smile slowly formed on Sturmer's lips...a genuine smile.

"I find your remark reassuring, Dieter. Thank you. Let's go inside and have a drink, shall we?" said Sturmer soothingly as he put his arm around Dieter's broad shoulders. Dieter had gambled and it paid off. Sturmer's megalomanic binge had subsided. "Now tell me, Dieter, how this Colonel Porter will arrive here?" he asked as they went inside. "What, if anything, do we know about him?"

*****

The steward gently shook Hamp's shoulder to awaken him. "We will be landing in Munich in about thirty minutes, sir. Would you like me to re-warm your dinner for you?" It took Hamp several seconds to remember where he was and what was happening. His sleep had been deep and dreamless.

"Yes. I would appreciate that," Hamp replied groggily. He freshened up in the small lavatory in the rear of the Jetstar, and then went forward to speak with the pilot and co-pilot. "You fellows fly so smoothly I slept like a baby all the way over," said Hamp with a smile.

"We're coming up on Munich now. That bright glow just off the left wing tip is greater Munich. We should be on the ground in about fifteen minutes. It's a little unusual for a US Air Force plane to land in Munich. They can't decide how to work us into the landing order, so we're just circling around until we get landing instructions," explained the pilot. He then answered a call from the Munich control tower giving him landing instructions and informing him that the aircraft and its passengers were exempt from going through customs. "Did you hear the word on customs, sir?"

"Yes. That's good news," replied Hamp. He knew that it was a simple matter of the CIA working out details with the German authorities. "You fellows know you will be hanging around here, don't you?" asked Hamp.

"Yes, sir. Our orders are to refuel the aircraft and wait for you. My boss said a CIA agent would contact us at the airport with detailed instructions. I assume someone will be watching the aircraft," said the pilot.

"The CIA agent will serve as liaison for you and will know my whereabouts and activities. They will also let you know when its time to wind up your engines. Meanwhile, the German authorities will provide security for the airplane," said Hamp.

"We'll be ready, sir."

The Jetstar made a silky smooth landing and followed the runway guide vehicle to a parking area in a remote part of the airport that was normally reserved for privately owned aircraft. While the steward lowered the door and extended the steps, a Mercedes sedan pulled up next to the Jetstar, and two men get out of the car and waited. A German police van pulled up behind the Mercedes and eight uniformed, armed policemen dismounted and took up positions in a circle around the airplane. Hamp walked down the ramp to meet whoever was waiting for him. "I'm Special Agent Art Kinzel and this is Karl Feifel, a representative of the German Government," explained the agent as he shook Hamp's hand. "We will be your liaison, guides, assistants, and only friends for the next few hours. Mr. Gibbs has briefed us thoroughly. I am prepared to meet your needs so far as possible, and Mr. Feifel will do the same within the operating constraints placed on him by his government." Kinzel opened the back door of the sedan and gestured for Hamp to enter first. The steward placed Hamp's bag in the open trunk, and Feifel slid behind the steering wheel.

As the Mercedes sped from the airport, Kinzel continued with a mini-briefing of the local situation. "Sturmer is presently in the Eagle's Nest with his operations officer, Dieter Obermyer. So far as we can tell, they are alone. The key players in NWO are all in their usual habitats, but I am afraid that Patterson's whereabouts remains a mystery. Feifel's people have pulled out all the stops but don't have inkling. Even more serious is that we have no idea where Sturmer is hiding the warhead. If the warhead is potent, we will be in deep trouble. In short, Colonel Porter, our intelligence effort in Pegasus has been a dismal failure."

"Well, we have several things going for us, Mr. Kinzel. First is that Sturmer obviously doesn't know the warhead is a dud. Second, we know Sturmer's location, and third, we have the money and the heroin. Now all I have to do is figure out how to use those three pieces of information to acquire Patterson's freedom. Any suggestions?" asked Hamp.

"Are you really walking into the Eagle's Nest without a plan?" Kinzel asked in disbelief.

"That about sums it up," replied Hamp. Feifel's reflection in the rear view mirror was one of shock while Kinzel stared speechless out the side window.

"All I can say is that someone in Washington has one hell of a lot of confidence in you, Colonel," retorted Kinzel.

"While we're in transit, would you mind giving me a run down on the architecture and layout of the Eagle's Nest, Mr. Kinzel?" asked Hamp, changing the subject.

"I'll leave that to Feifel. He's the resident expert on Nazi history," said Kinzel.

"I am a German Jew, if that tells you anything, Colonel Porter," remarked Feifel from the front seat. Feifel described the Eagle's Nest in great detail, from the road leading up to it from Berchestgaden, to the construction of the stone fireplace. His remarks were detailed, pertinent, and clear. By the time he finished, Hamp had formed a detailed mental picture of the famous structure. He could understand how a place like that could have a narcotic effect on a man like Sturmer. Hamp was beginning to lay the rudimentary foundation for a plan. He would have about forty-five minutes to complete the plan.

The CIA's psychological profile of Sturmer suggested a man of high intelligence; a man of radical political views; someone with a propensity for fanaticism; a person with a severe monomanic personality; and an intense proclivity toward anyone who holds views contrary to his own. The probability was very high that he is amoral and suffers from an asocial personality. He probably hates women, but is more than likely not homosexual. The profiler suggested that the best chance of persuading him to another point of view would be through an acknowledgement of his superior intelligence coupled with an appeal to his vision for humankind. "So I play to his ego," said Hamp aloud.

"What did you say, Colonel Porter?" responded Kinzel.

"Just thinking out loud," said Hamp with a weak smile. Hamp prayed silently that a plan of some sort would soon fall in place. Patterson's life depended on it.

Feifel turned off the autovon and followed the sign pointing the way to Berchtesgaden. It was mid-morning and the cobalt-colored alpine sky was totally clear. The air was so pure that it felt almost electric, and the meadows were lush with edelweiss and a vast array of wild flowers. Row after row of apple trees filled with white blossoms lined the hillsides. Snow still capped the mountaintops. In comparison to the grandeur before him, the affairs of Pegasus seemed dirty, surrealistic, and far, far away. Kinzel began speaking, jerking Hamp back to reality.

"Did you bring along a weapon?" he asked.

"No. I thought that would be too risky and would demonstrate bad form for someone who was supposed to be a negotiator. I did, however, bring a Kevlar vest," explained Hamp. General Stone's aide de camp had given the vest to Hamp assuring him that the pound and a half, seven layer, quarter inch thick Kevlar protective device was state of the art and would offer him adequate protection against a fatal gunshot wound.

"You have nerve," suggested Kinzel. What do you want us to do?"

"Just standby in the Eagle's Nest parking area, I suppose," replied Hamp. "Knowing you are there will be somewhat supportive."

"Will you at least wear a wire so we will know what's going on?" urged Kinzel.

"My government feels strongly about that, Colonel Porter," added Feifel. "We want you to do that."

"I don't think so. Sorry to disappoint you." replied Hamp firmly.

Feifel shrugged his shoulders in resignation. They fell silent, each man in his own world. The country side sped by as Feifel maintained a very high rate of speed on the narrow mountain road. They passed through Berchtesgaden and headed up the Eagle's Nest road in what seemed to Hamp just a few minutes. Feifel finally slowed down to a reasonable speed probably because the sharp switchback turns on the Eagle's Nest road were unprotected and the climb rate increases at the rate of 500 feet per kilometer. They pulled into the parking area near the big bronze doors. Two men, both armed with automatic weapons, were waiting for them at the doors. Hamp got out of the car and walked toward them. When he was within a few feet of them, one of the men held up a hand and ordered him to stop, while the other man searched him. Hamp was glad that he was not armed. When the man was satisfied that Hamp was unarmed, and not wearing a wire, he told Hamp to follow him, and they entered the doors leading to the elevator tunnel. The second man waited behind to make sure Kinzel and Feifel remained in the car. They walked the distance of the tunnel and rode the elevator to the Eagle's Nest in complete silence.

The elevator doors opened to reveal Sturmer standing near the fireplace, facing them with his hands behind his back, and Obermyer standing near the door leading to the deck. The room looked exactly as Feifel had described it, except for the furnishings that Feifel had not seen.

Sturmer did not move or speak. Hamp recognized this behavior as a demonstration of Sturmer's power and superiority. It would be up to Hamp to approach Sturmer. After all, Hamp represented the antagonists in this drama. After a brief pause in front of the elevator, Hamp made and maintained eye contact with Sturmer as he walked across the large room to where Sturmer was standing. Hamp did not offer his hand in greeting, nor did Sturmer, rather both men stared coldly into each other's eyes as though engaged in a battle of wills.

"My name is Porter. I believe we have business, sir, but before we begin may I say how honored I am to be in the presence of a truly great mind. Even though our views differ, I have deep respect for your intellect and vision. You are indeed a man of the times, Herr. Sturmer. May I shake your hand, sir?" asked Hamp with all the servility he could muster. Sturmer was clearly caught off guard. His eyes widened slightly and his mouth opened as though he were about to speak, but then he hesitated.

"Why, yes, of course," stammered Sturmer, as he extended his hand to Hamp. They shook hands firmly for a few seconds, and then Sturmer regained his self control. Hamp continued to press on.

"I hope that I have not caused you embarrassment, Herr. Sturmer. I simply could not pass up an opportunity that might never come my way again. Now that you have given me that pleasure and honor, I am ready to negotiate, sir."

"And what makes you think I intend to negotiate, Colonel Porter?"

"I know you will, because you are a man of honor, sir. No one of your character could possibly go back on his word. There is no doubt about that." Hamp was making himself nauseous. Plan or no, he was on a path of no return. He would have to follow his visceral instincts and play this thing to its conclusion.

"Come out on the deck with me, Colonel Porter. I find the alpine air conducive to clear thinking." Sturmer led the way, but did not hold the door for Hamp. Perhaps he had not yet earned Sturmer's respect.

"I agree, sir, we do need to think clearly to complete our business to everyone's satisfaction," replied Hamp following him through the door.

"It has been my experience, Colonel Porter, that pleasing everyone is neither desirable nor possible," quipped Sturmer. He placed his back against the deck railing, folded his arms across his chest, and stared pensively at Hamp. "Is it your aim to please everyone with these negotiations, Colonel Porter?"

"No, sir, it is not my aim. I only hope to please you and to gain the freedom of Colonel Patterson." Hamp was trying to show respect without sounding like a wimp, but had the feeling that he was not succeeding.

"And how will you please me, may I ask?"

"I have in the aircraft that brought me to Germany almost a billion US dollars and 2,000 pounds of heroin, your heroin, Herr. Sturmer." Sturmer motioned Dieter to his side and whispered something in his ear. Dieter went inside and made a phone call from the table just inside the door leading to the deck. He spoke a few words to someone and hung up.

"I have men at the airport to check the aircraft, Colonel Porter. I do hope the authorities will not delay their verification inspection."

"They will allow the inspection," Hamp assured him.

"Then we shall wait a few moments for them to do their job," replied Sturmer. Several minutes pass without words passing between them. Sturmer paced the deck with his hands behind his back. Hamp stood still and tried to think of how he would force the issue with Patterson. Finally, the phone rang and Dieter answered immediately. He spoke one word, hung up, and walked to Spangle.

"The heroin and money were on the aircraft, sir," announced Dieter.

"That is a good start, Colonel Porter, but what about Dieppe?"

Without a pause, and looking Sturmer unflinchingly in the eye, Hamp said: "Dieppe is dead, Herr. Sturmer. Joey Costellano murdered him because he was a Nazi." Sturmer did not flinch, but for just a fleeting second Hamp could see something akin to loss in his eyes. Hamp continued in the absence of a response from Sturmer. "You must remember, sir, that Costellano was a stupid man. For what it is worth, he, too, is dead."

"Heinrich is dead?" repeated Sturmer in a whisper. "Killed by a stupid Italian Neanderthal," said Sturmer raising his voice several octaves. "Well, at least I don't have to feel badly about telling you that Colonel Patterson is also dead," said Sturmer in a quiet voice. Sturmer's words hit Hamp like a sledgehammer. Sturmer's personality had undergone a complete change. Even his posture was different; he embraced himself with both arms and his lower jaw was thrust forward like Adolf Hitler. He began pacing with a little goose-step gait, his chin raised. Hamp didn't know what to expect next. "I killed him with a single shot to the head, because he failed to show me respect, and because his usefulness to me had ended."

Hamp tried not to show his feelings. He inhaled deeply to control the rage he felt inside. "Then our negotiations are over, Herr. Sturmer," he said firmly, and turned to leave the deck.

"Do not turn your back on me, little man," retorted Sturmer with a sneer. You really do not realize what this means, do you? You leave me no choice but to detonate the warhead."

Hamp turned abruptly and faced Sturmer. Obermyer moved toward the door to protect Sturmer, but Sturmer motioned him off.

"You are the one who fails to realize what has happened, Sturmer. It's simple. You loose. The warhead is a dud. They were all duds, Sturmer, every single one of them. Only God could detonate your warhead, you pompous Nazi ass. You can do with it whatever you want. You had a chance until you killed Patterson. That was very dumb for a smart man, Sturmer. Now you have nothing with which to bargain." Hamp turned again to leave the deck. Sturmer removed a Walther PPK from his jacket and fired three times into Hamp's back. The impact of the three shots knocked Hamp through the glass door leading to the great room. Hamp's world suddenly became topsy-turvy. He couldn't breathe or focus. He felt completely numb all over. With a lot of effort he rolled over on his back and looked toward Sturmer. Hamp managed to remain conscious just long enough to see Sturmer hand the pistol to Dieter, and then darkness overtook him.

* * * * *

The light was blinding and his back felt like someone pushed a telephone pole through it. He heard someone calling his name repeatedly, but the light was so bright he was unable to see anything.

"Colonel Porter, Art Kinzel here. Can you hear me?" He heard Kinzel's voice, but he could not make his mouth answer.

"Let's allow him to rest, Mr. Kinzel. He'll come around in a few minutes. I'm going to have him moved to a private room as soon as we

finish up here. I think he's out of danger now,"
said a strange voice, maybe a doctor, and then
darkness came again.

Later, Hamp was able to open his eyes. The
bright light was gone. He tried to raise his head
to look around, but his back and neck hurt too
much to move. "Where the hell am I? What
happened to me?" Hamp asked groggily.

"Welcome back to the living, Colonel
Porter," said Art Kinzel from somewhere. "You
are in a US Army hospital in Landstuhl, Germany.
We brought you here yesterday in pretty bad shape
with three gunshot wounds to the back. You're
going to be okay. I'm going to get the doctor;
he wanted me to let him know when you woke."
Kinzel left the room.

Slowly, but surely, events at the Eagle's
Nest came drifting back to Hamp's mind. "Oh,
yeah," said Hamp aloud to no one in particular.
"Now I remember. I forgot to put on the vest
before I went up to the Nest. How could I have
been so stupid?" yelled Hamp.

Kinzel and a doctor entered the room. The
doctor introduced himself. "You are a very lucky
man, Colonel Porter. One bullet passed through
your chest without touching anything important.
One bullet hit a rib and made a mess of your
right lung. The third bullet followed essentially
the same path as the second bullet and passed
through your chest about two inches away from
your spinal column and your heart. I'm afraid we
had to open you up pretty good to get at all the
damage, but you should heal quickly and without
many lasting effects," explained the doctor. "We
did have to remove about half of your right lung,
I'm sorry to say, but you can manage well enough
with what is left. You also sustained several
nasty glass cuts. I have asked a plastic surgeon
to see you tomorrow. We will talk again later
when you're feeling better. I'm sure you will

have questions after you've had time to digest what I've told you."

"Thank you doctor," replied Hamp weakly. He already had questions. "Say, Kinzel, I . . ..

"Don't worry, Porter, I promise not to tell anyone you forgot to put on your security blanket," interrupted Kinzel with a chuckle. "By the way, I almost forgot to tell you, General Stone will be arriving this evening. Rumor has it he's making the trip just to see you. You must be special, boy," said Kinzel.

"Not special, groaned Hamp, just stupid."

"Time for some sleep, Colonel Porter," commanded the nurse as she flitted into the room with a hypodermic syringe in her hand. "It's just a little Demerol for the pain so you can rest."

"Before I go out again, Kinzel, I want to say thanks for all your help. What happened after I went down?"

"About thirty minutes had passed after you left the parking lot, when this big German guy comes running out of the elevator tunnel shouting in German to the guard at the door. They both jumped into the other car and headed down the mountain, completely ignoring Feifel and me. We took off to the Eagle's Nest to see what was happening. When the elevator door opened at the Nest, we saw you lying unconscious with glass and blood all around you. As we were taking a look at you, Feifel spotted someone on the deck with half his skull blown away - maybe your buddy. A Walther PPK was lying beside him. Feifel used the phone in the Nest to alert the German authorities and to call for an ambulance. The Germans flew you from Berchtesgaden to Landstuhl in a German air ambulance. The doctors here say the crew on that helicopter saved your life. Feifel's people are out looking for Obermyer and other key NWO people. It looks like . . .Hamp, are you listening?" Hamp was out again. The Demerol was working as intended.

Talking just outside his room woke Hamp. He had no idea who was talking until the door opened and his doctor came in with General Stone.

"Heck, Hamp, I count at least five tubes in you. I will not ask how you are feeling; no one who looks like you right now could possibly feel good," quipped the General with a smile.

"Have a seat, sir, and bring me up to date. I'm a little behind on things."

"Thanks, but I'll stand. I've been sitting for hours. There really isn't that much to bring you up to date on, Hamp. Charo was found yesterday in his Miami home with a .22 caliber bullet hole behind the left ear. Clearly, the mob had made a retribution hit. Gibbs's people tell us Anatole and Popodopolus were found murdered. We think Dieppe was responsible for both. I think you already knew about Reifenstahl, Feltgeibell, and Costellano. Gregory is a happy camper, and the President is making a big deal of cracking down on neo-Nazi groups, and has taken full credit for the demise of the Charo and Costellano families."

"His price for keeping his generals quiet?" asked Hamp.

"Yes, something like that. My only real regret is the loss of B.J. Patterson." "Feifel's people found his body buried in the rubble of the General Walker Hotel tunnel complex." Hamp started to say something, but realized it would be inadequate. He was really sorry to hear that news.

"And how is Sully Sultoy?" asked Hamp, to change the subject.

"He ended up a hero with a little help from Colonel Carter and the State Department."

"I'm pleased to hear that," said Hamp.

"Oh! This will make you feel better. Estabo was killed in a government raid on one of his heroin factories just two days after he acquired his warheads. He probably never knew they were duds," grinned the General. And last, but not least, Gordon Beckman and I will be retiring at the end of next month. We both feel we can no longer support the President or his staff."

"I am truly sorry to hear that, sir."

"Don't be. It's time to let the youngsters run the Army. Listen, Hamp, Fran and I want you to do your convalescing at our farm in Virginia. The doctor tells me you will require some looking after for awhile."

"Thanks, General, but I really miss Steinhatchee. I have friends there that will look after me. Tell Fran thanks."

"Well, at least visit with us as soon as you can travel."

"It's a done deal, General."

"There's just one more thing, then I promised the nurse I would leave you alone. Patterson is being posthumously awarded the Congressional Medal of Honor at a ceremony at Fort Myer in about a month. The presentation will be the first ever peace-time award of the medal. Of course the public will never know the reason for which it is being presented. If you are up to it, General Beckman would like you to make the presentation to his wife."

"Tell the General I will be honored to do it," replied Hamp with tears in his eyes. "Is that a part of the deal with the President, sir?"

"Something like that. See you soon, Hamp," said the General as he took a packet from his brief case and laid it on Hamp's nightstand.

The nurse hurried into Hamp's room about half an hour after the General's departure. "You must really rate, Colonel. General Stone left

very explicit instructions with the hospital
commander as to how you were to be treated during
your stay with us. Are you related to the
General?"

"No, but I wish I were. Nurse, would you
mind handing me that package on the night stand,
please?" She cheerfully complied.

"Please allow me to open it for you," she
said with an exaggerated smile. She unwrapped
the package with a look of surprise on her face.
"Why, Colonel Porter, it's an award of some kind
I think. Shall I go ahead and read the
citation?"

"I suppose so," replied Hamp somewhat
puzzled. As she read the citation, Hamp opened
the box. It contained the Distinguished Service
Medal.

*****

Hamp was a patient at Landstuhl Hospital
for ten days, and then he was transferred to
Walter Reed Hospital in Washington, D.C. There he
underwent two weeks of treatment and plastic
surgery to minimize the effects of scars caused
by the glass cuts. Fran and General Stone
visited Hamp almost every day during his stay in
Washington, and he talked with Tom and Marian
several times while there, but he didn't speak to
Gwen.

Hamp was placed on convalescent leave from
Walter Reed, and flew to Moody Air Force Base on
the twice-weekly medical evacuation flight. Tom
Adams was waiting for him in the flight
operations building at Moody.

"Boy, you are one pitiful, skinny, wimpy
looking sight," exclaimed Tom with a frown on his
face.

"Thanks a heap. I'm so glad I have friends
like you. You make me feel so good about
myself."

"Come on. I'm taking you to Steinhatchee so Marian can get some victuals in you. Why did they starve you? You want to stop by McDonalds on the way home?" Tom was hyper, his way of saying "I'm glad to see you."

"I'm glad to see you, too," said Hamp with a laugh. It had been a while since he had smiled.

Chapter 22

The trip from Moody Air Force base to Steinhatchee took about two hours. Tom took several of his famous short cuts, some dirt roads, which Hamp could never remember, nor would he ever attempt to repeat. Their moods were reflective. Tom brought Hamp up to date on Steinhatchee news and events, and Hamp told Tom, as much as he could, about his final moments with Sturmer.

"We've not had a great deal of time together lately, Tom, but I don't want another day to pass without my saying thanks for all you did in conjunction with Pegasus. You didn't have to get involved at all, but the fact is I didn't trust anyone else out on the big pond. Can you forgive me for getting you involved?"

"Sure, I can forgive you; it was fun. Marian, however, might be another story. You might want to give her a lot of room on the port and starboard side for the next few days, if you know what I mean."

"Oh, heck! Am I really in trouble with her?" asked Hamp with genuine concern.

"Darned right you are, boy."

They rounded the curve near Roy's restaurant and made the final turn to Hamp's house. Hamp had dreaded seeing the house and the aftermath of the Gotcha bunch that had inhabited the place for several weeks. He would never get it back to normal. Tom pulled into the driveway.

"You want me to go in with you, ol' buddy?"

"No, I'll face the music alone. I would hate for anyone to see me cry."

Tom got out of the car laughing. Hamp was confused. "Come on, let's go see what's upstairs. Maybe it's not as bad as you think," said Tom, still laughing. Hamp was completely winded after climbing the 22 steps to his front door. He was in worse physical condition that he thought. He fumbled for a house key, and when he placed the key into the lock, the door swung open. He could not believe his eyes. There stood Marian in the middle of the cleanest house in Steinhatchee. Fresh flowers abounded and the house smelled of freshly peeled peaches. Even Mozart played quietly on the stereo system.

"Welcome home, sweetheart," said Marian as she gave him a gentle hug and a kiss on the cheek. "This is the part in the story where we leave, Tom," she said as she grabbed him by the hand and led him through the door. "See ya' later." Marian closed the door behind them. Hamp was confused, happy with what he saw, but confused by Marian and Tom's strange behavior. He had thought that they would stay and visit for awhile since he hadn't seen them in so long. "Maybe they thought I needed to rest," Hamp told himself. Truly feeling tired from the flight from Walter Reid to Moody and the drive from Moody to Steinhatchee, Hamp decided to take a shower and hit the sack for some sleep. He walked slowly to the bedroom in back of the house where he found the bedroom door open about two inches. Hamp noticed that a light was on in the room, too. "I guess Marian didn't want me stumbling around in the dark. She is so sweet," thought Hamp. He pushed the door open and then gasped because there was someone standing in the middle of the room, a beautiful someone—Gwen. If he didn't know better, Hamp would have thought that the Demerol was messing with his head.

"You look tired," Gwen said.

"You look gorgeous," said Hamp

"Oh Hamp, I see you still have your charm about you," she teased. "Why don't we sit down and let you rest," she said as her eyes filled and a tear slipped down her right cheek. Seeing

Hamp made her realize just how close to loosing him she had come.

Hamp, without saying a word more, walked over to where Gwen stood and embraced her first gently and then tightly. Feeling her in his arms made Hamp realize why she had been on his mind so much during this whole Pegasus business. He had not wanted to die not because he feared death so much, but because he wanted to love again. He wanted to be with Gwen. She had been his friend for more years than he could remember. Now, he knew that he wanted her to be his best friend forever.

They relaxed their embrace. Then, gently cupping Gwen's chin in his hand, Hamp looked into her eyes—the most beautiful, warm eyes he had ever seen. As their eyes remained transfixed, their thoughts twirled about in their heads posing all kind of questions: Would they kiss? Would they have a future? Can they be more than just friends? Then slowly, Hamp lifted Gwen's chin toward him, pausing and then continuing, until their lips met for the first time ever. Breathless, they looked at each other again. "Aren't you going to say anything?" asked Gwen, smiling.

"Yes. Would you be happy with a small wedding? Right here at Fellowship Baptist Church with just close friends and the children?" Gwen's smile turned into a wide grin. They embraced and kissed again, their second ever kiss.

Epilogue

The day was uncomfortably warm, but it was July 31 and it was supposed to be warm in Washington, D.C. and most everywhere else in the United States. As Hamp and Gwen walked down the second floor E·Ring corridor to General Beckman's office, Gwen stopped suddenly.

"What do I say? How do I address these military people?" Gwen's unfamiliarity with the military was manifesting itself in her sudden nervousness.

"Behave just as you would around anyone. Just be your usual charming self. They are just people like you and me who dress a bit differently," replied Hamp reassuringly.

They entered the anteroom of the Chief's office and were greeted by the aide de camp. "The General is expecting you, Colonel Porter. Please go on in to his office," he gestured toward an open door. They entered the Chief's office and Hamp was very surprised to see among the group of distinguished people in the room, the President of the United States.

"Mr. President, may I present Colonel and Mrs. Hampton Porter. I believe you remember Colonel Porter from previous briefings." The President nodded pleasantly and shook hands with Hamp and Gwen. Hamp thought it uncommon for the President to go elsewhere for such a presentation. He thought everyone went to the President. Then he remembered the strange politics involved in Pegasus. The President did not want to answer questions from the media regarding the presentation of a Congressional Medal of Honor.

"Colonel Porter, I believe you know the rest of these gentlemen, but they have not all had the pleasure of meeting Mrs. Porter. Mrs.

Porter, may I present Secretary of Defense Harrison Murphy, Secretary of the Army Martin Griffin, Deputy Director of the Central Intelligence Agency Walter Gibbs, Director of the Drug Enforcement Agency James Gregory, and I believe you already know General and Mrs. Stone." Everyone smiled politely and held Gwen's hand briefly. Fran and General Stone both gave Gwen a hug.

"Finally, Colonel and Mrs. Porter, I want to introduce you to a very special lady, Mrs. B.J. Patterson." Mrs. Patterson took Hamp's right hand in both her hands and looked into his eyes. For a brief moment, something special passed between them that did not require words. They shared something that neither would ever forget, and, now, Hamp knew why he had been selected to present the award to Mrs. Patterson.

*****

As Hamp and Gwen walked from the Pentagon to their car, Gwen surprised Hamp with an unexpected question, one that Hamp did not want to hear. "When will Sturmer interrupt our lives again? Will it be soon?"

"I don't know, but I have the uneasy feeling that he will."

Notes

CIA Factbook, Brazil. 1994 (With Modifications).

Farah, Douglas. "New Threats from Columbia: Heroin." The Washington Post, 27 March 1997: A01.

Hamburger, Philip. "Beauty and the Beast: Letter from Berchtesgaden." World Press Review, June 1995. 70-73.

Infield, Glenn B. "Hitler's Secret Life," Stein and Day, New York. 1979.

Rothchild, John. "The Day Drugs Came to Steinhatchee." Harper's, January 1983. 45-52.

The United States Department of Justice, Drug Enforcement Agency, DEA Press Release, "Columbian Heroin a Major Threat," 21 June 1995.

White Aryan Resistance Positions. February 1997. 6 April 1997
<http//:www.resist.com/Positionsone.gif>.

Author's Note

This is a work of fiction. Most of the places are real, however, with the exception of several historical personalities, the characters and incidents are the product of the author's imagination or are used fictitiously, and any resemblance to actual persons, living or dead, is entirely coincidental.

ISBN 1412037530-0

9 781412 037532